The Trail
of the
Serpent

MARY ELIZABETH BRADDON

THE TRAIL
OF THE
SERPENT

Edited by Chris Willis

Introduction by Sarah Waters

THE MODERN LIBRARY

NEW YORK

Modern Library Paperback Edition

Introduction copyright © 2003 by Sarah Waters
Biographical note, notes, editor's afterword, and reading group guide
copyright © 2003 by Random House, Inc.

LIBRARY OF CONGRESS CATALOGING-IN-PUBLICATION DATA
Braddon, M. E. (Mary Elizabeth), 1835–1915.
[Three times dead]
The trail of the serpent / Mary Elizabeth Braddon; edited by Chris Willis;
introduction by Sarah Waters.
p. cm.
ISBN 0-8129-6678-3
1. Bankers—Fiction.   2. Murderers—Fiction.   3. Foundlings—Fiction.
4. Mute persons—Fiction.   5. Paris (France)—Fiction.   6. Serial murders—
Fiction.   7. Judicial error—Fiction.   8. Yorkshire (England)—Fiction.
I. Willis, Chris, 1960–   II. Title.

PR4989.M4 T48 2003
823'.8—dc21   2002026594

Modern Library website address: www.modernlibrary.com

Printed in the United States of America

MARY ELIZABETH BRADDON

Actress, novelist, playwright, and poet, Mary Elizabeth Braddon (1835–1915) was one of the most fascinating women of the Victorian age. In her fifty-five-year writing career, she became one of Victorian England's best-loved writers, as well as being one of the most prolific. Her phenomenal output included more than eighty novels, five plays, and numerous poems and short stories.

Braddon was born in London on October 4, 1835 (a date she later sometimes gave as 1837). Her father, Henry, was an unsuccessful London solicitor who was perpetually on the brink of bankruptcy. He and her mother, Fanny, supplemented the family income by writing articles for *Pitman's Sporting Magazine* under the pseudonyms "Rough Robin" and "Gilbert Forester." The marriage was unhappy, and Fanny and Henry separated in 1840. By the 1850s, Henry's financial failures had left the family almost penniless. To support her mother and sister, Braddon embarked on a career as a professional actress with a touring repertory company, using the stage name Mary Seyton. This was a scandalous career for a Victorian woman: actresses were regarded as little better than prostitutes. Braddon safeguarded her reputation and her chastity by taking her mother on tour with her as chaperone.

From 1852 until early 1860, she appeared in plays in London and the provinces. During this time she tried her hand as a playwright and poet. Several of her poems were published in provincial newspapers, and her play *The Loves of Arcadia* was performed successfully in London. She later put her knowledge of the theatre to good use in her novels. Actress heroines often appear in her fiction, and her 1875 novel *A Strange World* gives a lively picture of a Victorian traveling theatre company.

In 1860, Braddon's first novel, *Three Times Dead*, was published in serial form, but sold badly. Shortly afterward, Braddon met London publisher John Maxwell, who was soon to become her lover and then her husband. Under his guidance, she rewrote *Three Times Dead* as *The Trail of the Serpent*. It sold one thousand copies within a week of publication, prompting George Eliot to complain to John Blackwood that it was populist trash while bitterly bemoaning the fact that it sold better than her own carefully crafted novels. Braddon now moved in with Maxwell and embarked on a career as a full-time writer and editor. To meet the demands of the market, she wrote melodramatic serials under a variety of pseudonyms for Maxwell's *Halfpenny Journal*. Braddon had no illusions about the literary merits of this hackwork, wryly commenting in a letter to her novelist friend Edward Bulwer Lytton that "the amount of crime, treachery, murder, slow poisoning & general infamy required by the halfpenny reader is something terrible."

But in 1862, *Lady Audley's Secret*, which is considered to be her masterpiece, brought Braddon firmly into mainstream publishing and turned her into one of the era's most popular novelists. The adventures of Braddon's beautiful, bigamous anti-heroine became an instant bestseller, running to nine editions within three months of publication. High-minded critics condemned *Lady Audley's Secret* as noxious and immoral, but their reaction only served to give the novel more publicity.

Braddon's output at this time was astounding. While writing *Lady Audley's Secret*, she also wrote another serial, *The Black Band*, which appeared in the *Halfpenny Journal* under the pseudonym

Lady Caroline Lascelles in 1861–62. This achievement is even more remarkable given that Braddon was heavily pregnant at the time. She gave birth to her first son, Gerald, on March 19, 1862. As the last installments of *Lady Audley's Secret* and *The Black Band* appeared, Braddon began another novel, *Aurora Floyd*. Another immediate bestseller, this book scandalized critics because of the notorious scene in which the beautiful heroine becomes passionately aroused while horsewhipping a male stable hand.

From the early 1860s until her death in 1915, Braddon wrote almost continually. Between 1861 and 1871 alone she wrote over twenty novels. Under constant pressure to publish, in 1864 she told Bulwer Lytton that she was "always divided between a noble desire to attain something like excellence—and a very ignoble wish to earn plenty of money." Whatever her misgivings about commercialism, she wrote for pleasure as well as profit. Toward the end of her career she told a *Daily Telegraph* interviewer, "What does surprise me is that every girl who is well educated and endowed with imagination does not long to express herself with her pen."

Her hectic work schedule, in addition to a series of personal tragedies, contributed to Braddon's having a nervous breakdown in 1868. During 1867–68, she had written and published eight books (*The Lady's Mile, Ralph the Bailiff, Circe, Rupert Godwin, Birds of Prey, Charlotte's Inheritance, Run to Earth,* and *Dead Sea Fruit*), as well as editing *Belgravia* magazine. Then in 1868, her sister Maggie died suddenly in Italy. Shortly afterward, her mother died. Heartbroken, Braddon suffered a yearlong breakdown and feared that she would never be able to write again. However, this experience led to her sensitive and moving portrayal of mental illness in *Strangers and Pilgrims* (1871–72), whose heroine has a breakdown after the death of her child.

In 1874, after the death of Maxwell's estranged wife, Mary Anne, Braddon and Maxwell finally married. Maxwell had been unable to obtain a divorce from his wife, who was alleged to be insane. Though Mary Anne was rumored to have been sent to a lunatic asylum, recent research by Braddon's biographer, Jennifer

Carnell, has uncovered no evidence of any such incarceration and indicates that, instead of being locked away, she may simply have gone home to her family in Ireland. At the time of their marriage, Braddon had already borne Maxwell six children (one of whom died in infancy) and had helped him raise his five children from his marriage to Mary Anne.

Having established her name as a sensation novelist, Braddon went on to write successfully in a variety of genres. *Eleanor's Victory* (1863) features one of fiction's earliest (and least efficient) female detectives. *The Doctor's Wife* (1864) is an English adaptation of Flaubert's *Madame Bovary* that focuses on the plight of a discontented, overimaginative woman trapped in a dull marriage in provincial English society. According to Professor C. Heywood and Robert Lee Wolff, it was a substantial influence on George Eliot's *Middlemarch* and Thomas Hardy's *The Return of the Native. Vixen* (1879) is a lively love story with an unconventional heroine. *Mount Royal* (1882) is a nineteenth-century reworking of the legend of Tristran and Iseult. *Gerard, or The World, the Flesh and the Devil* (1891) is based on the Faust story. *Rough Justice* (1898) and *His Darling Sin* (1899) are detective novels, written during the height of Sherlock Holmes's popularity. *The Rose of Life* (1905) is loosely based on the downfall of Oscar Wilde, who was a close friend. However, Edwardian convention dictated that she had to be suitably discreet about the nature of his offense. In Braddon's novel the hero commits fraud, not sodomy.

Condemned as a cheap sensationalist in the 1860s, by the turn of the century Braddon had become a respected literary figure. In September 1897, the *Windsor Magazine* said that "Miss Braddon's name is a household word." Her work, which was admired by Thackeray and Henry James and mentioned by James Joyce in *Ulysses,* was serialized in periodicals throughout Britain and appeared as far afield as Japan and Australia. Her earnings enabled her to buy luxurious homes in Hampshire's New Forest and the London suburb of Richmond, as well as purchasing her mother's beloved childhood home, Skisdon, in Cornwall. After Maxwell's death in 1895, she lived in their Richmond home, Lichfield House, where she continued writing until her death in 1915. Her last novel, *Mary,* was published posthumously. With many of her novels now being reprinted, and a new biography recently published, Braddon is likely to provide a fruitful source of study for many years.

CONTENTS

THE TRAIL OF THE SERPENT

BOOK THE FIRST. A RESPECTABLE YOUNG MAN

BOOK THE SECOND. A CLEARANCE OF ALL SCORES

INTRODUCTION

Sarah Waters

Mary Elizabeth Braddon is known to readers today—if she is known at all—primarily for the two bestselling novels written early in her career, *Lady Audley's Secret* (1861–62) and *Aurora Floyd* (1862–63). With these, and alongside writers such as Wilkie Collins, Charles Reade, and Mrs. Henry Wood, she helped to define and popularize that extraordinary mid-Victorian genre, the novel of "sensation." Like Collins's, her intrigue-based plots locate crime and the harboring of dreadful secrets at the heart of the middle-class household; like Reade, she sends her characters on extravagant narrative journeys; like Wood, she is interested in the oppressive social forces which might drive individuals—and women, in particular—into deceit, blackmail, bigamy, murder, and madness. And like all these writers, her contribution to the sensation genre made her vulnerable to conservative criticism which understood her fiction to be unhealthy and amoral, a gratuitous dwelling on "nasty sentiments and equivocal heroines,"[1] a pandering to the bourgeoisie's fascination with its own corruption, which was helping to make "the literature of the Kitchen the favourite reading of the Drawing room."[2]

The Trail of the Serpent occupies a fascinating place in relation both to Braddon's sensational œuvre and to the criticism that greeted it. Her first finished novel (she had previously written poetry, sentimental juvenile fiction, and a pastoral play, *The Loves of Arcadia*), it was begun at the instigation of a Yorkshire printer, C. H. Empson.[3] Empson had read and admired her work; what he sensed particularly, perhaps, was her burgeoning affinity with literary formula, for he encouraged her to write in more or less blatant imitation of the popular, plot-based fictions of Dickens and G.W.M. Reynolds.[4] The result—produced in the spring and summer of 1860—was this lurid, improbable story, originally entitled *Three Times Dead, or the Secret of the Heath*. Braddon wrote it swiftly, in what was clearly, for her, an exhilarating kind of professional innocence: by April 1863 she would have grown used to creating serialized novels for a demanding public and having "the printer at me all the time";[5] she wrote *Three Times Dead* "with all the freedom of one who feared not the face of a critic," with "a pen unchastened by experience...faster and more facile at that initial stage than it ever became after long practice."[6] Even so, the novel was not an immediate financial success. Issued by Empson in cheap serial form, it "could hardly have entered upon the world of books," she recalled later, "in a more profound obscurity."[7]

Within a year, however, Braddon had embarked upon a professional and romantic liaison with the more experienced and ambitious publisher, John Maxwell; more crucially, she had begun publication of the novel that was to make her famous, *Lady Audley's Secret*. On the strength of this success, *Three Times Dead* was reissued with a new title which, like the first, hinted at enigma, convolution, and surprise, but added another element: the subtle foregrounding of the process of detection through which the enigma was to be unraveled. In short, it was reinvented and secured more firmly within the genre that Braddon was even then helping to form—the genre of sensation. The tactics worked. With Maxwell's money behind it, and in its new guise as *The Trail of the Serpent*, the novel sold a thousand new copies in its first week.[8]

What strikes us about *The Trail of the Serpent* today, perhaps, is its likeness to that other great mid-Victorian popular cultural phenomenon, the melodrama. Braddon recognized this herself: "I gave loose," she wrote of the novel, "to all my leanings to the violent in melodrama. Death stalked in ghastliest form across my pages; and villainy reigned triumphant till the Nemesis of the last chapter."⁹ The twenty-four-year-old author's "leanings to the violent" were, as even the most casual reading of *The Trail of the Serpent* could not fail to discover, considerable. Two gruesome murders—one of a delirious child—take place before the end of book 1, chapter 3; by chapter 6, an abandoned woman has cast herself and her illegitimate baby into a river; within another seven chapters the novel's villain, Jabez North, has killed his own twin brother and set in motion the dastardly plot that will persuade a duped heiress to poison her husband. Much of this, of course, is the stock violence of popular literary and theatrical tradition, and leaves us relatively unmoved. Some images, however—for example, that of Jabez washing his blood-stained hands and then disposing of the "dark and ghastly" water by calmly drinking it—are more original, and more unsettling. Most shocking, I think, is the casualness with which violence, and violent, untimely deaths, are invoked. There is a preponderance of dead or vulnerable children in this novel—a grim reflection, perhaps, of nineteenth-century infant mortality rates; but consider the cynicism of Braddon's description of the Slopperton river, the Sloshy:

> It has quite a knack of swelling and bursting, this Sloshy; it overflows its banks and swallows up a house or two, or takes an impromptu snack off a few outbuildings, once or twice a year. It is inimical to children, and has been known to suck into its muddy bosom the hopes of divers families; and has afterwards gone down to the distant sea, flaunting on its breast Billy's straw hat or Johnny's pinafore, as a flag of triumph for having done a little amateur business for the gentleman on the pale horse.

This is not the tone we tend to associate with Victorian lady novelists; there is something almost Dickensian, in fact, about the mix of coolness and imaginative fancy, the controlled insouciance of that glorious final phrase, "a little amateur business for the gentleman on the pale horse." Equally memorable and troubling—and per-haps more truly Braddonesque, more "female"—is the recurrence throughout the novel of casual references to violent *domestic* crime. Note, for example, the man who "invited a friend to dinner and murdered him on the kitchen stairs while the first course was being dished." Note "John Boggins, weaver," who "beat out the brains of Sarah his wife, first with the heel of his clog and ultimately with a poker." Note the girl who poisoned her father with "the crust of a beef-steak pudding," the "boy of fourteen" who committed suicide "by hanging himself behind a door," the man who "cut his wife's throat…because she hadn't put no salt in the saucepan when she boiled the greens." Such references amount, collectively, to a kind of chorus or commentary, forming a counterpoint to Jabez's in-creasingly grandiose criminal career, his steady ascension into aris-tocratic villainy and the higher flights of melodrama.

In short, these references keep violence *ordinary*, reminding us of its grisly proximity to middle- as well as to "criminal"-class life. Jabez himself—like many sensation novel protagonists—is a respectable public figure with terrible secrets. Raised by the Slopperton Humane Society, whose founder—a "very excellent gentleman"—is known for "maltreating his wife and turning his el-dest son out of doors," he proves to be the abandoned son of a pow-erful man with a similarly shameful secret history. The very names "Slopperton" and "Sloshy"—silly as they might appear to us now—nevertheless have the important effect of establishing Braddon's town and its dark and "poisonous" river (poisoned, perhaps, through acts of industrial rather than domestic abuse, by the local mills and factories) as generic, emblematic locations, a sort of En-glish "anywhere." The "black-minded" weather of the novel's opening recalls the rain and the mud of London from the start of *Bleak House;* Braddon's breathtaking vision of the inhabitants of a county town driven to ideas and perhaps to deeds of murder, sui-cide, and madness by the depressing effects of the British climate is entirely her own. "Keep us from bad thoughts to-day," she writes, inclusively, in her first paragraph, "and keep us out of the Police Reports next week."

Of course, the sensation novelist's unhealthy dwelling on the stuff of police reports—and of coroners' courts and "low" newspapers—was exactly what the genre's critics so deplored. Braddon's implication of herself and her readers in a shared capacity for private and public violence effectively anticipates such criticisms and confronts them on their own terms. She even has a character give explicit voice to them: "I don't like these subjects," exclaims the Marquis de Cevennes, watching a performance of *Lucretia Borgia* at the Paris Opera with Valerie, his niece.

> "Even the handling of a Victor Hugo cannot make them otherwise than repulsive: and then again, there is something to be said on the score of their evil tendency. They set a dangerous example. Lucretia Borgia, in black velvet, avenging an insult according to the rules of high art and to the music of Donizetti is very charming, no doubt; but we don't want our wives and daughters to learn how they may poison us without fear of detection."

Here, distaste at the "repulsive" nature of melodramatic fictions becomes a distinctly gendered anxiety that such fictions might be setting patterns of transgression for emulation by the womenfolk of respectable men. With *Lady Audley's Secret* and *Aurora Floyd*, Braddon was soon to refine the formula that would allow her to trouble those anxieties more precisely; *The Trail of the Serpent* is dominated by men, but contains at least one magnificently vengeful female: it's a nice irony that when the Marquis makes his speech, Valerie has recently poisoned her opera-singer husband and is about to watch him apparently die on stage.

Increasingly, in fact, the novel revels in such ironies, as the casual calling up of images of domestic savagery gives way to a self-reflexive preoccupation with theatrical and literary code. Confronted with the details of his niece's abuses within her miserable (and, as it will turn out, bigamous) marriage to the fortune-seeking Jabez, the Marquis is philosophical. "I never," he says, "alarm myself when everything is hopelessly wrong, and villainy deliciously triumphant; for I know that somebody who died in the first act will come in at the centre doors, and make it all right before the curtain

falls." Joseph Peters, the detective on Jabez's trail, is knowing in a
different sort of way, but to a similar effect: his observations serve
to nudge Braddon's readers into an awareness of themselves *as*
readers by reminding them not just of the conventions of the
genre-bound book in their hands, but of the very establishment—
the private lending library, whose codes of taste and decency Braddon would become so skillful at negotiating—from which they
probably obtained it.

> "But the likeness?" said Dr. Tappenden. "That dead man was the very
> image of Jabez North."
>   "Very likely, sir. There's mysterious goin's-on, and some coinci-
> dences in this life, as well as in your story-books that's lent out at three
> half-pence a volume, keep 'em three days and return 'em clean."

This is more, I think, than simply Braddon having fun. The pleasures and the perils of *reading* are important matters throughout
The Trail of the Serpent. The novel bristles with systems of signs and
forms of communication; messages are translated—or resist translation—from one language or one medium to another, with crucial
consequences. Most memorable, perhaps, is Peters's "dumb," or
"dirty," alphabet. He manages, with this, to persuade Braddon's
hero, Richard Marwood, into feigning madness, so saving him from
being executed for a murder he did not commit; he is driven to this
extreme, however, because the proper system for the interpretation
of meaning—the reading of evidence in a public courtroom, the
determining of *truth*—has broken down. Jabez, meanwhile, pros-
pers in his career of villainy because he is adept both at manipulat-
ing his own public image ("Slopperton believed in Jabez North"),
and at orchestrating the signs through which the activities of others
are to be interpreted—stage-managing, Iago-like, the scene in
which Valerie believes her husband to be making love to another
woman. Alphabets, in this novel, emerge as "dumb" and "dirty" indeed: signs are terrifyingly vulnerable to misreading by the careless, and to manipulation by the unscrupulous; popular opinion is
dangerously prone to taking things at face value—and then as dan-

gerously prone to changing its mind. Ultimately, of course, Braddon's message is a reassuring one: Peters succeeds in disentangling reality from fiction; there are some signs, after all—the physical marks of heredity, for example—which speak an incontrovertible truth. What lingers, however, is our unease at the fact that misapprehension—individual and collective—can make signs function falsely to the extent that men might lose their lives by them, or women be provoked to devastating crimes of passion.

This is what makes *The Trail of the Serpent*, finally, a novel of social rather than psychological significance. Sensation literature has been criticized—in its own day as well as in ours—for privileging plot over character development and motivation. It has been derided, too, for its dramatic form, its unwillingness to penetrate the minds of its characters, so that they have to expose their emotional lives to us via swoons, mutterings, gnashings of teeth. (Thank heavens for Peters's extraordinary habit of "thinking aloud" on his fingers!) But the effect of this, of course, is to make us equal players with the characters in Braddon's story: we must learn, with them, the slipperiness of signs; we must ponder the proper management of those semipermeable social membranes through which we experience the lives of others and risk the under- or over-exposure of ourselves; and we must discover that personality, at some point, becomes opaque—that there are moments of psychic stress that language is incapable of containing or even describing, scenes, as Braddon puts it, "too painful and too sacred for many words."

I am suggesting, in short, that we look beyond what might seem to be the clichés and limitations of Braddon's prose—or rather, that we use those very clichés as our way into the culture from which Braddon's novels emerged. Consider, for example, the coincidences and contrivances with which *The Trail of the Serpent* is increasingly cluttered. Some—such as Richard's leaving Slopperton on the morning his uncle is murdered; Jabez seeing Valerie slip de Lancy the letter of assignation; Slosh taking the post of keeper's boy in Richard's asylum—are vital to the furthering of Braddon's plot. Others are curiously redundant—in particular, the fact that Jabez, having secured Valerie's fortune by blackmailing her into marriage, then discovers himself to be the abandoned son of her uncle the Marquis, and so legitimate heir to the fortune anyway.... The point, surely, is that if we attempt to apply the rules of realism to Braddon's text, we will fail to read it. As, again, in Dickens—and in a prefiguring, perhaps, of the novels of Hardy, in which the deeds and misdeeds of criminal and blameless characters alike invariably return to haunt them—coincidence and contrivance are invoked to remind us of the patterns and cycles in which individuals, communities, and sometimes whole societies can be fatally enmeshed.

This explains why the novel is filled with doubles: with shadows, echoes, and repetitions; it explains, too, the preoccupation with *revolution*—a word that suggests both the cyclical recurrence of events and the violent transformation of them. Jabez's seduction and abandonment of the suicide-bound young woman of the novel's first chapters replicates his father's treatment of his mother whilst an impoverished French refugee; his marriage to Valerie echoes the Marquis's bigamous post-Restoration marriage with the "wealthy widow of a Buonapartist general"; the fate of his son—who is thrown into the river, rescued, and brought up as a Slopperton "fondling"—exactly repeats his own. Crucially, however, Slosh is raised, as Jabez was not, by kind and considerate foster-parents, and the cycle of abuse leading to villainy is broken. He inherits the aristocratic features of the de Cevennes, along with a certain "undercurrent" of Jabez which, put at the service of the police, sets him on the road to becoming "the glory of his profession"—though we might well be made a little uneasy by the image of Slosh with which Peters jocularly leaves us: that of him bellowing "for three mortal hours because his father committed suicide, and disappointed the boy of seein' him hung." Here, in fact, at the very emergence of the detective literary tradition, Braddon is suggesting something that will become a troubling truism of the genre: that little distinguishes the criminal from the detective mastermind but the channeling of its powers into evil or into good; that the categories of "evil" and "good" themselves are sometimes worryingly liable to slip and blur.

Modern critics have suggested that sensation fiction can best be understood as having offered its contemporary audience an alternative to dominant Victorian values of rationality, containment, and social control;[10] but I wonder, too, whether the genre may not have spoken most intimately to its readers' daily experiences of a complicated modern life in which those values were looking increasingly inadequate. This was a world, after all, of gross distinction between poverty and wealth; a world in which friendless people really were at risk of being falsely incarcerated in asylums and subjected to all sorts of abuses whilst inside them; a world in which women—particularly working-class women—were routinely liable to seduction, rape, abandonment, and to the abuse of alcohol and drugs; a world in which orphans and other vulnerable children were at risk of neglect and exploitation. So, far from being hysterical or melodramatic, sensation fiction might ultimately be read as an entirely appropriate literary mode for such a world; and to the extent that that world still resembles our own, sensation novels like *The Trail of the Serpent*—astonishingly, out of print until now for almost a century—will retain their power to unsettle and impress.

———

SARAH WATERS has published articles on literature and cultural history, and is the author of three award-winning neo-Victorian novels: *Tipping the Velvet, Affinity,* and *Fingersmith*. She lives in London.

NOTES

1. [Oliphant, Margaret], "Novels," *Blackwoods,* Vol. CII, No. DCXXIII (Sept. 1867), pp. 257–80, p. 280.
2. [Rae, W. F.], "Sensation Novelists: Miss Braddon," *North British Review,* No. LXXXV (Sept. 1865), pp. 180–204, p. 204.
3. Wolff, Robert L., *Sensational Victorian: The Life and Fiction of Mary Elizabeth Braddon* (New York and London, 1979).
4. Braddon, Mary Elizabeth, "My First Novel: *The Trail of the Serpent,*" *The Idler Magazine,* Vol. III (Feb. to July 1893), pp. 19–30, p. 25.
5. Wolff, Robert L., "Devoted Disciple: The Letters of Mary Elizabeth Braddon to Sir Edward Bulwer-Lytton, 1862–73," *Harvard Library Bulletin,* Vol. XXII, No. I (Jan. 1974), pp. 5–35, p. 12.

6. Braddon, "My First Novel," p. 25.

7. Ibid., p. 26.

8. Wolff, *Sensational Victorian*.

9. Braddon, "My First Novel," p. 25.

10. For example, Hughes, W., *The Maniac in the Cellar: Sensation Novels of the 1860s* (Princeton, 1980), p. 13.

A NOTE ON THE TEXT

The Trail of the Serpent was first published in 1860 as *Three Times Dead* (London: W&M Clark; and Beverley, Empson). It was published in weekly parts starting in February 1860, but sold poorly. Under the guidance of London publisher John Maxwell, Braddon condensed and revised the book. (In "My First Novel" [reprinted on pp. 415–427 of this edition], Braddon recalls reducing the novel by around ten thousand words, but a comparison of the two texts indicates that the cuts were rather less substantial.) Reissued as *The Trail of the Serpent* in March 1861, it sold one thousand copies within a week of publication. It was serialized in the *Halfpenny Journal* in twenty-eight parts, from August 1, 1864, to February 28, 1865, and was reprinted several times during the following years.

This Modern Library Paperback Classic is set from the text of the 1890 Stereotyped Edition published by the London firm of Simpkin, Marshall, Hamilton, Kent & Co. A handful of typographical errors and minor inconsistencies have been silently corrected.

"Poor race of men, said the pitying Spirit,
 Dearly ye pay for your primal fall;
Some flowers of Eden ye yet inherit,
 But the trail of the Serpent is over them all."
Thomas Moore[1]

THE TRAIL
OF THE
SERPENT

BOOK THE FIRST

A RESPECTABLE
YOUNG MAN

THE GOOD SCHOOLMASTER

I don't suppose it rained harder in the good town of Slopperton-on-the-Sloshy than it rained anywhere else. But it did rain. There was scarcely an umbrella in Slopperton that could hold its own against the rain that came pouring down that November afternoon, between the hours of four and five. Every gutter in High Street, Slopperton; every gutter in Broad Street (which was of course the narrowest street); in New Street (which by the same rule was the oldest street); in East Street, West Street, Blue Dragon Street, and Windmill Street; every gutter in every one of these thoroughfares was a little Niagara, with a maelstrom at the corner, down which such small craft as bits of orange-peel, old boots and shoes, scraps of paper, and fragments of rag were absorbed—as better ships have been in the great northern whirlpool. That dingy stream, the Sloshy, was swollen into a kind of dirty Mississippi, and the graceful coal-barges which adorned its bosom were stripped of the clothes-lines and fluttering linen which usually were to be seen on their decks. A bad, determined, black-minded November day. A day on which the fog shaped itself into a demon, and lurked behind men's shoulders, whispering into their ears, "Cut your throat!—you know you've got a razor, and can't shave with it, because you've been drinking and your hand shakes; one little gash under the left ear, and the business is done. It's the best thing you can do. It is, really." A day on which the rain, the monotonous ceaseless persevering rain, has a voice as it comes down, and says, "Don't you think you could go melancholy mad? Look at me; be good enough to watch me for a couple of hours or so, and think, while you watch me, of the girl who jilted you ten years ago; and of what a much better man you would be to-day if she had only loved you truly. Oh, I think, if you'll only be so good as watch me, you might really contrive to go mad." Then again the wind. What does the wind say, as it comes cutting through the dark passage, and stabbing you, like a coward as it is, in the back, just between the shoulders—what does it say? Why, it whistles in your ear a reminder of the little bottle of laudanum[1] you've got upstairs, which you had for your toothache last week, and never used. A foggy wet windy November day. A bad day—a dangerous day. Keep us from bad thoughts to-day, and keep us out of the Police Reports[2] next week. Give us a glass of something hot and strong, and a bit of something nice for supper, and bear with us a little this day; for if the strings of yonder piano—an instrument fashioned on mechanical principles by mortal hands—if they are depressed and slackened by the influence of damp and fog, how do we know that there may not be some string in this more critical instrument, the human mind, not made on mechanical principles or by mortal hands, a little out of order on this bad November day?

But of course bad influences can only come to bad men; and of course he must be a very bad man whose spirits go up and down with every fluctuation of the weather-glass. Virtuous people no doubt are virtuous always; and by no chance, or change, or trial, or temptation, can they ever become other than virtuous. Therefore why should a wet day or a dark day depress them? No; they look out of the windows at houseless men and women and fatherless and motherless children wet through to the skin, and thank Heaven that they are not as other men:[3] like good Christians, punctual rate-payers, and unflinching church-goers as they are.

Thus it was with Mr. Jabez North, assistant and usher[4] at the academy of Dr. Tappenden. He was not in anywise affected by fog, rain, or wind. There was a fire at one end of the schoolroom, and Allecompain Major[5] had been fined sixpence, and condemned to a page of Latin grammar, for surreptitiously warming his worst chilblain at the bars thereof. But Jabez North did not want to go near the fire, though in his official capacity he might have done so; ay, even might have warmed his hands in moderation. He was not cold, or if he was cold, he didn't mind being cold. He was sitting at his desk, mending pens and hearing six red-nosed boys conjugate the verb *Amare*, "to love"—while the aforesaid boys were giving practical illustrations of the active verb "to shiver,"—and the passive ditto, "to be puzzled." He was not only a good young man, this Jabez North (and he must have been a very good young man, for his goodness was in almost every mouth in Slopperton—indeed, he was looked upon by many excellent old ladies as an incarnation of the adjective "pious")—but he was rather a handsome young man also. He had delicate features, a pale fair complexion, and, as young women said, very beautiful blue eyes; only it was unfortunate that these eyes, being, according to report, such a very beautiful colour, had a shifting way with them, and never looked at you long enough for you to find out their exact hue, or their exact expression either. He had also what was called a very fine head of fair curly hair, and what some people considered a very fine head—though it was a pity it shelved off on either side in the locality where prejudiced people place the organ of conscientiousness. A professor of phrenology,[6] lecturing at Slopperton, had declared Jabez North to be singularly wanting in that small virtue; and had even gone so far as to hint that he had never met with a parallel case of deficiency in the entire moral region, except in the skull of a very distinguished criminal, who invited a friend to dinner and murdered him on the kitchen stairs while the first course was being dished. But of course the Sloppertonians pronounced this professor to be an impostor, and his art a piece of charlatanism, as they were only too happy to pronounce any professor or any art that came in their way.

Slopperton believed in Jabez North. Partly because Slopperton had in a manner created, clothed, and fed him, set him on his feet; patted him on his head, and reared him under the shadow of Sloppertonian wings, to be the good and worthy individual he was.

The story was in this wise. Nineteen years before this bad November day, a little baby had been dragged, to all appearance drowned, out of the muddy waters of the Sloshy. Fortunately or unfortunately, as the case may be, he turned out to be less drowned than dirty, and after being subjected to very sharp treatment—such as being held head downwards, and scrubbed raw with a jack-towel,[7] by the Sloppertonian Humane Society, founded by a very excellent gentleman, somewhat renowned for maltreating his wife and turning his eldest son out of doors—this helpless infant set up a feeble squall, and evinced other signs of a return to life. He was found in a Slopperton river by a Slopperton bargeman, resuscitated by a Slopperton society, and taken by the Slopperton beadle to the Slopperton workhouse; he therefore belonged to Slopperton. Slopperton found him a species of barnacle rather difficult to shake off. The wisest thing, therefore, for Slopperton to do, was to put the best face on a bad matter, and, out of its abundance, rear this *un*-welcome little stranger. And truly virtue has its reward; for, from the workhouse brat to the Sunday-school teacher; from the Sunday-school teacher to the scrub at Dr. Tappenden's academy; from scrub to usher of the fourth form; and from fourth form usher to first assistant, pet toady, and factotum, were so many steps in the ladder of fortune which Jabez mounted, as in seven-leagued boots.

As to his name, Jabez North, it is not to be supposed that when some wretched drab[8] (mad with what madness, or wretched to what intensity of wretchedness, who shall guess?) throws her hapless and sickly offspring into the river—it is not, I say, to be supposed that she puts his card-case in his pocket, with his name and address inscribed in neat copper-plate[9] upon enamelled cards therein. No, the foundling of Slopperton was called by the board of the workhouse Jabez; first, because Jabez was a scriptural name; secondly, perhaps, because it was an ugly one, and agreed better with the cut of his clothes and the fashion of his appointments than Reginald, Conrad, or Augustus might have done. The gentlemen of the board further bestowed upon him the surname of North because he was found on the north bank of the Sloshy, and because North was an unobtrusive and commonplace cognomen, appropriate to a pauper; like whose impudence it would indeed be to write himself down Montmorency or Fitz-Harding.

Now there are many natures (God-created though they be) of so black and vile a tendency as to be soured and embittered by workhouse treatment; by constant keeping down; by days and days which grow into years and years, in which to hear a kind word is to hear a strange language—a language so strange as to bring a choking sensation into the throat, and not unbidden tears into the eyes. Natures there are, so innately wicked, as not to be improved by tyranny; by the dominion, the mockery, and the insult of little boys, who are wise enough to despise poverty, but not charitable enough to respect misfortune. And fourth-form ushers in a second-rate academy have to endure this sort of thing now and then. Some natures too may be so weak and sentimental as to sicken at a life without one human tie; a boyhood without father or mother; a youth without sister or brother. Not such the excellent nature of Jabez North. Tyranny found him meek, it is true, but it left him much meeker. Insult found him mild, but it left him lamb-like. Scornful speeches glanced away from him; cruel words seemed drops of water on marble, so powerless were they to strike or wound. He would take an insult from a boy whom with his powerful right hand he could have strangled: he would smile at the insolence of a brat whom he could have thrown from the window with one uplifting of his strong arm almost as easily as he threw away a bad pen. But he was a good young man; a benevolent young man; giving in secret, and generally getting his reward openly. His left hand scarcely knew what his right hand did; but Slopperton always knew it before long. So every citizen of the borough praised and applauded this model young man, and many were the prophecies of the day when the pauper boy should be one of the greatest men in that greatest of all towns, the town of Slopperton.

The bad November day merged into a bad November night. Dark night at five o'clock, when candles, few and far between, flickering in Dr. Tappenden's schoolroom, and long rows of half-pint mugs—splendid institutions for little boys to warm their hands at, being full of a boiling and semi-opaque liquid, *par excellence* milk-and-water—ornamented the schoolroom table. Darker night still, when the half-pint mugs have been collected by a red maid-servant, with nose, elbows, and knuckles picked out in purple; when all traces of the evening meal are removed; when the six red-nosed first-form boys have sat down to Virgil[10]—for whom they entertain a deadly hatred, feeling convinced that he wrote with a special view to their being flogged from inability to construe[11] him. Of course, if he hadn't been a spiteful beast he would have written in English, and then he wouldn't have had to be construed. Darker night still at eight o'clock, when the boys have gone to bed, and perhaps would have gone to sleep, if Allecompain Major had not a supper-party in his room, with Banbury cakes, pigs' trotters, periwinkles, acid rock,[12] and ginger-beer powders, laid out upon the bolster. Not so dark by the head assistant's desk, at which Jabez sits, his face ineffably calm, examining a pile of exercises. Look at his face by that one candle; look at the eyes, which are steady now, for he does not dream that any one is watching him—steady and luminous with a subdued fire, which might blaze out some day into a deadly flame. Look at the face, the determined mouth, the thin lips, which form almost an arch—and say, is that the face of a man to be content with a life of dreary and obscure monotony? A somewhat intellectual face; but not the face of a man with an intellect seeking no better employment than the correcting of French and Latin exercises. If we could look into his heart, we might find the answers to these questions. He raises the lid of his desk; a deep desk that holds many things—paper, pens, letters: and what?—a thick coil of rope. A strange object in the assistant's desk, this coil of rope! He looks at it as if to assure himself that it is safe; shuts his desk quickly, locks it, puts the key in his waistcoat-pocket; and when at half-past nine he goes up into his little bedroom at the top of the house, he will carry the desk under his arm.

CHAPTER II

GOOD FOR NOTHING

The November night is darkest, foggiest, wettest, and windiest out on the open road that leads into Slopperton. A dreary road at the best of times, this Slopperton road, and dreariest of all in one spot about a mile and a half out of the town. Upon this spot stands a solitary house, known as the Black Mill. It was once the cottage of a miller, and the mill still stands, though in disuse.

The cottage had been altered and improved within the last few years, and made into a tolerable-sized house; a dreary, rambling, tumble-down place, it is true, but still with some pretension about it. It was occupied at this time by a widow lady, a Mrs. Marwood, once the owner of a large fortune, which had nearly all been squandered by the dissipation of her only son. This son had long left Slopperton. His mother had not heard of him for years. Some said he had gone abroad. She tried to hope this, but sometimes she mourned him as dead. She lived in modest style, with one old female servant, who had been with her since her marriage, and had been faithful through every change of fortune—as these common and unlearned creatures, strange to say, sometimes are. It happened that at this very time Mrs. Marwood had just received the visit of a brother, who had returned from the East Indies[1] with a large fortune. This brother, Mr. Montague Harding, had on his landing in England hastened to seek out his only sister, and the arrival of the wealthy nabob at the solitary house on the Slopperton road had been a nine days' wonder for the good citizens of Slopperton. He brought with him only one servant, a half-caste;[2] his visit was to be a short one, as he was about buying an estate in the south of England, on which he intended to reside with his widowed sister.

Slopperton had a great deal to say about Mr. Harding. Slopperton gave him credit for the possession of uncounted and uncountable lacs of rupees;[3] but Slopperton wouldn't give him credit for the possession of the hundredth part of an ounce of liver.[4] Slopperton left cards at the Black Mill, and had serious thoughts of getting up a deputation to invite the rich East Indian to represent its inhabitants at the great congress of Westminster. But both Mr. Harding and Mrs. Marwood kept aloof from Slopperton, and were set down accordingly as mysterious, not to say dark-minded individuals, forthwith.

———

The brother and sister are seated in the little, warm, lamp-lit drawing-room at the Black Mill this dark November night. She is a woman who has once been handsome, but whose beauty has been fretted away by anxieties and suspenses, which wear out the strongest hope, as water wears away the hardest rock. The Anglo-Indian[5] very much resembles her; but though his face is that of an invalid, it is not care-worn. It is the face of a good man, who has a hope so strong that neither fear nor trouble can disquiet him.

He is speaking—"And you have not heard from your son?"

"For nearly seven years. Seven years of cruel suspense; seven years, during which every knock at yonder door seems to have beaten a blow upon my heart—every footstep on yonder garden-walk seems to have trodden down a hope."

"And you do not think him dead?"

"I hope and pray not. Not dead, impenitent; not dead, without my blessing; not gone away from me for ever, without one pressure of the hand, one prayer for my forgiveness, one whisper of regret for all he has made me suffer."

"He was very wild, then, very dissipated?"

"He was a reprobate and a gambler. He squandered his money like water. He had bad companions, I know; but was not himself wicked at heart. The very night he ran away, the night I saw him for the last time, I'm sure he was sorry for his bad courses. He said something to that effect; said his road was a dark one, but that it had only one end, and he must go on to the end."

"And you made no remonstrance?"

"I was tired of remonstrance, tired of prayer, and had wearied out my soul with hope deferred."

"My dear Agnes! And this poor boy, this wretched misguided boy, Heaven have pity upon him and restore him! Heaven have pity upon every wanderer, this dismal and pitiless night!"

Heaven, indeed, have pity upon that wanderer, out on the bleak highroad to Slopperton; out on the shelterless Slopperton road, a mile away from the Black Mill! The wanderer is a young man, whose garments, of the shabby-genteel order, are worst of all fitted to keep out the cruel weather; a handsome young man, or a man who has once been handsome, but on whom riotous days and nights, drunkenness, recklessness, and folly, have had their dire effects. He is struggling to keep a bad cigar alight, and when it goes out, which is about twice in five minutes, he utters expressions which in Slopperton are thought very wicked, and consigns that good city, with its virtuous citizens, to a very bad neighbourhood.

He talks to himself between his struggles with the cigar. "Foot-sore and weary, hungry and thirsty, cold and ill; it is not a very hopeful way for the only son of a rich man to come back to his native place after seven years' absence. I wonder what star presides over my vagabond existence; if I knew, I'd shake my fist at it," he muttered, as he looked up at two or three feeble luminaries glimmering through the rain and fog. "Another mile to the Black Mill—and then what will she say to me? What can she say to me but to curse me? What have I earned by such a life as mine except a mother's curse?" His cigar chose this very moment of all others to go out. If the bad three-halfpenny Havannah[6] had been a sentient thing with reasoning powers, it might have known better. He threw it aside into a ditch with an oath. He slouched his hat over his eyes, thrust one hand into the breast of his coat—(he had a stick cut from some hedgerow in the other)—and walked with a determined though a weary air onward through slush and mire towards the Black Mill, from which already the lighted windows shone through the darkness like so many beacons.

On through slush and mire, with a weary and slouching step.

No matter. It is the step for which his mother has waited for seven long years; it is the step whose ghostly echo on the garden-walk has smitten so often on her heart and trodden out the light of hope. But surely the step comes on now—full surely, and for good or ill. Whether for good or ill comes this long-watched-for step, this bad November night, who shall say?

In a quarter of an hour the wanderer stands in the little garden of the Black Mill. He has not courage to knock at the door; it might be opened by a stranger; he might hear something he dare not whisper to his own heart—he might hear something which would strike him down dead upon the threshold.

He sees the light in the drawing-room windows. He approaches, and hears his mother's voice.

It is a long time since he has uttered a prayer: but he falls on his knees by the long French window and breathes a thanksgiving.

That voice is not still!

What shall he do? What can he hope from his mother, so cruelly abandoned?

At this moment Mr. Harding opens the window to look out at the dismal night. As he does so, the young man falls fainting, exhausted, into the room.

Draw a curtain over the agitation and the bewilderment of that scene. The almost broken-hearted mother's joy is too sacred for words. And the passionate tears of the prodigal son—who shall measure the remorseful agony of a man whose life has been one long career of recklessness, and who sees his sin written in his mother's face?

———

The mother and son sit together, talking gravely, hand in hand, for two long hours. He tells her, not of all his follies, but of all his regrets—his punishment, his anguish, his penitence, and his resolutions for the future.

Surely it is for good, and good alone, that he has come over a long and dreary road, through toil and suffering, to kneel here at his mother's feet and build up fair schemes for the future.

The old servant, who has known Richard from a baby, shares in his mother's joy. After the slight supper which the weary wanderer is induced to eat, her brother and her son persuade Mrs. Marwood to retire to rest; and left *tête-à-tête*, the uncle and nephew sit down to discuss a bottle of old madeira by the sea-coal[7] fire.

"My dear Richard"—the young man's name is Richard—("Daredevil Dick" he has been called by his wild companions)—"My dear Richard," says Mr. Harding very gravely, "I am about to say something to you, which I trust you will take in good part."

"I am not so used to kind words from good men that I am likely to take anything you can say amiss."

"You will not, then, doubt the joy I feel in your return this night, if I ask you what are your plans for the future?"

The young man shook his head. Poor Richard! he had never in his life had any definite plan for the future, or he might not have been what he was that night.

"My poor boy, I believe you have a noble heart, but you have led a wasted life. This must be repaired."

Richard shook his head again. He was very hopeless of himself.

"I am good for nothing," he said; "I am a bad lot. I wonder they don't hang such men as me."

"I wonder they don't hang such men." He uttered this reckless speech in his own reckless way, as if it would be rather a good joke to be hung up out of the way and done for.

"My dear boy, thank Heaven you have returned to us. Now I have a plan to make a man of you yet."

Richard looked up this time with a hopeful light in his dark eyes. He was hopeless at five minutes past ten; he was radiant when the minute hand had moved on to the next figure on the dial. He was one of those men whose bad and good angels have a sharp fight and a constant struggle, but whom we all hope to see saved at last.

"I have a plan which has occurred to me since your unexpected arrival this evening," continued his uncle. "Now, if you stay here, your mother, who has a trick (as all loving mothers have) of fancying you are still a little boy in a pinafore and frock[8]—your mother will be for having you loiter about from morning till night with nothing to do and nothing to care for; you will fall in again with all your old Slopperton companions, and all those companions' bad habits. This isn't the way to make a man of you, Richard."

Richard, very radiant by this time, thinks not.

"My plan is, that you start off to-morrow morning before your mother is up, with a letter of introduction which I will give you to an old friend of mine, a merchant in the town of Gardenford, forty miles from here. At my request, he will give you a berth in his office, and will treat you as if you were his own son. You can come over here to see your mother as often as you like; and if you choose to work hard as a merchant's clerk, so as to make your own fortune, I know an old fellow just returned from the East Indies, with not enough liver to keep him alive many years, who will leave you another fortune to add to it. What do you say, Richard? Is it a bargain?"

"My dear generous uncle!" Richard cries, shaking the old man by the hand.

Was it a bargain? Of course it was. A merchant's office—the very thing for Richard. He *would* work hard, work night and day to repair the past, and to show the world there was stuff in him to make a man, and a good man yet.

Poor Richard, half an hour ago wishing to be hung and put out of the way, now full of radiance and hope, while the good angel has the best of it!

"You must not begin your new life without money, Richard: I shall, therefore, give you all I have in the house. I think I cannot better show my confidence in you, and my certainty that you will not return to your old habits, than by giving you this money." Richard looks—he cannot speak his gratitude.

The old man conducts his nephew up stairs to his bedroom, an old-fashioned apartment, in one window of which is a handsome cabinet, half desk, half bureau. He unlocks this, and takes from it a pocket-book containing one hundred and thirty-odd pounds in small notes and gold, and two bills for one hundred pounds each on an Anglo-Indian bank in the city.

"Take this, Richard. Use the broken cash as you require it for present purposes—in purchasing such an outfit as becomes my nephew; and on your arrival in Gardenford, place the bills in the bank for future exigencies. And as I wish your mother to know nothing of our little plan until you are gone, the best thing you can do is to start before any one is up—to-morrow morning."

"I will start at day-break. I can leave a note for my mother."

"No, no," said the uncle, "I will tell her all. You can write directly you reach your destination. Now, you will think it cruel of me to ask you to leave your home on the very night of your return to it; but it is quite as well, my dear boy, to strike while the iron's hot. If you remain here your good resolutions may be vanquished by old influences; for the best resolution, Richard, is but a seed, and if it doesn't bear the fruit of a good action, it is less than worthless, for it is a lie, and promises what it doesn't perform. I've a higher opinion of you than to think that you brought no better fruit of your penitence home to your loving mother than empty resolutions. I believe you have a steady determination to reform."

"You only do me justice in that belief, sir. I ask nothing better than the opportunity of showing that I am in earnest."

Mr. Harding is quite satisfied, and once more suggests that Richard should depart very early the next day.

"I will leave this house at five in the morning," said the nephew; "a train starts for Gardenford about six. I shall creep out quietly, and not disturb any one. I know the way out of the dear old house—I can get out of the drawing-room window, and need not unlock the hall-door; for I know that good stupid old woman Martha sleeps with the key under her pillow.

"Ah, by the bye, where does Martha mean to put you to-night?"

"In the little back parlour, I think she said; the room under this."

———

The uncle and nephew went down to this little parlour, where they found old Martha making up a bed on the sofa.

"You will sleep very comfortably here for to-night, Master Richard," said the old woman; "but if my mistress doesn't have this ceiling mended before long there'll be an accident some day."

They all looked up at the ceiling. The plaster had fallen in several places, and there were one or two cracks of considerable size.

"If it was daylight," grumbled the old woman, "you could see through into Mister Harding's bedroom, for his worship won't have a carpet."

His worship said he had not been used to carpets in India, and liked the sight of Mrs. Martha's snow-white boards.

"And it's hard to keep them white, sir, I can tell you; for when I scour the floor of that room the water runs through and spoils the furniture down here."

But Daredevil Dick didn't seem to care much for the dilapidated ceiling. The madeira, his brightened prospects, and the excitement he had gone through, all combined to make him thoroughly wearied out. He shook his uncle's hand with a brief but energetic expression of gratitude, and then flung himself half dressed upon the bed.

"There is an alarum clock in my room," said the old man, "which I will set for five o'clock. I always sleep with my door open; so you will be sure to hear it go down. It won't disturb your mother, for she sleeps at the other end of the house. And now good night, and God bless you, my boy!"

———

He is gone, and the returned prodigal is asleep. His handsome face has lost half its look of dissipation and care, in the renewed light of hope; his black hair is tossed off his broad forehead, and it is a fine candid countenance, with a sweet smile playing round the mouth. Oh, there is stuff in him to make a man yet, though he says they should hang such fellows as he!

His uncle has retired to his room, where his half-caste servant assists at his toilette for the night. This servant, who is a Lascar,[9] and cannot speak one word of English (his master converses with him in Hindostanee), and is thought to be as faithful as a dog, sleeps in a little bed in the dressing-room adjoining his master's apartment.

So, on this bad November night, with the wind howling round the walls as if it were an angry unadmitted guest that clamoured to come in; with the rain beating on the roof, as if it had a special purpose and was bent on flooding the old house; there is peace and happiness, and a returned and penitent wanderer at the desolate old Black Mill.

The wind this night seems to howl with a peculiar significance, but nobody has the key to its strange language; and if, in every shrill dissonant shriek, it tries to tell a ghastly secret or to give a timely warning, it tries in vain, for no one heeds or understands.

CHAPTER III

THE USHER WASHES HIS HANDS

Mr. Jabez North had not his little room quite to himself at Dr. Tappenden's. There are some penalties attendant even on being a good young man, and our friend Jabez sometimes found his very virtues rather inconvenient. It happened that Allecompain Junior was ill of a fever—sometimes delirious; and as the usher was such an excel-

lent young person, beloved by the pupils and trusted implicitly by
the master, the sick little boy was put under his especial care, and a
bed was made up for him in Jabez's room.

This very November night, when the usher comes up stairs, his
great desk under one arm (he is very strong, this usher), and a little
feeble tallow candle in his left hand, he finds the boy very ill indeed.
He does not know Jabez, for he is talking of a boat-race—a race
that took place in the bright summer gone by. He is sitting up on
the pillow, waving his little thin hand, and crying out at the top of
his feeble voice, "Bravo, red! Red wins! Three cheers for red! Go
it—go it, red! Blue's beat—I say blue's beat! George Harris has won
the day. I've backed George Harris. I've bet six-pennorth of toffey
on George Harris! Go it, red!"

"We're worse to-night, then," said the usher; "so much the better.
We're off our head, and we're not likely to take much notice; so
much the better;" and this benevolent young man began to undress.
To undress, but not to go to bed; for from a small trunk he takes out
a dark smock-frock,[1] a pair of leather gaiters,[2] a black scratch wig,[3]
and a countryman's slouched hat. He dresses himself in these
things, and sits down at a little table with his desk before him.

The boy rambles on. He is out nutting in the woods with his little sister in the glorious autumn months gone by.

"Shake the tree, Harriet, shake the tree; they'll fall if you only
shake hard enough. Look at the hazel-nuts! so thick you can't count
'em. Shake away, Harriet; and take care of your head, for they'll
come down like a shower of rain!"

The usher takes the coil of rope from his desk, and begins to un-
wind it; he has another coil in his little trunk, another hidden away
under the mattress of his bed. He joins the three together, and they
form a rope of considerable length. He looks round the room; holds
the light over the boy's face, but sees no consciousness of passing
events in those bright feverish eyes.

He opens the window of his room; it is on the second story, and
looks out into the playground—a large space shut in from the lane
in which the school stands by a wall of considerable height. About
half the height of this room are some posts erected for gymnastics;

they are about ten feet from the wall of the house, and the usher looks at them dubiously. He lowers the rope out of the window and attaches one end of it to an iron hook in the wall—a very convenient hook, and very secure apparently, for it looks as if it had been only driven in that very day.

He surveys the distance beneath him, takes another dubious look at the posts in the playground, and is about to step out of the window, when a feeble voice from the little bed cries out—not in any delirious ramblings this time—"What are you doing with that rope? Who are you? What are you doing with that rope?"

Jabez looks round, and although so good a young man, mutters something very much resembling an oath.

"Silly boy, don't you know me? I'm Jabez, your old friend——"

"Ah, kind old Jabez; you won't send me back in Virgil, because I've been ill; eh, Mr. North?"

"No, no! See, you want to know what I am doing with this rope; why, making a swing, to be sure."

"A swing? Oh, that's capital. Such a jolly thick rope too! When shall I be well enough to swing, I wonder? It's so dull up here. I'll try and go to sleep; but I dream such bad dreams."

"There, there, go to sleep," says the usher, in a soothing voice. This time, before he goes to the window, he puts out his tallow candle; the rushlight on the hearth he extinguishes also; feels for something in his bosom, clutches this something tightly; takes a firm grasp of the rope, and gets out of the window.

A curious way to make a swing! He lets himself down foot by foot, with wonderful caution and wonderful courage. When he gets on a level with the posts of the gymnasium he gives himself a sudden jerk, and swinging over against them, catches hold of the highest post, and his descent is then an easy one for the post is notched for the purpose of climbing, and Jabez, always good at gymnastics, descends it almost as easily as another man would an ordinary staircase. He leaves the rope still hanging from his bedroom window, scales the playground wall, and when the Slopperton clocks strike twelve is out upon the highroad. He skirts the town of Slopperton by a circuitous route, and in another half hour is on the other side of it, bearing towards the Black Mill. A curious manner of making a swing this midnight ramble. Altogether a curious ramble for this good young usher; but even good men have sometimes strange fancies, and this may be one of them.

One o'clock from the Slopperton steeples: two o'clock: three o'clock. The sick little boy does not go to sleep, but wanders, oh, how wearily, through past scenes in his young life. Midsummer rambles, Christmas holidays, and merry games; the pretty speeches of the little sister who died three years ago; unfinished tasks and puzzling exercises, all pass through his wandering mind; and when the clocks chime the quarter after three, he is still talking, still rambling on in feeble accents, still tossing wearily on his pillow.

As the clocks chime the quarter, the rope is at work again, and five minutes afterwards the usher clambers into the room.

Not very good to look upon, either in costume or countenance; bad to look upon, with his clothes mud-bespattered and torn; wet to the skin; his hair in matted locks streaming over his forehead; worse to look upon, with his light blue eyes, bright with a dangerous and wicked fire—the eyes of a wild beast baulked of his prey; dreadful to look upon, with his hands clenched in fury, and his tongue busy with half-suppressed but terrible imprecations.

"All for nothing!" he mutters. "All the toil, the scheming, and the danger for nothing—all the work of the brain and the hands wasted—nothing gained, nothing gained!"

He hides away the rope in his trunk, and begins to unbutton his mud-stained gaiters. The little boy cries out in a feeble voice for his medicine.

The usher pours a tablespoonful of the mixture into a wineglass with a steady hand, and carries it to the bedside.

The boy is about to take it from him, when he utters a sudden cry.

"What's the matter?" asks Jabez, angrily.

"Your hand!—your hand! What's that upon your hand?"

A dark stain scarcely dry—a dark stain, at the sight of which the boy trembles from head to foot.

"Nothing, nothing!" answers the tutor. "Take your medicine, and go to sleep."

No, the boy cries hysterically, he won't take his medicine; he will never take anything again from that dreadful hand. "I know what that horrid stain is. What have you been doing? Why did you climb out of the window with a rope? It wasn't to make a swing; it must have been for something dreadful! Why did you stay away three hours in the middle of the night? I counted the hours by the church clocks. Why have you got those strange clothes on? What does it all mean? I'll ask the Doctor to take me out of this room! I'll go to him this moment, for I'm afraid of you."

The boy tries to get out of bed as he speaks; but the usher holds him down with one powerful hand, which he places upon the boy's mouth, at the same time keeping him from stirring and preventing him from crying out.

With his free right hand he searches among the bottles on the table by the bedside.

He throws the medicine out of the glass, and pours from another bottle a few spoonfuls of a dark liquid labelled, "Opium—Poison!"[4]

"Now, sir, take your medicine, or I'll report you to the principal to-morrow morning."

The boy tries to remonstrate, but in vain; the powerful hand throws back his head, and Jabez pours the liquid down his throat.

For a little time the boy, quite delirious now, goes on talking of the summer rambles and the Christmas games, and then falls into a deep slumber.

Then Jabez North sets to work to wash his hands. A curious young man, with curious fashions for doing things—above all, a curious fashion of washing his hands.

He washes them very carefully in a small quantity of water, and when they are quite clean, and the water has become a dark and ghastly colour, he drinks it, and doesn't make even one wry face at the horrible draught.

"Well, well," he mutters, "if nothing is gained by to-night's work, I have at least tried my strength, and I now know what I'm made of."

Very strange stuff he must have been made of—very strange and perhaps not very good stuff, to be able to look at the bed on which the innocent and helpless boy lay in a deep slumber, and say,—

"At any rate, *he* will tell no tales."

No! he will tell no tales, nor ever talk again of summer rambles, or of Christmas holidays, or of his dead sister's pretty words. Perhaps he will join that wept-for little sister in a better world, where there are no such good young men as Jabez North.

That worthy gentleman goes down aghast, with a white face, next morning, to tell Dr. Tappenden that his poor little charge is dead, and that perhaps he had better break the news to Allecompain Major, who is sick after that supper, which, in his boyish thoughtlessness, and his certainty of his little brother's recovery, he had given last night.

"Do, yes, by all means, break the sad news to the poor boy; for I know, North, you'll do it tenderly."

CHAPTER IV

RICHARD MARWOOD LIGHTS HIS PIPE

Daredevil Dick hears the alarum at five o'clock, and leaves his couch very cautiously. He would like, before he leaves the house, to go to his mother's door, if it were only to breathe a prayer upon the threshold. He would like to go to his uncle's bedside, to give one farewell look at the kind face; but he has promised to be very cautious, and to awaken no one; so he steals quietly out through the drawing-room window—the same window by which he entered so strangely the preceding evening—into the chill morning, dark as night yet. He pauses in the little garden-walk for a minute while he lights his pipe, and looks up at the shrouded windows of the familiar house. "God bless her!" he mutters; "and God reward that good old man, for giving a scamp like me the chance of redeeming his honour!"

There is a thick fog, but no rain. Daredevil Dick knows his way so well, that neither fog nor darkness are any hindrance to him, and he trudges on with a cheery step, and his pipe in his mouth, towards the Slopperton railway station. The station is half an hour's walk out of the town, and when he reaches it the clocks are striking six. Learning that the train will not start for half an hour, he walks up and down the platform, looking, with his handsome face and shabby dress, rather conspicuous. Two or three trains for different destinations start while he is waiting on the platform, and several people stare at him, as he strides up and down, his hands in his pockets, and his weather-beaten hat slouched over his eyes—(for he does not want to be known by any Slopperton people yet awhile, till his position is better)—and when one man, with whom he had been intimate before he left the town, seemed to recognize him, and approached as if to speak to him, Richard turned abruptly on his heel and crossed to the other side of the station.

If he had known that such a little incident as that could have a dark and dreadful influence on his life, surely he would have thought himself foredoomed and set apart for a cruel destiny.

He strolled into the refreshment-room, took a cup of coffee, changed a sovereign[1] in paying for his ticket, bought a newspaper, seated himself in a second-class carriage, and in a few minutes was out of Slopperton.

There was only one other passenger in the carriage—a commercial traveller;[2] and Richard and he smoked their pipes in defiance of the guards at the stations they passed. When did ever Daredevil Dick quail before any authorities? He had faced all Bow Street, chaffed Marlborough Street out of countenance, and had kept the station-house awake all night singing, "We won't go home till morning."

It is rather a dull journey at the best of times from Slopperton to Gardenford, and on this dark foggy November morning, of course, duller than usual. It was still dark at half-past six. The station was lighted with gas, and there was a little lamp in the railway carriage, but for which the two travellers would not have seen each other's faces. Richard looked out of the window for a few minutes, got up a little conversation with his fellow traveller, which soon flagged (for the young man was rather out of spirits at leaving his mother directly after their reconciliation), and then, being sadly at a loss to amuse himself, took out his uncle's letter to the Gardenford merchant, and looked at the superscription. The letter was not sealed, but he did not take it from the envelope. "If he said any good of me, it's a great deal more than I deserve," said Richard to himself; "but I'm young yet, and there's plenty of time to redeem the past."

Time to redeem the past! O poor Richard!

He twisted the letter about in his hands, lighted another pipe, and smoked till the train arrived at the Gardenford station. Another foggy November day had set in.

If Richard Marwood had been a close observer of men and manners, he might have been rather puzzled by the conduct of a short, thick-set man, shabbily dressed, who was standing on the platform when he descended from the carriage. The man was evidently waiting for some one to arrive by this train: and as surely that some one had arrived, for the man looked perfectly satisfied when he had scanned, with a glance marvellously rapid, the face of every passenger who alighted. But who this some one was, for whom the man was waiting, it was rather difficult to discover. He did not speak to any one, nor approach any one, nor did he appear to have any particular purpose in being there after that one rapid glance at all the travellers. A very minute observer might certainly have detected in him a slight interest in the movements of Richard Marwood; and when that individual left the station the stranger strolled out after him, and walked a few paces behind him down the back street that led from the station to the town. Presently he came up closer to him, and a few minutes afterwards suddenly and unceremoniously hooked his arm into that of Richard.

"Mr. Richard Marwood, I think," he said.

"I'm not ashamed of my name," replied Daredevil Dick, "and that *is* my name. Perhaps you'll oblige me with yours, since you're so uncommonly friendly." And the young man tried to withdraw his arm from that of the stranger; but the stranger was of an affectionate turn of mind, and kept his arm tightly hooked in his.

"Oh, never mind my name," he said: "you'll learn my name fast enough, I dare say. But," he continued, as he caught a threatening look in Richard's eye, "if you want to call me anything, why, call me Jinks."

"Very well then, Mr. Jinks, since I didn't come to Gardenford to make your acquaintance, and as now, having made your acquaintance, I can't say I much care about cultivating it further, why I wish you a very good morning!" As he said this, Richard wrenched his arm from that of the stranger, and strode two or three paces forward.

Not more than two or three paces though, for the affectionate Mr. Jinks caught him again by the arm, and a friend of Mr. Jinks, who had also been lurking outside the station when the train arrived, happening to cross over from the other side of the street at this very moment, caught hold of his other arm, and poor Daredevil Dick, firmly pinioned by these two new-found friends, looked with a puzzled expression from one to the other.

"Come, come," said Mr. Jinks, in a soothing tone, "the best thing you can do is to take it quietly, and come along with me."

"Oh, I see," said Richard. "Here's a spoke in the wheel of my reform; it's those cursed Jews,[3] I suppose, have got wind of my coming down here. Show us your writ,[4] Mr. Jinks, and tell us at whose suit it is, and for what amount? I've got a considerable sum about me, and can settle it on the spot."

"Oh, you have, have you?" Mr. Jinks was so surprised by this last speech of Richard's that he was obliged to take off his hat, and rub his hand through his hair before he could recover himself. "Oh!" he continued, staring at Richard, "Oh! you've got a considerable sum of money about you, have you? Well, my friend, you're either very green, or you're very cheeky; and all I can say is, take care how you commit yourself. I'm not a sheriff's officer. If you'd done me the honour to reckon up my nose you might have knowed it" (Mr. Jinks's olfactory organ was a decided snub); "and I ain't going to arrest you for debt."

"Oh, very well then," said Dick; "perhaps you and your affectionate friend, who both seem to be afflicted with rather an overlarge allowance of the organ of adhesiveness,[5] will be so very obliging as to let me go. I'll leave you a lock of my hair, as you've taken such a wonderful fancy to me." And with a powerful effort he shook the two strangers off him; but Mr. Jinks caught him again by the arm, and Mr. Jinks's friend, producing a pair of handcuffs, locked them on Richard's wrists with railroad rapidity.

"Now, don't you try it on," said Mr. Jinks. "I didn't want to use these, you know, if you'd have come quietly. I've heard you belong to a respectable family, so I thought I wouldn't ornament you with these here objects of *bigotry*" (it is to be presumed Mr. Jinks means *bijouterie*);[6] "but it seems there's no help for it, so come along to the station; we shall catch the eight-thirty train, and be in Slopperton before ten. The inquest won't come on till to-morrow."

Richard looked at his wrists, from his wrists to the faces of the two men, with an utterly hopeless expression of wonder.

"Am I mad," he said, "or drunk, or dreaming? What have you put these cursed things upon me for? Why do you want to take me back to Slopperton? What inquest? Who's dead?"

Mr. Jinks put his head on one side, and contemplated the prisoner with the eye of a connoisseur.

"Don't he come the *h*innocent dodge stunnin'?" he said, rather to himself than to his companion, who, by the bye, throughout the affair had never once spoken. "Don't he do it beautiful? Wouldn't he be a first-rate actor up at the Wictoria Theayter in London?[7] Wouldn't he be prime in the 'Suspected One,' or 'Gonsalvo the Guiltless?'[8] Vy," said Mr. Jinks, with intense admiration, "he'd be worth his two-pound-ten a week and a clear half benefit every month to any manager as is."

As Mr. Jinks made these complimentary remarks, he and his friend walked on. Richard, puzzled, bewildered, and unresisting, walked between them towards the railway station; but presently Mr. Jinks condescended to reply to his prisoner's questions, in this wise:—

"You want to know what inquest? Well, a inquest on a gentleman what's been barbarously murdered. You want to know who's dead? Why, your uncle is the gent as has been murdered. You want to know why we are going to take you back to Slopperton? Well, because we've got a warrant to arrest you upon suspicion of having committed the murder."

"My uncle murdered!" cried Richard, with a face that now for the first time since his arrest betrayed anxiety and horror; for throughout his interview with Mr. Jinks he had never once seemed frightened. His manner had expressed only utter bewilderment of mind.

"Yes, murdered; his throat cut from ear to ear."

"It cannot be," said Richard. "There must be some horrid mistake here. My uncle, Montague Harding, murdered! I bade him good-bye at twelve last night in perfect health."

"And this morning he was found murdered in his bed; with the cabinet in his room broken open, and rifled of a pocket-book known to contain upwards of three hundred pounds."

"Why, he gave me that pocket-book last night. He gave it to me. I have it here in my breast-pocket."

"You'd better keep that story for the coroner," said Mr. Jinks. "Perhaps *he'll* believe it."

"I must be mad, I must be mad," said Richard.

They had by this time reached the station, and Mr. Jinks having glanced into two or three carriages of the train about to start, selected one of the second-class, and ushered Richard into it. He seated himself by the young man's side, while his silent and unobtrusive friend took his place opposite. The guard locked the door, and the train started.

Mr. Jinks's quiet friend was exactly one of those people adapted to pass in a crowd. He might have passed in a hundred crowds, and no one of the hundreds of people in any of those hundred crowds would have glanced aside to look at him.

You could only describe him by negatives. He was neither very tall nor very short, he was neither very stout nor very thin, neither dark nor fair, neither ugly nor handsome; but just such a medium between the two extremities of each as to be utterly commonplace and unnoticeable.

If you looked at his face for three hours together, you would in those three hours find only one thing in that face that was any way out of the common—that one thing was the expression of the mouth.

It was a compressed mouth with thin lips, which tightened and drew themselves rigidly together when the man thought—and the man was almost always thinking: and this was not all, for when he thought most deeply the mouth shifted in a palpable degree to the left side of his face. This was the only thing remarkable about the man, except, indeed, that he was dumb but not deaf, having lost the use of his speech during a terrible illness which he had suffered in his youth.

Throughout Richard's arrest he had watched the proceedings with unswerving intensity, and he now sat opposite the prisoner, thinking deeply, with his compressed lips drawn on one side.

The dumb man was a mere scrub,[9] one of the very lowest of the police force, a sort of outsider and *employé* of Mr. Jinks, the Gardenford detective; but he was useful, quiet, and steady, and above all, as his patrons said, he was to be relied on, because he could not talk.

He could talk though, in his own way, and he began to talk presently in his own way to Mr. Jinks; he began to talk with his fingers with a rapidity which seemed marvellous. The fingers were more active than clean, and made rather a dirty alphabet.

"Oh, hang it," said Mr. Jinks, after watching him for a moment, "you must do it a little slower, if you want me to understand. I am not an electric telegraph."

The scrub nodded, and began again with his fingers, very slowly.

This time Richard too watched him; for Richard knew this dumb alphabet. He had talked whole reams of nonsense with it, in days gone by, to a pretty girl at a boarding-school, between whom and himself there had existed a platonic attachment, to say nothing of a high wall and broken glass bottles.

Richard watched the dirty alphabet.

First, two grimy fingers laid flat upon the dirty palm, N. Next, the tip of the grimy forefinger of the right hand upon the tip of the grimy third finger of the left hand, O; the next letter is T, and the man snaps his fingers—the word is finished, NOT. Not what? Richard found himself wondering with an intense eagerness, which, even in the bewildered state of his mind, surprised him.

The dumb man began another word—

G—U—I—L—

Mr. Jinks cut him short.

"Not guilty? Not fiddlesticks! What do *you* know about it, I should like to know? Where did you get your experience? Where did you get your sharp practice? What school have you been formed in, I wonder, that you can come out so positive with your opinion; and what's the value you put your opinion at, I wonder? I should be glad to hear what you'd take for your opinion."

Mr. Jinks uttered the whole of this speech with the most intense sarcasm; for Mr. Jinks was a distinguished detective, and prided himself highly on his acumen; and was therefore very indignant that his sub and scrub should dare to express an opinion.

"My uncle murdered!" said Richard; "my good, kind, generous-hearted uncle! Murdered in cold blood! Oh, it is too horrible!"

The scrub's mouth was very much on one side as Richard muttered this, half to himself.

"And I am suspected of the murder?"

"Well, you see," said Mr. Jinks, "there's two or three things tell pretty strong against you. Why were you in such a hurry this morning to cut and run to Gardenford?"

"My uncle had recommended me to a merchant's office in that town: see, here is the letter of introduction—read it."

"No, it ain't my place," said Mr. Jinks. "The letter's not sealed, I see, but *I* mustn't read it, or if I do, I stand the chance of gettin' snubbed and lectured for goin' beyond my dooty: howsumdever, you can show it to the coroner. I'm sure I should be very glad to see you clear yourself, for I've heard you belong to one of our good old county families, and it ain't quite the thing to hang such as you."

Poor Richard! His reckless words of the night before came back to him: "I wonder they don't hang such fellows as I am."

"And now," says Jinks, "as I should like to make all things comfortable, if you're willing to come along quietly with me and my friend here, why, I'll move those bracelets, because they are not quite so ornamental as they're sometimes useful; and as I'm going to light my pipe, why, if you like to blow a cloud, too, you can."

With this Mr. Jinks unlocked and removed the handcuffs, and

produced his pipe and tobacco. Richard did the same, and took from his pocket a match-box in which there was only one match.

"That's awkward," said Jinks, "for I haven't a light about me."

They filled the two pipes, and lighted the one match.

Now, all this time Richard had held his uncle's letter of introduction in his hand, and when there was some little difficulty in lighting the tobacco from the expiring lucifer, he, without a moment's thought, held the letter over the flickering flame, and from the burning paper lighted his pipe.

In a moment he remembered what he had done.

The letter of introduction! the one piece of evidence in his favour! He threw the blazing paper on the ground and stamped on it, but in vain. In spite of all his efforts a few black ashes alone remained.

"The devil must have possessed me," he exclaimed. "I have burnt my uncle's letter."

"Well," says Mr. Jinks, "I've seen many dodges in my time, and I've seen a many knowing cards; but if that isn't the neatest dodge, and if you ain't the knowingest card I ever did see, blow me."

"I tell you that letter was in my uncle's hand; written to his friend, the merchant at Gardenford; and in it he mentions having given me the very money you say has been stolen from his cabinet."

"Oh, the letter was all that, was it? And you've lighted your pipe with it. You'd better tell that little story before the coroner. It will be so very conwincing to the jury."

The scrub, with his mouth very much to the left, spells out again the two words, "Not guilty!"

"Oh," says Mr. Jinks, "you mean to stick to your opinion, do you, now you've formed it? Upon my word, you're too clever for a country-town practice; I wonder they don't send for you up at Scotland Yard; with your talents, you'd be at the top of the tree in no time, I've no doubt."

During the journey, the thick November fog had been gradually clearing away, and at this very moment the sun broke out with a bright and sudden light that shone full upon the threadbare coat-sleeve of Daredevil Dick.

"Not guilty!" cried Mr. Jinks, with sudden energy. "Not guilty! Why, look here! I'm blest if his coat-sleeve isn't covered with blood!"

Yes, on the shabby worn-out coat the sunlight revealed dark and ghastly stains; and, stamped and branded by those hideous marks as a villain and a murderer, Richard Marwood re-entered his native town.

CHAPTER V

THE HEALING WATERS

The Sloshy is not a beautiful river, unless indeed mud is beautiful, for it is very muddy. The Sloshy is a disagreeable kind of compromise between a river and a canal. It is like a canal which (after the manner of the mythic frog that wanted to be an ox)[1] had seen a river, and swelled itself to bursting in imitation thereof. It has quite a knack of swelling and bursting, this Sloshy; it overflows its banks and swallows up a house or two, or takes an impromptu snack off a few outbuildings, once or twice a year. It is inimical to children, and has been known to suck into its muddy bosom the hopes of divers families; and has afterwards gone down to the distant sea, flaunting on its breast Billy's straw hat or Johnny's pinafore, as a flag of triumph for having done a little amateur business for the gentleman on the pale horse.[2]

It has been a soft pillow of rest, too, this muddy breast of the Sloshy; and weary heads have been known to sleep more soundly in that loathsome, dark, and slimy bed than on couches of down.

Oh, keep us ever from even whispering to our own hearts that our best chance of peaceful slumber might be in such a bed!

An ugly, dark, and dangerous river—a river that is always telling you of trouble, and anguish, and weariness of spirit—a river that to some poor impressionable mortal creatures, who are apt to be saddened by a cloud or brightened by a sunbeam, is not healthy to look upon.

I wonder what that woman thinks of the river? A badly-dressed woman carrying a baby, who walks with a slow and restless step up and down by one of its banks, on the afternoon of the day on which the murder of Mr. Montague Harding took place.

It is a very solitary spot she has chosen, on the furthest outskirts of the town of Slopperton; and the town of Slopperton being at best a very ugly town, is ugliest at the outskirts, which consist of two or three straggling manufactories, a great gaunt gaol—the stoniest of stone jugs—and a straggling fringe of shabby houses, some new and only half-built, others ancient and half fallen to decay, which hang all round Slopperton like the rags that fringe the edges of a dirty garment.

The woman's baby is fretful, and it may be that the damp foggy atmosphere on the banks of the Sloshy is scarcely calculated to engender either high spirits or amiable temper in the bosom of infant or adult. The woman hushes it impatiently to her breast, and looks down at the little puny features with a strange unmotherly glance. Poor wretch! Perhaps she scarcely thinks of that little load as a mother is apt to think of her child. She may remember it only as a shame, a burden, and a grief. She has been pretty; a bright country beauty, perhaps, a year ago; but she is a faded, careworn-looking creature now, with a pale face, and hollow circles round her eyes. She has played the only game a woman has to play, and lost the only stake a woman has to lose.

"I wonder whether he will come, or whether I must wear out my heart through another long long day.—Hush, hush! As if my trouble was not bad enough without your crying."

This is an appeal to the fretful baby; but that young gentleman is engaged at fisticuffs with his cap, and has just destroyed a handful of its tattered border.

There is on this dingy bank of the Sloshy a little dingy public-house, very old-fashioned, though surrounded by newly-begun houses. It is a little, one-sided, pitiful place, ornamented with the cheering announcements of "Our noted Old Tom at 4*d.* per quartern;" and "This is the only place for the real Mountain Dew."[3] It is a wretched place, which has never seen better days, and never

hopes to see better days. The men who frequent it are a few stragglers from a factory near, and the colliers whose barges are moored
in the neighbourhood. These shamble in on dark afternoons, and
play at all-fours, or cribbage, in a little dingy parlour with dirty
dog's-eared cards, scoring their points with beer-marks on the
sticky tables. Not a very attractive house of entertainment this; but
it has an attraction for the woman with the baby, for she looks at it
wistfully, as she paces up and down. Presently she fumbles in her
pocket, and produces two or three halfpence—just enough, it
seems, for her purpose, for she sneaks in at the half-open door, and
in a few minutes emerges in the act of wiping her lips.

As she does so, she almost stumbles against a man wrapped in a
great coat, and with the lower part of his face muffled in a thick
handkerchief.

"I thought you would not come," she said.

"Did you? Then you see you thought wrong. But you might have
been right, for my coming was quite a chance: I can't be at your
beck and call night and day."

"I don't expect you to be at my beck and call. I've not been used
to get so much attention, or so much regard from you as to expect
that, Jabez."

The man started, and looked round as if he expected to find all
Slopperton at his shoulder; but there wasn't a creature about.

"You needn't be quite so handy with my name," he said; "there's
no knowing who might hear you. Is there any one in there?" he
asked, pointing to the public-house.

"No one but the landlord."

"Come in, then; we can talk better there. This fog pierces one to
the bones."

He seems never to consider that the woman and the child have
been exposed to that piercing fog for an hour and more, as he is
above an hour after his appointment.

He leads the way through the bar into the little parlour. There
are no colliers playing at all-fours to-day, and the dog's-eared cards
lie tumbled in a heap on one of the sticky tables among broken
clay-pipes and beer-stains. This table is near the one window

which looks out on the river, and by this window the woman sits, Jabez placing himself on the other side of the table.

The fretful baby has fallen asleep, and lies quietly in the woman's lap.

"What will you take?"

"A little gin," she answers, not without a certain shame in her tone.

"So you've found out *that* comfort, have you?" He says this with a glance of satisfaction he cannot repress.

"What other comfort is there for such as me, Jabez? It seemed at first to make me forget. Nothing can do that now—except——"

She did not finish this sentence, but sat looking with a dull vacant stare at the black waters of the Sloshy, which, as the tide rose, washed with a hollow noise against the brickwork of the pathway close to the window.

"Well, as I suppose you didn't ask me to meet you here for the sole purpose of making miserable speeches, perhaps you'll tell me what you want with me. My time is precious, and if it were not, I can't say I should much care about stopping long in this place; it's such a deliciously lively hole and such a charming neighbourhood."

"I live in this neighbourhood—at least, I *starve* in this neighbourhood, Jabez."

"Oh, now we're coming to it," said the gentleman, with a very gloomy face, "we're coming to it. You want some money. That's how this sort of thing always ends."

"I hoped a better end than that, Jabez. I hoped long ago, when I thought you loved me——"

"Oh, we're going over that ground again, are we?" said he; and with a gesture of weariness, he took up the dog's-eared cards on the sticky table before him, and began to build a house with them, such as children build in their play.

Nothing could express better than this action his thorough determination not to listen to what the woman might have to say; but in spite of this she went on—

"You see I was a foolish country girl, Jabez, or I might have known better. I had been accustomed to take my father and my brother's word of mouth as Bible truth, and had never known that word to be belied. I did not think, when the man I loved with all my heart and soul—to utter forgetfulness of every other living creature on the earth, of every duty that I knew to man and heaven—I did not think when the man I loved so much said this or that, to ask him if he meant it honestly, or if it was not a cruel and a wicked lie. Being so ignorant, I did not think of that, and I thought to be your wife, as you swore I should be, and that this helpless little one lying here might live to look up to you as a father, and be a comfort and an honour to you."

To be a comfort and an honour to you! The fretful baby awoke at the words, and clenched its tiny fists with a spiteful action.

If the river, as a thing eternal in comparison to man—if the river had been a prophet, and had had a voice in its waters wherewith to prophesy, I wonder whether it would have cried—

"A shame and a dishonour, an enemy and an avenger in the days to come!"

Jabez's card-house had risen to three stories; he took the dog's-eared cards one by one in his white hands with a slow deliberate touch that never faltered.

The woman looked at him with a piteous but tearless glance; from him to the river; and back again to him.

"You don't ask to look at the child, Jabez."

"I don't like children," said he. "I get enough of children at the Doctor's. Children and Latin grammar—and the end so far off yet,"—he said the last words to himself, in a gloomy tone.

"But your own child, Jabez—your own."

"As *you* say," he muttered.

She rose from her chair and looked full at him—a long long gaze which seemed to say, "And this is the man I loved; this is the man for whom I am lost!" If he could have seen her look! But he was stooping to pick up a card from the ground—his house of cards was five stories high by this time. "Come," he said, in a hard resolute tone, "you've written to me to beg me to meet you here, for you were dying of a broken heart; that's to say you have taken to drinking gin (I dare say it's an excellent thing to nurse a child upon), and you want to be bought off. How much do you expect? I thought to have a sum of money at my command to-day. Never you mind how; it's no business of yours." He said this savagely, as if in answer to a look of inquiry from her; but she was standing with her back turned to him, looking steadily out of the window.

"I thought to have been richer to-day," he continued, "but I've had a disappointment. However, I've brought as much as I could afford; so the best thing you can do is to take it, and get out of Slopperton as soon as you can, so that I may never see your wretched white face again."

He counted out four sovereigns on the sticky table, and then, adding the sixth story to his card-house, looked at the frail erection with a glance of triumph.

"And so will I build my fortune in days to come," he muttered.

A man who had entered the dark little parlour very softly passed behind him and brushed against his shoulder at this moment; the house of cards shivered, and fell in a heap on the table.

Jabez turned round with an angry look.

"What the devil did you do that for?" he asked.

The man gave an apologetic shrug, pointed with his fingers to his lips, and shook his head.

"Oh," said Jabez, "deaf and dumb! So much the better."

The strange man seated himself at another table, on which the landlord placed a pint of beer; took up a newspaper, and seemed absorbed in it; but from behind the cover of this newspaper he watched Jabez with a furtive glance, and his mouth, which was very much on one side, twitched now and then with a nervous action.

All this time the woman had never touched the money—never indeed turned from the window by which she stood; but she now came up to the table, and took the sovereigns up one by one.

"After what you have said to me this day, I would see this child starve, hour by hour, and die a slow death before my eyes, before I would touch one morsel of bread bought with your money. I have heard that the waters of that river are foul and poisonous, and death to those who live on its bank; but I know the thoughts of your wicked heart to be so much more foul and so much bitterer a poison, that I would go to that black river for pity and help rather than to you." As she said this, she threw the sovereigns into his face with such a strong and violent hand, that one of them, striking him above the eyebrow, cut his forehead to the bone, and brought the blood gushing over his eyes.

The woman took no notice of his pain, but turning once more to the window, threw herself into a chair and sat moodily staring out at the river, as if indeed she looked to that for pity.

The dumb man helped the landlord to dress the cut on Jabez's forehead. It was a deep cut, and likely to leave a scar for years to come.

Mr. North didn't look much the better, either in appearance or temper, for this blow. He did not utter a word to the woman, but began, in a hang-dog manner, to search for the money, which had rolled away into the corners of the room. He could only find three sovereigns; and though the landlord brought a light, and the three men searched the room in every direction, the fourth could not be found; so, abandoning the search, Jabez paid his score and strode out of the place without once looking at the woman.

"I've got off cheap from that tiger-cat," he said to himself; "but it has been a bad afternoon's work. What can I say about my cut face to the governor?" He looked at his watch, a homely silver one attached to a black ribbon. "Five o'clock; I shall be at the Doctor's by tea-time. I can get into the gymnasium the back way, take a few minutes' turn with the poles and ropes, and say the accident happened in climbing. They always believe what I say, poor dolts."

His figure was soon lost in the darkness and the fog—so dense a fog that very few people saw the woman with the fretful baby when she emerged from the public-house, and walked along the river-bank, leaving even the outskirts of Slopperton behind, and wandered on and on till she came to a dreary spot, where dismal pollard willows stretched their dark and ugly shadows, like the bare arms of withered hags, over the dismal waters of the lonely Sloshy.

O river, sometimes so pitiless when thou devourest youth, beauty, and happiness, wilt thou be pitiful and tender to-night, and take a poor wretch, who has no hope of mortal pity, to peace and quiet on thy breast?

O merciless river, so often bitter foe to careless happiness, wilt thou to-night be friend to reckless misery and hopeless pain?

God made thee, dark river, and God made the wretch who stands shivering on thy bank: and may be, in His boundless love and compassion for the creatures of His hand, He may have pity even for those so lost as to seek forbidden comfort in thy healing waters.

CHAPTER VI

Two Coroner's Inquests

There had not been since the last general election, when George Augustus Slashington, the Liberal member, had been returned against strong Conservative opposition, in a blaze of triumph and a shower of rotten eggs and cabbage-stumps—there had not been since that great day such excitement in Slopperton as there was on the discovery of the murder of Mr. Montague Harding.

A murder was always a great thing for Slopperton. When John Boggins, weaver, beat out the brains of Sarah his wife, first with the heel of his clog and ultimately with a poker, Slopperton had a great deal to say about it—though, of course, the slaughter of one "hand" by another was no great thing out of the factories. But this murder at the Black Mill was something out of the common. Uncommonly cruel, cowardly, and unmanly, and moreover occurring in a respectable rank of life.

Round that lonely house on the Slopperton road there was a crowd and a bustle throughout that short foggy day on which Richard Marwood was arrested.

Gentlemen of the Press were there, sniffing out, with miraculous acumen, particulars of the murder, which as yet were known to none but the heads of the Slopperton police force.

How many lines at three-halfpence per line these gentlemen

wrote concerning the dreadful occurrence, without knowing anything whatever about it, no one unacquainted with the mysteries of
their art would dare to say.

The two papers which appeared on Friday had accounts varying
in every item, and the one paper which appeared on Saturday had
a happy amalgamation of the two conflicting accounts—demon-
strating thereby the triumph of paste and scissors over penny-a-
liners' copy.[1]

The head officials of the Slopperton police, attired in plain
clothes, went in and out of the Black Mill from an early hour on
that dark November day. Every time they came out, though none of
them ever spoke, by some strange magic a fresh report got current
among the crowd. I think the magical process was this: Some one
man, auguring from such and such a significance in their manner,
whispered to his nearest neighbour his suggestion of what *might*
have been revealed to them within; and this whispered suggestion
was repeated from one to another till it grew into a fact, and was
still repeated through the crowd, while with every speaker it gathered interest until it grew into a series of imaginary facts.

Of one thing the crowd was fully convinced—that was, that
those grave men in plain clothes, the Slopperton detectives, knew
all, and could tell all, if they only chose to speak. And yet I doubt if
there was beneath the stars more than one person who really knew
the secret of the dreadful deed.

The following day the coroner's inquisition was held at a respectable hostelry near the Black Mill, whither the jury went, accompanied by the medical witness, to contemplate the body of the
victim. With solemn faces they hovered round the bed of the murdered man: they took depositions, talked to each other in low
hushed tones; and exchanged a few remarks, in a low voice, with
the doctor who had probed the deep gashes in that cold breast.

All the evidence that transpired at the inquest only amounted to
this—

The servant Martha, rising at six o'clock on the previous morning, went, as she was in the habit of doing, to the door of the old

East Indian to call him—he being always an early riser, and getting up even in winter to study by lamp-light.

Receiving, after repeated knocking at the door, no answer the old woman had gone into the room, and there had beheld, by the faint light of her candle, the awful spectacle of the Anglo-Indian lying on the floor by the bed-side, his throat cut, cruel stabs upon his breast, and a pool of blood surrounding him; the cabinet in the room broken open and ransacked, and the pocket-book and money which it was known to contain missing. The papers of the murdered gentleman were thrown into confusion and lay in a heap near the cabinet; and as there was no blood upon them, the detectives concluded that the cabinet had been rifled prior to the commission of the murder.

The Lascar had been found lying insensible on his bed in the little dressing-room, his head cruelly beaten; and beyond this there was nothing to be discovered. The Lascar had been taken to the hospital, where little hope was given by the doctors of his recovery from the injuries he had received.

In the first horror and anguish of that dreadful morning Mrs. Marwood had naturally inquired for her son; had expressed her surprise at his disappearance; and when questioned had revealed the history of his unexpected return the night before. Suspicion fell at once upon the missing man. His reappearance after so many years on the return of his rich uncle; his secret departure from the house before any one had risen—everything told against him. Inquiries were immediately set on foot at the turnpike gates on the several roads out of Slopperton; and at the railway station from which he had started for Gardenford by the first train.

In an hour it was discovered that a man answering to Richard's description had been seen at the station; half an hour afterwards a man appeared, who deposed to having seen and recognized him on the platform—and deposed, too, to Richard's evident avoidance of him. The railway clerks remembered giving a ticket to a handsome young man with a dark moustache, in a shabby suit, having a pipe in his mouth. Poor Richard! the dark moustache and pipe tracked him at every stage. "Dark moustache—pipe—shabby dress—tall—handsome face." The clerk who played upon the electric-telegraph wires, as other people play upon the piano, sent these words shivering down the line to the Gardenford station; from the Gardenford station to the Gardenford police-office the words were carried in less than five minutes; in five minutes more Mr. Jinks the detective was on the platform, and his dumb assistant, Joe Peters, was ready outside the station; and they both were ready to recognize Richard the moment they saw him.

O wonders of civilized life! cruel wonders, when you help to track an innocent man to a dreadful doom.

Richard's story of the letter only damaged his case with the jury. The fact of his having burned a document of such importance seemed too incredible to make any impression in his favour.

Throughout the proceedings there stood in the background a shabbily-dressed man, with watchful observant eyes, and a mouth very much on one side.

This man was Joseph Peters, the scrub of the detective force of Gardenford. He rarely took his eyes from Richard, who, with pale bewildered face, dishevelled hair, and slovenly costume, looked perhaps as much like guilt as innocence.

The verdict of the coroner's jury was, as every one expected it would be, to the effect that the deceased had been wilfully murdered by Richard Marwood his nephew; and poor Dick was removed immediately to the county gaol on the outskirts of Slopperton, there to lie till the assizes.

The excitement in Slopperton, as before observed, was immense. Slopperton had but one voice—a voice loud in execration of the innocent prisoner, horror of the treachery and cruelty of the dreadful deed, and pity for the wretched mother of this wicked son, whose anguish had thrown her on a sick bed—but who, despite of every proof repeated every hour, expressed her assurance of her unfortunate son's innocence.

The coroner had plenty of work on that dismal November day: for from the inquest on the unfortunate Mr. Harding he had to hurry down to a little dingy public-house on the river's bank, there to inquire into the cause of the untimely death of a wretched outcast found by some bargemen in the Sloshy.

This sort of death was so common an event in the large and thickly-populated town of Slopperton, that the coroner and the jury (lighted by two guttering tallow candles with long wicks, at four o'clock on that dull afternoon) had very little to say about it.

One glance at that heap of wet, torn, and shabby garments—one half-shuddering, half-pitying look at the white face, blue lips, and damp loose auburn hair, and a merciful verdict—"Found drowned."[2]

One juryman, a butcher—(we sometimes think them hard-hearted, these butchers)—lays a gentle hand upon the auburn hair, and brushes a lock of it away from the pale forehead.

Perhaps so tender a touch had not been laid upon that head for two long years. Perhaps not since the day when the dead woman left her native village, and a fond and happy mother for the last time smoothed the golden braids beneath her daughter's Sunday bonnet.

In half an hour the butcher is home by his cheerful fireside; and I think he has a more loving and protecting glance than usual for the fair-haired daughter who pours out his tea.

No one recognizes the dead woman. No one knows her story; they guess at it as a very common history, and bury her in a parish burying-ground—a damp and dreary spot not far from the river's brink, in which many such as she are laid.

Our friend Jabez North, borrowing the Saturday's paper of his principal in the evening after school-hours, is very much interested in the accounts of these two coroner's inquests.

CHAPTER VII

THE DUMB DETECTIVE A PHILANTHROPIST

The dreary winter months pass by. Time, slow of foot to some, and fast of wing to others, is a very chameleon, such different accounts do different people give of him.

He is very rapid in his flight, no doubt, for the young gentlemen from Dr. Tappenden's home for the Christmas holidays: rapid enough perhaps for the young gentlemen's papas, who have to send their sons back to the academy armed with Dr. Tappenden's little account—which is not such a very little account either, when you reckon up all the extras, such as dancing, French, gymnastics, drill-serjeant, hair-cutting, stationery, servants, and pew at church.

Fast enough, perhaps, is the flight of Time for Allecompain Major, who goes home in a new suit of mourning, and who makes it sticky about the cuffs and white about the elbows before the holidays are out. I don't suppose he forgets his little dead brother; and I dare say, by the blazing hearth, where the firelight falls dullest upon his mother's black dress, he sometimes thinks very sadly of the little grave out in the bleak winter night, on which the snow falls so purely white. But "cakes and ale"[1] are eternal institutions; and if you or I, reader, died to-morrow, the baker would still bake, and Messrs. Barclay and Perkins would continue to brew the ale and stout for which they are so famous, and the friends who were sorriest for us would eat, drink, ay and be merry too, before long.

Who shall say how slow of foot is Time to the miserable young man awaiting his trial in the dreary gaol of Slopperton?

Who shall say how slow to the mother awaiting in agony the result of that trial?

The assizes take place late in February. So, through the fog and damp of gloomy November; through long, dark, and dreary December nights; through January frost and snow—(of whose outward presence he has no better token than the piercing cold within)—Richard paces up and down his narrow cell, and broods upon the murder of his uncle, and of his trial which is to come.

Ministers of religion come to convert him, as they say. He tells them that he hopes and believes all they can teach him, for that it was taught him in years gone by at his mother's knee.

"The best proof of my faith," he says, "is that I am not mad. Do you think, if I did not believe in an All-seeing Providence, I should not go stark staring mad, when, night after night, through hours which are as years in duration, I think, and think, of the situation in which I am placed, till my brain grows wild and my senses reel? I have no hope in the result of my trial, for I feel how every circumstance tells against me: but I have hope that Heaven, with a mighty hand, and an instrument of its own choosing, may yet work out the saving of an innocent man from an ignominious death."

The dumb detective Peters had begged to be transferred from Gardenford to Slopperton, and was now in the employ of the police force of that town. Of very little account this scrub among the officials. His infirmity, they say, makes him scarcely worth his salt, though they admit that his industry is unfailing.

So the scrub awaits the trial of Richard Marwood, in whose fortunes he takes an interest which is in no way abated since he spelt out the words "Not guilty" in the railway carriage.

He had taken up his Slopperton abode in a lodging in a small street of six-roomed houses yclept[2] Little Gulliver Street. At No. 5, Little Gulliver Street, Mr. Peters's attention had been attracted by the announcement of the readiness and willingness of the occupier of the house to take in and do for a single gentleman. Mr. Peters was a single gentleman, and he accordingly presented himself at No. 5, expressing the amiable desire of being forthwith taken in and done for.

The back bedroom of that establishment, he was assured by its proprietress, was an indoor garden-of-Eden for a single man; and certainly, looked at by the light of such advantages as a rent of four-and-sixpence a week, a sofa-bedstead—(that deliciously innocent white lie in the way of furniture which never yet deceived anybody); a Dutch oven,[3] an apparatus for cooking anything, from a pheasant to a red herring;[4] and a little high-art in the way of a young gentleman in red-and-yellow making honourable proposals to a young lady in yellow-and-red, in picture number one; and the same lady and gentleman perpetuating themselves in picture number two, by means of a red baby in a yellow cradle;—taking into consideration such advantages as these, the one-pair back was a paradise calculated to charm a virtuously-minded single man. Mr. Peters therefore took immediate possession by planting his honest gingham in a corner of the room, and by placing two-and-sixpence in the hands of the proprietress by way of deposit. His luggage was more convenient than extensive—consisting of a parcel in the crown of his hat, containing the lighter elegancies of his costume; a small bundle in a red cotton pocket handkerchief, which held the heavier articles of his wardrobe; and a comb, which he carried in his pocket-book.

The proprietress of the indoor Eden was a maiden lady of mature age, with a sharp red nose and metallic pattens. It was with some difficulty that Mr. Peters made her understand, by the aid of pantomimic gestures and violent shakings of the head, that he was dumb, but not deaf; that she need be under no necessity of doing violence to the muscles of her throat, as he could hear her with perfect ease in her natural key. He then—still by the aid of pantomime—made known a desire for pencil and paper, and on being supplied with these articles wrote the one word "baby," and handed that specimen of caligraphy to the proprietress.

That sharp-nosed damsel's maidenly indignation sent new roses to join the permanent blossoms at the end of her olfactory organ, and she remarked, in a voice of vinegar, that she let her lodgings to single men, and that single men as were single men, and not impostors, had no business with babies.

Mr. Peters again had recourse to the pencil, "Not mine—fondling;[5] to be brought up by hand;[6] would pay for food and nursing."

The maiden proprietress had no objection to a fondling, if paid for its requirements; liked children in their places; would call Kuppins; and did call Kuppins.

A voice at the bottom of the stairs responded to the call of Kuppins; a boy's voice most decidedly; a boy's step upon the stairs announced the approach of Kuppins; and Kuppins entered the room with a boy's stride and a boy's slouch; but for all this, Kuppins was a girl.

Not very much like a girl about the head, with that shock of dark rough short hair; not much like a girl about the feet, in high-lows,[7] with hob-nailed soles; but a girl for all that, as testified by short petticoats and a long blue pinafore, ornamented profusely with every variety of decoration in the way of three-cornered slits and grease-spots.

Kuppins was informed by her mistress that the gent had come to lodge; and moreover that the gent was dumb. It is impossible to describe Kuppins's delight at the idea of a dumb lodger.

Kuppins had knowed a dumb boy as lived three doors from mother's (Kuppins's mother understood); this 'ere dumb boy was wicious, and when he was gone agin, 'owled 'orrid.

Was told that the gent wasn't vicious and never howled, and seemed, if anything, disappointed. Understood the dumb alphabet, and had conversed in it for hours with the aforesaid dumb boy. The author, as omniscient, may state that Kuppins and the vicious boy had had some love-passages in days gone by. Mr. Peters was delighted to find a kindred spirit capable of understanding his dirty alphabet, and explained his wish that a baby, "a fondling" he intended to bring up, might be taken in and done for as well as himself.

Kuppins doated on babies; had nursed nine brothers and sisters, and had nursed outside the family circle, at the rate of fifteen-pence a week, for some years. Kuppins had been out in the world from the age of twelve, and was used up as to Slopperton at sixteen.

Mr. Peters stated by means of the dirty alphabet—(more than usually dirty to-day, after his journey from Gardenford, whence he had transplanted his household goods, namely, the gingham umbrella, the bundle, parcel, pocket-book, and comb)—that he would go and fetch the baby. Kuppins immediately proved herself an adept in the art of construing this manual language, and nodded triumphantly a great many times in token that she understood the detective's meaning.

The baby was apparently not far off, for Mr. Peters returned in five minutes with a limp bundle smothered in an old pea-jacket,[8] which on close inspection turned out to be the "fondling."

Mr. Peters had lately purchased the pea-jacket second-hand, and believed it to be an appropriate outer garment for a baby in long-clothes.[9]

The fondling soon evinced signs of a strongly-marked character, not to say a vindictive disposition, and fought manfully with Kuppins, smiting that young lady in the face, and abstracting handfuls of her hair with an address beyond his years.

"Ain't he playful?" asked that young person, who was evidently experienced in fretful babies, and indifferent to the loss of a stray tress or so from her luxuriant locks. "Ain't he playful, pretty hinnercent! Lor! he'll make the place quite cheerful!"

In corroboration of which prediction the "fondling" set up a dismal wail, varied with occasional chokes and screams.

Surely there never could have been, since the foundation-stones of the hospitals for abandoned children in Paris and London were laid, such a "fondling" to choke as this fondling. The manner in which his complexion would turn—from its original sickly sallow to a vivid crimson, from crimson to dark blue, and from blue to black—was something miraculous; and Kuppins was promised much employment in the way of shakings and pattings on the back, to keep the "fondling" from an early and unpleasant death. But Kuppins, as we have remarked, liked a baby—and, indeed, would have given the preference to a cross baby—a cross baby being, as it were, a battle to fight, and a victory to achieve.

In half an hour she had conquered the fondling in a manner wonderful to behold. She laid him across her knee while she lighted a fire in the smoky little grate; for the in-door Eden offered a Hobson's choice to its inhabitants, of smoke or damp; and Mr. Peters preferred smoke. She carried the infant on her left arm, while she fetched a red herring, an ounce of tea, and other comestibles from the chandler's at the corner; put him under her arm while she cooked the herring and made the tea, and waited on Mr. Peters at his modest repast with the fondling choking on her shoulder.

Mr. Peters, having discussed his meal, conversed with Kuppins as she removed the tea-things. The alphabet by this time had acquired a piscatorial flavour, from his having made use of the five vowels to remove the bones of his herring.

"That baby's a rare fretful one," says Mr. Peters with rapid fingers.

Kuppins had nursed a many fretful babies. "Orphants was generally fretful; supposed the 'fondling' was a orphant."

"Poor little chap!—yes," said Peters. "He's had his trials, though he is a young 'un. I'm afeard he'll never grow up a tee-totaller. He's had a little too much of the water already."

Has had too much of the water? Kuppins would very much like to know the meaning of this observation. But Mr. Peters relapses into profound thought, and looks at the "fondling" (still choking) with the eye of a philanthropist and almost the tenderness of a father.

He who provides for the young ravens[10] had, perhaps, in the marvellous fitness of all things of His creation, given to this helpless little one a better protector in the dumb scrub of the police force than he might have had in the father who had cast him off, whoever that father might be.

Mr. Peters presently remarks to the interested Kuppins, that he shall "ederkate,"—he is some time deciding on the conflicting merits of a *c* or a *k* for this word—he shall "ederkate the fondling, and bring him up to his own business."

"What is his business?" asks Kuppins naturally.

"Detecktive," Mr. Peters spells, embellishing the word with an extraneous *k*.

"Oh, perlice," said Kuppins. "Criky, how jolly! Shouldn't I like to be a perliceman, and find out all about this 'ere 'orrid murder!"

Mr. Peters brightens at the word "murder," and he regards Kuppins with a friendly glance.

"So you takes a hinterest in this 'ere murder, do yer?" he spells out.

"Oh, don't I? I bought a Sunday paper. Shouldn't I like to see that there young man as killed his uncle scragged[11]—that's all!"

Mr. Peters shook his head doubtfully, with a less friendly glance at Kuppins. But there were secrets and mysteries of his art he did not trust at all times to the dirty alphabet; and perhaps his opinion on the subject of the murder of Mr. Montague Harding was one of them.

Kuppins presently fetched him a pipe; and as he sat by the smoky fire, he watched alternately the blue cloud that issued from his lips and the clumsy figure of the damsel pacing up and down with the "fondling" (asleep after the exhaustion attendant on a desperate choke) upon her arms.

"If," mused Mr. Peters, with his mouth very much to the left of his nose—"if that there baby was grow'd up, he might help me to find out the rights and wrongs of this 'ere murder."

Who so fit? or who so unfit? Which shall we say? If in the wonderful course of events, this little child shall ever have a part in dragging a murderer to a murderer's doom, shall it be called a monstrous and a terrible outrage of nature, or a just and a fitting retribution?

CHAPTER VIII

SEVEN LETTERS ON THE DIRTY ALPHABET

The 17th of February shone out bright and clear, and a frosty sunlight illumined the windows of the court where Richard Marwood stood to be tried for his life.

Never, perhaps, had that court been so crowded; never, perhaps, had there been so much anxiety felt in Slopperton for the result of any trial as was felt that day for the issue of the trial of Richard Marwood.

The cold bright sunlight streaming in at the windows seemed to fall brightest and coldest on the wan white face of the prisoner at the bar.

Three months of mental torture had done their work, and had written their progress in such characters upon that young and once radiant countenance, as Time, in his smooth and peaceful course, would have taken years to trace. But Richard Marwood was calm to-day, with the awful calmness of that despair which is past all hope. Suspense had exhausted him. But he had done with suspense, and felt that his fate was sealed; unless, indeed, Heaven—infinite both in mercy and in power—raised up as by a miracle some earthly instrument to save him.

The court was one vast sea of eager faces; for, to the spectators, this trial was as a great game of chance, which the counsel for the prosecution, the judge, and the jury, played against the prisoner and his advocate, and at which the prisoner staked his life.

There was but one opinion in that vast assemblage; and that was, that the accused would lose in this dreadful game, and that he well deserved to lose.

There had been betting in Slopperton on the result of this awful hazard. For the theory of chances is to certain minds so delightful, that the range of subjects for a wager may ascend from a maggot-race to a trial for murder. Some adventurous spirits had taken desperate odds against the outsider "Acquittal;" and many enterprising gentlemen had made what they considered "good books," by putting heavy sums on the decided favourite, "Found Guilty." As, however, there might be a commutation of the sentence of death to transportation for life, some speculators had bet upon the chance of the prisoner being found guilty, but not executed; or, as it had been forcibly expressed, had backed "Penal Servitude" against "Gallows."

So there were private interests, as well as a public interest, among that swelling ocean of men and women; and Richard had but very few backers in the great and terrible game that was being played.

In a corner of the gallery of the court, high up over the heads of the multitude, there was a little spot railed off from the public, and accessible only to the officials, or persons introduced by them. Here, among two or three policemen, stood our friend Mr. Joseph Peters, with his mouth very much on one side, and his eyes fixed intently upon the prisoner at the bar. The gallery in which he stood faced the dock, though at a great distance from it.

If there was one man in that vast assembly who, next to the prisoner, was most wretched, that man was the prisoner's counsel. He was young, and this was only his third or fourth brief; and this was, moreover, the first occasion upon which he had ever been intrusted with an important case. He was an intensely nervous and excitable man, and failure would be to him worse than death; and he felt failure inevitable. He had not one inch of ground for the defence; and, in spite of the prisoner's repeated protestations of his innocence, he believed that prisoner to be guilty. He was an earnest man; and this belief damped his earnestness. He was a conscientious man; and he felt that to defend Richard Marwood was something like a dishonest action.

The prisoner pleaded "Not guilty" in a firm voice. We read of this whenever we read of the trial of a great criminal; we read of the firm voice, the calm demeanour, the composed face, and the dignified bearing; and we wonder. Would it not be more wonderful were it otherwise? If we consider the pitch to which that man's feelings have been wrought; the tension of every nerve; the exertion of every force, mental and physical, to meet those five or six desperate hours, we wonder no longer. The man's life has become a terrible drama, and he is playing his great act. That mass of pale and watchful faces carries him through the long agony. Or perhaps it is less an agony than an excitement. It may be that his mind is mercifully darkened, and that he cannot see beyond the awful present into the more awful future. He is not busy with the vision of a ghastly structure of wood and iron; a dangling rope swinging loose in the chill morning air, till it is tightened and strained by a quivering and palpitating figure, which so soon grows rigid. He does not, it is to be hoped, see this. Life for him to-day stands still, and there is not room in his breast—absorbed with the one anxious desire to preserve a proud and steady outward seeming—for a thought of that dreadful future which may be so close at hand.

So, Richard Marwood, in an unfaltering voice, pleaded "Not guilty."

There was among that vast crowd but one person who believed him.

Ay, Richard Marwood, thou mightest reverence those dirty hands, for they have spelt out the only language, except that of thy wretched mother, that ever spoke conviction of thy innocence.

Now the prisoner, though firm and collected in his manner,

spoke in so low and subdued a voice as to be only clearly audible to those near him. It happened that the judge, one of the celebrities of the bench, was afflicted with a trifling infirmity, which he would never condescend to acknowledge. That infirmity was partial deafness. He was what is called hard of hearing on one side, and his—to use a common expression—*game* ear happened to be nearest Richard.

"Guilty," said the judge. "So, so—Guilty. Very good."

"Pardon me, my lord," said the counsel for the defence, "the prisoner pleaded *not* guilty."

"Nonsense, sir. Do you suppose me deaf?" asked his lordship; at which there was a slight titter among the habitués of the court.

The barrister gave his head a deprecatory shake. Of course, a gentleman in his lordship's position could not be deaf.

"Very well, then," said the judge, "unless I am deaf, the prisoner pleaded guilty. I heard him, sir, with my own ears—my own ears."

The barrister thought his lordship should have said "my own ear," as the *game* organ ought not to count.

"Perhaps," said the judge, "perhaps the prisoner will be good enough to repeat his plea; and this time he will be good enough to speak out."

"Not guilty," said Richard again, in a firm but not a loud voice—his long imprisonment, with days, weeks, and months of slow agony, had so exhausted his physical powers, that to speak at all, under such circumstances, was an effort.

"Not guilty?" said the judge. "Why, the man doesn't know his own mind. The man must be a born idiot—he can't be right in his intellect."

Scarcely had the words passed his lordship's lips, when a long low whistle resounded through the court.

Everybody looked up towards a corner of the gallery from which the sound came, and the officials cried "Order!"

Among the rest the prisoner raised his eyes, and looking to the spot from which this unexampled and daring interruption proceeded, recognized the face of the man who had spelt out the words "Not guilty" in the railway carriage. Their eyes met: and the man signalled to Richard to watch his hands, whilst with his fingers he spelt out several words slowly and deliberately.

This occurred during the pause caused by the endeavours of the officials to discover what contumacious[1] person had dared to whistle at the close of his lordship's remark.

The counsel for the prosecution stated the case—a very clear case it seemed too—against Richard Marwood.

"Here," said the barrister, "is the case of a young man, who, after squandering a fortune, and getting deeply in debt in his native town, leaves that town, as it is thought by all, never to return. For seven years he does not return. His widowed and lonely mother awaits in anguish for any tidings of this heartless reprobate; but, for seven long years, by not so much as one line or one word, sent through any channel whatever, does he attempt to relieve her anxiety. His townsmen believe him to be dead; his mother believes him to be dead; and it is to be presumed from his conduct that he wishes to be lost sight of by all to whom he once was dear. But at the end of this seven years, his uncle, his mother's only brother, a man of large fortune, returns from India and takes up his temporary abode at the Black Mill. Of course all Slopperton knows of the arrival of this gentleman, and knows also the extent of his wealth. We are always interested in rich people, gentlemen of the jury. Now, it is not very difficult to imagine, that through some channel or other the prisoner at the bar was made aware of his uncle's return, and his residence at the Black Mill. The fact was mentioned in every one of the five enterprising journals which are the pride of Slopperton. The prisoner may have seen one of these journals; he may have had some former boon companion resident in Slopperton, with whom he may have been in correspondence. Be that as it may, gentlemen, on the eighth night after Mr. Montague Harding's arrival, the prisoner at the bar appears, after seven years' absence, with a long face and a penitent story, to beg his mother's forgiveness. Gentlemen, we know the boundless power of maternal love; the inexhaustible depth of affection in a mother's breast. His mother forgave him. The fatted calf was killed; the returned wanderer was welcomed to the home he had rendered desolate; the past was wiped out; and seven long years of neglect and desertion were forgotten. The family retired to rest. That night, gentlemen, a murder was committed of a deeper and darker dye than guilt ordinarily wears: a murder which in centuries hence will stand amongst the blackest chapters in the gloomy annals of crime. Under the roof whose shelter he had sought for the repose of his old age, Montague Harding was cruelly and brutally murdered.

"Now, gentlemen, who committed this outrage? Who was the monster in human form that perpetrated this villanous, cowardly, and bloodthirsty deed? Suspicion, gentlemen of the jury, only points to one man; and to that man suspicion points with so unerring a finger, that the criminal stands revealed in the broad glare of detected guilt. That man is the prisoner at the bar. On the discovery of the murder, the returned wanderer, the penitent and dutiful son, was of course sought for. But was he to be found? No, gentlemen. The bird had flown. The affectionate son, who, after seven years' desertion, had returned to his mother's feet—as it was of course presumed never again to leave her—had departed, secretly, in the dead of the night; choosing to sneak out of a window like a burglar, rather than to leave by the door, as the legitimate master of the house. Suspicion at once points to him; he is sought and found—where, gentlemen? Forty miles from the scene of the murder, with the money rifled from the cabinet of the murdered man in his possession, and with his coat-sleeve stained by the blood of his victim. These, gentlemen, are, in brief, the circumstances of this harrowing case; and I think you will agree with me that never did circumstantial evidence so clearly point out the true criminal. I shall now proceed to call the witnesses for the crown."

There was a pause and a little bustle in the court, the waves of the human sea were agitated for a moment. The backers of the favourites, "Guilty" and "Gallows," felt they had made safe books. During this pause, a man pushed his way through the crowd, up to the spot where the prisoner's counsel was seated, and put a little dirty slip of paper into his hand. There was written on it only one word, a word of three letters. The counsel read it, and then tore the slip of paper into the smallest atoms it was possible to reduce it to, and threw the fragments on the floor at his feet; but a warm flush mounted to his face, hitherto so pale, and he prepared himself to watch the evidence.

Richard Marwood, who knew the strength of the evidence against him, and knew his powerlessness to controvert it, had listened to its recapitulation with the preoccupied air of a man whom the proceedings of the day in no way concerned. His abstracted manner had been noticed by the spectators, and much commented upon.

It was singular, but at this most important crisis it appeared as if his chief attention was attracted by Joseph Peters, for he kept his eyes intently fixed upon the corner where that individual stood. The eyes of the people, following the direction of Richard's eyes, saw nothing but a little group of officials leaning over a corner of the gallery.

The crowd did not see what Richard saw, namely, the fingers of Mr. Peters slowly shaping seven letters—two words—four letters in the first word, and three letters in the second.

There lay before the prisoner a few sprigs of rue;[2] he took them up one by one, and gathering them together into a little bouquet, placed them in his button-hole—the eyes of the multitude staring at him all the time.

Strange to say, this trifling action appeared to be so pleasing to Mr. Joseph Peters, that he danced, as involuntarily, the first steps of an extempore hornpipe, and being sharply called to order by the officials, relapsed into insignificance for the remainder of the trial.

CHAPTER IX

"MAD, GENTLEMEN OF THE JURY"

The first witness called was Richard's mother. From one to another amidst the immense number of persons in that well-packed courtroom there ran a murmur of compassion for that helpless woman with the white, anguish-worn face, and the quivering lip which tried so vainly to be still. All in Slopperton who knew anything of Mrs. Marwood, knew her to be a proud woman; they knew how silently she had borne the wild conduct of her son; how deeply she had loved that son; and they could guess now the depth of the bitterness of her soul when called upon to utter words which must help to condemn him.

After the witness had been duly sworn, the counsel for the prosecution addressed her thus:

"We have every wish, madam, to spare your feelings; I know there is not one individual present who does not sympathize with you in the position in which you now stand. But the course of Justice is as inevitable as it is sometimes painful, and we must all of us yield to its stern necessities. You will be pleased to state how long it is since your son left his home?"

"Seven years—seven years last August."

"Can you also state his reasons for leaving his home?"

"He had embarrassments in Slopperton—debts, which I have since his departure liquidated."

"Can you tell me what species of debts?"

"They were—" she hesitated a little, "chiefly debts of honour."

"Then am I to understand your son was a gambler?"

"He was unfortunately much addicted to cards."

"To any other description of gambling?"

"Yes, to betting on the events of the turf."

"He had fallen, I imagine, into bad companionship?"

She bowed her head, and in a faltering voice replied, "He had."

"And he had acquired in Slopperton the reputation of being a scamp—a ne'er-do-well?"

"I am afraid he had."

"We will not press you further on this very painful subject; we will proceed to his departure from home. Your son gave you no intimation of his intention of leaving Slopperton?"

"None whatever. The last words he said to me were, that he was sorry for the past, but that he had started on a bad road, and must go on to the end."

In this manner the examination proceeded, the account of the discovery of the murder being elicited from the witness, whose horror at having to give the details was exceedingly painful to behold.

The prisoner's counsel rose and addressed Mrs. Marwood.

"In examining you, madam, my learned friend has not asked you whether you had looked upon your son, the prisoner at the bar, as a good or a bad son. Will you be kind enough to state your impression on this subject?"

"Apart from his wild conduct, he was a good son. He was kind and affectionate, and I believe it was his regret for the grief his dissipation had caused me that drove him away from his home."

"He was kind and affectionate. I am to understand, then, that his disposition was naturally good?"

"Naturally he had a most excellent disposition. He was universally beloved as a boy; the servants were excessively attached to him; he had a great love of animals—dogs followed him instinctively, as I believe they always do follow people who like them."

"A very interesting trait, no doubt, in the prisoner's disposition; but if we are to have so much charmingly minute description, I'm afraid we shall never conclude this trial," said the opposite counsel. And a juryman, who had a ticket for a public dinner at four o'clock in his pocket, forgot himself so far that he applauded with the heels of his boots.

The prisoner's counsel, regardless of the observation of his "learned friend," proceeded.

"Madam," he said, "had your son, before his departure from home, any serious illness?"

"The question is irrelevant," said the judge.

"Pardon me, my lord. I shall not detain you long. I believe the question to be of importance. Permit me to proceed."

Mrs. Marwood looked surprised by the question, but it came from her son's advocate, and she did her best to answer it.

"My son had, shortly before his leaving home, a violent attack of brain-fever."[1]

"During which he was delirious?"

"Everybody is delirious in brain-fever," said the judge. "This is trifling with the court, sir."

The judge was rather inclined to snub the prisoner's counsel; first, because he was a young and struggling man, and therefore ought to be snubbed; and secondly, because he had in a manner inferred that his lordship was deaf.

"Pardon me, my lord; you will see the drift of my question by-and-by."

"I hope so, sir," said his lordship, very testily.

"Was your son, madam, delirious during this fever?"

"Throughout it, sir."

"And you attributed the fever——"

"To his bad conduct having preyed upon his mind."

"Were you alarmed for his life during his illness?"

"Much alarmed. But our greatest fear was for his reason."

"Did the faculty apprehend the loss of his reason?"

"They did."

"The doctors who attended him were resident in Slopperton?"

"They were, and are so still. He was attended by Dr. Morton and Mr. Lamb."

The prisoner's counsel here beckoned to some officials near him—whispered some directions to them, and they immediately left the court.

Resuming the examination of this witness, the counsel said:

"You repeated just now the words your son made use of on the night of his departure from home. They were rather singular words—'he had started on a dark road, and he must go on to the end of it.' "

"Those were his exact words, sir."

"Was there any wildness in his manner in saying these words?" he asked.

"His manner was always wild at this time—perhaps wilder that night than usual."

"His manner, you say, was always wild. He had acquired a reputation for a wild recklessness of disposition from an early age, had he not?"

"He had, unfortunately—from the time of his going to school."

"And his companions, I believe, had given him some name expressive of this?"

"They had."

"And that name was———"

"Daredevil Dick."

Martha, the old servant, was next sworn. She described the finding of the body of Mr. Harding.

The examination by the prisoner's counsel of this witness elicited nothing but that—

Master Dick had always been a wild boy, but a good boy at heart; that he had been never known to hurt so much as a worm; and that she, Martha, was sure he'd never done the murder. When asked if she had any suspicion as to who had done the deed, she became nebulous in her manner, and made some allusions to "the French"—having lived in the days of Waterloo, and being inclined to ascribe any deed of darkness, from the stealing of a leg of mutton to the exploding of an infernal machine, to the emissaries of Napoleon.

Mr. Jinks, who was then examined, gave a minute and rather discursive account of the arrest of Richard, paying several artful compliments to his own dexterity as a detective officer.

The man who met Richard on the platform at the railway station deposed to the prisoner's evident wish to avoid a recognition; to his even crossing the line for that purpose.

"There is one witness," said the counsel for the crown, "I am sorry to say I shall be unable to produce. That witness is the half-caste servant of the murdered gentleman, who still lies in a precarious state at the county hospital, and whose recovery from the injuries inflicted on him by the murderer of his master is pronounced next to an impossibility."

The case for the prosecution closed; still a very clear case against Richard Marwood, and still the backers of the "Gallows" thought they had made a very good book.

The deposition of the Lascar, the servant of the murdered man, had been taken through an interpreter, at the hospital. It threw little light on the case. The man said, that on the night of the murder he had been awoke by a sound in Mr. Harding's room, and had spoken in Hindostanee, asking if his master required his assistance, when he received in the darkness a blow on the head, which immediately deprived him of his senses. He could tell nothing of the person who struck the blow, except that at the moment of striking it a hand passed across his face—a hand which was peculiarly soft and delicate, and the fingers of which were long and slender.

As this passage in the deposition was read, every eye in court was turned to the prisoner, who at that moment happened to be leaning forward with his elbow on the ledge of the dock before him, and his hand shading his forehead—a very white hand, with long slender fingers. Poor Richard! In the good days gone by he had been rather proud of his delicate and somewhat feminine hand.

The prisoner's counsel rose and delivered his speech for the defence. A very elaborate defence. A defence which went to prove that the prisoner at the bar, though positively guilty, was not morally guilty, or legally guilty—"because, gentlemen of the jury, he is, and for some time has been, *insane.* Yes, *mad,* gentlemen of the jury. What has been every action of his life but the action of a madman? His wild boyhood; his reckless extravagant youth; his dissipated and wasted manhood, spent among drunken and dangerous companions. What was his return? Premeditated during the sufferings of delirium tremens, and premeditated long before the arrival of his rich uncle at Slopperton, as I shall presently prove to you. What was this, but the sudden repentance of a madman? Scarcely recovered from this frightful disease—a disease during which men have been known frequently to injure themselves, and those very dear to them, in the most terrible manner—scarcely recovered from this disease, he starts on foot, penniless, for a journey of upwards of two hundred miles. He accomplishes that journey—how, gentlemen, in that dreary November weather, I tremble even to think—he accomplishes that long and painful journey; and on the evening of the eighth day from that on which he left London he falls fainting at his mother's feet. I shall prove to you, gentlemen, that the prisoner left London on the very day on which his uncle arrived in Slopperton; it is therefore impossible he could have had any knowledge of that arrival when he started. Well, gentlemen, the prisoner, after the fatigue, the extreme privation, he has suffered, has yet another trial to undergo—the terrible agitation caused by a reconciliation with his beloved mother. He has eaten scarcely anything for two days, and is injudiciously allowed to drink nearly a bottle of old madeira. That night, gentlemen of the jury, a cruel murder is perpetrated; a murder as certain of immediate discovery, as clumsy in execution, as it is frightful in detail. Can there be any doubt that if it was committed by my unhappy client, the prisoner at the bar, it was perpetrated by him while labouring under an access of delirium, or insanity—temporary, if you will, but unmitigated insanity—aggravated by excessive fatigue, unprecedented mental excitement, and the bad effects of the wine he had been drinking? It has been proved that the cabinet was rifled, and that the pocket-book stolen therefrom was found in the prisoner's possession. This may have been one of those strange flashes of method which are the distinguishing features of madness. In his horror at the crime he had in his delirium committed, the prisoner's endeavour was to escape. For this escape he required money—hence the plunder of the cabinet. The manner of his attempting to escape again proclaims the madman. Instead of flying to Liverpool, which is only thirty miles from this town—whence he could have sailed for any part of the globe, and thus defied pursuit—he starts without any attempt at disguise for a small inland town, whence escape is next to an impossibility, and is captured a few hours after the crime has been committed, with the blood of his unhappy victim upon the sleeve of his coat. Would a man in his senses, gentlemen, not have removed, at any rate, this fatal evidence of his guilt? Would a man in his senses not have endeavoured to disguise himself, and to conceal the money he had stolen? Gentlemen of the jury, I have perfect confidence in your coming to a just decision respecting this most unhappy affair. Weighing well the antecedents of the prisoner, and the circumstances of the crime, I can have not one shadow of a doubt that your verdict will be to the effect that the wretched man before you is, alas! too certainly his uncle's murderer, but that he is as certainly irresponsible for a deed committed during an aberration of intellect."

Strange to say, the counsel did not once draw attention to the singular conduct of the prisoner while in court; but this conduct had not been the less remarked by the jury, and did not the less weigh with them.

The witnesses for the defence were few in number. The first who mounted the witness-box was rather peculiar in his appearance. If you include amongst his personal attractions a red nose (which shone like the danger-signal on a railway through the dusky air of the court); a black eye—not that admired darkness of the organ itself which is the handiwork of liberal nature, but that peculiarly mottled purple-and-green appearance about the region which bears witness to the fist of an acquaintance; a bushy moustache of a fine blue-black dye; a head of thick black hair, not too intimately acquainted with that modern innovation on manly habits, the comb—you may perhaps have some notion of his physical qualifications. But nothing could ever give a full or just idea of the recklessness, the effrontery of his manner, the twinkle in his eye, the expression in every pimple of that radiant nose, or the depth of meaning he could convey by one twitch of his moustache, or one shake of his forest of black ringlets.

His costume inclined towards the fast and furious, consisting of a pair of loose Scotch plaid unmentionables,[2] a bright blue greatcoat, no under-coat[3] or waistcoat, a great deal of shirt ornamented with death's-heads and pink ballet-dancers—to say nothing of coffee and tobacco stains, and enough sham gold chain meandering over his burly breast to make up for every deficiency. While he was being duly sworn, the eyes of the witness wandered with a friendly and pitying glance towards the wretched prisoner at the bar.

"You are a member of the medical profession?"

"I am."

"You were, I believe, in the company of the prisoner the night of his departure from London for this town?"

"I was."

"What was the conduct of the prisoner on that night?"

"Rum."

On being further interrogated, the witness stated that he had known Mr. Richard Marwood for many years, being himself originally a Slopperton man.

"Can you tell what led the prisoner to determine on returning to his mother's house in the month of November last?"

"Blue devils,"[4] replied the witness, with determined conciseness.

"Blue devils?"

"Yes, he'd been in a low way for three months, or more; he'd had a sharp attack of delirium tremens, and a touch of his old complaint—"

"His old complaint?"

"Yes, brain-fever. During the fever he talked a great deal of his mother; said he had killed her by his bad conduct, but that he'd beg her forgiveness if he walked to Slopperton on his bare feet."

"Can you tell me at what date he first expressed this desire to come to Slopperton?"

"Some time during the month of September."

"Did you during this period consider him to be in a sound mind?"

"Well, several of my friends at Guy's used to think rather the reverse. It was customary amongst us to say he had a loose slate somewhere."

The counsel for the prosecution taking exception to this phrase "loose slate," the witness went on to state that he thought the prisoner very often off his nut; had hidden his razors during his illness, and piled up a barricade of furniture before the window. The prisoner was remarkable for reckless generosity, good temper, a truthful disposition, and a talent for doing everything, and always doing it better than anybody else. This, and a great deal more, was elicited from him by the advocate for the defence.

He was cross-examined by the counsel for the prosecution.

"I think you told my learned friend that you were a member of the medical profession?"

"I did."

Was first apprenticed to a chemist and druggist at Slopperton, and was now walking one of the hospitals in London with a view to attaining a position in the profession; had not yet attained eminence, but hoped to do so; had operated with some success in a desperate case of whitlow[5] on the finger of a servant-girl, and should have effected a surprising cure, if the girl had not grown impatient and allowed her finger to be amputated by a rival practitioner before the curative process had time to develop itself; had always entertained a sincere regard for the prisoner; had at divers[6] times borrowed money of him; couldn't say he remembered ever returning any; perhaps he never had returned any, and that might account for his not remembering the circumstance; had been present at the election of, and instrumental in electing the prisoner a member of a convivial club called the "Cheerful Cherokees." No "Cheerful Cherokee" had ever been known to commit a murder, and the club was convinced of the prisoner's innocence.

"You told the court and jury a short time ago, that the prisoner's state on the last night you saw him in London was 'rum,' " said the learned gentleman conducting the prosecution; "will you be good enough to favour us with the meaning of that adjective—you intend it for an adjective, I presume?"

"Certainly," replied the witness. "Rum, an adjective when applied to a gentleman's conduct; a substantive when used to denominate his tipple."

The counsel for the prosecution doesn't clearly understand the meaning of the word "tipple."

The witness thinks the learned gentleman had better buy a dictionary before he again assists in a criminal prosecution.

"Come, come, sir," said the judge; "you are extremely impertinent. We don't want to be kept here all night. Let us have your evidence in a straightforward manner."

The witness squared his elbows, and turned that luminary, his nose, full on his lordship, as if it had been a bull's-eye lantern.

"You used another strange expression," said the counsel, "in answer to my friend. Will you have the kindness to explain what you mean by the prisoner having 'a loose slate'?"

"A tile off. Something wrong about the roof—the garret—the upper story—the nut."

The counsel for the prosecution confessed himself to be still in the dark.

The witness declared himself sorry to hear it—he could undertake to give his evidence; but he could not undertake to provide the gentleman with understanding.

"I will trouble you to be respectful in your replies to the counsel for the crown," said the judge.

The medical student's variegated eye looked defiantly at his lordship; the counsel for the crown had done with him, and he retired from the witness-box, after bowing to the judge and jury with studious politeness.

The next witnesses were two medical gentlemen of a different stamp to the "Cheerful Cherokee," who had now taken his place amongst the spectators.

These gentlemen gave evidence of having attended the prisoner some years before, during brain-fever, and having very much feared the fever would have resulted in the loss of the patient's reason.

The trial had by this time lasted so long, that the juryman who had a ticket for the public dinner began to feel that his card of admission to the festive board was so much waste paste-board, and that the green fat of the turtle[7] and the prime cut from the haunch of venison were not for him.

The counsel for the prosecution delivered himself of his second address to the jury, in which he endeavoured to demolish the superstructure which his "learned friend" had so ingeniously raised for the defence. Why should the legal defender of a man whose life is in the hands of the jury not be privileged to address that jury in favour of his client as often, at least, as the legal representative of the prosecutor?

The judge delivered his charge to the jury.

The jury retired, and in an hour and fifteen minutes returned.

They found that the prisoner, Richard Marwood, had murdered his uncle, Montague Harding, and had further beaten and injured a half-caste servant in the employ of his uncle, while suffering from aberration of intellect—or, in simple phraseology, they found the prisoner "Not Guilty, on the ground of insanity."

The prisoner seemed little affected by the verdict. He looked with a vacant stare round the court, removed the bouquet of rue from his button-hole and placed it in his bosom; and then said, with a clear distinct enunciation—

"Gentlemen of the jury, I am extremely obliged to you for the politeness with which you have treated me. Thanks to your powerful sense of justice, I have won the battle of Arcola,[8] and I think I have secured the key of Italy."

It is common for lunatics to fancy themselves some great and distinguished person. This unhappy young man believed himself to be Napoleon the First.[9]

BOOK THE SECOND

A CLEARANCE
OF ALL SCORES

BLIND PETER

The favourite, "Gallows," having lost in the race with Richard Marwood, there was very little more interest felt in Slopperton about poor Daredevil Dick's fate. It was known that he was in the county lunatic asylum, a prisoner for life, or, as it is expressed by persons learned in legal matters, during the pleasure of the sovereign. It was known that his poor mother had taken up her abode near the asylum, and that at intervals she was allowed the melancholy pleasure of seeing the wreck of her once light-hearted boy. Mrs. Marwood was now a very rich woman, inheritress of the whole of her poor murdered brother's wealth—for Mr. Montague Harding's will had been found to bequeath the whole of his immense fortune to his only sister. She spent little, however, and what she did expend was chiefly devoted to works of charity; but even her benevolence was limited, and she did little more for the poor than she had done before from her own small income. The wealth of the East Indian remained accumulating in the hands of her bankers. Mrs. Marwood was, therefore, very rich, and Slopperton accordingly set her down as a miser.

So the nine-days' wonder died out, and the murder of Mr. Harding was forgotten. The sunshine on the factory chimneys of Slopperton grew warmer every day. Every day the "hands" appertaining to the factories felt more and more the necessity of frequent application to the public-house, as the weather grew brighter and brighter—till the hot June sun blazed down upon the pavement of every street in Slopperton, baking and grilling the stones; till the sight of a puddle or an overflowing gutter would have been welcome as pools of water in the great desert of Sahara; till the people who lived on the sunny side of the way felt spitefully disposed towards the inhabitants of the shady side; till the chandler[1] at the corner, who came out with a watering-pot and sprinkled the pavement before his door every evening, was thought a public benefactor; till the baker, who added his private stock of caloric to the great firm of Sunshine and Co., and baked the pavement above his oven on his own account, was thought a public nuisance, and hot bread an abomination; till the butter Slopperton had for tea was no longer butter, but oil, and eluded the pursuit of the knife, or hid itself in a cowardly manner in the holes of the quartern loaf when the housewife attempted to spread it thereon; till cattle standing in pools of water were looked upon with envy and hatred; and till—wonder of wonders!—Slopperton paid up the water-rate sharp, in fear and anguish at the thought of the possible cutting-off of that refreshing fluid.

The 17th of June ushered in the midsummer holidays at Dr. Tappenden's establishment, and on the evening of that day Dr. Tappenden broke up. Of course, this phrase, breaking up, is only a schoolboy's slang. I do not mean that the worthy Doctor (how did he ever come to be a doctor, I wonder? or where did he get his degree?) experienced any physical change when he broke up; or that he underwent the moral change of going into the *Gazette*[2] and coming out thereof better off than when he went in—which is, I believe, the custom in most cases of bankruptcy; I merely mean to say, that on the evening of the 17th of June Dr. Tappenden gave a species of ball, at which Mr. Pranskey, the dancing-master, assisted with his pumps and his violin; and at which the young gentlemen appeared also in pumps, a great deal of wrist-band and shirt-collar, and shining faces—in a state of painfully high polish, from the effect of the yellow soap that had been lavished upon them by the respectable young person who looked to the wardrobe department, and mended the linen of the young gentlemen.

By the evening of the 18th, Dr. Tappenden's young gentlemen, with the exception of two little fellows with dark complexions and frizzy hair, whose nearest connections were at Trinidad, all departed to their respective family circles; and Mr. Jabez North had the schoolroom to himself for the whole of the holidays—for, of course, the little West Indians, playing at a sea-voyage on one of the forms, with a cricket-bat for a mast, or reading Sinbad the Sailor in a corner, were no hindrance to that gentleman's proceedings.

Our friend Jabez is as calm-looking as ever. The fair pale complexion may be, perhaps, a shade paler, and the arched mouth a trifle more compressed—(that absurd professor of phrenology had declared that both the head and face of Jabez bespoke a marvellous power of secretiveness)—but our friend is as placid as ever. The pale face, delicate aquiline nose, the fair hair and rather slender figure, give a tone of aristocracy to his appearance which even his shabby black suit cannot conceal. But Jabez is not too well pleased with his lot. He paces up and down the schoolroom in the twilight of the June evening, quite alone, for the little West Indians have retired to the long dormitory which they now inhabit in solitary grandeur. Dr. Tappenden has gone to the sea-side with his slim only daughter, familiarly known amongst the scholars, who have no eyes for ethereal beauty, as "Skinny Jane." Dr. Tappenden has gone to enjoy himself; for Dr. Tappenden is a rich man. He is said to have some twenty thousand pounds in a London bank. He doesn't bank his money in Slopperton. And of "Skinny Jane," it may be observed, that there are young men in the town who would give something for a glance from her insipid grey eyes, and who think her ethereal figure the very incarnation of the poet's ideal, when they add to that slender form the bulky figures that form the sum-total of her father's banking account.

Jabez paces up and down the long schoolroom with a step so light that it scarcely wakes an echo (those crotchety physiologists call this light step another indication of a secretive disposition)—up and down, in the darkening summer evening.

"Another six months' Latin grammar," he mutters, "another half-year's rudiments of Greek, and all the tiresome old fables of Paris and Helen, and Hector and Achilles, for entertainment! A nice life for a man with my head—for those fools who preached about my deficient moral region were right perhaps when they told me my intellect might carry me anywhere. What has it done for me yet? Well, at the worst, it has taken me out of loathsome parish rags; it has given me independence. And it shall give me fortune. But how? What is to be the next trial? This time it must be no failure. This time my premises must be sure. If I could only hit upon some scheme! There is a way by which I could obtain a large sum of money; but then, the fear of detection! Detection, which if eluded to-day might come to-morrow! And it is not a year or two's riot and dissipation that I want to purchase; but a long life of wealth and luxury, with proud men's necks to trample on, and my old patrons to lick the dust off my shoes. This is what I must fight for, and this is what I must attain—but how? How?"

He takes his hat up, and goes out of the house. He is quite his own master during these holidays. He comes in and goes out as he likes, provided he is always at home by ten o'clock, when the house is shut up for the night.

He strolls with a purposeless step through the streets of Slopperton. It is half-past eight o'clock, and the factory hands fill the streets, enjoying the coolness of the evening, but quiet and subdued in their manner, being exhausted by the heat of the long June day. Jabez does not much affect these crowded streets, and turns out of one of the most busy quarters of the town into a little lane of old houses, which leads to a great old-fashioned square, in which stand two ancient churches with very high steeples, an antique-looking town-hall (once a prison), a few quaint houses with peaked roofs and projecting upper stories, and a gaunt gump. Jabez soon leaves this square behind him, and strolls through two or three dingy, narrow, old-fashioned streets, till he comes to a labyrinth of tumbledown houses, pigstyes, and dog-kennels, known as Blind Peter's Alley. Who Blind Peter was, or how he ever came to have this alley—or whether, as a place possessing no thoroughfare and admitting very little light, it had not originally been called Peter's Blind Alley—nobody living knew. But if Blind Peter was a myth, the alley was a reality, and a dirty loathsome fetid reality, with regard to which the Board of Health seemed as if smitten with the aforesaid Peter's own infirmity, ignoring the horror of the place with fatal blindness. So Blind Peter was the Alsatia[3] of Slopperton, a refuge for crime and destitution—since destitution cannot pick its company, but must be content often, for the sake of shelter, to jog cheek by jowl with crime. And thus no doubt it is on the strength of that golden adage about birds of a feather that destitution and crime are thought by numerous wise and benevolent persons to mean one and the same thing. Blind Peter had risen to popularity once or twice—on the occasion of a girl poisoning her father in the crust of a beef-steak pudding, and a boy of fourteen committing suicide by hanging himself behind a door. Blind Peter, on the first of these occasions, had even had his portrait taken for a Sunday paper; and very nice indeed he had looked in a woodcut—so nice, that he had found some difficulty in recognizing himself; which perhaps was scarcely wonderful, when it is taken into consideration that the artist, who lived in the neighbourhood of Holborn, had sketched Blind Peter from a mountain gorge in the Tyrol, broken up with three or four houses out of Chancery Lane.

Certainly Blind Peter had a peculiar wildness in his aspect, being built on the side of a steep hill, and looked very much like a London alley which had been removed from its site and pitched haphazard on to a Slopperton mountain.

It is not to be supposed for a moment that so highly respectable an individual as Mr. Jabez North had any intention of plunging into the dirty obscurity of Blind Peter. He had come thus far only on his way to the outskirts of the town, where there was a little brick-bestrewn, pseudo country, very much more liberally ornamented by oyster-shells, broken crockery, and scaffolding, than by trees or wild flowers—which natural objects were wondrous rarities in this part of the Sloppertonian outskirts.

So Jabez pursued his way past the mouth of Blind Peter—which was adorned by two or three broken-down and rusty iron railings that looked like jagged teeth—when he was suddenly arrested by a hideous-looking woman, who threw her arms about him, and addressed him in a shrill voice thus—

"What, he's come back to his best friends, has he? He's come back to his old granny, after frightening her out of her poor old wits by staying away four days and four nights. Where have you been, Jim, my deary? And where did you get your fine toggery?"

"Where did I get my fine toggery? What do you mean, you old hag? I don't know you, and you don't know me. Let me pass, will you? or I'll knock you down!"

"No, no," she screamed; "he wouldn't knock down his old granny; he wouldn't knock down his precious granny that nursed him, and brought him up like a gentleman, and will tell him a secret one of these days worth a mint of money, if he treats her well."

Jabez pricked up his ears at the words "mint of money," and said in rather a milder tone—

"I tell you, my good woman, you mistake me for somebody else. I never saw you before."

"What! you're not my Jim?"

"No. My name is Jabez North. If you're not satisfied, here's my card," and he took out his card-case.

The old woman stuck her arms a kimbo, and stared at him with a gaze of admiration.

"Lor'," she cried, "don't he do it nat'ral? Ain't he a born genius? He's been a-doing the respectable reduced tradesman, or the young man brought up to the church, what waits upon the gentry with a long letter, and has a wife and two innocent children staying in another town, and only wants the railway fare to go to 'em. Eh, Jim, that's what you've been a-doing, ain't it now? And you've brought home the swag like a good lad to your grandmother, haven't you now?" she said in a wheedling tone.

"I tell you, you confounded old fool, I'm not the man you take me for."

"What, not my Jim! And you can look at me with his eyes and tell me so with his voice. Then, if you're not him, he's dead, and you're his ghost."

Jabez thought the old woman was mad; but he was no coward, and the adventure began to interest him. Who was this man who was so like him, and who was to learn a secret some day worth a mint of money?

"Will you come with me, then," said the old woman, "and let me get a light, and see whether you are my Jim or not?"

"Where's the house?" asked Jabez.

"Why, in Blind Peter, to be sure. Where should it be?"

"How should I know?" said Jabez, following her. He thought himself safe even in Blind Peter, having nothing of value about him, and having considerable faith in the protecting power of his strong right arm.

The old woman led the way into the little mountain gorge, choked up with rickety hovels lately erected, or crazy old houses which had once been goodly residences, in the days when the site of Blind Peter had been a pleasant country lane. The house she entered was of this latter class; and she led the way into a stone-paved room, which had once been a tolerably spacious entrance-hall.

It was lighted by one feeble little candle with a long drooping wick, stuck in an old ginger-beer bottle; and by this dim light Jabez saw, seated on a heap of rubbish by the desolate hearth, his own reflection—a man dressed, unlike him, in the rough garments of a labourer, but whose face gave back as faithfully as ever glass had done the shadow of his own.

CHAPTER II

LIKE AND UNLIKE

The old woman stared aghast, first at one of the young men, then at the other.

"Why, then, he isn't Jim!" she exclaimed.

"Who isn't Jim, grandmother? What do you mean? Here I am, back again; a bundle of aching bones, old rags, and empty pockets. I've done no good where I've been; so you needn't ask me for any money, for I haven't earned a farthing either by fair means or foul."

"But the other," she said,—"this young gentleman. Look at him, Jim."

The man took up the candle, snuffed it with his fingers, and walked straight to Jabez. He held the light before the face of the usher, and surveyed him with a leisurely stare. That individual's blue eyes winked and blinked at the flame like an owl's in the sunshine, and looked every way except straight into the eyes looking into his.

"Why, curse his impudence!" said the man, with a faint sickly laugh; "I'm blest if he hasn't been and boned my mug.[1] I hope it'll do him more good than it's done me," he added, bitterly.

"I can't make out the meaning of this," mumbled the old woman. "It's all dark to me. I saw where the other one was put myself. I saw it done, and safely done too. Oh, yes, of course—"

"What do you mean by 'the other one'?" asked the man, while Jabez listened intently for the answer.

"Why, my deary, that's a part of the secret you're to know some of these days. Such a secret. Gold, gold, gold, as long as it's kept; and gold when it's told, if it's told at the right time, deary."

"If it's to be told at the right time to do me any good, it had better be told soon, then," said Jim, with a dreary shiver. "My bones ache, and my head's on fire, and my feet are like lumps of ice. I've walked twenty miles to-day, and I haven't had bite nor sup since last night. Where's Sillikens?"

"At the factory, Jim deary. Somebody's given her a piece of work—one of the regular hands; and she's to bring home some money to-night. Poor girl, she's been a fretting and a crying her eyes out since you've been gone, Jim."

"Poor lass. I thought I might do some good for her and me both by going away where I did; but I haven't; and so I've come back to eat her starvation wages, poor lass. It's a cowardly thing to do, and if I'd had strength I should have gone on further, but I couldn't."

As he was saying these words a girl came in at the half-open door, and running up to him, threw her arms round his neck.

"O Jim, you've come back! I said you would; I knew you'd never stop away; I knew you couldn't be so cruel."

"It's crueller to come back, lass," he said; "it's bad to be a burden on a girl like you."

"A burden, Jim!" she said, in a low reproachful voice, and then dropped quietly down amongst the dust and rubbish at his feet, and laid her head caressingly against his knee.

She was not what is generally called a pretty girl. Hers had not

been the delicate nurture which nourishes so frail an exotic as
beauty. She had a pale sickly face; but it was lighted up by large
dark eyes, and framed by a heavy mass of dark hair.

She took the man's rough hand in hers, and kissed it tenderly. It
is not likely that a duchess would have done such a thing; but if she
had, she could scarcely have done it with better grace.

"A burden, Jim!" she said,—"a burden! Do you think if I worked
for you day and night, and never rested, that I should be weary? Do
you think, if I worked my fingers to the bone for you, that I should
ever feel the pain? Do you think, if my death could make you a
happy man, I should not be glad to die? Oh, you don't know, you
don't know!"

She said this half-despairingly, as if she knew there was no
power in his soul to fathom the depth of love in hers.

"Poor lass, poor lass," he said, as he laid the other rough hand
gently on her black hair. "If it's as bad as this, I'm sorry for it—more
than ever sorry to-night."

"Why, Jim?" She looked up at him with a sudden glance of alarm.
"Why, Jim? Is anything the matter?"

"Not much, lass; but I don't think I'm quite the thing to-night."
His head drooped as he spoke. The girl put it on her shoulder, and
it lay there as if he had scarcely power to lift it up again.

"Grandmother, he's ill—he's ill! why didn't you tell me this before? Is that gentleman the doctor?" she asked, looking at Jabez,
who still stood in the shadow of the doorway, watching the scene
within.

"No; but I'll fetch the doctor, if you like," said that benevolent
personage, who appeared to take a wonderful interest in this family
group.

"Do, sir, if you will be so good," said the girl imploringly; "he's
very ill, I'm sure. Jim, look up, and tell us what's the matter?"

The man lifted his heavy eyelids with an effort, and looked up
with bloodshot eyes into her face. No, no! Never could he fathom
the depth of this love which looks down at him now with more than
a mother's tenderness, with more than a sister's devotion, with
more than a wife's self-abnegation. This love, which knows no

change, which would shelter him in those entwining arms a thief or a murderer, and which could hold him no dearer were he a king upon a throne.

Jabez North goes for a doctor, and returns presently with a gentleman, who, on seeing Jim the labourer, pronounces that he had better go to bed at once; "for," as he whispers to the old woman, "he's got rheumatic fever,[2] and got it pretty sharp, too."

The girl they call Sillikens bursts out crying on hearing this announcement, but soon chokes down her tears—(as tears are wont to be choked down in Blind Peter, whose inhabitants have little time for weeping)—and sets to work to get ready a poor apology for a bed—a worn-out mattress and a thin patch-work counterpane; and on this they lay the bundle of aching bones known to Blind Peter as Jim Lomax.

The girl receives the doctor's directions, promises to fetch some medicine from his surgery in a few minutes, and then kneels down by the sick man.

"O Jim, dear Jim," she says, "keep a good heart, for the sake of those who love you."

She might have said for the sake of her who loves you, for it never surely was the lot of any man, from my lord the marquis to Jim the labourer, to be twice in his life loved as this man was loved by her.

Jabez North on his way home must go the same way as the doctor; so they walk side by side.

"Do you think he will recover?" asks Jabez.

"I doubt it. He has evidently been exposed to great hardship, wet, and fatigue. The fever is very strong upon him; and I'm afraid there's not much chance of his getting over it. I should think something might be done for him, to make him a little more comfortable. You are his brother, I presume, in spite of the apparent difference between you in station?"

Jabez laughed a scornful laugh. "His brother! Why, I never saw the man till ten minutes before you did."

"Bless me!" said the old doctor, "you amaze me. I should have taken you for twin brothers. The likeness between you is something wonderful; in spite, too, of the great difference in your clothes. Dressed alike, it would be impossible to tell one from the other."

"You really think so?"

"The fact must strike any one."

Jabez North was silent for a little time after this. Presently, as he parted from the doctor at a street-corner, he said—

"And you really think there's very little chance of this poor man's recovery?"

"I'm afraid there is positively none. Unless a wonderful change takes place for the better, in three days he will be a dead man. Good night."

"Good night," says Jabez, thoughtfully. And he walked slowly home.

It would seem about this time that he was turning his attention to his personal appearance, and in some danger of becoming a fop; for the next morning he bought a bottle of hair-dye, and tried some experiments with it on one or two of his own light ringlets, which he cut off for that purpose.

It would seem a very trivial employment for so superior and intellectual a man as Jabez North, but it may be that every action of this man's life, however apparently trivial, bore towards one deep and settled purpose.

CHAPTER III

A GOLDEN SECRET

Mr. Jabez North, being of such a truly benevolent character, came the next day to Blind Peter, full of kind and sympathetic inquiries for the sick man. For once in a way he offered something more than sympathy, and administered what little help he could afford from his very slender purse. Truly a good young man, this Jabez.

The dilapidated house in Blind Peter looked still more dreary and dilapidated in the daylight, or in such light as was called daylight by the denizens of that wretched alley. By this light, too, Jim

Lomax looked none the better, with hungry pinched features, bloodshot eyes, and two burning crimson spots on his hollow cheeks. He was asleep when Jabez entered. The girl was still seated by his side, never looking up, or taking her large dark eyes from his face—never stirring, except to re-arrange the poor bundle of rags which served as a pillow for the man's weary head, or to pour out his medicine, or moisten his hot forehead with wet linen. The old woman sat by the great gaunt fireplace, where she had lighted a few sticks, and made the best fire she could, by the doctor's orders; for the place was damp and draughty, even in this warm June weather. She was rocking herself to and fro on a low three-legged stool, and muttering some disconnected jargon.

When Jabez had spoken a few words to the sick man, and made his offer of assistance, he did not leave the place, but stood on the hearth, looking with a thoughtful face at the old woman.

She was not quite right in her mind, according to general opinion in Blind Peter; and if a Commission of Lunacy had been called upon to give a return of her state of intellect on that day, I think that return would have agreed with the opinion openly expressed in a friendly manner by her neighbours.

She kept muttering to herself, "And so, my deary, this is the other one. The water couldn't have been deep enough. But it's not my fault, Lucy dear, for I saw it safely put away."

"What did you see so safely put away?" asked Jabez, in so low a voice as to be heard neither by the sick man nor the girl.

"Wouldn't you like to know, deary?" mumbled the old hag, looking up at him with a malicious grin. "Don't you very much want to know, my dear? But you never will; or if you ever do, you must be a rich man first; for it's part of the secret, and the secret's gold—as long as it is kept, my dear, and it's been kept a many years, and kept faithful."

"Does *he* know it?" Jabez asked, pointing to the sick man.

"No, my dear; he'd want to tell it. I mean to sell it some day, for it's worth a mint of money! A mint of money! He doesn't know it— nor she—not that it matters to her; but it does matter to him."

"Then you had best let him know before three days are over or he'll never know it!" said the schoolmaster.

"Why not, deary?"

"Never you mind! I want to speak to you; and I don't want those two to hear what I say. Can we go anywhere hereabouts where I can talk to you without the chance of being overheard?"

The old woman nodded assent, and led the way with feeble tottering steps out of the house, and through a gap in a hedge to some broken ground at the back of Blind Peter. Here the old crone seated herself upon a little hillock, Jabez standing opposite her, looking her full in the face.

"Now," said he, with a determined look at the grinning face before him, "now tell me,—what was the *something* that was put away so safely? And what relation is that man in there to me? Tell me, and tell me the truth, or——" He only finishes the sentence with a threatening look, but the old woman finishes it for him,—

"Or you'll kill me—eh, deary? I'm old and feeble, and you might easily do it—eh? But you won't—you won't, deary! You know better than that! Kill me, and you'll never know the secret!—the secret that may be gold to *you* some day, and that nobody alive but me can tell. If you'd got some very precious wine in a glass bottle, my dear, you wouldn't smash the bottle now, would you? because, you see, you couldn't smash the bottle without spilling the wine. And you won't lay so much as a rough finger upon me, I know."

The usher looked rather as if he would have liked to lay the whole force of ten very rough fingers upon the most vital part of the grinning hag's anatomy at that moment—but he restrained himself, as if by an effort, and thrust his hands deep into his trousers-pockets, in order the better to resist temptation.

"Then you don't mean to tell me what I asked you?" he said impatiently.

"Don't be in a hurry, my dear! I'm an old woman, and I don't like to be hurried. What is it you want to know?"

"What that man in there is to me."

"Own brother—twin brother, my dear—that's all. And I'm your

grandmother—your mother's mother. Ain't you pleased to find your relations, my blessed boy?"

If he were, he had a strange way of showing pleasure; a very strange manner of welcoming newly-found relations, if his feelings were to be judged by that contracted brow and moody glance.

"Is this true?" he asked.

The old harridan looked at him and grinned. "That's an ugly mark you've got upon your left arm, my dear," she said, "just above the elbow; it's very lucky, though, it's under your coat-sleeve, where nobody can see it."

Jabez started. He had indeed a scar upon his arm, though very few people knew of it. He remembered it from his earliest days in the Slopperton workhouse.

"Do you know how you came by that mark?" continued the old woman. "Shall I tell you? Why, you fell into the fire, deary, when you were only three weeks old. We'd been drinking a little bit, my dear, and we weren't used to drinking much then, nor to eating much either, and one of us let you tumble into the fireplace, and before we could get you out, your arm was burnt; but you got over it, my dear, and three days after that you had the misfortune to fall into the water."

"You threw me in, you old she-devil!" he exclaimed fiercely.

"Come, come," she said, "you are of the same stock, so I wouldn't call names if I were you. Perhaps I did throw you into the Sloshy. I don't want to contradict you. If you say so, I dare say I did. I suppose you think me a very unnatural old woman?"

"It wouldn't be so strange if I did."

"Do you know what choice we had, your mother and me, as to what we were to do with our youngest hope—you're younger by two hours than your brother in there? Why, there was the river on one side, and a life of misery, perhaps starvation, perhaps worse, on the other. At the very best, such a life as he in there has led—hard labour and bad food, long toilsome days and short nights, and bad words and black looks from all who ought to help him. So we thought one was enough for that, and we chose the river for the other. Yes, my precious boy, I took you down to the river-side one very dark night and dropped you in where I thought the water was deepest; but, you see, it wasn't deep enough for you. Oh, dear," she said, with an imbecile grin, "I suppose there's a fate in it, and you were never born to be drowned."[1]

Her hopeful grandson looked at her with a savage frown.

"Drop that!" he said, "I don't want any of your cursed wit."

"Don't you, deary? Lor, I was quite a wit in my young days. They used to call me Lively Betty; but that's a long time ago."

There was sufficient left, however, of the liveliness of a long time ago to give an air of ghastly mirth to the old woman's manner, which made that manner extremely repulsive. What can be more repulsive than old age, which, shorn of the beauties and graces, is yet not purified from the follies or the vices of departed youth?

"And so, my dear, the water wasn't deep enough, and you were saved. How did it all come about? Tell us, my precious boy?"

"Yes; I dare say you'd like to know," replied her "precious boy,"— "but you can keep your secret, and I can keep mine. Perhaps you'll tell me whether my mother is alive or dead?"

Now this was a question which would have cruelly agitated some men in the position of Jabez North; but that gentleman was a philosopher, and he might have been inquiring the fate of some cast-off garment, for all the fear, tenderness, or emotion of any kind that his tone or manner betrayed.

"Your mother's been dead these many years. Don't you ask me how she died. I'm an old woman, and my head's not so right but what some things will set it wrong. Talking of that is one of 'em. She's dead. I couldn't save her, nor help her, nor set her right. I hope there's more pity where she's gone than she ever got here; for I'm sure if trouble can need it, she needed it. Don't ask me anything about her."

"Then I won't," said Jabez. "My relations don't seem such an eligible lot that I should set to work to write the history of the family. I suppose I had a father of some kind or other. What's become of him? Dead or——"

"Hung, eh, deary?" said the old woman, relapsing into the malicious grin.

"Take care what you're about," said the fascinating Mr. North, "or you'll tempt me to shake the life out of your shrivelled old carcass."

"And then you'll never know who your father was. Eh? Ha, ha! my precious boy; that's part of the golden secret that none but me can tell."

"Then you won't tell me my father's name?"

"Perhaps I've forgotten it, deary; perhaps I never knew it—who knows?"

"Was he of your class—poor, insignificant, and wretched, the scum of the earth, the mud in the streets, the slush in the gutters, for other people to trample upon with their dirty boots? Was he that sort of thing? Because if he was, I shan't put myself out of the way to make any tender inquiries about him."

"Of course not, deary. You'd like him to have been a fine gentleman—a baronet, or an earl, or a marquis, eh, my blessed boy? A marquis is about the ticket for you, eh? What do you say to a marquis?"

It was not very polite, certainly, what he did say; not quite the tone of conversation to be pleasing to any marquis, or to any noble or potentate whatever, except one, and him, by the laws of polite literature, I am not allowed to mention.

Puzzled by her mysterious mumblings, grinnings, and gesticulations, our friend Jabez stared hard in the old crone's face for about three minutes—looking very much as if he would have liked to throttle her; but he refrained from that temptation, turned on his heel, and walked off in the direction of Slopperton.

The old woman apostrophized his receding figure.

"Oh, yes, deary, you're a nice young man, and a clever, civil-spoken young man, and a credit to them that reared you; but you'll never have the golden secret out of me till you've got the money to pay for it."

CHAPTER IV

JIM LOOKS OVER THE BRINK OF THE TERRIBLE GULF

The light had gone down on the last of the days through which, according to the doctor's prophecy, Jim Lomax was to live to see that light.

Poor Jim's last sun sank to his rest upon such cloud-pillows of purple and red, and drew a curtain of such gorgeous colours round him in the western sky, as it would have very much puzzled any earthly monarch to have matched, though Ruskin himself had chosen the colours, and Turner had been the man to lay them on. Of course some of this red sunset flickered and faded upon the chimney-pots and window-panes—rare luxuries, by the bye, those window-panes—of Blind Peter; but there it came in a modified degree only—this blessed sign-manual of an Almighty Power—as all earthly and heavenly blessings should come to the poor.

One ray of the crimson light fell full upon the face of the sick man, and slanted from him upon the dark hair of the girl, who sat on the ground in her old position by the bed-side. This light, which fell on them and on no other object in the dusky room, seemed to unite them, as though it were a messenger from the sky that said, "They stand alone in the world, and never have been meant to stand asunder."

"It's a beautiful light, lass," said the sick man, "and I wonder I never cared more to notice or to watch it than I have. Lord, I've seen it many a time sinking behind the sharp edge of ploughed land, as if it had dug its own grave, and was glad to go down to it, and I've thought no more of it than a bit of candle; but now it seems such a beautiful light, and I feel as if I should like to see it again, lass."

"And you will—you will see it again, Jim." She drew his head upon her bosom, and stroked the rough hair away from his damp forehead. She was half dead herself, with want, anxiety, and fatigue; but she spoke in a cheerful voice. She had not shed a tear throughout his illness. "Lord help you, Jim dear, you'll live to see many and many a bright sunset—live to see it go down upon our wedding-day, perhaps."

"No, no, lass; that's a day no sun will ever shine upon. You must get another sweetheart, and a better one, maybe. I'm sure you deserve a better one, for you're true, lass, true as steel."

The girl drew his head closer to her breast, and bending over him, kissed his dry lips. She never thought, or cared to know, what fever or what poison she might inhale in that caress. If she had thought about it, perhaps she would have prayed that the same fever which had struck him down might lay her low beside him. He spoke again, as the light, with a lingering glow, brightened, and flickered, and then faded out.

"It's gone; it's gone for ever; it's behind me now, lass, and I must look straight before——"

"At what, Jim?—at what?"

"At a terrible gulf, my lass. I'm a-standing on the edge of it, and I'm a-looking down to the bottom of it—a cold dark lonesome place. But perhaps there's another light beyond it, lass; who knows?"

"Some say they do know, Jim," said the girl; "some say they do know, and that there is another light beyond, better than the one we see here, and always shining. Some people do know all about it, Jim."

"Then why didn't they tell us about it?" asked the man, with an angry expression in his hollow eyes. "I suppose those as taught them meant them to teach us; but I suppose they didn't think us worth the teaching. How many will be sorry for me, lass, when I am gone? Not grandmother; her brain's crazed with that fancy of hers of a golden secret—as if she wouldn't have sold it long before this if she'd had a secret—sold it for bread, or more likely for gin. Not anybody in Blind Peter—they've enough to do to think of the bit of food to put inside them, or of the shelter to cover their unfortunate heads. Nobody but you, lass, nobody but you, will be sorry for me; and I think you will."

He thinks she will be sorry. What has been the story of her life but one long thought and care for him, in which her every sorrow and her every joy have taken their colour from joys and sorrows of his?

While they are talking, Jabez comes in, and, seating himself on a low stool by the bed, talks to the sick man.

"And so," says Jim, looking him full in the face with a curious glance—"so you're my brother—the old woman's told me all about it—my twin brother; so like me, that it's quite a treat to look at you. It's like looking in a glass, and that's a luxury I've never been accustomed to. Light a candle, lass; I want to see my brother's face."

His brother was against the lighting of the candle—it might hurt the eyes of the sufferer, he suggested; but Jim repeated his request, and the girl obeyed.

"Now come here and hold the candle, lass, and hold it close to my brother's face, for I want to have a good look at him."

Mr. Jabez North seemed scarcely to relish the unflinching gaze of his newly-found relation; and again those fine blue eyes, for which he was distinguished, winked and shifted, and hid themselves, under the scrutiny of the sick man.

"It's a handsome face," said Jim; "and it looks like the face of one of your fine high-born gentlemen too, which is rather queer, considering who it belongs to; but for all that, I can't say it's a face I much care about. There's something under—something behind the curtain. I say, brother, you're hatching of some plot to-night, and a very deep-laid plot it is too, or my name isn't Jim Lomax."

"Poor fellow," murmured the compassionate Jabez, "his mind wanders sadly."

"Does it?" asked the sick man; "does my mind wander, lad? I hope it does; I hope I can't see very clear to-night, for I didn't want to think my own brother a villain. I don't want to think bad of thee, lad, if it's only for my dead mother's sake."

"You hear!" said Jabez, with a glance of appeal to the girl, "you hear how delirious he is?"

"Stop a bit, lad," cried Jim, with sudden energy, laying his wasted hand upon his brother's wrist; "stop a bit. I'm dying fast; and before it's too late I've one prayer to make. I haven't made so many either to God or man that I need forget this one. You see this lass; we've been sweethearts, I don't know how long, now—ever since she was a little toddling thing that I could carry on my shoulder; and, one of these days, when wages got to be better, and bread cheaper, and hopes brighter, somehow, for poor folks like us, we was to have been married; but that's over now. Keep a good heart, lass, and don't look so white; perhaps it's better as it is. Well, as I was saying, we've been sweethearts for a many year, and often when I haven't been able to get work, maybe sometimes when I haven't been willing, when I've been lazy, or on the drink, or among bad companions, this lass has kept a shelter over me, and given me bread to eat with the labour of her own hands. She's been true to me. I could tell you how true, but there's something about the corners of your mouth that makes me think you wouldn't care to hear it. But if you want me to die in peace, promise me this—that as long as you've got a shilling she shall never be without a sixpence; that as long as you've got a roof to cover your head she shall never be without a shelter. Promise!"

He tightened his grasp convulsively upon his brother's wrist. That gentleman made an effort to look him full in the face; but not seeming to relish the searching gaze of the dying man's eyes, Mr. Jabez North was compelled to drop his own.

"Come," said Jim; "promise—swear to me, by all you hold sacred, that you'll do this."

"I swear!" said Jabez, solemnly.

"And if you break your oath," added his brother, "never come anigh the place where I'm buried, for I'll rise out of my grave and haunt you."

The dying man fell back exhausted on his pillow. The girl poured out some medicine and gave it to him, while Jabez walked to the door, and looked up at the sky.

A very dark sky for a night in June. A wide black canopy hung over the earth, and as yet there was not one feeble star to break the inky darkness. A threatening night—the low murmuring of whose sultry wind moaned and whispered prophecies of a coming storm. Never had the blindness of Blind Peter been darker than to-night. You could scarcely see your hand before you. A wretched woman who had just fetched half-a-quartern of gin from the nearest public-house, though a denizen of the place, and familiar with every broken flag-stone and crumbling brick, stumbled over her own threshold, and spilt a portion of the precious liquid.

It would have been difficult to imagine either the heavens or the earth under a darker aspect in the month of June. Not so, however, thought Mr. Jabez North; for, after contemplating the sky for some moments in silence, he exclaimed—"A fine night! A glorious night! It could not be better!"

A figure, one shade darker than the night, came between him and the darkness. It was the doctor, who said—

"Well, sir, I'm glad you think it a fine night; but I must beg to differ with you on the subject, for I never remember seeing a blacker sky, or one that threatened a more terrible storm at this season of the year."

"I was scarcely thinking of what I was saying, doctor. That poor man in there——"

"Ah, yes; poor fellow! I doubt if he'll witness the storm, near as it seems to be. I suppose you take some interest in him on account of his extraordinary likeness to you?"

"That would be rather an egotistical reason for being interested in him. Common humanity induced me to come down to this wretched place, to see if I could be of any service to the poor creature."

"The action does you credit, sir," said the doctor. "And now for my patient."

It was with a very grave face that the medical man looked at poor Jim, who had, by this time, fallen into a fitful and restless slumber; and when Jabez drew him aside to ask his opinion, he said,—"If he lives through the next half-hour I shall be surprised. Where is the old woman—his grandmother?"

"I haven't seen her this evening," answered Jabez. And then, turning to the girl, he asked her if she knew where the old woman was.

"No; she went out some time ago, and didn't say where she was going. She's not quite right in her mind, you know, sir, and often goes out after dark."

The doctor seated himself on a broken chair, near the mattress on which the sick man lay. Only one feeble guttering candle, with a long, top-heavy wick, lighted the dismal and comfortless room. Jabez paced up and down with that soft step of which we have before spoken. Although in his character of a philosopher the death of a fellow-creature could scarcely have been very distressing to him, there was an uneasiness in his manner on this night which he could not altogether conceal. He looked from the doctor to the girl, and from the girl to his sick brother. Sometimes he paused in his walk up and down the room to peer out at the open door. Once he stooped over the feeble candle to look at his watch. There was a listening expression too in his eyes; an uneasy twitching about his mouth; and at times he could scarcely suppress a tremulous action of his slender fingers, which bespoke impatience and agitation. Presently the clocks of Slopperton chimed the first quarter after ten. On hearing this, Jabez drew the medical man aside, and whispered to him,—

"Are there no means," he said, "of getting that poor girl out of the way? She is very much attached to that unfortunate creature; and if he dies, I fear there will be a terrible scene. It would be an act of mercy to remove her by some stratagem or other. How can we get her away till it is all over?"

"I think I can manage it," said the doctor. "My partner has a surgery at the other end of the town; I will send her there."

He returned to the bedside, and presently said,—

"Look here, my good girl; I am going to write a prescription for something which I think will do our patient good. Will you take it for me, and get the medicine made up?"

The girl looked at him with an appealing glance in her mournful eyes.

"I don't like to leave him, sir."

"But if it's for his good, my dear?"

"Yes, yes, sir. You're very kind. I will go. I can run all the way. And you won't leave him while I'm gone, will you, sir?"

"No, my good girl, I won't. There, there; here's the prescription.

It's written in pencil, but the assistant will understand it. Now listen, while I tell you where to find the surgery."

He gave her the direction; and after a lingering and mournful look at her lover, who still slept, she left the house, and darted off in the direction of Slopperton.

"If she runs as fast as that all the way," said Jabez, as he watched her receding figure, "she will be back in less than an hour."

"Then she will find him either past all help, or better," replied the doctor.

Jabez's pale face turned white as death at this word "better."

"Better!" he said. "Is there any chance of his recovery?"

"There are wonderful chances in this race between life and death. This sleep may be a crisis. If he wakes, there may be a faint hope of his living."

Jabez's hand shook like a leaf. He turned his back to the doctor, walked once up and down the room, and then asked, with his old calmness,—

"And you, sir—you, whose time is of such value to so many sick persons—you can afford to desert them all, and remain here, watching this man?"

"His case is a singular one, and interests me. Besides, I do not know that I have any patient in imminent danger to-night. My assistant has my address, and would send for me were my services peculiarly needed."

"I will go out and smoke a cigar," said Jabez, after a pause. "I can scarcely support this sick room, and the suspense of this terrible conflict between life and death."

He strode out into the darkness, was absent about five minutes, and returned.

"Your cigar did not last long," remarked the doctor. "You are a quick smoker. Bad for the system, sir."

"My cigar was a bad one. I threw it away."

Shortly afterwards there was a knock at the door, and a ragged vagabond-looking boy, peeping in, asked,—

"Is Mr. Saunders the doctor here?"

"Yes, my lad. Who wants me?"

"A young woman up in Hill Fields, sir, what's took poison, they say. You're wanted very bad."

"Poison! that's urgent," said Mr. Saunders. "Who sent you here for me?"

The lad looked with a puzzled expression at Jabez standing in the shadow, who, unperceived by the doctor, whispered something behind his hand.

"Surgery, sir," answered the boy, still looking at Jabez.

"Oh, you were sent from the surgery. I must be off, for this is no doubt a desperate case. I must leave you to look after this poor fellow. If he wakes, give him two teaspoonfuls of that medicine there. I could do no more if I stopped myself. Come, my lad."

The doctor left the house, followed by the boy, and in a few moments both were lost in the darkness, and far out of the ken of Blind Peter.

Five minutes after the departure of the medical man Jabez went to the door, and after looking out at the squalid houses, which were all dark, gave a long low whistle.

A figure crept out of the darkness, and came up to where he stood. It was the old woman, his grandmother.

"All's right, deary," she whispered. "Bill Withers has got everything ready. He's a waiting down by the wall yonder. There's not a mortal about; and I'll keep watch. You'll want Bill's help. When you're ready for him, you're to whistle softly three times running. He'll know what it means—and I'm going to watch while he helps you. Haven't I managed beautiful, deary? and shan't I deserve the golden sovereigns you've promised me? They was guineas always when I was young, deary. Nothing's as good now as it used to be."

"Don't let us have any chattering," said Jabez, as he laid a rough hand upon her arm; "unless you want to wake everybody in the place."

"But, I say, deary, is it all over? Nothing unfair, you know. Remember your promise."

"All over? Yes; half an hour ago. If you hinder me here with your talk, the girl will be back before we're ready for her."

"Let me come in and close his eyes, deary," supplicated the old woman. "His mother was my own child. Let me close his eyes."

"Keep where you are, or I'll strangle you!" growled her dutiful grandson, as he shut the door upon his venerable relation, and left her mumbling upon the threshold.

Jabez crept cautiously towards the bed on which his brother lay. Jim at this moment awoke from his restless slumber; and, opening his eyes to their widest extent, looked full at the man by his side. He made no effort to speak, pointed to his lips, and, stretching out his hand towards the bottles on the table, made signs to his brother. These signs were a supplication for the cooling draught which always allayed the burning heat of the fever.

Jabez never stirred. "He has awoke," he murmured. "This is the crisis of his life, and of my fate."

The clocks of Slopperton chimed the quarter before eleven.

"It's a black gulf, lass," gasped the dying man; "and I'm fast sinking into it."

There was no friendly hand, Jim, to draw you back from that terrible gulf. The medicine stood untouched upon the table; and, perhaps as guilty as the first murderer,[1] your twin brother stood by your bed-side.

CHAPTER V

MIDNIGHT BY THE SLOPPERTON CLOCKS

The clouds and the sky kept their promise, and as the clocks chimed the quarter before twelve the storm broke over the steeples at Slopperton.

Blue lightning-flashes lit up Blind Peter, and attendant thunder-claps shook him to his very foundation; while a violent shower of rain gave him such a washing-down of every flagstone, chimney-pot, and door-step, as he did not often get. Slopperton in bed was almost afraid to go to sleep; and Slopperton not in bed did not seem to care about going to bed. Slopperton at supper was nervous as to handling of glittering knives and steel forks; and Slopperton going to windows to look out at the lightning was apt to withdraw hurriedly at the sight thereof. Slopperton in general was depressed by the storm; thought there would be mischief somewhere; and had a vague idea that something dreadful would happen before the night was out.

In Dr. Tappenden's quiet household there was consternation and alarm. Mr. Jabez North, the principal assistant, had gone out early in the evening, and had not returned at the appointed hour for shutting up the house. This was such an unprecedented occurrence, that it had occasioned considerable uneasiness—especially as Dr. Tappenden was away from home, and Jabez was, in a manner, deputy-master of the house. The young woman who looked after the gentlemen's wardrobes had taken compassion upon the housemaid, who sat up awaiting Mr. North's return, and had brought her workbox, and a lapful of young gentlemen's dilapidated socks, to the modest chamber in which the girl waited.

"I hope," said the housemaid, "nothing ain't happened to him through the storm. I hope he hasn't been getting under no trees."

The housemaid had a fixed idea that to go under a tree in a thunderstorm was to encounter immediate death.

"Poor dear young gentleman," said the lady of the wardrobes; "I tremble to think what can keep him out so. Such a steady young man; never known to be a minute after time either. I'm sure every sound I hear makes me expect to see him brought in on a shutter."

"Don't now, Miss Smithers!" cried the housemaid, looking behind her as if she expected to see the ghost of Jabez North pointing to a red spot on his left breast at the back of her chair. "I wish you wouldn't now! Oh, I hope he ain't been murdered. There's been such a many murders in Slopperton since I can remember. It's only three years and a half ago since a man cut his wife's throat down in Windmill Lane, because she hadn't put no salt in the saucepan when she boiled the greens."

The frightful parallel between the woman who boiled the greens without salt and Jabez North two hours after his time, struck such terror to the hearts of the young women, that they were silent for some minutes, during which they both looked uneasily at a thief in the candle which neither of them had the courage to take out—their nerves not being equal to the possible clicking of the snuffers.

"Poor young man!" said the housemaid, at last. "Do you know, Miss Smithers, I can't help thinking he has been rather low lately."

Now this word "low" admits of several applications, so Miss Smithers replied, rather indignantly,—

"Low, Sarah Anne! Not in his language, I'm sure. And as to his manners, they'd be a credit to the nobleman that wrote the letters."[1]

"No, no, Miss Smithers; I mean his spirits. I've fancied lately he's been a fretting about something; perhaps he's in love, poor dear."

Miss Smithers coloured up. The conversation was getting interesting. Mr. North had lent her *Rasselas*,[2] which she thought a story of thrilling interest; and she had kept his stockings and shirt buttons in order for three years. Such things had happened; and Mrs. Jabez North sounded more comfortable than Miss Smithers, at any rate.

"Perhaps," said Sarah Anne, rather maliciously—"perhaps he's been forgetting his situation and giving way to thoughts of marrying our young missus. She's got a deal of money, you know, Miss Smithers, though her figure ain't much to look at."

Sarah Anne's figure was plenty to look at, having a tendency to break out into luxuriance where you least expected it.

It was in vain that Sarah Anne or Miss Smithers speculated on the probable causes of the usher's absence. Midnight struck from the Dutch clock in the kitchen, the eight-day clock on the staircase, the time-piece in the drawing-room—a liberal and complicated piece of machinery which always struck eighteen to the dozen—and eventually from every clock in Slopperton; and yet there was no sign of Jabez North.

No sign of Jabez North. A white face and a pair of glazed eyes staring up at the sky, out on a dreary heath three miles from Slopperton, exposed to the fury of a pitiless storm; a man lying alone on a wretched mattress in a miserable apartment in Blind Peter—but no Jabez North.

—

Through the heartless storm, dripping wet with the pelting rain, the girl they have christened Sillikens hastens back to Blind Peter. The feeble glimmer of the candle, with the drooping wick sputtering in a pool of grease, is the only light which illumes that cheerless neighbourhood. The girl's heart beats with a terrible flutter as she approaches that light, for an agonizing doubt is in her soul about that *other light* which she left so feebly burning, and which may be now extinct. But she takes courage; and pushing open the door, which opposes neither bolts nor bars to any deluded votary of Mercury,[3] she enters the dimly-lighted room. The man lies with his face turned to the wall; the old woman is seated by the hearth, on which a dull and struggling flame is burning. She has on the table among the medicine-bottles, another, which no doubt contains spirits, for she has a broken teacup in her hand, from which ever and anon she sips consolation, for it is evident she has been crying.

"Mother, how is he—how is he?" the girl asks, with a hurried agitation painful to witness, since it reveals how much she dreads the answer.

"Better, deary, better—Oh, ever so much better," the old woman answers in a crying voice, and with another application to the broken teacup.

"Better! thank Heaven!—thank Heaven!" and the girl, stealing softly to the bed-side, bends down and listens to the sick man's breathing, which is feeble, but regular.

"He seems very fast asleep, grandmother. Has he been sleeping all the time?"

"Since when, deary?"

"Since I went out. Where's the doctor?"

"Gone, deary. Oh, my blessed boy, to think that it should come to this, and his dead mother was my only child! O dear, O dear!" And the old woman burst out crying, only choking her sobs by the aid of the teacup.

"But he's better, grandmother; perhaps he'll get over it now. I always said he would. Oh, I'm so glad—so glad." The girl sat down in her wet garments, of which she never once thought, on the little stool by the side of the bed. Presently the sick man turned round and opened his eyes.

"You've been away a long time, lass," he said.

Something in his voice, or in his way of speaking, she did not know which, startled her; but she wound her arm round his neck, and said—

"Jim, my own dear Jim, the danger's past. The black gulf you've been looking down is closed for these many happy years to come, and maybe the sun will shine on our wedding-day yet."

"Maybe, lass—maybe. But tell me, what's the time?"

"Never mind the time, Jim. Very late, and a very dreadful night; but no matter for that! You're better, Jim; and if the sun never shone upon the earth again, I don't think I should be able to be sorry, now you are safe."

"Are all the lights out in Blind Peter, lass?" he asked.

"All the lights out? Yes, Jim—these two hours. But why do you ask?"

"And in Slopperton did you meet many people, lass?"

"Not half-a-dozen in all the streets. Nobody would be out in such a night, Jim, that could help it."

He turned his face to the wall again, and seemed to sleep. The old woman kept moaning and mumbling over the broken teacup,—

"To think that my blessed boy should come to this—on such a night too, on such a night!"

The storm raged with unabated fury, and the rain pouring in at the dilapidated door threatened to flood the room. Presently the sick man raised his head a little way from the pillow.

"Lass," he said, "could you get me a drop o' wine? I think, if I could drink a drop o' wine, it would put some strength into me somehow."

"Grandmother," said the girl, "can I get him any? You've got some money; it's only just gone twelve; I can get in at the public-house. I *will* get in, if I knock them up, to get a drop o' wine for Jim."

The old woman fumbled among her rags and produced a sixpence, part of the money given her from the slender purse of the benevolent Jabez, and the girl hurried away to fetch the wine.

The public-house was called the Seven Stars; the seven stars being represented on a signboard in such a manner as to bear rather a striking resemblance to seven yellow hot-cross buns on a very blue background. The landlady of the Seven Stars was putting her hair in papers when the girl called Sillikens invaded the sanctity of her private life. Why she underwent the pain and grief of curling her hair for the admiration of such a neighbourhood as Blind Peter is one of those enigmas of this dreary existence to solve which the Œdipus[+] has not yet appeared. I don't suppose she much cared about suspending her toilet, and opening her bar, for the purpose of selling sixpennyworth of port wine; but when she heard it was for a sick man, she did not grumble. The girl thanked her heartily, and hurried homewards with her pitiful measure of wine.

Through the pitiless rain, and under the dark sky, it was almost impossible to see your hand before you; but as Sillikens entered the mouth of Blind Peter, a flash of lightning revealed to her the figure of a man gliding with a soft step between the broken iron railings. In the instantaneous glimpse she caught of him under the blue light, something familiar in his face or form quickened the beating of her heart, and made her turn to look back at him; but it was too dark for her to see more than the indistinct figure of a man hurrying away in the direction of Slopperton. Wondering who could be leaving Blind Peter on such a night and at such an hour, she hastened back to carry her lover the wine.

The old woman still sat before the hearth. The sputtering candle had gone out, and the light from the miserable little fire only revealed the dark outlines of the wretched furniture and the figure of Jim's grandmother, looking, as she sat mumbling over the broken teacup, like a wicked witch performing an incantation over a portable cauldron.

The girl hurried to the bed-side—the sick man was not there.

"Grandmother! Jim—Jim! Where is he?" she asked, in an alarmed voice; for the figure she had met hurrying through the storm flashed upon her with a strange distinctness. "Jim! Grandmother! tell me where he is, or I shall go mad! Not gone—not gone out on such a night as this, and in a burning fever?"

"Yes, lass, he's gone. My precious boy, my darling boy. His dead mother was my only child, and he's gone for ever and ever, and on this dreadful night. I'm a miserable old woman."

No other explanation than this, no other words than these, chattered and muttered again and again, could the wretched girl extort from the old woman, who, half imbecile and more than half tipsy, sat grinning and grunting over the teacup till she fell asleep in a heap on the cold damp hearth, still hugging the empty teacup, and still muttering, even in her sleep,—

"His dead mother was my only child; and it's very cruel it should come to this at last, and on such a night."

CHAPTER VI

THE QUIET FIGURE ON THE HEATH

The morning after the storm broke bright and clear, promising a hot summer's day, but also promising a pleasant breeze to counterbalance the heat of the sun. This was the legacy of the storm, which, dying out about three o'clock, after no purposeless fury, had left behind it a better and purer air in place of the sultry atmosphere which had heralded its coming.

Mr. Joseph Peters, seated at breakfast this morning, attended by Kuppins nursing the "fondling," has a great deal to say by means of the dirty alphabet (greasy from the effects of matutinal[1] bacon) about last night's storm. Kuppins has in nowise altered since we last saw her, and four months have made no change in the inscrutable physiognomy of the silent detective; but four months have made a difference in the "fondling," now familiarly known as "baby." Baby is short-coated;[2] baby takes notice. This accomplishment of taking notice appears to consist chiefly in snatching at every article within its reach, from Kuppins's luxuriant locks to the hot bowl of Mr. Peters's pipe. Baby also is possessed of a marvellous pair of shoes, which are alternately in his mouth, under the fender, and upon his feet—to say nothing of their occasionally finding their way out of the window, on to the dust-heap, and into divers other domestic recesses too numerous to mention. Baby is also possessed of a cap with frills, which it is Kuppins's delight to small-plait, and the delight of baby to demolish. Baby is devotedly attached to Kuppins, and evinces his affection by such pleasing demonstrations as poking his fists down her throat, hanging on to her nose, pushing a tobacco-pipe up her nostrils, and other equally gratifying proofs of infantine regard. Baby is, in short, a wonderful child; and the eye of Mr. Peters at breakfast wanders from his bacon and his watercresses to his young adopted, with a look of pride he does not attempt to conceal.

Mr. Peters has risen in his profession since last February. He has assisted at the discovery of two or three robberies, and has evinced on those occasions such a degree of tact, triumphing so completely over the difficulties he labours under from his infirmity, as to have won for himself a better place in the police force of Slopperton—and of course a better salary. But business has been dull lately, and Mr. Joseph Peters, who is ambitious, has found no proper field for his abilities as yet.

"I should like an iron-safe case, a regular out-and-out burglary," he muses, "or a good forgery, say to the tune of a thousand or so. Or a bit of bigamy; that would be something new. But a jolly good poisoning case might make my fortune. If that there little 'un was growed up," he mentally ejaculated, as Kuppins's charge gave an unusually loud scream, "his lungs might be a fortune to me. Lord," he continued, waxing metaphysical, "I don't look upon that hinfant as a hinfant. I looks upon him as a voice."

The "voice" was a very powerful one just at this moment; for in an interval of affectionate weakness Kuppins had regaled the "fondling" on the rind of Mr. Peters's rasher, which, not harmonizing with the limited development of his swallowing apparatus, had brought out the purple tints in his complexion with alarming violence.

For a long time Mr. Peters mused, and at last, after signalling Kuppins, as was his wont on commencing a conversation, with a loud snap of his finger and thumb, he began thus:

"There's a case of shop-lifting at Halford's Heath, and I've got to go over and look up some evidence in the village. I'll tell you what I'll do with you; I'll take you and baby over in Vorkins's trap—he said as how he'd lend it me whenever I liked to ask him for the loan of it; and I'll stand treat to the Rosebush tea-gardens."

Never had the dirty alphabet fashioned such sweet words. A drive in Mr. Vorkins's trap, and the Rosebush tea-gardens! If Kuppins had been a fairy changeling, and had awoke one morning to find herself a queen, I don't think she would have chosen any higher delight wherewith to celebrate her accession to the throne.

Kuppins had, during the few months of Mr. Peters's residence in the indoor Eden of No. 5, Little Gulliver Street, won a very high place in that gentleman's regards. The elderly proprietress of the Eden was as nothing in the eyes of Mr. Peters when compared with Kuppins. It was Kuppins whom he consulted when giving his orders for dinner; Kuppins, whose eye he knew to be infallible as regarded a chop, either mutton or pork; whose finger was as the finger of Fate in the matter of hard or soft-roed herrings. It was by Kuppins's advice he purchased some mysterious garment for the baby, or some prodigious wonder in the shape of a bandanna or a neck-handkerchief for himself; and this tea-garden treat he had long contemplated as a fitting reward for the fidelity of his handmaiden.

Mr. Vorkins was one of the officials of the police force, and Mr. Vorkins's trap was a happy combination of the cart of a vender of feline provisions and the gig of a fast young man of half a century gone by—that is to say, it partook of the disadvantages of each, without possessing the capabilities of either: but Mr. Peters looked at it with respect, and in the eye of Kuppins it was a gorgeous and fashionable vehicle, which the most distinguished member of the peerage might have driven along the Lady's Mile,[3] at six o'clock on a midsummer afternoon, with pride and delight.

At two o'clock on this June afternoon, behold Mr. Vorkins's trap at the door of No. 5, Little Gulliver Street, with Kuppins in a miraculous bonnet, and baby in a wonderful hat, seated therein. Mr. Peters, standing on the pavement, contemplated the appointments of the equipage with some sense of pride, and the juvenile population of the street hovered around, absorbed in admiration of the turn-out.

"Mind your bonnet don't make the wehicle top-heavy, miss," said one youthful votary of the renowned Joe Miller; "it's big enough, anyways."

Miss Kuppins (she was Miss Kuppins in her Sunday costume) flung a Parthian[4] glance at the young barbarian, and drew down a green veil, which, next to the "fondling," was the pride of her heart. Mr. Peters, armed with a formidable whip, mounted to his seat by her side, and away drove the trap, leaving the juvenile population aforesaid venting its envy in the explosion of a perfect artillery of *jeux de mots.*

Mr. Vorkins's trap was as a fairy vehicle to Kuppins, and Mr. Vorkins's elderly pony an enchanted quadruped, under the strokes of whose winged hoofs Slopperton flew away like a smoky dream, and was no more seen—an enchanted quadruped, by whose means the Slopperton suburbs of unfinished houses, scaffolding, barren ground for sale in building lots, ugly lean streets, and inky river, all melted into the distance, giving place to a road that intersected a broad heath, in the undulations of which lay fairy pools of blue water, in whose crystal depths the good people might have admired their tiny beauties as in a mirror. Indeed, it was pleasant to ride in Mr. Vorkins's jingling trap through the pure country air, scented with the odours of distant bean-fields, and, looking back, to see the smoke of Sloppertonian chimneys a mere black daub on the blue sky, and to be led almost to wonder how, on the face of such a fair and lovely earth, so dark a blot as Slopperton could be.

The Rosebush tea-gardens were a favourite resort of Slopperton on a Sunday afternoon; and many teachers there were in that great city who did not hesitate to say that the rosebushes of those gardens were shrubs planted by his Satanic Majesty, and that the winding road over Halford's Heath, though to the ignorant eye bordered by bright blue streams and sweet-smelling wild flowers, lay in reality between two lakes of fire and brimstone. Some gentlemen, however, dared to say—gentlemen who wore white neckcloths[5] too, and were familiar and welcome in the dwellings of the poor—that

Slopperton might go to more wicked places than Rosebush gardens, and might possibly be led into more evil courses than the consumption of tea and watercresses at ninepence a-head. But in spite of all differences of opinion, the Rosebush gardens prospered, and Rosebush tea and bread-and-butter were pleasant in the mouth of Slopperton.

Mr. Peters deposited his fair young companion, with the baby in her arms, at the gate of the gardens—after having authorized her to order two teas, and to choose an arbour—and walked off himself into the village of Halford to transact his official business.

The ordering of the teas and the choosing of the arbour were a labour of love with the fair Kuppins. She selected a rustic retreat, over which the luxuriant tendrils of a hop-vine fell like a thick green curtain. It was a sight to see Kuppins skirmishing with the earwigs and spiders in their sylvan bower, and ultimately routing those insects from the nests of their fathers. Mr. Peters returned from the village in about an hour, hot and dusty, but triumphant as to the issue of the business he had come about, and with an inordinate thirst for tea at ninepence a-head. I don't know whether Rosebush gardens made much out of the two teas at ninepence, but I know the bread-and-butter and watercresses disappeared by the aid of the detective and his fair companion as if by magic. It was pleasant to watch the "fondling" during this humble *fête champêtre*.[6] He had been brought up by hand, which would be better expressed as by *spoon*, and had been fed on every variety of cosmestible, from pap and farinaceous[7] food to beef-steaks and onions and the soft roes of red herrings—to say nothing of sugar-sticks, bacon rinds, and the claws of shell-fish; he therefore, immediately upon the appearance of the two teas, laid violent hands on a bunch of watercresses and a slice of bread-and-butter, wiping the buttered side upon his face—so as to give himself the appearance of an infant in a violent perspiration—preparatory to its leisurely consumption. He also made an onslaught on Mr. Peters's cup of steaming tea, but scalding his hands therewith, withdrew to the bosom of Kuppins, and gave vent to his indignation in loud screams, which the detective said made the gardens quite lively. After the two teas, Mr. Peters, attended by Kuppins and the infant, strolled round the gardens, and peered into the arbours, very few of which were tenanted this week-day afternoon. The detective indulged in a gambling speculation with some wonderful machine, the distinguishing features of which were numbers and Barcelona nuts;[8] and by the aid of which you might lose as much as threepence halfpenny before you knew where you were, while you could not by any possibility win anything. There was also a bowling-green, and a swing, which Kuppins essayed to mount, and which repudiated that young lady, by precipitating her forward on her face at the first start.

Having exhausted the mild dissipations of the gardens, Mr. Peters and Kuppins returned to their bower, where the gentleman sat smoking his clay pipe, and contemplating the infant, with a perfect serenity and calm enjoyment delightful to witness. But there was more on Mr. Peters's mind that summer's evening than the infant. He was thinking of the trial of Richard Marwood, and the part he had taken in that trial by means of the dirty alphabet; he was thinking, perhaps, of the fate of Richard—poor unlucky Richard, a hopeless and incurable lunatic, imprisoned for life in a dreary asylum, and comforting himself in that wretched place by wild fancies of imaginary greatness. Presently Mr. Peters, with a preparatory snap of his fingers, asks Kuppins if she can "call to mind that there story of the lion and the mouse."[9]

Kuppins *can* call it to mind, and proceeds to narrate with volubility, how a lion, once having rendered a service to a mouse, found himself caught in a great net, and in need of a friend; how this insignificant mouse had, by sheer industry and perseverance, effected the escape of the mighty lion. Whether they lived happy ever afterwards Kuppins couldn't say, but had no doubt they did; that being the legitimate conclusion of every legend, in this young lady's opinion.

Mr. Peters scratched his head violently during this story, to which he listened with his mouth very much round the corner; and when it was finished he fell into a reverie that lasted till the distant Slopperton clocks chimed the quarter before eight—at which time he laid down his pipe, and departed to prepare Mr. Vorkins's trap for the journey home.

Perhaps of the two journeys, the journey home was almost the more pleasant. It seemed to Kuppins's young imagination as if Mr. Peters was bent on driving Mr. Vorkins's trap straight into the sinking sun, which was going down in a sea of crimson behind a ridge of purple heath. Slopperton was yet invisible, except as a dark cloud on the purple sky. This road across the heath was very lonely on every evening except Sunday, and the little party only met one group of haymakers returning from their work, and one stout farmer's wife, laden with groceries, hastening home from Slopperton. It was a still evening, and not a sound rose upon the clear air, except the last song of a bird or the chirping of a grasshopper. Perhaps, if Kuppins had been with anybody else, she might have been frightened, for Kuppins had a confused idea that such appearances as highwaymen and ghosts are common to the vesper[10] hour; but in the company of Mr. Peters, Kuppins would have fearlessly met a regiment of highwaymen, or a churchyard full of ghosts: for was he not the law and the police in person, under whose shadow there could be no fear?

Mr. Vorkins's trap was fast gaining on the sinking sun, when Mr. Peters drew up, and paused irresolutely between two roads. These diverging roads met at a point a little further on, and the Sunday afternoon pleasure-seekers crossing the heath took sometimes one, sometimes the other; but the road to the left was the least frequented, being the narrower and more hilly, and this road Mr. Peters took, still driving towards the dark line behind which the red sun was going down.

The broken ground of the heath was all a-glow with the warm crimson light; a dissipated skylark and an early nightingale were singing a duet, to which the grasshoppers seemed to listen with suspended chirpings; a frog of an apparently fretful disposition was keeping up a captious croak in a ditch by the side of the road; and beyond these voices there seemed to be no sound beneath the sky. The peaceful landscape and the tranquil evening shed a benign influence upon Kuppins, and awakened the dormant poetry in that young lady's breast.

"Lor', Mr. Peters," she said, "it's hard to think in such a place as this, that gents of your purfession should be wanted. I do think now, if I was ever led to feel to want to take and murder somebody, which I hopes ain't likely—knowin' my duty to my neighbour better— I do think, somehow, this evening would come back to my mind, and I should hear them birds a-singing, and see that there sun a-sinking, till I shouldn't be able to do it, somehow."

Mr. Peters shakes his head dubiously: he is a benevolent man and a philanthropist; but he doesn't like his profession run down, and a murder and bread-and-cheese are inseparable things in his mind.

"And, do you know," continued Kuppins, "it seems to me as if, when this world is so beautiful and quiet, it's quite hard to think there's one wicked person in it to cast a shadow on its peace."

As Kuppins said this, she and Mr. Peters were startled by a shadow which came between them and the sinking sun—a distorted shadow thrown across the narrow road from the sharp outline of the figure of a man lying upon a hillock a little way above them. Now, there is not much to alarm the most timid person in the sight of a man asleep upon a summer's evening among heath and wild flowers; but something in this man's appearance startled Kuppins, who drew nearer to Mr. Peters, and held the "fondling," now fast asleep and muffled in a shawl, closer to her bosom. The man was lying on his back, with his face upturned to the evening sky, and his arms straight down at his sides. The sound of the wheels of Mr. Vorkins's trap did not awaken him; and even when Mr. Peters drew up with a sudden jerk, the sleeping man did not raise his head. Now, I don't know why Mr. Peters should stop, or why either he or Kuppins should feel any curiosity about this sleeping man; but they certainly did feel considerable curiosity. He was dressed rather shabbily, but still like a gentleman; and it was perhaps a strange thing for a gentleman to be sleeping so soundly in such a lonely spot as this. Then again, there was something in his attitude— a want of ease, a certain stiffness, which had a strange effect upon both Kuppins and Mr. Peters.

"I wish he'd move," said Kuppins; "he looks so awful quiet, lying there all so lonesome."

"Call to him, my girl," said Mr. Peters with his fingers.

Kuppins essayed a loud "Hilloa," but it was a dismal failure, on which Mr. Peters gave a long shrill whistle, which must surely have disturbed the peaceful dreams of the seven sleepers,[11] though it might not have awakened them. The man on the hillock never stirred. The pony, taking advantage of the halt, drew nearer to the heath and began to crop the short grass by the road-side, thus bringing Mr. Vorkins's trap a little nearer the sleeper.

"Get down, lass," said the fingers of the detective; "get down, my lass, and have a look at him, for I can't leave this 'ere pony."

Kuppins looked at Mr. Peters; and Mr. Peters looked at Kuppins, as much as to say, "Well, what then?" So Kuppins to whom the laws of the Medes and Persians would have been mild compared to the word of Mr. Peters, surrendered the infant to his care, and descending from the trap, mounted the hillock, and looked at the still reclining figure.

She did not look long, but returning rapidly to Mr. Peters, took hold of his arm, and said—

"I don't think he's asleep—leastways, his eyes is open; but he don't look as if he could see anything, somehow. He's got a little bottle in his hand."

Why Kuppins should keep so tight a hold on Mr. Peters's arm while she said this it is difficult to tell; but she did clutch his coat-sleeve very tightly, looking back while she spoke with her white face turned towards that whiter face under the evening sky.

Mr. Peters jumped quickly from the trap, tied the elderly pony to a furze-bush, mounted the hillock, and proceeded to inspect the sleeping figure. The pale set face, and the fixed blue eyes, looked up at the crimson light melting into the purple shadows of the evening sky, but never more would earthly sunlight or shadow, or night or morning, or storm or calm, be of any account to that quiet figure lying on the heath. Why the man was there, or how he had come there, was a part of the great mystery under the darkness of which he lay; and that mystery was Death! He had died apparently by poison administered by his own hand; for on the grass by his side there was a little empty bottle labelled "Opium," on which his fingers lay, not clasping it, but lying as if they had fallen over it. His clothes were soaked through with wet, so that he must in all probability have lain in that place through the storm of the previous night. A silver watch was in the pocket of his waistcoat, which Mr. Peters found, on looking at it, to have stopped at ten o'clock—ten o'clock of the night before, most likely. His hat had fallen off, and lay at a little distance, and his curling light hair hung in wet ringlets over his high forehead. His face was handsome, the features well chiselled, but the cheeks were sunken and hollow, making the large blue eyes seem larger.

Mr. Peters, in examining the pockets of the suicide, found no clue to his identity; a handkerchief, a little silver, a few half-pence, a penknife wrapped in a leaf torn out of a Latin Grammar, were the sole contents.

The detective reflected for a few moments, with his mouth on one side, and then, mounting the highest hillock near, looked over the surrounding country. He presently descried a group of haymakers at a little distance, whom he signalled with a loud whistle. To them, through Kuppins as interpreter, he gave his directions; and two of the tallest and strongest of the men took the body by the head and feet and carried it between them, with Kuppins's shawl spread over the still white face. They were two miles from Slopperton, and those two miles were by no means pleasant to Kuppins, seated in Mr. Vorkins's trap, which Mr. Peters drove slowly, so as to keep pace with the two men and their ghastly burden. Kuppins's shawl, which of course would never be any use as a shawl again, was no good to conceal the sharp outline of the face it covered; for Kuppins had seen those blue eyes, and once to see was always to see them as she thought. The dreary journey came at last to a dreary end at the police-office, where the men deposited their dreadful load, and being paid for their trouble, departed rejoicing. Mr. Peters was busy enough for the next half-hour giving an account of the finding of the body, and issuing handbills of "Found dead, &c."

Kuppins and the "fondling" returned to Little Gulliver Street, and if ever there had been a heroine in that street, that heroine was Kuppins. People came from three streets off to see her, and to hear the story, which she told so often that she came at last to tell it mechanically, and to render it slightly obscure by the vagueness of her punctuation. Anything in the way of supper that Kuppins would accept, and two or three dozen suppers if Kuppins would condescend to partake of them, were at Kuppins's service; and her reign as heroine-in-chief of this dark romance in real life was only put an end to by the appearance of Mr. Peters, the hero, who came home by-and-by, hot and dusty, to announce to the world of Little Gulliver Street, by means of the alphabet, very grimy after his exertions, that the dead man had been recognized as the principal usher of a great school up at the other end of the town, and that his name was, or had been, Jabez North. His motive for committing suicide he had carried a secret with him into the dark and mysterious region to which he was a voluntary traveller; and Mr. Peters, whose business it was to pry about the confines of this shadowy land, though powerless to penetrate the interior, could only discover some faint rumour of an ambitious love for his master's daughter as being the cause of the young usher's untimely end. What secrets this dead man had carried with him into the shadow-land, who shall say? There might be one, perhaps, which even Mr. Peters, with his utmost acuteness, could not discover.

CHAPTER VII

THE USHER RESIGNS HIS SITUATION

On the very day on which Mr. Peters treated Kuppins and the "fondling" to tea and watercresses, Dr. Tappenden and Jane his daughter returned to their household gods at Slopperton.

Who shall describe the ceremony and bustle with which that great dignitary, the master of the house, was received? He had announced his return by the train which reached Slopperton at seven o'clock; so at that hour a well-furnished tea-table was ready laid in the study—that terrible apartment which little boys entered with red eyes and pale cheeks, emerging therefrom in a pleasant glow, engendered by a specific peculiar to schoolmasters whose desire it is not to spoil the child. But no ghosts of bygone canings, no infantine whimpers from shadow-land—(though little Allecompain, dead and gone, had received correction in this very room)—haunted the Doctor's sanctorum—a cheerful apartment, warm in winter, and cool in summer, and handsomely furnished at all times. The silver teapot reflected the evening sunshine; and reflected too Sarah Jane laying the table, none the handsomer for being represented upside down, with a tendency to become collapsed or elongated, as she hovered about the tea-tray. Anchovy-paste, pound-cake,[1] Scotch marmalade and fancy bread, all seemed to cry aloud for the arrival of the doctor and his daughter to demolish them; but for all that there was fear in the hearts of the household as the hour for that arrival drew near. What would he say to the absence of his factotum? Who should tell him? Every one was innocent enough, certainly; but in the first moment of his fury might not the descending avalanche of the Doctor's wrath crush the innocent? Miss Smithers—who, as well as being presiding divinity of the young gentlemen's wardrobes, was keeper of the keys of divers presses and cupboards, and had sundry awful trusts connected with tea and sugar and butchers' bills—was elected by the whole household, from the cook to the knife-boy, as the proper person to make the awful announcement of the unaccountable disappearance of Mr. Jabez North. So, when the doctor and his daughter had alighted from the fly which brought them and their luggage from the station, Miss Smithers hovered timidly about them, on the watch for a propitious moment.

"How have you enjoyed yourself, miss? Judging by your looks I should say very much indeed, for never did I see you looking better," said Miss Smithers, with more enthusiasm than punctuation, as she removed the shawl from the lovely shoulders of Miss Tappenden.

"Thank you, Smithers, I am better," replied the young lady, with

The Usher Resigns His Situation · 113

languid condescension. Miss Tappenden, on the strength of never having anything the matter with her, was always complaining, and passed her existence in taking sal-volatile[2] and red lavender,[3] and reading three volumes a day from the circulating library.[4]

"And how," asked the ponderous voice of the ponderous Doctor, "how is everything going on, Smithers?" By this time they were seated at the tea-table, and the learned Tappenden was in the act of putting five lumps of sugar in his cup, while the fair Smithers lingered in attendance.

"Quite satisfactory, sir, I'm sure," replied that young lady, growing very much confused. "Everything quite satisfactory, sir; leastways——"

"What do you mean by *leastways*, Smithers?" asked the Doctor, impatiently. "In the first place it isn't English; and in the next it sounds as if it meant something unpleasant. For goodness sake, Smithers, be straightforward and business-like. Has anything gone wrong? What is it? And why wasn't I informed of it?"

Smithers, in despair at her incapability of answering these three questions at once, as no doubt she ought to have been able to do, or the Doctor would not have asked them, stammered out,—

"Mr. North, sir——"

" 'Mr. North, sir'! Well, what of 'Mr. North, sir'? By the bye, where is Mr. North? Why isn't he here to receive us?"

Smithers feels that she is in for it; so, after two or three nervous gulps, and other convulsive movements of the throat, she continues thus—"Mr. North, sir, didn't come home last night, sir. We sat up for him till one o'clock this morning—last night, sir."

The rising storm in the Doctor's face is making Smithers's English more *un*-English every moment.

"Didn't come last night? Didn't return to my house at the hour of ten, which hour has been appointed by me for the retiring to rest of every person in my employment?" cried the Doctor, aghast.

"No, sir! Nor yet this morning, sir! Nor yet this afternoon, sir! And the West-Indian pupils have been looking out of the window, sir, and would, which we told them not till we were hoarse, sir."

"The person intrusted by me with the care of my pupils abandoning his post, and my pupils looking out of the window!" exclaimed Dr. Tappenden, in the tone of a man who says—"The glory of England has departed! You wouldn't, perhaps, believe it; but it has!"

"We didn't know what to do, sir, and so we thought we'd better not do it," continued the bewildered Smithers. "And we thought as you was coming back to-day, we'd better leave it till you did come back—and please, sir, will you take any new-laid eggs?"

"Eggs!" said the Doctor; "new-laid eggs! Go away, Smithers. There must be some steps taken immediately. That young man was my right hand, and I would have trusted him with untold gold; or," he added, "with my cheque-book."

As he uttered the words "cheque-book," he, as it were instinctively, laid his hand upon the pocket which contained that precious volume; but as he did so, he remembered that he had used the last leaf but one when writing a cheque for a midsummer butcher's bill, and that he had a fresh book in his desk untouched. This desk was always kept in the study, and the Doctor gave an involuntary glance in the direction in which it stood.

It was a very handsome piece of furniture, ponderous, like the Doctor himself; a magnificent construction of shining walnut-wood and dark green morocco, with a recess for the Doctor's knees, and on either side of this recess two rows of drawers, with brass handles and Bramah locks. The centre drawer on the left-hand side contained an inner and secret drawer, and towards the lock of this drawer the Doctor looked, for this contained his new cheque-book. The walnut-wood round the lock of this centre drawer seemed a little chipped; the Doctor thought he might as well get up and look at it; and a nearer examination showed the brass handle to be slightly twisted, as if a powerful hand had wrenched it out of shape. The Doctor, taking hold of the handle to pull it straight, drew the drawer out, and scattered its contents upon the floor; also the contents of the inner drawer, and amongst them the cheque-book, half-a-dozen leaves of which had been torn out.

"So," said the Doctor, "this man, whom I trusted, has broken open my desk, and finding no money, he has taken blank cheques, in the hope of being able to forge my name. To think that I did not know this man!"

To think that you did not, Doctor; to think, too, that you do not even now, perhaps, know half this man may have been capable of.

But it was time for action, not reflection; so the Doctor hurried to the railway station, and telegraphed to his bankers in London to stop any cheques presented in his signature, and to have the person presenting such cheques immediately arrested. From the railway station he hurried, in an undignified perspiration, to the police-office, to institute a search for the missing Jabez, and then returned home, striking terror into the hearts of his household, ay, even to the soul of his daughter, the lovely Jane, who took an extra dose of sal-volatile, and went to bed to read "Lady Clarinda, or the Heart-breaks of Belgravia."

With the deepening twilight came a telegraphic message from the bank to say that cheques for divers sums had been presented and cashed by different people in the course of the day. On the heels of this message came another from the police-station, announcing that a body had been found upon Halford Heath answering to the description of the missing man.

———

The bewildered schoolmaster, hastening to the station, recognises, at a glance, the features of his late assistant. The contents of the dead man's pocket, the empty bottle with the too significant label, are shown him. No, some other hand than the usher's must have broken open the desk in the study, and the unfortunate young man's reputation had been involved in a strange coincidence. But the motive for his rash act? That is explained by a most affecting letter in the dead man's hand, which is found in his desk. It is addressed to the Doctor, expresses heartfelt gratitude for that worthy gentleman's past kindnesses, and hints darkly at a hopeless attachment to his daughter, which renders the writer's existence a burden too heavy for him to bear. For the rest, Jabez North has passed a threshold, over which the boldest and most inquisitive scarcely care to follow him. So he takes his own little mystery with him into the land of the great mystery.

There is, of course, an inquest, at which two different chemists, who sold laudanum to Jabez North on the night before his disappearance, give their evidence. There is another chemist, who deposes to having sold him, a day or two before, a bottle of patent hair-dye, which is also a poisonous compound; but surely he never could have thought of poisoning himself with hair-dye.

The London police are at fault in tracing the presenters of the cheques; and the proprietors of the bank, or the clerks, who maintain a common fund to provide against their own errors, are likely to be considerable losers. In the mean while the worthy Doctor announces, by advertisements in the Slopperton papers, that "his pupils assemble on the 27th of July."

BOOK THE THIRD

A HOLY INSTITUTION

THE VALUE OF AN OPERA-GLASS

Paris!—City of fashion, pleasure, beauty, wealth, rank, talent, and indeed all the glories of the earth. City of palaces, in which La Vallière smiled, and Scarron sneered; under whose roofs the echoes of Bossuet's[1] voice have resounded, while folly, coming to be amused, has gone away in tears, only to forget to-morrow what it has heard to-night. Glorious city, in which a *bon mot*[2] is more famous than a good action; which is richer in the records of Ninon de Lenclos than in those of Joan of Arc; for which Beaumarchais wrote, and Marmontel moralised; which Scottish John Law infected with a furious madness, in those halcyon days when jolly, good-tempered, accomplished, easy-going Philippe of Orleans held the reins of power. Paris, which young Arouet, afterwards Voltaire, ruled with the distant jingle of his jester's wand, from the far retreat of Ferney. Paris, in which Madame du Deffand dragged out those weary, brilliant, dismal, salon-keeping years, quarrelling with Mademoiselle de l'Espinasse, and corresponding with Horace Walpole;[3] *ce cher*[4] Horace, who described those brilliant French ladies as women who neglected all the duties of life, and gave very pretty suppers.

Paris, in which Bailly spoke, and Madame Roland dreamed; in which Marie Antoinette despaired, and gentle Princess Elizabeth laid down her saintly life; in which the son of St. Louis[5] went calmly to the red mouth of that terrible machine invented by the charitable doctor[6] who thought to benefit his fellow creatures. City, under whose roofs bilious Robespierre[7] suspected and feared; beneath whose shadow the glorious twenty-two went hand in hand to death, with the psalm of freedom swelling from their lips. Paris, which rejoiced when Marengo was won, and rang joy-bells for the victories of Lodd, Arcola, Austerlitz, Auerstadt, and Jena;[8] Paris, which mourned over fatal Waterloo, and opened its arms, after weary years of waiting, to take to its heart only the ashes of the ruler of its election; Paris, the marvellous; Paris, the beautiful, whose streets are streets of palaces—fairy wonders of opulence and art;—can it be that under some of thy myriad roofs there are such incidental trifles as misery, starvation, vice, crime, and death? Nay, we will not push the question, but enter at once into one of the most brilliant of the temples of that goddess whose names are Pleasure, Fashion, Folly, and Idleness: and what more splendid shrine can we choose whereat to worship the divinity called Pleasure than the Italian Opera House?

To-night the house is thronged with fashion and beauty. Bright uniforms glitter in the backgrounds of the boxes, and sprinkle the crowded parterre. The Citizen King[9] is there—not King of France; no such poor title will he have, but King of the French. His throne is based, not on the broad land, but on the living hearts of his people. May it never prove to be built on a shallow foundation! In eighteen hundred and forty-two all is well for Louis Philippe and his happy family.

In the front row of the stalls, close to the orchestra, a young man lounges, with his opera-glass in his hand. He is handsome and very elegant, and is dressed in the most perfect taste and the highest fashion. Dark curling hair clusters round his delicately white forehead; his eyes are of a bright blue, shaded by auburn lashes, which contrast rather strangely with his dark hair. A very dark and thick moustache only reveals now and then his thin lower lip and a set of dazzling white teeth. His nose is a delicate aquiline, and his features altogether bear the stamp of aristocracy. He is quite alone, this elegant lounger, and of the crowd of people of rank and fashion around him not one turns to speak to him. His listless white hand is thrown on the cushion of the stall on which he leans, as he glances round the house with one indifferent sweep of his opera-glass. Presently his attention is arrested by the conversation of two gentlemen close to him, and without seeming to listen, he hears what they are saying.

"Is the Spanish princess here to-night?" asks one.

"What, the marquis's niece, the girl who has that immense property in Spanish America? Yes, she is in the box next to the king's; don't you see her diamonds? They and her eyes are brilliant enough to set the curtains of the box on fire."

"She is immensely rich, then?"

"She is an Eldorado. The Marquis de Cevennes has no children, and all his property will go to her; her Spanish American property comes from her mother. She is an orphan, as you know, and the marquis is her guardian."

"She is handsome; but there's just a little too much of the demon in those great almond-shaped black eyes and that small determined mouth. What a fortune she would be to some intriguing adventurer!"

"An adventurer! Valerie de Cevennes the prize of an adventurer! Show me the man capable of winning her, without rank and fortune equal to hers; and I will say you have found the eighth wonder of the world."

The listener's eyes light up with a strange flash, and lifting his glass, he looks for a few moments carelessly round the house, and then fixes his gaze upon the box next to that occupied by the royal party.

The Spanish beauty is indeed a glorious creature; of a loveliness rich alike in form and colour, but with hauteur and determination expressed in every feature of her face. A man of some fifty years of age is seated by her side, and behind her chair two or three gentlemen stand, the breasts of whose coats glitter with stars and orders. They are speaking to her; but she pays very little attention to them. If she answers, it is only by a word, or a bend of her proud head, which she does not turn towards them. She never takes her eyes from the curtain, which presently rises. The opera is *La Sonnambula*.[10] The Elvino is the great singer of the day—a young man whose glorious voice and handsome face have made him the rage of the musical world. Of his origin different stories are told. Some say he was originally a shoemaker, others declare him to be the son of a prince. He has, however, made his fortune at seven-and-twenty, and can afford to laugh at these stories. The opera proceeds, and the powerful glass of the lounger in the stalls records the minutest change in the face of Valerie de Cevennes. It records one faint quiver, and then a firmer compression of the thin lips, when the Elvino appears; and the eyes of the lounger fasten more intently, if possible, than before upon the face of the Spanish beauty.

Presently Elvino sings the grand burst of passionate reproach, in which he upbraids Amina's fancied falsehood. As the house applauds at the close of the scene, Valerie's bouquet falls at the feet of the Amina. Elvino, taking it in his hand, presents it to the lady, and as he does so, the lounger's glass—which, more rapidly than the bouquet has fallen, has turned to the stage—records a movement so quick as to be almost a feat of legerdemain. The great tenor has taken a note from the bouquet. The lounger sees the triumphant glance towards the box next the king's, though it is rapid as lightning. He sees the tiny morsel of glistening paper crumpled in the singer's hand; and after one last contemplative look at the proud brow and set lips of Valerie de Cevennes, he lowers the glass.

"My glass is well worth the fifteen guineas I paid for it," he whispers to himself. "That girl can command her eyes; they have not one traitorous flash. But those thin lips cannot keep a secret from a man with a decent amount of brains."

When the opera is over, the lounger of the stalls leaves his place by the orchestra, and loiters in the winter night outside the stage-door. Perhaps he is enamoured of some lovely *coryphée*[11]—lovely in all the gorgeousness of flake white and liquid rouge; and yet that can scarcely be, or he would be still in the stalls, or hovering about the side-scenes, for the *ballet* is not over. Two or three carriages, belonging to the principal singers, are waiting at the stage-door. Presently a tall, stylish-looking man, in a loose over-coat, emerges; a groom opens the door of a well-appointed little brougham, but the gentleman says—

"No, Farée, you can go home. I shall walk."

"But, monsieur," remonstrates the man, "monsieur is not aware that it rains."

Monsieur says he is quite aware of the rain; but that he has an umbrella, and prefers walking. So the brougham drives off with the distressed Farée, who consoles himself at a café high up on the boulevard, where he plays *écarté* with a limp little pack of cards, and drinks effervescing lemonade.

The lounger of the stalls, standing in the shadow, hears this little dialogue, and sees also, by the light of the carriage-lamps, that the gentleman in the loose coat is no less a personage than the hero of the opera. The lounger also seems to be indifferent to the rain, and to have a fancy for walking; for when Elvino crosses the road and turns into an opposite street, the lounger follows. It is a dark night, with a little drizzling rain—a night by no means calculated to tempt an elegantly-dressed young man to brave all the disagreeables and perils of dirty pavements and overflowing gutters; but neither Elvino nor the lounger seem to care for mud or rain, for they walk at a rapid pace through several streets—the lounger always a good way behind and always in the shadow. He has a light step, which wakes no echo on the wet pavement; and the fashionable tenor has no idea that he is followed. He walks through long narrow streets to the Rue Rivoli, thence across one of the bridges. Presently he enters a very aristocratic but retired street, in a lonely quarter of the city. The distant roll of carriages and the tramp of a passing *gendarme* are the only sounds that break the silence. There is not a creature to be seen in the wide street but the two men. Elvino turns to look about him, sees no one, and walks on till he comes to a mansion at the corner, screened from the street by a high wall, with great gates and a porter's lodge. Detached from the house, and sheltered by an angle of the wall, is a little pavilion, the windows of which look into the courtyard or garden within. Close to this pavilion is a narrow low door of carved oak, studded with great iron nails, and almost hidden in the heavy masonry of the wall which frames it. The house in early times has been a convent, and is now the property of the Marquis de Cevennes. Elvino, with one more glance up and down the dimly-lighted street, approaches this doorway, and stooping down to the key-hole whistles softly three bars of a melody from Don Giovanni—*La ci darem la mano.*[12]

"So!" says the lounger, standing in the shadow of a house opposite, "we are getting deeper into the mystery; the curtain is up, and the play is going to begin."

As the clocks of Paris chime the half-hour after eleven the little door turns on its hinges, and a faint light in the courtyard within falls upon the figure of the fashionable tenor. This light comes from a lamp in the hand of a pretty-looking, smartly-dressed girl, who has opened the door.

"She is not the woman I took her for, this Valerie," says the lounger, "or she would have opened that door herself. She makes her waiting-maid her confidante—a false step, which proves her either stupid or inexperienced. Not stupid; her face gives the lie to that. Inexperienced then. So much the better."

As the spy meditates thus, Elvino passes through the doorway, stooping as he crosses the threshold, and the light disappears.

"This is either a private marriage, or something worse," mutters the lounger. "Scarcely the last. Hers is the face of a woman capable of a madness, but not of degradation—the face of a Phædra[13] rather than a Messalina.[14] I have seen enough of the play for to-night."

CHAPTER II

WORKING IN THE DARK

Early the next morning a gentleman rings the bell of the porter's lodge belonging to the mansion of the Marquis de Cevennes, and on seeing the porter addresses him thus—

"The lady's-maid of Mademoiselle Valerie de Cevennes is perhaps visible at this early hour?"

The porter thinks not; it is very early, only eight o'clock; Mademoiselle Finette never appears till nine. The toilette of her mistress is generally concluded by twelve; after twelve, the porter thinks monsieur may succeed in seeing Mademoiselle Finette—before twelve, he thinks not.

The stranger rewards the porter with a five-franc piece for this valuable information; it is very valuable to the stranger, who is the lounger of the last night, to discover that the name of the girl who held the lamp is Finette.

The lounger seems to have as little to do this morning as he had last night; for he leans against the gateway, his cane in his hand, and a half-smoked cigar in his mouth, looking up at the house of the marquis with lazy indifference.

The porter, conciliated by the five-franc piece, is inclined to gossip.

"A fine old building," says the lounger, still looking up at the house, every window of which is shrouded by ponderous Venetian shutters.

"Yes, a fine old building. It has been in the family of the marquis for two hundred years, but was sadly mutilated in the first revolution; monsieur may see the work of the cannon amongst the stone decorations."

"And that pavilion to the left, with the painted windows and Gothic decorations—a most extraordinary little edifice," says the lounger.

Yes, monsieur has observed it? It is a great deal more modern than the house; was built so lately as the reign of Louis the Fifteenth, by a dissipated old marquis who gave supper-parties at which the guests used to pour champagne out of the windows, and pelt the servants in the courtyard with the empty bottles. It is certainly a curious little place; but would monsieur believe something more curious?

Monsieur declares that he is quite willing to believe anything the porter may be good enough to tell him. He says this with a well-bred indifference, as he lights a fresh cigar, which is quite aristocratic, and which might stamp him a scion of the noble house of De Cevennes itself.

"Then," replies the porter, "monsieur must know that Mademoiselle Valerie, the proud, the high-born, the beautiful, has lately taken it into her aristocratic head to occupy that pavilion, attended only by her maid Finette, in preference to her magnificent apartments, which monsieur may see yonder on the first floor of the mansion—a range of ten windows. Does not monsieur think this very extraordinary?"

Scarcely. Young ladies have strange whims. Monsieur never allows himself to be surprised by a woman's conduct, or he might pass his life in a state of continual astonishment.

The porter perfectly agrees with monsieur. The porter is a married man, "and, monsieur——?" the porter ventures to ask with a shrug of interrogation.

Monsieur says he is not married yet.

Something in monsieur's manner emboldens the porter to say— "But monsieur is perhaps contemplating a marriage?"

Monsieur takes his cigar from his mouth, raises his blue eyes to the level of the range of ten windows, indicated just now by the porter, takes one long and meditative survey of the magnificent mansion opposite him, and then replies, with aristocratic indifference—

"Perhaps. These Cevennes are immensely rich?"

"Immensely! To the amount of millions." The porter is prone to extravagant gesticulation, but he cannot lift either his eyebrows or his shoulders high enough to express the extent of the wealth of the De Cevennes.

The lounger takes out his pocket-book, writes a few lines, and, tearing the leaf out, gives it to the porter, saying—

"You will favour me, my good friend, by giving this to Mademoiselle Finette at your earliest convenience. You were not always a married man; and can therefore understand that it will be as well to deliver my little note secretly."

Nothing can exceed the intense significance of the porter's wink as he takes charge of the note. The lounger nods an indifferent good-day, and strolls away.

"A marquis at the least," says the porter. "O, Mademoiselle Finette, you do not wear black satin gowns and a gold watch and chain for nothing."

The lounger is ubiquitous, this winter's day. At three o'clock in the afternoon he is seated on a bench in the gardens of the Luxembourg, smoking a cigar. He is dressed as before, in the last Parisian fashion; but his greatcoat is a little open at the throat, displaying a loosely-tied cravat of a peculiarly bright blue.

A young person of the genus lady's-maid, tripping daintily by, is apparently attracted by this blue cravat, for she hovers about the bench for a few moments and then seats herself at the extreme end of it, as far as possible from the indifferent lounger, who has not once noticed her by so much as one glance of his cold blue eyes.

His cigar is nearly finished, so he waits till it is quite done; then, throwing away the stump, he says, scarcely looking at his neighbour—

"Mademoiselle Finette, I presume?"

"The same, monsieur."

"Then perhaps, mademoiselle, as you have condescended to favour me with an interview, and as the business on which I have to address you is of a strictly private nature, you will also condescend to come a little nearer to me?"

He says this without appearing to look at her, while he lights another cigar. He is evidently a desperate smoker, and caresses his cigar, looking at the red light and blue smoke almost as if it were his familiar spirit, by whose aid he could work out wonderful calculations in the black art, and without which he would perhaps be powerless. Mademoiselle Finette looks at him with a great deal of surprise and not a little indignation, but obeys him, nevertheless, and seats herself close by his side.

"I trust monsieur will believe that I should never have consented to afford him this interview, had I not been assured—"

"Monsieur will spare you, mademoiselle, the trouble of telling him why you come here, since it is enough for him that you are here. I have nothing to do, mademoiselle, either with your motives or your scruples. I told you in my note that I required you to do me a service, for which I could afford to pay you handsomely; that, on the other hand, if you were unwilling to do me this service, I had it in my power to cause your dismissal from your situation. Your coming here is a tacit declaration of your willingness to serve me. So much and no more preface is needed. And now to business."

He seems to sweep this curt preface away, as he waves off a cloud of the blue smoke from his cigar with one motion of his small hand. The lady's-maid, thoroughly subdued by a manner which is quite new to her, awaits his pleasure to speak, and stares at him with surprised black eyes.

He is not in a hurry. He seems to be consulting the blue smoke prior to committing himself by any further remark. He takes his cigar from his mouth, and looks into the bright red spot at the lighted end, as if it were the lurid eye of his familiar demon. After consulting it for a few seconds he says, with the same indifference with which he would make some observation on the winter's day—

"So, your mistress, Mademoiselle Valerie de Cevennes, has been so imprudent as to contract a secret marriage with an opera-singer?"

He has determined on hazarding his guess. If he is right, it is the best and swiftest way of coming at the truth; if wrong, he is no worse off than before. One glance at the girl's face tells him he has struck home, and has hit upon the entire truth. He is striking in the dark; but he is a mathematician, and can calculate the effect of every blow.

"Yes, a secret marriage, of which you were the witness." This is his second blow; and again the girl's face tells him he has struck home.

"Father Pérot has betrayed us, then, monsieur, for he alone could tell you this," said Finette.

The lounger understands in a moment that Father Pérot is the priest who performed the marriage. Another point in his game. He continues, still stopping now and then to take a puff at his cigar, and speaking with an air of complete indifference—

"You see, then, that this secret marriage, and the part you took with regard to it, have, no matter whether through the worthy priest, Father Pérot——" (he stops at this point to knock the ashes from his cigar, and a sidelong glance at the girl's face tells him that he is right again, Father Pérot *is* the priest)—"or some other channel, come to my knowledge. Though a French woman, you may be acquainted with the celebrated aphorism of one of our English neighbours, 'Knowledge is power.'[1] Very well, mademoiselle, how if I use my power?"

"Monsieur means that he can deprive me of my present place,

and prevent my getting another." As she said this, Mademoiselle Finette screwed out of one of her black eyes a small bead of water, which was the best thing she could produce in the way of a tear, but which, coming into immediate contact with a sticky white compound called pearl-powder, used by the lady's-maid to enhance her personal charms, looked rather more like a digestive pill than anything else.

"But, on the other hand, I may not use my power; and, indeed, I should deeply regret the painful necessity which would compel me to injure a lady."

Mademoiselle Finette, encouraged by this speech, wiped away the digestive pill.

"Therefore, mademoiselle, the case resolves itself to this: serve me, and I will reward you; refuse to do so, and I can injure you."

A cold glitter in the blue eyes converts the words into a threat, without the aid of any extra emphasis from the voice.

"Monsieur has only to command," answers the lady's-maid; "I am ready to serve him."

"This Monsieur Elvino will be at the gate of the little pavilion to-night——?"

"At a quarter to twelve."

"Then *I* will be there at half-past eleven. You will admit me instead of him. That is all."

"But my mistress, monsieur: she will discover that I have betrayed her, and she will kill me. You do not know Mademoiselle de Cevennes."

"Pardon me, I think I do know her. She need never learn that you have betrayed her. Remember, I have discovered the appointed signal;—you are deceived by my use of that signal, and you open the door to the wrong man. For the rest I will shield you from all harm. Your mistress is a glorious creature; but perhaps that high spirit may be taught to bend."

"It must first be broken, monsieur," says Mademoiselle Finette.

"Perhaps," answers the lounger, rising as he speaks. "Mademoiselle, *au revoir.*" He drops five twinkling pieces of gold into her hand, and strolls slowly away.

The lady's-maid watches the receding figure with a bewildered stare. Well may Finette Léris be puzzled by this man: he might mystify wiser heads than hers. As he walks with his lounging gait through the winter sunset, many turn to look at his aristocratic figure, fair face, and black hair. If the worst man who looked at him could have seen straight through those clear blue eyes into his soul, would there have been something revealed which might have shocked and revolted even this worst man? Perhaps. Treachery is revolting, surely, to the worst of us. The worst of us might shrink appalled from the contemplation of those hideous secrets which are hidden in the plotting brain and the unflinching heart of the cold-blooded traitor.

CHAPTER III

THE WRONG FOOTSTEP

Half-past eleven from the great booming voice of Notre Dame the magnificent. Half-past eleven from every turret in the vast city of Paris. The musical tones of the timepiece over the chimney in the boudoir of the pavilion testify to the fact five minutes afterwards. It is an elegant timepiece, surmounted by a group from the hand of a fashionable sculptor, a group in which a golden Cupid has hushed a grim bronze Saturn to sleep, and has hidden the old man's hourglass under one of his lacquered wings—a pretty design enough, though the sand in the glass will never move the slower, or wrinkles and gray hairs be longer coming, because of the prettiness of that patrician timepiece; for the minute-hand on the best dial-plate that all Paris can produce is not surer in its course than that dark end which spares not the brightest beginning, that weary awakening which awaits the fairest dream.

This little apartment in the pavilion belonging to the house of the Marquis de Cevennes is furnished in the style of the Pompadour days of elegance, luxury, and frivolity. Oval portraits of the reigning beauties of that day are let into the panels of the walls, and

"Louis the Well-beloved"[1] smiles an insipid Bourbon[2] smile above the mantelpiece. The pencil of Boucher[3] has immortalized those frail goddesses of the Versailles Olympus,[4] and their coquettish loveliness lights the room almost as if they were living creatures, smiling unchangingly on every comer. The chimney-piece is of marble, exquisitely carved with lotuses and water-nymphs. A wood fire burns upon the gilded dogs which ornament the hearth. A priceless Persian carpet covers the centre of the polished floor; and a golden Cupid, suspended from the painted ceiling in an attitude which suggests such a determination of blood to the head as must ultimately result in apoplexy, holds a lamp of alabaster, which floods the room with a soft light.

Under this light the mistress of the apartment, Valerie de Cevennes, looks gloriously handsome. She is seated in a low arm-chair by the hearth—looking sometimes into the red blaze at her feet, with dreamy eyes, whose profound gaze, though thoughtful, is not sorrowful. This girl has taken a desperate step in marrying secretly the man she loves; but she has no regret, for she *does* love; and loss of position seems so small a thing in the balance when weighed against this love, which is as yet unacquainted with sorrow, that she almost forgets she has lost it. Even while her eyes are fixed upon the wood fire at her feet, you may see that she is listening; and when the clocks have chimed the half-hour, she turns her head towards the door of the apartment, and listens intently. In five minutes she hears something—a faint sound in the distance, the sound of an outer door turning on its hinges. She starts, and her eyes brighten; she glances at the timepiece, and from the timepiece to the tiny watch at her side.

"So soon!" she mutters; "he said a quarter to twelve. If my uncle had been here! And he only left me at eleven o'clock!"

She listens again; the sounds come nearer—two more doors open, and then there are footsteps on the stairs. At the sound of these footsteps she starts again, with a look of anxiety in her face.

"Is he ill," she says, "that he walks so slowly? Hark!"

She turns pale and clasps her hands tightly upon her breast.

"It is not his step!"

She knows she is betrayed; and in that one moment she prepares herself for the worst. She leans her hand upon the back of the chair from which she has risen, and stands, with her thin lips firmly set, facing the door. She may be facing her fate for aught she knows, but she is ready to face anything.

The door opens, and the lounger of the morning enters. He wears a coat and hat of exactly the same shape and colour as those worn by the fashionable tenor, and he resembles the tenor in build and height. An easy thing, in the obscurity of the night, for the faithful Finette to admit this stranger without discovering her mistake. One glance at the face and attitude of Valerie de Cevennes tells him that she is not unprepared for his appearance. This takes him off his guard. Has he, too, been betrayed by the lady's-maid? He never guesses that his light step betrayed him to the listening ear which love has made so acute. He sees that the young and beautiful girl is prepared to give him battle. He is disappointed. He had counted upon her surprise and confusion, and he feels that he has lost a point in his game. She does not speak, but stands quietly waiting for him to address her, as she might were he an ordinary visitor.

"She is a more wonderful woman than I thought," he says to himself, "and the battle will be a sharp one. No matter! The victory will be so much the sweeter."

He removes his hat, and the light falls full upon his pale fair face. Something in that face, she cannot tell what, seems in a faint, dim manner, familiar to her—she has seen some one like this man, but when, or where, she cannot remember.

"You are surprised, madame, to see me," he says, for he feels that he must begin the attack, and that he must not spare a single blow, for he is to fight with one who can parry his thrusts and strike again. "You are surprised. You command yourself admirably in repressing any demonstration of surprise, but you are not the less surprised."

"I am certainly surprised, monsieur, at receiving any visitor at such an hour." She says this with perfect composure.

"Scarcely, madame," he looks at the timepiece; "for in five minutes from this your husband will—or should—be here."

Her lips tighten, and her jaw grows rigid in spite of herself. The secret is known, then—known to this stranger, who dares to intrude himself upon her on the strength of this knowledge.

"Monsieur," she says, "people rarely insult Valerie de Cevennes with impunity. You shall hear from my uncle to-morrow morning; for to-night—" she lays her hand upon the mother-of-pearl handle of a little bell; he stops her, saying, smilingly,

"Nay, madame, we are not playing a farce. You wish to show me the door? You would ring that bell, which no one can answer but Finette, your maid, since there is no one else in this charming little establishment. I shall not be afraid of Finette, even if you are so imprudent as to summon her; and I shall not leave you till you have done me the honour of granting me an interview. For the rest, I am not talking to Valerie de Cevennes, but to Valerie de Lancy; Valerie, the wife of Elvino; Valerie, the lady of Don Giovanni."

De Lancy is the name of the fashionable tenor. This time the haughty girl's thin lips quiver, with a rapid, convulsive movement. What stings her proud soul is the contempt with which this man speaks of her husband. Is it such a disgrace, then, this marriage of wealth, rank, and beauty, with genius and art?

"Monsieur," she says, "you have discovered my secret. I have been betrayed either by my servant, or the priest who married me—no matter which of them is the traitor. You, who, from your conduct of to-night, are evidently an adventurer, a person to whom it would be utterly vain to speak of honour, chivalry, and gentlemanly feeling—since they are doubtless words of which you do not even know the meaning—you wish to turn the possession of this secret to account. In other words, you desire to be bought off. You know, then, what I can afford to pay you. Be good enough to say how much will satisfy you, and I will appoint a time and place at which you shall receive your earnings. You will be so kind as to lose no time. It is on the stroke of twelve; in a moment Monsieur De Lancy will be here. He may not be disposed to make so good a bargain with you as I am. He might be tempted to throw you out of the window."

She has said this with entire self-possession. She might be talking to her *modiste,* so thoroughly indifferent is she in her high-bred ease and freezing contempt for the man to whom she is speaking. As she finishes she sinks quietly into her easy-chair. She takes up a book from a little table near her, and begins to cut the leaves with a jewelled-handled paper-knife. But the battle has only just begun, and she does not yet know her opponent.

He watches her for a moment; marks the steady hand with which she slowly cuts leaf after leaf, without once notching the paper; and then he deliberately seats himself opposite to her in the easy-chair on the other side of the fireplace. She lifts her eyes from the book, and looks him full in the face with an expression of supreme disdain; but as she looks, he can see how eagerly she is also listening for her husband's step. He has a blow to strike which he knows will be a heavy one.

"Do not, madame," he says, "distract yourself by listening for your husband's arrival. He will not be here to-night."

This is a terrible blow. She tries to speak, but her lips only move inarticulately.

"No, he will not be here. You do not suppose, madame, that when I contemplated, nay, contrived and arranged an interview with so charming a person as yourself, I could possibly be so deficient in foresight as to allow that interview to be disturbed at the expiration of one quarter of an hour? No; Monsieur Don Giovanni will not be here to-night."

Again she tries to speak, but the words refuse to come. He continues, as though he interpreted what she wants to say,—

"You will naturally ask what other engagement detains him from his lovely wife's society? Well, it is, as I think, a supper at the *Trois Frères.* As there are ladies invited, the party will no doubt break up early; and you will, I dare say, see Monsieur de Lancy by four or five o'clock in the morning."

She tries to resume her employment with the paper-knife, but this time she tears the leaves to pieces in her endeavours to cut them. Her anguish and her womanhood get the better of her pride and her power of endurance. She crumples the book in her clenched hands, and throws it into the fire. Her visitor smiles. His blows are beginning to tell.

For a few minutes there is silence. Presently he takes out his cigar-case.

"I need scarcely ask permission, madame. All these opera-singers smoke, and no doubt you are indulgent to the weakness of our dear Elvino?"

"Monsieur de Lancy is a gentleman, and would not presume to smoke in a lady's presence. Once more, monsieur, be good enough to say how much money you require of me to ensure your silence?"

"Nay, madame," he replies, as he bends over the wood fire, and lights his cigar by the blaze of the burning book, "there is no occasion for such desperate haste. You are really surprisingly superior to the ordinary weakness of your sex. Setting apart your courage, self-endurance, and determination, which are positively wonderful, you are so entirely deficient in curiosity."

She looks at him with a glance which seems to say she scorns to ask him what he means by this.

"You say your maid, Finette, or the good priest, Monsieur Pérot, must have betrayed your confidence. Suppose it was from neither of those persons I received my information?"

"There is no other source, monsieur, from which you could obtain it."

"Nay, madame, reflect. Is there no other person whose vanity may have prompted him to reveal this secret? Do you think it, madame, so utterly improbable that Monsieur de Lancy himself may have been tempted to boast over his wine of his conquest of the heiress of all the De Cevennes?"

"It is a base falsehood, monsieur, which you are uttering."

"Nay, madame, I make no assertion. I am only putting a case. Suppose at a supper at the *Maison Dorée*, amongst his comrades of the Opera and his admirers of the stalls—to say nothing of the *coryphées*, who, somehow or other, contrive to find a place at these *recherché*[5] little banquets—suppose our friend, Don Giovanni, imprudently ventures some allusion to a lady of rank and fortune whom his melodious voice or his dark eyes have captivated? This little party is not, perhaps, satisfied with an allusion; it requires facts; it is incredulous; it lays heavy odds that Elvino cannot name the lady; and in the end the whole story is told, and the health of Valerie de Cevennes is drunk in Cliquot's finest brand of champagne. Suppose this, madame, and you may, perhaps, guess whence I got my information."

Throughout this speech Valerie has sat facing him, with her eyes fixed in a strange and ghastly stare. Once she lifts her hand to her throat, as if to save herself from choking; and when the schemer has finished speaking she slides heavily from her chair, and falls on her knees upon the Persian hearth-rug, with her small hands convulsively clasped about her heart. But she is not insensible, and she never takes her eyes from his face. She is a woman who neither weeps nor faints—she suffers.

"I am here, madame," the lounger continues—and now she listens to him eagerly; "I am here for two purposes. To help myself before all things; to help you afterwards, if I can. I have had to use a rough scalpel, madame, but I may not be an unskilful physician. You love this tenor singer very deeply; you must do so; since for his sake you were willing to brave the contempt of that which you also love very much—the world—the great world in which you move."

"I did love him, monsieur—O God! how deeply, how madly, how blindly! Nay, it is not to such an eye as yours that I would reveal the secrets of my heart and mind. Enough, I loved him! But for the man who could degrade the name of the woman who had sacrificed so much for his sake, and hold the sacrifice so lightly—for the man who could make that woman's name a jest among the companions of a tavern, Valerie de Cevennes has but one sentiment, and that is—contempt."

"I admire your spirit, madame; but then, remember, the subject can scarcely be so easily dismissed. A husband is not to be shaken off so lightly; and is it likely that Monsieur de Lancy will readily resign a marriage which, as a speculation, is so brilliantly advantageous? Perhaps you do not know that it has been, ever since his *début,* his design to sell his handsome face to the highest bidder; that he has—pardon me, madame—been for two years on the look-out for an heiress possessed of more gold than discrimination, whom a few pretty namby-pamby speeches selected from the librettos of the operas he is familiar with would captivate and subdue."

The haughty spirit is bent to the very dust. This girl, truth itself, never for a moment questions the words which are breaking her heart. There is something too painfully probable in this bitter humiliation.

"Oh, what have I done," she cries, "what have I done, that the golden dream of my life should be broken by such an awakening as this?"

"Madame, I have told you that I wish, if I can, to help you. I pretend no disinterested or Utopian generosity. You are rich, and can afford to pay me for my services. There are only three persons who, besides yourself, were witnesses of or concerned in this marriage— Father Pérot, Finette, and Monsieur de Lancy. The priest and the maid-servant may be silenced; and for Don Giovanni—we will talk of him to-morrow. Stay, has he any letters of yours in his possession?"

"He returns my letters one by one as he receives them," she mutters.

"Good—it is so easy to retract what one has said; but so difficult to deny one's handwriting."

"The De Cevennes do not lie, monsieur!"

"Do they not? What, madame, have you acted no lies, though you may not have spoken them? Have you never lied with your face, when you have worn a look of calm indifference, while the mental effort with which you stopped the violent beating of your heart produced a dull physical torture in your breast; when, in the crowded opera-house, you heard *his* step upon the stage? Wasted lies, madame; wasted torture; for your idol was not worth them. Your god laughed at your worship, because he was a false god, and the attributes for which you worshipped him—truth, loyalty, and genius, such as man never before possessed—were not his, but the offspring of your own imagination, with which you invested him, because you were in love with his handsome face. Bah! madame, after all, you were only the fool of a chiselled profile and a melodious voice. You are not the first of your sex so fooled; Heaven forbid you should be the last!"

"You have shown me why I should hate this man; show me my revenge, if you wish to serve me. My countrywomen do not forgive. O Gaston de Lancy, to have been the slave of your every word; the blind idolator of your every glance; to have given so much; and, as my reward, to reap only your contempt!"

There are no tears in her eyes as she says this in a hoarse voice. Perhaps long years hence she may come to weep over this wild infatuation—now, her despair is too bitter for tears.

The lounger still preserves the charming indifference which stamps him of her own class. He says, in reply to her entreaty,—

"I can lead you to your revenge, madame, if your noble Spanish blood does not recoil from the ordeal. Dress yourself to-morrow night in your servant's clothes, wearing of course a thick veil; take a hackney coach, and at ten o'clock be at the entrance to the Bois de Boulogne. I will join you there. You shall have your revenge, madame, and I will show you how to turn that revenge (which is in itself an expensive luxury) to practical account. In a few days you may perhaps be able to say, 'There is no such person as Gaston de Lancy: the terrible delusion was only a dream; I have awoke, and I am free!' "

She passes her trembling hand across her brow, and looks at the speaker, as if she tried in vain to gather the meaning of his words.

"At ten o'clock, at the entrance to the Bois de Boulogne? I will be there," she murmurs faintly.

"Good! And now, madame, adieu! I fear I have fatigued you by this long interview. Stay! You should know the name of the man to whom you allow the honour of serving you."

He takes out his card-case, lays a card on the tiny table at her side, bows low to her, and leaves her—leaves her stricken to the dust. He looks back at her as he opens the door, and watches her for a moment, with a smile upon his face. His blows have had their full effect.

O Valerie, Valerie! loving so wildly, to be so degraded, humiliated, deceived! Little wonder that you cry to-night. There is no light in the sky—there is no glory in the world! Earth is weary, heaven is dark, and death alone is the friend of the broken heart!

CHAPTER IV

OCULAR DEMONSTRATION

Inscribed on the card which the lounger leaves on the table of Mademoiselle de Cevennes, or Madame de Lancy, is the name of Raymond Marolles. The lounger, then, is Raymond Marolles, and it is he whom we must follow, on the morning after the stormy interview in the pavilion.

He occupies a charming apartment in the Champs Elysées; small, of course, as befitting a bachelor, but furnished in the best taste. On entering his rooms there is one thing you could scarcely fail to notice; and this is the surprising neatness, the almost mathematical precision, with which everything is arranged. Books, pictures, desks, pistols, small-swords, boxing-gloves, riding-whips, canes, and guns—every object is disposed in an order quite unusual in a bachelor's apartment. But this habit of neatness is one of the idiosyncrasies of Monsieur Marolles. It is to be seen in his exquisitely-appointed dress; in his carefully-trimmed moustache; it is to be heard even in the inflexions of his voice, which rise and fall with rather monotonous though melodious regularity, and which are never broken by anything so vulgar as anger or emotion.

At ten o'clock this morning he is still seated at breakfast. He has eaten nothing, but he is drinking his second cup of strong coffee, and it is easy to see that he is thinking very deeply.

"Yes," he mutters, "I must find a way to convince her; she must be thoroughly convinced before she will be induced to act. My first blows have told so well, I must not fail in my master-stroke. But how to convince her—words alone will not satisfy her long; there must be ocular demonstration."

He finishes his cup of coffee, and sits playing with the tea-spoon, clinking it with a low musical sound against the china teacup.

Presently he hits it with one loud ringing stroke. That stroke is a note of triumph. He has been working a problem and has found the solution. He takes up his hat and hurries out of the house; but as soon as he is out of doors he slackens his step, and resumes his usual lounging gait. He crosses the Place de la Concorde, and makes his way to the Boulevard, and only turns aside when he reaches the Italian Opera House. It is to the stage-door he directs his steps. An old man, the doorkeeper, is busy in the little dark hall, manufacturing a *pot à feu*,[1] and warming his hands at the same time at a tiny stove in a corner. He is quite accustomed to the apparition of a stylish young man; so he scarcely looks up when the shadow of Raymond Marolles darkens the doorway.

"Good morning, Monsieur Concierge," says Raymond; "you are very busy, I see."

"A little domestic avocation, that is all, monsieur, being a bachelor."

The doorkeeper is rather elderly, and somewhat snuffy for a bachelor; but he is very fond of informing the visitors of the stage-door that he has never sacrificed his liberty at the shrine of Hymen. He thinks, perhaps, that they might scruple to give their messages to a married man.

"Not too busy, then, for a little conversation, my friend?" asks the visitor, slipping a five-franc piece into the porter's dingy hand.

"Never too busy for that, monsieur;" and the porter abandons the *pot à feu* to its fate, and dusts with his coloured handkerchief a knock-kneed-looking easy-chair, which he presents to monsieur.

Monsieur is very condescending, and the doorkeeper is very communicative. He gives monsieur a great deal of useful information about the salaries of the principal dancers; the bouquets and diamond bracelets thrown to them; the airs and graces indulged in by them; and divers other interesting facts. Presently monsieur, who has been graciously though rather languidly interested in all this, says—"Do you happen to have amongst your supernumeraries or choruses, or any of your insignificant people, one of those mimics so generally met with in a theatre?"

"Ah," says the doorkeeper, chuckling, "I see monsieur knows

theatre. We have indeed two or three mimics; but one above all—a chorus-singer, a great man, who can strike off an imitation which is life itself; a drunken, dissolute fellow, monsieur, or he would have taken to principal characters and made himself a name. A fellow with a soul for nothing but dominoes and vulgar wine-shops; but a wonderful mimic."

"Ah! and he imitates, I suppose, all your great people—your prima donna, your basso, your tenor—" hazards Monsieur Raymond Marolles.

"Yes, monsieur. You should hear him mimic this new tenor, this Monsieur Gaston de Lancy, who has made such a sensation this season. He is not a bad-looking fellow, pretty much the same height as De Lancy, and he can assume his manner, voice, and walk, so completely that——"

"Perhaps in a dark room you could scarcely tell one from the other, eh?"

"Precisely, monsieur."

"I have rather a curiosity about these sort of people; and I should like to see this man, if——" he hesitates, jingling some silver in his pocket.

"Nay, monsieur," says the porter; "nothing more easy, this Moucée is always here about this time. They call the chorus to rehearsal while the great people are lounging over their breakfasts. We shall find him either on the stage, or in one of the dressing-rooms playing dominoes. This way, monsieur."

Raymond Marolles follows the doorkeeper down dark passages and up innumerable flights of stairs; till, very high up, he stops at a low door, on the other side of which there is evidently a rather noisy party. This door the porter opens without ceremony, and he and Monsieur Marolles enter a long low room, with bare white-washed walls, scrawled over with charcoal caricatures of prima donnas and tenors, with impossible noses and spindle legs. Seated at a deal table is a group of young men, shabbily dressed, playing at dominoes, while others look on and bet upon the game. They are all smoking tiny cigarettes, which look like damp curl-papers, and which last about two minutes each.

"Pardon me, Monsieur Moucée," says the porter, addressing one of the domino players, a good-looking young man, with a pale dark face and black hair—"pardon me that I disturb your pleasant game; but I bring a gentleman who wishes to make your acquaintance."

The chorus-singer rises, gives a lingering look at a double-six he was just going to play, and advances to where Monsieur Marolles is standing.

"At monsieur's service," he says, with an unstudied but graceful bow.

Raymond Marolles, with an ease of manner all his own, passes his arm through that of the young man, and leads him out into the passage.

"I have heard, Monsieur Moucée, that you possess a talent for mimicry which is of a very superior order. Are you willing to assist with this talent in a little farce I am preparing for the amusement of a lady? If so you will have a claim (which I shall not forget) on my gratitude and on my purse."

This last word makes Paul Moucée prick up his ears. Poor fellow! his last coin has gone for the half-ounce of tobacco he has just consumed. He expresses himself only too happy to obey the commands of monsieur.

Monsieur suggests that they shall repair to an adjoining *café*, at which they can have half-an-hour's quiet conversation. They do so; and at the end of the half-hour, Monsieur Marolles parts with Paul Moucée at the door of this *café*. As they separate Raymond looks at his watch—"Half-past eleven; all goes better than I could have even hoped. This man will do very well for our friend Elvino, and the lady shall have ocular demonstration. Now for the rest of my work; and to-night, my proud and beautiful heiress, for you."

As the clocks strike ten that night, a hackney-coach stops close to the entrance of the Bois de Boulogne; and as the coachman checks his horse, a gentleman emerges from the gloom, and goes up to the door of the coach, which he opens before the driver can dismount. This gentleman is Monsieur Raymond Marolles, and Valerie de Lancy is seated in the coach.

"Punctual, madame!" he says. "Ah, in the smallest matters you are superior to your sex. May I request you to step out and walk with me for some little distance?"

The lady, who is thickly veiled, only bows her head in reply; but she is by his side in a moment. He gives the coachman some directions, and the man drives off a few paces; he then offers his arm to Valerie.

"Nay, monsieur," she says, in a cold, hard voice, "I can follow you, or I can walk by your side. I had rather not take your arm."

Perhaps it is as well for this man's schemes that it is too dark for his companion to see the smile that lifts his black moustache, or the glitter in his blue eyes. He is something of a physiologist as well as a mathematician, this man; and he can tell what she has suffered since last night by the change in her voice alone. It has a dull and monotonous sound, and the tone seems to have gone out of it for ever. If the dead could speak, they might speak thus.

"This way, then, madame," he says. "My first object is to convince you of the treachery of the man for whom you have sacrificed so much. Have you strength to live through the discovery?"

"I lived through last night. Come, monsieur, waste no more time in words, or I shall think you are a charlatan. Let me hear from *his* lips that I have cause to hate him."

"Follow me, then, and softly."

He leads her into the wood. The trees are very young as yet, but all is obscure to-night. There is not a star in the sky; the December night is dark and cold. A slight fall of snow has whitened the ground, and deadens the sound of footsteps. Raymond and Valerie might be two shadows, as they glide amongst the trees. After they have walked about a quarter of a mile, he catches her by the arm, and draws her hurriedly into the shadow of a group of young pine-trees. "Now," he says, "now listen."

She hears a voice whose every tone she knows. "At first there is a rushing sound in her ears, as if all the blood were surging from her heart up to her brain; but presently she hears distinctly; presently too, her eyes grow somewhat accustomed to the gloom; and she sees a few paces from her the dim outline of a tall figure, familiar to her. It is Gaston de Lancy, who is standing with one arm round the slight waist of a young girl, his head bending down with the graceful droop she knows so well, as he looks in her face.

Marolles' voice whispers in her ear, "The girl is a dancer from one of the minor theatres, whom he knew before he was a great man. Her name, I think, is Rosette, or something like it. She loves him very much; perhaps almost as much as you do, in spite of the quarterings on your shield."[2]

He feels the slender hand, which before disdained to lean upon his arm, now clasp his wrist, and tighten, as if each taper finger were an iron vice.

"Listen," he says again. "Listen to the drama, madame. I am the chorus!"

It is the girl who is speaking. "But, Gaston, this marriage, this marriage, which has almost broken my heart."

"Was a sacrifice to our love, my Rosette. For your sake alone would I have made such a sacrifice. But this haughty lady's wealth will make us happy in a distant land. She little thinks, poor fool, for whose sake I endure her patrician airs, her graces of the old *régime*, her caprices, and her folly. Only be patient, Rosette, and trust me. The day that is to unite us for ever is not far distant, believe me."

It is the voice of Gaston de Lancy. Who should better know those tones than his wife? Who should better know them than she to whose proud heart they strike death?

The girl speaks again. "And you do not love this fine lady, Gaston? Only tell me that you do not love her!"

Again the familiar voice speaks. "Love her! Bah! We never love these fine ladies who give us such tender glances from opera-boxes. We never admire these great heiresses, who fall in love with a handsome face, and have not enough modesty to keep the sentiment a secret; who think they honour us by a marriage which they are ashamed to confess; and who fancy we must needs be devoted to them, because, after their fashion, they are in love with us."

"Have you heard enough?" asked Raymond Marolles.

"Give me a pistol or a dagger!" she gasped, in a hoarse whisper; "let me shoot him dead, or stab him to the heart, that I may go away and die in peace!"

"So," muttered Raymond, "she has heard enough. Come, madame. Yet—stay, one last look. You are sure that is Monsieur de Lancy?"

The man and the girl are standing a few yards from them; his back is turned to Valerie, but she would know him amongst a thousand by the dark hair and the peculiar bend of the head.

"Sure!" she answers. "Am I myself?"

"Come, then; we have another place to visit to-night. You are satisfied, are you not, madame, now that you have had ocular demonstration?"

CHAPTER V

THE KING OF SPADES

When Monsieur Marolles offers his arm to lead Valerie de Cevennes back to the coach, it is accepted passively enough. Little matter now what new degradation she endures. Her pride can never fall lower than it has fallen. Despised by the man she loved so tenderly, the world's contempt is nothing to her.

In a few minutes they are both seated in the coach driving through the Champs Elysées.

"Are you taking me home?" she asks.

"No, madame, we have another errand, as I told you."

"And that errand?"

"I am going to take you where you will have your fortune told."

"*My* fortune!" she exclaims, with a bitter laugh.

"Bah! madame," says her companion. "Let us understand each other. I hope I have not to deal with a romantic and lovesick girl. I will not gall your pride by recalling to your recollection in what a contemptible position I have found you. I offer my services to rescue you from that contemptible position; but I do so in the firm belief that you are a woman of spirit, courage, and determination, and——"

"And that I can pay you well," she adds, scornfully.

"And that you can pay me well. I am no Don Quixote, madame; nor have I any great respect for that gentleman. Believe me, I intend that you shall pay me well for my services, as you will learn by-and-by."

Again there is the cold glitter in the blue eyes, and the ominous smile which a moustache does well to hide.

"But," he continues, "if you have a mind to break your heart for an opera-singer's handsome face, go and break it in your boudoir, madame, with no better confidante than your lady's-maid; for you are not worthy of the services of Raymond Marolles."

"You rate your services very high, then, monsieur?"

"Perhaps. Look you madame: you despise me because I am an adventurer. Had I been born in the purple—lord, even in my cradle, of wide lands and a great name, you would respect me. Now, I respect myself because I am an adventurer; because by the force alone of my own mind I have risen from what I was, to be what I am. I will show you my cradle some day. It had no tapestried coverlet or embroidered curtains, I can assure you."

They are driving now through a dark street, in a neighbourhood utterly unknown to the lady.

"Where are you taking me?" she asks again, with something like fear in her voice.

"As I told you before, to have your fortune told. Nay, madame, unless you trust me, I cannot serve you. Remember, it is to my interest to serve you well: you can therefore have no cause for fear."

As he speaks they stop before a ponderous gateway in the blank wall of a high dark-looking house. They are somewhere in the neighbourhood of Notre Dame, for the grand old towers loom dimly in the darkness. Monsieur Marolles gets out of the coach and rings a bell, at the sound of which the porter opens the door. Raymond assists Valerie to dismount, and leads her across a courtyard into a little hall, and up a stone staircase to the fifth story of the house. At another time her courage might have failed her in this strange house, at so late an hour, with this man, of whom she knows nothing; but she is reckless to-night.

There is nothing very alarming in the aspect of the room into which Raymond leads her. It is a cheerful little apartment lighted with gas. There is a small stove, near a table, before which is seated a gentlemanly-looking man, of some forty years of age. He has a very pale face, a broad forehead, from which the hair is brushed away behind the ears: he wears blue spectacles, which entirely conceal his eyes, and in a manner shade his face. You cannot tell what he is thinking of; for it is a peculiarity of this man that the mouth, which with other people is generally the most expressive feature, has with him no expression whatever. It is a thin, straight line, which opens and shuts as he speaks, but which never curves into a smile, or contracts when he frowns.

He is deeply engaged, bending over a pack of cards spread out on the green cloth which covers the table, as if he were playing *écarté* without an opponent, when Raymond opens the door; but he rises at the sight of the lady, and bows low to her. He has the air of a student rather than of a man of the world.

"My good Blurosset," says Raymond, "I have brought a lady to see you, to whom I have been speaking very highly of your talents."

"With the pasteboard or the crucible?" asks the impassible mouth.

"Both, my dear fellow; we shall want both your talents. Sit down, madame; I must do the honours of the apartment, for my friend Laurent Blurosset is too much a man of science to be a man of gallantry. Sit down, madame; place yourself at this table—there, opposite Monsieur Blurosset, and then to business."

This Raymond Marolles, of whom she knows absolutely nothing, has a strange influence over Valerie; an influence against which she no longer struggles. She obeys him passively, and seats herself before the little green baize-covered table.

The blue spectacles of Monsieur Laurent Blurosset look at her attentively for two or three minutes. As for the eyes behind the spectacles, she cannot even guess what might be revealed in their light. The man seems to have a strange advantage in looking at every one as from behind a screen. His own face, with hidden eyes and inflexible mouth, is like a blank wall.

"Now then, Blurosset, we will begin with the pasteboard.

Madame would like to have her fortune told. She knows of course that this fortune-telling is mere charlatanism, but she wishes to see one of the cleverest charlatans."

"Charlatanism! Charlatan! Well, it doesn't matter. *I* believe in what I read here, because I find it true. The first time I find a false meaning in these bits of pasteboard I shall throw them into that fire, and never touch a card again. They've been the hobby of twenty years, but you know I could do it, Englishman!"

"Englishman!" exclaimed Valerie, looking up with astonishment.

"Yes," answered Raymond, laughing; "a surname which Monsieur Blurosset has bestowed upon me, in ridicule of my politics, which happened once to resemble those of our honest neighbour, John Bull."

Monsieur Blurosset nods an assent to Raymond's assertion, as he takes the cards in his thin yellow-white hands and begins shuffling them. He does this with a skill peculiar to himself, and you could almost guess in watching him that these little pieces of pasteboard have been his companions for twenty years. Presently he arranges them in groups of threes, fives, sevens, and nines, on the green baize, reserving a few cards in his hand; then the blue spectacles are lifted and contemplate Valerie for two or three seconds.

"Your friend is the queen of spades," he says, turning to Raymond.

"Decidedly," replies Monsieur Marolles. "How the insipid diamond beauties fade beside this gorgeous loveliness of the south!"

Valerie does not hear the compliment, which at another time she would have resented as an insult. She is absorbed in watching the groups of cards over which the blue spectacles are so intently bent.

Monsieur Blurosset seems to be working some abstruse calculations with these groups of cards, assisted by those he has in his hand. The spectacles wander from the threes to the nines; from the sevens to the fives; back again; across again; from five to nine, from three to seven; from five to three, from seven to nine. Presently he says—

"The king of spades is everywhere here." He does not look up as he speaks—never raising the spectacles from the cards. His manner of speaking is so passionless and mechanical, that he might almost be some calculating automaton.

"The king of spades," says Raymond, "is a dark and handsome young man."

"Yes," says Blurosset, "he's everywhere beside the queen of spades."

Valerie in spite of herself is absorbed by this man's words. She never takes her eyes from the spectacles and the thin pale lips of the fortune-teller.

"I do not like his influence. It is bad. This king of spades is dragging the queen down, down into the very mire." Valerie's cheeks can scarcely grow whiter than it has been ever since the revelation of the Bois de Boulogne, but she cannot repress a shudder at these words.

"There is a falsehood," continues Monsieur Blurosset; "and there is a fair woman here."

"A fair woman! That girl we saw to-night is fair," whispers Raymond. "No doubt Monsieur Don Giovanni admires blondes, having himself the southern beauty."

"The fair woman is always with the king of spades," says the fortune-teller. "There is here no falsehood—nothing but devotion. The king of spades can be true; he is true to this diamond woman; but for the queen of spades he has nothing but treachery."

"Is there anything more on the cards?" asks Raymond.

"Yes! A priest—a marriage—money. Ah! this king of spades imagines that he is within reach of a great fortune."

"Does he deceive himself?"

"Yes! Now the treachery changes sides. The queen of spades is in it now—— But stay—the traitor, the real traitor is here; this fair man—the knave of diamonds——"

Raymond Marolles lays his white hand suddenly upon the card to which Blurosset is pointing, and says, hurriedly,—

"Bah! You have told us all about yesterday; now tell us of to-morrow." And then he adds, in a whisper, in the ear of Monsieur Blurosset,—

"Fool! Have you forgotten your lesson?"

"*They* will speak the truth," mutters the fortune-teller. "I was carried away by them. I will be more careful."

This whispered dialogue is unheard by Valerie, who sits immovable, awaiting the sentence of the oracle, as if the monotonous voice of Monsieur Blurosset were the voice of Nemesis.

"Now then for the future," says Raymond. "It is possible to tell what *has* happened. We wish to pass the confines of the possible: tell us, then, what is *going* to happen."

Monsieur Blurosset collects the cards, shuffles them, and rearranges them in groups, as before. Again the blue spectacles wander. From three to nine; from nine to seven; from seven to five; Valerie following them with bright and hollow eyes. Presently the fortune-teller says, in his old mechanical way,—

"The queen of spades is very proud."

"Yes," mutters Raymond in Valerie's ear. "Heaven help the king who injures such a queen!"

She does not take her eyes from the blue spectacles of Monsieur Blurosset; but there is a tightening of her determined mouth which seems like an assent to this remark.

"She can hate as well as love. The king of spades is in danger," says the fortune-teller.

There is, for a few minutes, dead silence, while the blue spectacles shift from group to group of cards; Valerie intently watching them, Raymond intently watching her.

This time there seems to be something difficult in the calculation of the numbers. The spectacles shift hither and thither, and the thin white lips move silently and rapidly, from seven to nine, and back again to seven.

"There is something on the cards that puzzles you," says Raymond, breaking the deathly silence. "What is it?"

"A death!" answers the passionless voice of Monsieur Blurosset. "A violent death, which bears no outward sign of violence. I said, did I not, that the king of spades was in danger?"

"You did."

From three to five, from five to nine, from nine to seven, from seven to nine: the groups of cards form a circle: three times round the circle, as the sun goes; back again, and three times round the circle in a contrary direction: across the circle from three to seven, from seven to five, from five to nine, and the blue spectacles come to a dead stop at nine.

"Before twelve o'clock to-morrow night the king of spades will be dead!" says the monotonous voice of Monsieur Blurosset. The voices of the clocks of Paris seem to take up Monsieur Blurosset's voice as they strike the hour of midnight.

Twenty-four hours for the king of spades!

Monsieur Blurosset gathers up his cards and drops them into his pocket. Malicious people say that he sleeps with them under his pillow; that he plays *écarté* by himself in his sleep; and that he has played *piquet* with a very tall dark gentleman, whom the porter never let either in or out, and who left a sulphureous and suffocating atmosphere behind him in Monsieur Blurosset's little apartment.

"Good!" says Monsieur Raymond Marolles. "So much for the pasteboard. Now for the crucible."

For the first time since the discovery of the treachery of her husband Valerie de Lancy smiles. She has a beautiful smile, which curves the delicate lips without distorting them, and which brightens in her large dark eyes with a glorious fire of the sunny south. But for all that, Heaven save the man who has injured her from the light of such a smile as hers of to-night.

"You want my assistance in some matters of chemistry?" asks Blurosset.

"Yes! I forgot to tell you, madame, that my friend Laurent Blurosset—though he chooses to hide himself in one of the most obscure streets of Paris—is perhaps one of the greatest men in this mighty city. He is a chemist who will one day work a revolution in the chemical science; but he is a fanatic, madame, or, let me rather say, he is a lover, and his crucible is his mistress. This blind devotion to a science is surely only another form of the world's great madness—love! Who knows what bright eyes a problem in Euclid may have replaced? Who can tell what fair hair may not have been forgotten in the search after a Greek root?"

Valerie shivers. Heaven help that shattered heart! Every word that touches on the master-passion of her life is a wound that pierces it to the core.

"You do not smoke, Blurosset. Foolish man you do not know how to live. Pardon, madame." He lights his cigar at the green-shaded gas-lamp, seats himself close to the stove, and smokes for a few minutes in silence.

Valerie, still seated before the little table, watches him with fixed eyes, waiting for him to speak.

In the utter shipwreck of her every hope this adventurer is the only anchor to which she can cling. Presently he says, in his most easy and indifferent manner,—

"It was the fashion at the close of the fifteenth and throughout the sixteenth century for the ladies of Italy to acquire a certain knowledge of some of the principles of chemistry. Of course, at the head of these ladies we must place Lucretia Borgia."[1]

Monsieur Blurosset nods an assent. Valerie looks from Raymond to the blue spectacles; but the face of the chemist testifies no shade of surprise at the singularity of Raymond's observation.

"Then," continued Monsieur Marolles, "if a lady was deeply injured or cruelly insulted by the man she loved; if her pride was trampled in the dust, or her name and her weakness held up to ridicule and contempt—then she knew how to avenge herself and to defy the world. A tender pressure of the traitor's hand; a flower or a ribbon given as a pledge of love; the leaves of a book hastily turned over with the tips of moistened fingers—people had such vulgar habits in those days—and behold the gentleman died, and no one was any the wiser but the worms, with whose constitutions *aqua tofana*[2] at second hand may possibly have disagreed."

"Vultures have died from the effects of poisoned carrion," muttered Monsieur Blurosset.

"But in this degenerate age," continued Raymond, "what can our Parisian ladies do when they have reason to be revenged on a traitor? The poor blunderers can only give him half a pint of laudanum, or an ounce or so of arsenic, and run the risk of detection half an hour after his death! I think that time is a circle, and that we retreat as we advance, in spite of our talk of progress."

His horrible words, thrice horrible when contrasted with the coolness of his easy manner, freeze Valerie to the very heart; but she does not make one effort to interrupt him.

"Now, my good Blurosset," he resumes, "what I want of you is this. Something which will change a glass of wine into a death-warrant, but which will defy the scrutiny of a college of physicians. This lady wishes to take a lesson in chemistry. She will, of course, only experimentalise on rabbits, and she is so tender-hearted that, as you see, she shudders even at the thought of that little cruelty. For the rest, to repay you for your trouble, if you will give her pen and ink, she will write you an order on her banker for five thousand francs.

Monsieur Blurosset appears no more surprised at this request than if he had been asked for a glass of water. He goes to a cabinet, which he opens, and after a little search selects a small tin box, from which he takes a few grains of white powder, which he screws carelessly in a scrap of newspaper. He is so much accustomed to handling these compounds that he treats them with very small ceremony.

"It is a slow poison," he says. "For a full-grown rabbit use the eighth part of what you have there; the whole of it would poison a man; but death in either case would not be immediate. The operation of the poison occupies some hours before it terminates fatally."

"Madame will use it with discretion," says Raymond; "do not fear."

Monsieur Blurosset holds out the little packet as if expecting Valerie to take it; she recoils with a ghastly face, and shudders as she looks from the chemist to Raymond Marolles.

"In this degenerate age," says Raymond, looking her steadily in the face, "our women cannot redress their own wrongs, however deadly those wrongs may be; they must have fathers, brothers, or uncles to fight for them, and the world to witness the struggle. Bah! There is not a woman in France who is any better than a sentimental schoolgirl."

Valerie stretches out her small hand to receive the packet.

"Give me the pen, monsieur," says she; and the chemist presents her a half-sheet of paper, on which she writes hurriedly an order on her bankers, which she signs in full with her maiden name.

—

Monsieur Blurosset looked over the paper as she wrote.

"Valerie de Cevennes!" he exclaimed. "I did not know I was honoured by so aristocratic a visitor."

Valerie put her hand to her head as if bewildered. "My name!" she muttered, "I forgot, I forgot."

"What do you fear, madame?" asked Raymond, with a smile. "Are you not among friends?"

"For pity's sake, monsieur," she said, "give me your arm, and take me back to the carriage! I shall drop down dead if I stay longer in this room."

The blue spectacles contemplated her gravely for a moment. Monsieur Blurosset laid one cold hand upon her pulse, and with the other took a little bottle from the cabinet, out of which he gave his visitor a few drops of a transparent liquid.

"She will do now," he said to Raymond, "till you get her home; then see that she takes this," he added, handing Monsieur Marolles another phial; "it is an opiate which will procure her six hours' sleep. Without that she would go mad."

Raymond led Valerie from the room; but, once outside, her head fell heavily on his shoulder, and he was obliged to carry her down the steep stairs.

"I think," he muttered to himself as he went out into the courtyard with his unconscious burden, "I think we have sealed the doom of the king of spades!"

CHAPTER VI

A Glass of Wine

Upon a little table in the boudoir of the pavilion lay a letter. It was the first thing Valerie de Lancy beheld on entering the room, with Raymond Marolles by her side, half an hour after she had left the apartment of Monsieur Blurosset. This letter was in the handwriting of her husband, and it bore the postmark of Rouen. Valerie's face told her companion whom the letter came from before she took it in her hand.

"Read it," he said, coolly. "It contains his excuses, no doubt. Let us see what pretty story he has invented. In his early professional career his companions surnamed him Baron Munchausen."[1]

Valerie's hand shook as she broke the seal; but she read the letter carefully through, and then turning to Raymond she said—

"You are right; his excuse is excellent, only a little too transparent: listen.

" 'The reason of my absence from Paris'—(absence from Paris, and to-night in the Bois de Boulogne)—'is most extraordinary. At the conclusion of the opera last night, I was summoned to the stage-door, where I found a messenger waiting for me, who told me he had come post-haste from Rouen, where my mother was lying dangerously ill, and to implore me, if I wished to see her before her death, to start for that place immediately. Even my love for you, which you well know, Valerie, is the absorbing passion of my life, was forgotten in such a moment. I had no means of communicating with you without endangering our secret. Imagine, then, my surprise on my arrival here, to find that my mother is in perfect health, and had of course sent no messenger to me. I fear in this mystery some conspiracy which threatens the safety of our secret. I shall be in Paris to-night, but too late to see you. To-morrow, at dusk, I shall be at the dear little pavilion, once more to be blest by a smile from the only eyes I love.—Gaston de Lancy.' "

"Rather a blundering epistle," muttered Raymond. "I should really have given him credit for something better. You will receive him to-morrow evening, madame?"

She knew so well the purport of this question that her hand almost involuntarily tightened on the little packet given her by Monsieur Blurosset, which she had held all this time, but she did not answer him.

"You will receive him to-morrow; or by to-morrow night all Paris will know of this romantic but rather ridiculous marriage; it will be in all the newspapers—caricatured in all the print-shops; Charivari[2] will have a word or two about it, and little boys will cry it in the streets, a full, true, and particular account for only one sous. But then, as I said before, you are superior to your sex, and perhaps you will not mind this kind of thing."

"I shall see him to-morrow evening at dusk," she said, in a hoarse whisper not pleasant to hear; "and I shall never see him again after to-morrow."

"Once more, then, good night," says Raymond. "But stay, Monsieur begs you will take this opiate. Nay," he muttered with a laugh as she looked at him strangely, "you may be perfectly assured of its harmlessness. Remember, I have not been paid yet."

He bowed, and left the room. She did not lift her eyes to look at him as he bade her adieu. Those hollow tearless eyes were fixed on the letter she held in her left hand. She was thinking of the first time she saw this handwriting, when every letter seemed a character inscribed in fire, because *his* hand had shaped it; when the tiniest scrap of paper covered with the most ordinary words was a precious talisman, a jewel of more price than the diamonds of all the Cevennes.

———

The short winter's day died out, and through the dusk a young man, in a thick greatcoat, walked rapidly along the broad quiet street in which the pavilion stood. Once or twice he looked round to assure himself that he was unobserved. He tried the handle of the little wooden door, found it unfastened, opened it softly, and went in. In a few minutes he was in the boudoir, and by the side of Valerie. The girl's proud face was paler than when he had last seen it; and when he tenderly asked the reason of this change, she said,—

"I have been anxious about you, Gaston. You can scarcely wonder."

"The voice too, even your voice is changed," he said anxiously. "Stay, surely I am the victim of no juggling snare. It is—it is Valerie."

The little boudoir was only lighted by the wood fire burning on the low hearth. He drew her towards the blaze, and looked her full in the face.

"You would scarcely believe me," he said; "but for the moment I half doubted if it were really you. The false alarm, the hurried journey, one thing and another have upset me so completely, that you seemed changed—altered; I can scarcely tell you how, but altered very much."

She seated herself in the easy-chair by the hearth. There was an embroidered velvet footstool at her feet, and he placed himself on this, and sat looking up in her face. She laid her slender hands on his dark hair, and looked straight into his eyes. Who shall read her thoughts at this moment? She had learnt to despise him, but she had never ceased to love him. She had cause to hate him; but she could scarcely have told whether the bitter anguish which rent her heart were nearer akin to love or hate.

"Pshaw, Gaston!" she exclaimed, "you are full of silly fancies tonight. And I, you see, do not offer to reproach you once for the uneasiness you have caused me. See how readily I accept your excuse for your absence, and never breathe one doubt of its truth. Now, were I a jealous or suspicious woman, I might have a hundred doubts. I might think you did not love me, and fancy that your absence was a voluntary one. I might even be so foolish as to picture you with another whom you loved better than me."

"Valerie!" he said, reproachfully, raising her small hand to his lips.

"Nay," she cried, with a light laugh, "this might be the thought of a jealous woman. But could I think so of you, Gaston?"

"Hark!" he said, starting and rising hastily; "did you not hear something?"

"What?"

"A rustling sound by that door—the door of your dressing-room. Finette is not there, is she? I left her in the anteroom below."

"No, no, Gaston; there is no one there; this is another of your silly fancies."

He glanced uneasily towards the door, but re-seated himself at her feet, and looked once more upward to the proudly beautiful face. Valerie did not look at her companion, but at the fire. Her dark eyes were fixed upon the blaze, and she seemed almost unconscious of Gaston de Lancy's presence. What did she see in the red light? Her shipwrecked soul? The ruins of her hopes? The ghost of her dead happiness? The image of a long and dreary future, in which the love on whose foundation she had built a bright and peaceful life to come could have no part? What did she see? A warning arm stretched out to save her from the commission of a dreadful deed, which, once committed, must shut her out from all earthly sympathy, though not perhaps from heavenly forgiveness; or a stern finger pointing to the dark end to which she hastens with a purpose in her heart so strange and fearful to her she scarcely can believe it is her own, or that she is herself?

With her left hand still upon the dark hair—which even now she could not touch without a tenderness, that, having no part in her nature of to-day, seemed like some relic of the wreck of the past—she stretched out her right arm towards a table near her, on which there were some decanters and glasses that clashed with a silvery sound under her touch.

"I must try and cure you of your fancies, Gaston. My physician insists on my taking every day at luncheon a glass of that old Madeira of which my uncle is so fond. They have not removed the wine—you shall take some; pour it out yourself. See, here is the decanter. I will hold the glass for you."

She held the antique diamond-cut glass with a steady hand while Gaston poured the wine into it. The light from the wood fire flickered, and he spilt some of the Madeira over her dress. They both laughed at this, and her laugh rang out the clearer of the two.

There was a third person who laughed; but his was a silent laugh. This third person was Monsieur Marolles, who stood within the half-open door that led into Valerie's dressing-room.

"So," he says to himself, "this is even better than I had hoped. I feared his handsome face would shake her resolution. The light in those dark eyes is very beautiful, no doubt, but it has not long to burn."

As the firelight flashed upon the glass, Gaston held it for a moment between his eyes and the blaze.

"Your uncle's wine is not very clear," he said; "but I would drink the vilest vinegar from the worst tavern in Paris, if you poured it out for me, Valerie."

As he emptied the glass the little time-piece struck six.

"I must go, Valerie. I play Gennaro in Lucretia Borgia,[3] and the King is to be at the theatre to-night. You will come? I shall not sing well if you are not there."

"Yes, yes, Gaston." She laid her hand upon her head as she spoke.

"Are you ill?" he asked, anxiously.

"No, no, it is nothing. Go, Gaston; you must not keep his Majesty waiting," she said.

I wonder whether as she spoke there rose the image in her mind of a King who reigns in undisputed power over the earth's wide face; whose throne no revolution ever shook; whose edict no creature ever yet set aside, and to whom all terrible things give place, owning in him the King of Terrors!

The young man took his wife in his arms and pressed his lips to her forehead. It was damp with a deadly cold perspiration.

"I am sure you are ill, Valerie," he said.

She shivered violently, but pushing him towards the door, said, "No, no, Gaston; go, I implore you; you will be late; at the theatre you will see me. Till then, adieu."

He was gone. She closed the door upon him rapidly, and with one long shudder fell to the ground, striking her head against the gilded moulding of the door. Monsieur Marolles emerged from the shadow, and lifting her from the floor, placed her in the chair by the hearth. Her head fell heavily back upon the velvet cushions, but her large black eyes were open. I have said before, this woman was not subject to fainting-fits.

She caught Raymond's hand in hers with a convulsive grasp.

"Madame," he said, "you have shown yourself indeed a daughter of the haughty line of the De Cevennes. You have avenged yourself most nobly."

The large black eyes did not look at him. They were fixed on vacancy. Vacancy? No! there could be no such thing as vacancy for this woman. Henceforth for her the whole earth must be filled with one hideous phantom.

There were two wine-glasses on the table which stood a little way behind the low chair in which Valerie was seated—very beautiful glasses, antique, exquisitely cut, and emblazoned with the arms of the De Cevennes. In one of those glasses, the one from which Gaston de Lancy had drunk, there remained a few drops of wine, and a little white sediment. Valerie did not see Raymond, as with a stealthy hand he removed this glass from the table, and put it in the pocket of his greatcoat.

He looked once more at her as she sat with rigid mouth and staring eyes, and then he said, as he moved towards the door,—

"I shall see you at the opera, madame! I shall be in the stalls. You will be, with more than your wonted brilliancy and beauty, the centre of observation in the box next to the King's. Remember, that until to-night is over, your play will not be played out. *Au revoir,* madame. To-morrow I shall say *mademoiselle!* For to-morrow the secret marriage of Valerie de Cevennes with an opera-singer will only be a foolish memory of the past."

CHAPTER VII

The Last Act of Lucretia Borgia

Two hours after this interview in the pavilion Raymond Marolles is seated in his old place in the front row of the stalls. Several times during the prologue and the first act of the opera his glass seeks the box next to that of the King, always to find it empty. But after the curtain has fallen on the *finale* to the first act, the quiet watcher raises his glass once more, and sees Valerie enter, leaning on her uncle's arm. Her dark beauty loses nothing by its unusual pallor, and her eyes to-night have a brilliancy which, to the admiring crowd, who know so little and so little care to know the secrets of her proud soul, is very beautiful. She wears a high dress of dark green velvet, fastened at the throat with one small diamond ornament, which trembles and emits bright scintillations of rainbow light. This sombre dress, her deadly pallor, and the strange fire in her eyes, give to her beauty of to-night a certain peculiarity which renders her more than usually the observed of all observers.

She seats herself directly facing the stage, laying down her costly bouquet, which is of one pure white, being composed entirely of orange-flowers, snowdrops, and jasmine, a mixture of winter, summer, and hot-house blossoms for which her florist knows how to charge her. She veils the intensity which is the distinctive character of her face with a weary listless glance to-night. She does not once look round the house. She has no need to look, for it seems as if without looking she can see the pale face of Monsieur Marolles, who lounges with his back to the orchestra, and his opera-glass in his hand.

The Marquis de Cevennes glances at the programme of the opera, and throws it away from him with a dissatisfied air.

"That abominable poisoning woman!" he says; "when will the Parisians be tired of horrors?"

His niece raises her eyebrows slightly, but does not lift her eyelids as she says—"Ah, when, indeed!"

"I don't like these subjects," continued the marquis. "Even the handling of a Victor Hugo[1] cannot make them otherwise than repulsive: and then again, there is something to be said on the score of their evil tendency. They set a dangerous example. Lucretia Borgia, in black velvet, avenging an insult according to the rules of high art and to the music of Donizetti[2] is very charming, no doubt; but we don't want our wives and daughters to learn how they may poison us without fear of detection. What do you say, Rinval?" he asked, turning to a young officer who had just entered the box. "Do you think I am right?"

"Entirely, my dear marquis. The representation of such a hideous subject is a sin against beauty and innocence," he said, bowing to Valerie. "And, though the music is very exquisite——"

"Yes," said Valerie, "my uncle cannot help admiring the music. How have they been singing to-night?"

"Why, strange to say, for once De Lancy has disappointed his admirers. His Gennaro is a very weak performance."

"Indeed!" She takes her bouquet in her hand and plays with the drooping blossom of a snowdrop. "A weak performance? You surprise me really!" She might be speaking of the flowers she holds, from the perfect indifference of her tone.

"They say he is ill," continues Monsieur Rinval. "He almost broke down in the 'Pescator ignobile.'³ But the curtain has risen—we shall have the poison scene soon, and you can judge for yourself."

She laughs. "Nay," she says, "I have never been so enthusiastic an admirer of this young man as you are, Monsieur Rinval. I should not think the world had come to an end if he happened to sing a false note."

—

The young Parisian bent over her chair, admiring her grace and beauty—admiring, perhaps, more than all, the haughty indifference with which she spoke of the opera-singer, as if he were something too far removed from her sphere for her to be in earnest about him even for one moment. Might he not have wondered even more, if he had admired her less, could he have known that as she looked up at him with a radiant face, she could not even see him standing close beside her; that to her clouded sight the opera-house was only a confusion of waving lights and burning eyes; and that, in the midst of a chaos of blood and fire, she saw the vision of her lover and her husband dying by the hand that had caressed him?

"Now for the banquet scene," exclaimed Monsieur Rinval. "Ah! there is Gennaro. Is he not gloriously handsome in ruby velvet and gold? That clubbed Venetian wig becomes him. It is a wig, I suppose."

"Oh, no doubt. That sort of people owe half their beauty to wigs, and white and red paint, do they not?" she asked, contemptuously; and even as she spoke she was thinking of the dark hair which her white fingers had smoothed away from the broad brow so often, in that time which, gone by a few short days, seemed centuries ago to her. She had suffered the anguish of a lifetime in losing the bright dream of her life.

"See," said Monsieur Rinval, "Gennaro has the poisoned goblet in his hand. He is acting very badly. He is supporting himself with one hand on the back of that chair, though he has not yet drunk the fatal draught."

De Lancy was indeed leaning on an antique stage-chair for support. Once he passed his hand across his forehead, as if to collect his scattered senses, but he drank the wine, and went on with the music. Presently, however, every performer in the orchestra looked up as if thunderstruck. He had left off singing in the middle of a concerted piece; but the Maffeo Orsini[4] took up the passage, and the opera proceeded.

"He is either ill, or he does not know the music," said Monsieur Rinval. "If the last, it is really shameful; and he presumes on the indulgence of the public."

"It is always the case with these favourites, is it not?" asked Valerie.

At this moment the centre of the stage was thrown open. There entered first a procession of black and shrouded monks singing a dirge. Next, pale, haughty, and vengeful, the terrible Lucretia burst upon the scene.

Scornful and triumphant she told the companions of Gennaro that their doom was sealed, pointing to where, in the ghastly background, were ranged five coffins, waiting for their destined occupants. The audience, riveted by the scene, awaited that thrilling question of Gennaro, "Then, madame, where is the sixth?" and as De Lancy emerged from behind his comrades every eye was fixed upon him.

He advanced towards Lucretia, tried to sing, but his voice broke on the first note; he caught with his hand convulsively at his throat, staggered a pace or two forward, and then fell heavily to the floor. There was immediate consternation and confusion on the stage; chorus and singers crowded round him; one of the singers knelt down by his side, and raised his head. As he did so, the curtain fell suddenly.

"I was certain he was ill," said Monsieur Rinval, "I fear it must be apoplexy."

"It is rather an uncharitable suggestion," said the marquis; "but do you not think it just possible that the young man may be tipsy?"

There was a great buzz of surprise amongst the audience, and in about three minutes one of the performers came before the curtain, and announced that in consequence of the sudden and alarming illness of Monsieur de Lancy it was impossible to conclude the opera. He requested the indulgence of the audience for a favourite ballet which would commence immediately.

The orchestra began the overture of the ballet, and several of the audience rose to leave the house.

"Will you stop any longer, Valerie? or has this dismal *finale* dispirited you?" said the marquis.

"A little," said Valerie; "besides, we have promised to look in at Madame de Vermanville's concert before going to the duchess's ball."

Monsieur Rinval helped to muffle her in her cloak, and then offered her his arm. As they passed from the great entrance to the carriage of the marquis, Valerie dropped her bouquet. A gentleman advanced from the crowd and restored it to her.

"I congratulate you alike on your strength of mind, as on your beauty, *mademoiselle!*" he said, in a whisper too low for her companions to hear, but with a terrible emphasis on the last word.

As she stepped into the carriage, she heard a bystander say—

"Poor fellow, only seven-and-twenty! And so marvellously handsome and gifted!"

"Dear me," said Monsieur Rinval, drawing up the carriage window, "how very shocking! De Lancy is dead!"

Valerie did not utter one exclamation at this announcement. She was looking steadily out of the opposite window. She was counting the lamps in the streets through the mist of a winter's night.

"Only twenty-seven!" she cried hysterically, "only twenty-seven! It might have been thirty-seven, forty-seven, fifty-seven! But he despised her love; he trampled out the best feelings of her soul; so it was only twenty-seven! Marvellously handsome, and only twenty-seven!"

"For heaven's sake open the windows and stop the carriage, Rinval!" cried the marquis—"I'm sure my niece is ill."

She burst into a long, ringing laugh.

"My dear uncle, you are quite mistaken. I never was better in my life; but it seems to me as if the death of this opera-singer has driven everybody mad."

They drove rapidly home, and took her into the house. The maid Finette begged that her mistress might be carried to the pavilion, but the marquis overruled her, and had his niece taken into her old suite of apartments in the mansion. The first physicians in Paris were sent for, and when they came they pronounced her to be seized by a brain-fever,[5] which promised to be a very terrible one.

CHAPTER VIII ·

BAD DREAMS AND A WORSE WAKING

The sudden and melancholy death of Gaston de Lancy caused a considerable sensation throughout Paris; more especially as it was attributed by many to poison. By whom administered, or from what motive, none could guess. There was one story, however, circulated that was believed by some people, though it bore very little appearance of probability. It was reported that on the afternoon preceding the night on which De Lancy died, a stranger had obtained admission behind the scenes of the opera-house, and had been seen in earnest conversation with the man whose duty it was to provide the goblets of wine for the poison scene in Lucretia Borgia. Some went so far as to say, that this stranger had bribed the man to put the contents of a small packet into the bottom of the glass given on the stage to De Lancy. But so improbable a story was believed by very few, and, of course, stoutly denied by the man in question. The doctors attributed the death of the young man to apoplexy. There was no inquest held on his remains; and at the wish of his mother he was buried at Rouen, and his funeral was no doubt a peculiarly quiet one, for no one was allowed to know when the ceremonial took place. Paris soon forgot its favourite. A few engravings of him, in one or two of his great characters, lingered for some time in the windows of the fashionable print-shops. Brief memoirs of him appeared in several papers, and in one or two magazines; and in a couple of weeks he was forgotten. If he had been a great general, or a great minister, it is possible that he would not have been remembered much longer. The new tenor had a fair complexion and blue eyes, and had two extra notes of falsetto. So the opera-house was as brilliant as ever, though there was for the time being a prejudice among opera-goers and opera-singers against Lucretia Borgia, and that opera was put on the shelf for the remainder of the season.

A month after the death of De Lancy the physician pronounced Mademoiselle de Cervennes sufficiently recovered to be removed from Paris to her uncle's château in Normandy. Her illness had been a terrible one. For many days she had been delirious. Ah, who shall paint the fearful dreams of that delirium!—dreams, of the anguish of which her disjointed sentences could tell so little? The face of the man she had loved had haunted her in every phase, wearing every expression—now thoughtful, now sparkling with vivacity, now cynical, now melancholy; but always distinct and palpable, and always before her night and day. The scene of her first meeting with him; her secret marriage; the little chapel a few miles out of Paris; the old priest; the bitter discovery in the Bois de Boulogne—the scene of his treachery; the lamp-lit apartment of Monsieur de Blurosset; the cards and the poisons. Every action of this dark period of her life she acted over in her disordered brain again and again a hundred times through the long day, and a hundred times more through the still longer night. So when at the expiration of a month, she was strong enough to walk from one room into another, it was but a wreck of his proud and lovely heiress which met her uncle's eyes.

The château of the marquis, some miles from the town of Caen,[1] was situated in a park which was as wild and uncultivated as a wood. A park full of old timber, and marshy reedy grounds dotted with pools of stagnant water, which in the good days of the old *régime* were beaten nightly by the submissive peasantry, that monseigneur, the marquis might sleep on his bedstead of ormolu and buhl à la Louis Quatorze,[2] undisturbed by the croaking of the frogs.

Everything around was falling into ruin; the château had been sacked, and one wing of it burnt down, in the year 1793; and the present marquis, then a very little boy, had fled with his father to the hospitable shores of England, where for more than twenty years of his life he had lived in poverty and obscurity, teaching sometimes his native language, sometimes mathematics, sometimes music, sometimes one thing, sometimes another, for his daily bread. But with the restoration of the Bourbons came the restoration of the marquis to title and fortune. A wealthy marriage with the widow of a rich Buonapartist restored the house of De Cevennes to its former grandeur; and looking now at the proud and stately head of that house, it was a difficult thing to imagine that this man had ever taught French, music, and mathematics, for a few shillings a lesson, in the obscure academics of an English manufacturing town.

The dreary park, which surrounded the still more dreary and tumble-down château, was white with the fallen snow, through which the servants, or their servants the neighbouring peasantry, coming backwards and forwards with some message or commission from the village, waded knee-deep, or well nigh lost themselves in some unsuspected hollow where the white drifts had swept and lay collected in masses whose depth was dangerous. The dark oak-panelled apartments appropriated to Valerie looked out upon the snow-clad wilderness; and very dismal they seemed in the dying February day.

Grim pictures of dead-and-gone branches of this haughty house stared and frowned from their heavy frames at the pale girl, half seated, half reclining in a great easy-chair in the deep embayed window. One terrible mail-clad baron, who had fought and fallen at disastrous Agincourt, held an uplifted axe, and in the evening shadow it seemed to Valerie as if he raised it with a threatening glance beneath his heavy brows, which took a purpose and a meaning as the painted eyes met hers. And turn which way she would, the eyes of these dark portraits seemed to follow her; sometimes threateningly, sometimes reproachfully, sometimes with a melancholy look fraught with a strange and ominous sadness that chilled her to the soul.

Logs of wood burned on the great hearth, supported by massive iron dogs, and their flickering light falling now here now there, left always the corners of the large room in shadow. The chill white night looking in at the high window strove with the firelight for mastery, and won it, so that the cheery beams playing bo-peep among the quaint oak carving of the panelled walls and ceiling hid themselves abashed before the chill stare of the cold steel-blue winter sky. The white face of the sick girl under this dismal light looked almost as still and lifeless as the face of her grandmother, in powder and patches, simpering down at her from the wall. She sat alone—no book near her, no sign of any womanly occupation in the great chamber, no friend to watch or tend her (for she had refused all companionship); she sat with listless hands drooping upon the velvet cushions of her chair, her head thrown back, as if in utter abandonment of all things on the face of the wide earth, and her dark eyes staring straight before her out into the dead waste of winter snow.

So she has sat since early morning; so she will sit till her maid comes to her and leads her to her dreary bedchamber. So she sits when her uncle visits her, and tries every means in his power to awaken a smile, or bring one look of animation into that dead face. Yes, it is the face of a dead woman. Dead to hope, dead to love, dead to the past; still more utterly dead to a future, which, since it cannot restore the dead, can give her nothing.

So the short February days, which seem so long to her, fade into the endless winter nights; and for her the morning has no light, nor the darkness any shelter. The consolations of that holy Church, on which for ages past her ancestors have leant for succour as on a rock of mighty and eternal strength, she dare not seek. Her uncle's chaplain, a white-haired old man who had nursed her in his arms a baby, and who resides at the château, beloved and honoured by all around, comes to her every morning, and on each visit tries anew to win her confidence; but in vain. How can she pour into the ears of this good and benevolent old man her dismal story? Surely he would cast her from him with contumely and horror. Surely he would tell her that for her there is no hope; that even a merciful Heaven, ready to hear the prayer of every sinner, would be deaf to the despairing cries of such a guilty wretch as she.

So, impenitent and despairing, she wears out the time, and waits for death. Sometimes she thinks of the arch tempter who smoothed the path of crime and misery in which she had trodden, and, who, in doing so seemed so much a part of herself, and so closely linked with her anguish and her revenge, that she often, in the weakness of her shattered mind, wondered if there were indeed such a person, or whether he might not be only the hideous incarnation of her own dark thoughts. He had spoken though of payment, of reward for his base services. If he were indeed human as her wretched self, why did he not come to claim his due?

———

As the lonely impenitent woman pondered thus in the wintry dusk, her uncle entered the chamber in which she sat.

"My dear Valerie," he said, "I am sorry to disturb you, but a person has just arrived on horseback from Caen. He has travelled, he says, all the way from Paris to see you, and he knows that you will grant him an interview. I told him it was not likely you would do so, and that you certainly would not with my consent. Who can this person be who has the impertinence to intrude at such a time as this? His name is entirely unknown to me."

He gave her a card. She looked at it, and read aloud—

" 'Monsieur Raymond Marolles.' The person is quite right, my dear uncle; I will see him."

"But, Valerie——!" remonstrated the marquis.

She looked at him, with her mother's proud Spanish blood mantling in her pale cheek.

"My dear uncle," she said quietly, "it is agreed between us, is it not, that I am in all things my own mistress, and that you have entire confidence in me? When you cease to trust me, we had better bid each other farewell, for we can then no longer live beneath the same roof."

He looked with one imploring glance at the inflexible face, but it was fixed as death.

"Tell them," she said, "to conduct Monsieur Marolles to this apartment. I must see him, and alone."

The marquis left her, and in a few moments Raymond entered the room, ushered in by the groom of the chambers.

He had the old air of well-bred and fashionable indifference which so well became him, and carried a light gold-headed riding-whip in his hand.

"Mademoiselle," he said, "will perhaps pardon my intrusion of this evening, which can scarcely surprise her, if she will be pleased to remember that more than a month has elapsed since a melancholy occurrence at the Royal Italian Opera House, and that I have some right to be impatient."

She did not answer him immediately; for at this moment a servant entered, carrying a lamp, which he placed on the table by her side, and afterwards drew the heavy velvet curtains across the great window, shutting out the chill winter night.

"You are very much altered, mademoiselle," said Raymond, as he scrutinized the wan face under the lamp-light.

"That is scarcely strange," she answered, in a chilling tone. "I am not yet accustomed to crime, and cannot wear the memory of it lightly."

Her visitor was dusting his polished riding-boot with his handkerchief as he spoke. Looking up with a smile, he said,—

"Nay, mademoiselle, I give you credit for more philosophy. Why use ugly words? Crime—poison—murder!" He paused between each of these three words, as if every syllable had been some sharp instrument—as if every time he spoke he stabbed her to the heart and stopped to calculate the depth of the wound. "There are no such words as those for beauty and high rank. A person far removed from our sphere offends us, and we sweep him from our path. We might as well regret the venomous insect which, having stung us, we destroy."

She did not acknowledge his words by so much as one glance or gesture, but said coldly,—

"You were so candid as to confess, monsieur, when you served me, yonder in Paris, that you did so in the expectation of a reward. You are here, no doubt, to claim that reward?"

He looked up at her with so strange a light in his blue eyes, and so singular a smile curving the dark moustache which hid his thin arched lips, that in spite of herself she was startled into looking at him anxiously. He was determined that in the game they were playing she should hold no hidden cards, and he was therefore resolved to see her face stripped of its mask of cold indifference. After a minute's pause he answered her question,—

"I am."

"It is well, monsieur. Will you be good enough to state the amount you claim for your *services?*"

"You are determined, mademoiselle, it appears," he said, with the strange light still glittering in his eyes, "you are determined to give me credit for none but the most mercenary sentiments. Suppose I do not claim any amount of money in repayment of my services?"

"Then, monsieur, I have wronged you. You are a disinterested villain, and, as such, worthy of the respect of the wicked. But since this is the case, our interview is at end. I am sorry you decline the reward you have earned so worthily, and I have the honour to wish you good evening."

He gave a low musical laugh. "Pardon me, mademoiselle," he said, "but really your words amuse me. 'A disinterested villain!' Believe me, when I tell you that disinterested villany is as great an impossibility as disinterested virtue. You are mistaken, mademoiselle, but only as to the nature of the reward I come to claim. You would confine the question to one of money. Cannot you imagine that I have acted in the hope of a higher reward than any recompense your banker's book could afford me?"

She looked at him with a puzzled expression, but his face was hidden. He was trifling with his light riding-whip, and looking down at the hearth. After a minute's pause he lifted his head, and glanced at her with the same dangerous smile.

"You cannot guess, then, mademoiselle, the price I claim for my services yonder?" he asked.

"No."

"Nay, mademoiselle, reflect."

"It would be useless. I might anticipate your claiming half my fortune, as I am, in a manner, in your power——"

"Oh, yes," he murmured softly, interrupting her, "you are, in a manner, in my power certainly."

"But the possibility of your claiming from me anything except money has never for a moment occurred to me."

"Mademoiselle, when first I saw you I looked at you through an opera-glass from my place in the stalls of the Italian Opera. The glass, mademoiselle, was an excellent one, for it revealed every line and every change in your beautiful face. From my observation of that face I made two or three conclusions about your character, which I now find were not made upon false premises. You are impulsive, mademoiselle, but you are not far-seeing. You are strong in your resolutions when once your mind is fixed; but that mind is easily influenced by others. You have passion, genius, courage—rare and beautiful gifts which distinguish you from the rest of womankind; but you have not that power of calculation, that inductive science, which never sees the effect without looking for the cause, which men have christened mathematics. I, mademoiselle, am a mathematician. As such, I sat down to play a deep and dangerous game with you; and as such, now that the hour has come at which I can show my hand, you will see that I hold the winning cards."

"I cannot understand, monsieur——"

"Perhaps not, yet. When you first honoured me with an interview you were pleased to call me 'an adventurer.' You used the expression as a term of reproach. Strange to say, I never held it in that light. When it pleased Heaven, or Fate—whichever name you please to give the abstraction—to throw me out upon a world with which my life has been one long war, it pleased that Power to give me nothing but my brains for weapons in the great fight. No rank, no rent-roll, neither mother nor father, friend nor patron. All to win, and nothing to lose. How much I had won when I first saw you it would be hard for you, born in those great saloons to which I have struggled from the mire of the streets—it would be very hard, I say, for you to guess. I entered Paris one year ago, possessed of a sum of money which to me was wealth, but which might, perhaps, to you, be a month's income. I had only one object—to multiply that sum a hundredfold. I became, therefore, a speculator, or, as you call it, 'an adventurer.' As a speculator, I took my seat in the stalls of the Opera House the night I first saw you."

She looked at him in utter bewilderment, as he sat in his most careless attitude, playing with the gold handle of his riding-whip, but she did not attempt to speak, and he continued,—

"I happened to hear from a bystander that you were the richest woman in France. Do you know, mademoiselle, how an adventurer, with a tolerably handsome face and a sufficiently gentlemanly address, generally calculates on enriching himself? Or, if you do not know, can you guess?"

"No," she muttered, looking at him now as if she were in a trance, and he had some strange magnetic power over her.

"Then, mademoiselle, I must enlighten you. The adventurer who does not care to grow grey and decrepit in making a fortune by that slow and uncertain mode which people call 'honest industry,' looks about him for a fortune ready made and waiting for him to claim it. He makes a wealthy marriage."

"A wealthy marriage?" She repeated the words after him, as if mechanically.

"Therefore, mademoiselle, on seeing you, and on hearing the extent of your fortune, I said to myself, 'That is the woman I must marry!'"

"Monsieur!" She started indignantly from her reclining attitude; but the effort was too much for her shattered frame, and she sank back exhausted.

"Nay, mademoiselle, I did not say 'That is the woman I will marry,' but rather, 'That is the woman I must try to marry;' for as yet, remember, I did not hold one card in the great game I had to play. I raised my glass, and looked long at your face. A very beautiful face, mademoiselle, as you and your glass have long decided between you. I was—pardon me—disappointed. Had you been an ugly woman, my chances would have been so much better. Had you been disfigured by a hump—(if it had been but the faintest elevation of one white shoulder, prouder, perhaps, than its fellow)—had your hair been tinged with even a suspicion of the ardent hue which prejudice condemns,[3] it would have been a wonderful advantage to me. Vain hope to win you by flattery, when even the truth must sound like flattery. And then, again, one glance told me that you were no pretty simpleton, to be won by a stratagem, or bewildered by romantic speeches. And yet, mademoiselle, I did not despair. You were beautiful; you were impassioned. In your veins ran the purple blood of a nation whose children's love and hate are both akin to madness! You had, in short, a soul, and you might have a secret!"

"Monsieur!"

"At any rate it would be no lost time to watch you. I therefore watched. Two or three gentlemen were talking to you; you did not listen to them; you were asked the same question three times, and on the second repetition of it you started, and replied as by an effort. You were weary, or indifferent. Now, as I have told you, mademoiselle, in the science of mathematics we acknowledge no effect without a cause; there was a cause, then, for this distraction on your part. In a few minutes the curtain rose. You were no longer absent-minded. Elvino came on the stage—you were all attention. You tried, mademoiselle, not to appear attentive; but your mouth, the most flexible feature in your face, betrayed you. The cause, then, of your late distraction was Elvino, otherwise the fashionable tenor, Gaston de Lancy."

"Monsieur, for pity's sake——" she cried imploringly.

"This was card number one. My chances were looking up. In a few minutes I saw you throw your bouquet on the stage. I also saw the note. You had a secret, mademoiselle, and I possessed the clue to it. My cards were good ones. The rest must be done by good play. I knew I was no bad player, and I sat down to the game with the determination to rise a winner."

"Finish the recital of your villany, monsieur, I beg—it really becomes wearisome." She tried as she spoke to imitate his own indifference of manner; but she was utterly subdued and broken down,

and waited for him to continue as the victim might wait the pleasure of the executioner, and with as little thought of opposing him.

"Then, mademoiselle, I have little more to say, except to claim
my reward. That reward is—your hand." He said this as if he never
even dreamt of the possibility of a refusal.

"Are you mad, monsieur?" She had for some time anticipated this
climax, and she felt how utterly powerless she was in the hands of an
unscrupulous villain. How unscrupulous she did not yet know.

"Nay, mademoiselle, remember! A man has been poisoned. Easy
enough to set suspicion, which has already pointed to foul play,
more fully at work. Easy enough to prove a certain secret marriage,
a certain midnight visit to that renowned and not too highly-
respected chemist, Monsieur Blurosset. Easy enough to produce
the order for five thousand francs signed by Mademoiselle de
Cevennes. And should these proofs not carry with them conviction,
I am the fortunate possessor of a wine-glass emblazoned with the
arms of your house, in which still remains the sediment of a poison
well known to the more distinguished members of the medical science. I think, mademoiselle, these few evidences, added to the powerful motive revealed by your secret marriage, would be quite
sufficient to set every newspaper in France busy with the details of
a murder unprecedented in the criminal annals of this country. But,
mademoiselle, I have wearied you; you are pale, exhausted. I have
no wish to hurry you into a rash acceptance of my offer. Think of
it, and to-morrow let me hear your decision. Till then, adieu." He
rose as he spoke.

She bowed her head in assent to his last proposition, and he left
her.

Did he know, or did he guess, that there might be another reason
to render her acceptance of his hand possible? Did he think that
even his obscure name might be a shelter to her in days to come?

O Valerie, Valerie, for ever haunted by the one beloved creature
gone out of this world never to return! For ever pursued by the
image of the love which never was—which at its best and brightest
was—but a false dream. Most treacherous when most tender, most

cruel when most kind, most completely false when it most seemed a holy truth. Weep, Valerie, for the long years to come, whose dismal burden shall for ever be, "Oh, never, never more!"

CHAPTER IX

A MARRIAGE IN HIGH LIFE

A month from the time at which this interview took place, everyone worth speaking of in Paris is busy talking of a singular marriage about to be celebrated in that smaller and upper circle which forms the apex of the fashionable pyramid. The niece and heiress of the Marquis de Cevennes is about to marry a gentleman of whom the Faubourg St. Germain[1] knows very little. But though the faubourg knows very little, the faubourg has, notwithstanding, a great deal to say; perhaps all the more from the very slight foundation it has for its assertions. Thus, on Tuesday the faubourg affirms that Monsieur Raymond Marolles is a German, and a political refugee. On Wednesday the faubourg rescinds: he is not a German, he is a Frenchman, the son of an illegitimate son of Philip Egalité,[2] and, consequently, nephew to the king, by whose influence the marriage has been negotiated. The faubourg, in short, has so many accounts of Monsieur Raymond Marolles, that it is quite unnecessary for the Marquis de Cevennes to give any account of him whatever, and he alone, therefore, is silent on the subject. Monsieur Marolles is a very worthy man—a gentleman, of course—and his niece is very much attached to him; beyond this, the marquis does not condescend to enlighten his numerous acquaintance. How much more might the faubourg have to say if it could for one moment imagine the details of a stormy scene which took place between the uncle and niece at the château in Normandy, when, kneeling before the cross, Valerie swore that there was so dreadful a reason for this strange marriage, that, did her uncle know it, he would himself kneel at her feet and implore her to sacrifice herself to save the honour of her noble house. What might have been suggested to the mind of the marquis by these dark hints no one knew; but he ceased to oppose the marriage of the only scion of one of the highest families in France with a man who could tell nothing of himself, except that he had received the education of a gentleman, and had a will strong enough to conquer fortune.

The religious solemnization of the marriage was performed with great magnificence at the Madeleine.³ Wealth, rank, and fashion were equally represented at the *dejeûner* which succeeded the ceremonial, and Monsieur Marolles found himself the centre of a circle of the old nobility of France. It would have been very difficult, even for an attentive observer, to discover one triumphant flash in those light blue eyes, or one smile playing round the thin lips, by which a stranger might divine that the bridegroom of to-day was the winner of a deep-laid and villainous scheme. He bore his good fortune, in fact, with such well-bred indifference, that the faubourg immediately set him down as a great man, even if not one of the set which was the seventh heaven in that Parisian paradise. And it would have been equally difficult for any observer to read the secret of the pale but beautiful face of the bride. Cold, serene, and haughty, she smiled a stereotyped smile upon all, and showed no more agitation during the ceremony than she might have done had she been personating a bride in an acted charade.

It may be, that the hour when any event, however startling, however painful, could move her from this cold serenity, had for ever passed away. It may be, that having outlived all the happiness of her life, she had almost outlived the faculty of feeling or of suffering, and must henceforth exist only for the world—a distinguished actress in the great comedy of fashionable life.

She is standing in a window filled with exotics, which form a great screen of dark green leaves and tropical flowers, through which the blue spring sky looks in, clear, bright, and cold. She is talking to an elderly duchess, a languid and rather faded personage, dressed in ruby velvet, and equally distinguished for the magnificence of her lace and the artful composition of her complexion, which is as near an approach to nature as can be achieved by pearl-powder. "And you leave France in a month, to take possession of your estates in South America?" she asks.

"In a month, yes," says Valerie, playing with the large dark leaf of a magnolia. "I am anxious to see my mother's native country. I am tired of Paris."

"Really? You surprise me!" The languid duchess cannot conceive the possibility of any one being tired of a Parisian existence. She is deep in her thirty-fourth platonic attachment—the object, a celebrated novelist of the transcendental school; and as at this moment she sees him entering the room by a distant door, she strolls away from the window, carrying her perfumed complexion through the delighted crowd.

———

Perhaps Monsieur Raymond Marolles, standing talking to an old Buonapartist general, whose breast is one constellation of stars and crosses, had only been waiting for this opportunity, for he advanced presently with soft step and graceful carriage towards the ottoman on which his bride had seated herself. She was trifling with her costly bridal bouquet as the bridegroom approached her, plucking the perfumed petals one by one, and scattering them on the ground at her feet in very wantonness.

"Valerie," he said, bending over her, and speaking in tones which, by reason of the softness of their intonation, might have been tender, but for the want of some diviner melody from within the soul of the man; not having which, they had the false jingle of a spurious coin.

The spot in which the bride was seated was so sheltered by the flowers and the satin hangings which shrouded the window, that it formed a little alcove, shut out from the crowded room.

"Valerie!" he repeated; and finding that she did not answer, he laid his white ungloved hand upon her jewelled wrist.

She started to her feet, drawing herself up to her fullest height, and shaking off his hand with a gesture which, had he been the foulest and most loathsome reptile crawling upon the earth's wide face, could not have bespoken a more intense abhorrence.

"There could not be a better time than this," she said, "to say what I have to say. You may perhaps imagine that to be compelled to speak to you at all is so abhorrent to me, that I shall use the fewest words I can, and use those words in their very fullest sense. You are the incarnation of misery and crime. As such you can perhaps understand how deeply I hate you. You are a villain; and so mean and despicable a villain, that even in the hour of your success you are a creature to be pitied; since from the very depth of your degradation you lack the power to know how much you are degraded! As such I scorn and loathe you, as we loathe those venemous reptiles which, from their noxious qualities, defy our power to handle and exterminate them."

"And as your husband, madame?" Her bitter words discomposed him so little, that he stooped to pick up a costly flower which in her passion she had thrown down, and placed it carefully in his button-hole. "As your husband, madame? The state of your feelings towards me in that character is perhaps a question more to the point."

"You are right," she said, casting all assumption of indifference aside, and trembling with scornful rage. "That is the question. Your speculation has been a successful one."

"Entirely successful," he replied, still arranging the flower in his coat.

"You have the command of my fortune——"

"A fortune which many princes might be proud to possess," he interposed, looking at the blossom, not at her. He may possibly have been a brave man, but he was not distinguished for looking in people's faces, and he did not care about meeting her eyes to-day.

"But if you think the words whose sacred import has been prostituted by us this day have any meaning for you or me; if you think there is a lacquey or a groom in this vast city, a ragged mendicant standing at a church-door whom I would not sooner call my husband than the wretch who stands beside me now, you neither know me nor my sex. My fortune you are welcome to. Take it, squander it, scatter it to the winds, spend it to the last farthing on the low vices that are pleasure to such men as you. But dare to address me with but one word from your false lips, dare to approach me so near as to touch but the hem of my dress, and that moment I proclaim the story of our marriage from first to last. Believe me when I say—and if you look me in the face you will believe me—the restraining influence is very slight that holds me back from standing now in the centre of this assembly to proclaim myself a vile and cruel murderess, and you my tempter and accomplice. Believe me when I tell you that it needs but one look of yours to provoke me to blazon this hideous secret, and cry its details in the very market-place. Believe this, and rest contented with the wages of your work."

Exhausted by her passion, she sank into her seat. Raymond looked at her with a supercilious sneer. He despised her for this sudden outbreak of rage and hatred, for he felt how much his calculating brain and icy temperament made him her superior.

"You are somewhat hasty, madame, in your conclusions. Who said I was discontented with the wages of my work, when for those wages alone I have played the game in which, as you say, I am the conqueror? For the rest, I do not think I am the man to break my heart for love of any woman breathing, as I never quite understood what this same weakness of the brain, which men have christened love, really is; and even were the light of dark eyes necessary to my happiness, I need scarcely tell you, madame, that beauty is very indulgent to a man with such a fortune as I am master of to-day. There is nothing on earth to prevent our agreeing remarkably well; and perhaps this marriage, which you speak of so bitterly, may be as happy as many other unions, which, were I Asmodeus[4] and you my pupil, we could look down on to-day through the housetops of this good city of Paris."

I wonder whether Monsieur Marolles was right? I wonder whether this thrice-sacred sacrament, ordained by an Almighty Power for the glory and the happiness of the earth, is ever, by any chance, profaned and changed into a bitter mockery or a wicked lie? Whether, by any hazard, these holy words were ever used in any dark hour of this world's history, to join such people as had been happier far asunder, though they had been parted in their graves; or whether, indeed, this solemn ceremonial has not so often united such people, with a chain no time has power to wear or lengthen, that it has at last, unto some ill-directed minds, sunk to the level of a pitiful and worn-out farce?

CHAPTER X

ANIMAL MAGNETISM[1]

Nearly a month has passed since this strange marriage, and Monsieur Blurosset is seated at his little green-covered table, the lamplight falling full upon the outspread pack of cards, over which the blue spectacles bend with the same intent and concentrated gaze as on the night when the fate of Valerie hung on the lips of the professor of chemistry and pasteboard. Every now and then, with light and careful fingers, Monsieur Blurosset changes the position of some card or cards. Sometimes he throws himself back in his chair and thinks deeply. The expressionless mouth, which betrays no secrets, tells nothing of the nature of his thoughts. Sometimes he makes notes on a long slip of paper; rows of figures, and problems in algebra, over which he ponders long. By-and-by, for the first time, he looks up and listens.

His little apartment has two doors. One, which leads out on to the staircase; a second, which communicates with his bedchamber. This door is open a very little, but enough to show that there is a feeble light burning within the chamber. It is in the direction of this door that the blue spectacles are fixed when Monsieur Blurosset suspends his calculations in order to listen; and it is to a sound within this room that he listens intently.

That sound is the laboured and heavy breathing of a man. The room is tenanted.

"Good," says Monsieur Blurosset, presently, "the respiration is certainly more regular. It is really a most wonderful case."

As he says this, he looks at his watch. "Five minutes past eleven—time for the dose," he mutters.

He goes to the little cabinet from which he took the drug he gave to Valerie, and busies himself with some bottles, from which he mixes a draught in a small medicine-glass; he holds it to the light, puts it to his lips, and then passes with it into the next room.

There is a sound as if the person to whom he gave the medicine made some faint resistance, but in a few minutes Monsieur Blurosset emerges from the room carrying the empty glass.

He reseats himself before the green table, and resumes his contemplation of the cards. Presently a bell rings. "So late," mutters Monsieur Blurosset; "it is most likely some one for me." He rises, sweeps the cards into one pack, and going over to the door of his bedroom, shuts its softly. When he has done so, he listens for a moment with his ear close to the woodwork. There is not a sound of the breathing within.

He has scarcely done so when the bell rings for the second time. He opens the door communicating with the staircase, and admits a visitor. The visitor is a woman, very plainly dressed, and thickly veiled.

"Monsieur Blurosset?" she says, inquiringly.

"The same, madame. Pray enter, and be good enough to be seated." He hands her a chair at a little distance from the green table, and as far away as he can place it from the door of the bedchamber: she sits down, and as he appears to wait for her to speak, she says,—

"I have heard of your fame, monsieur, and come——"

"Nay, madame," he says, interrupting her, "you can raise your veil if you will. I perfectly remember you; I never forget voices, Mademoiselle de Cevennes."

There is no shade of impertinence in his manner as he says this; he speaks as though he were merely stating a simple fact which it is as well for her to know. He has the air, in all he does or says, of a scientific man who has no existence out of the region of science.

Valerie—for it is indeed she—raises her veil.

"Monsieur," she says, "you are candid with me, and it will be the best for me to be frank with you. I am very unhappy—I have been so for some months past; and I shall be so until my dying day. One reason alone has prevented my coming to you long ere this, to offer you half my fortune for such another drug as that which you sold to me some time past. You may judge, then, that reason is a very powerful one, since, though death alone can give me peace, I yet do not wish to die. But I wish to have at my command a means of certain death. I may never use it at all: I swear never to use it on anyone but myself!"

All this time the blue spectacles have been fixed on her face, and now Monsieur Blurosset interrupts her—

"And now for such a drug, mademoiselle, you would offer me a large sum of money?" he asks.

"I would, monsieur."

"I cannot sell it you," he says, as quietly as though he were speaking of some unimportant trifle.

"You cannot?" she exclaims.

"No, mademoiselle. I am a man absorbed entirely in the pursuit of science. My life has been so long devoted to science only, that perhaps I may have come to hold everything beyond the circle of my little laboratory too lightly. You asked me some time since for a poison, or at least you were introduced to me by a pupil of mine, at whose request I sold you a drug. I had been twenty years studying the properties of that drug. I may not know them fully yet, but I expect to do so before this year is out. I gave it to you, and, for all I know to the contrary, it may in your hands have done some mischief." He pauses here and looks at her for a moment; but she has borne the knowledge of her crime so long, and it has become so much a part of her, that she does not flinch under his scrutiny.

"I placed a weapon in your hands," he continues, "and I had no right to do so. I never thought of this at that time; but I have thought of it since. For the rest, I have no inducement to sell you the drug you ask for. Money is of little use to me except in the necessary expenses of the chemicals I use. These"—he points to the cards—"give me enough for those expenses; beyond those, my wants amount to some few francs a week."

"Then you will not sell me this drug? You are determined?" she asks.

"Quite determined."

She shrugs her shoulders. "As you please. There is always some river within reach of the wretched; and you may depend, monsieur, that they who cannot support life will find a means of death. I will wish you good evening."

She is about to leave the room, when she stops, with her hand upon the lock of the door, and turns round.

She stands for a few minutes motionless and silent, holding the handle of the door, and with her other hand upon her heart. Monsieur Blurosset has the faintest shadow of a look of surprise in his expressionless countenance.

"I don't know what is the matter with me to-night," she says, "but something seems to root me to this spot. I cannot leave this room."

"You are ill, mademoiselle, perhaps. Let me give you some restorative."

"No, no, I am not ill."

Again she is silent; her eyes are fixed, not on the chemist, but with a strange vacant gaze upon the wall before her. Suddenly she asks him,—

"Do you believe in animal magnetism?"

"Madame, I have spent half my lifetime in trying to answer that question, and I can only answer it now by halves. Sometimes no; sometimes yes."

"Do you believe it possible for one soul to be gifted with a mysterious prescience of the emotions of another soul?—to be sad when that is sad, though utterly unconscious of any cause for sadness; and to rejoice when that is happy, having no reason for rejoicing?"

"I cannot answer your question, madame, because it involves another. I never yet have discovered what the soul really is. Animal magnetism, if it ever become a science, will be a material science, and the soul escapes from all material dissection."

"Do you believe, then, that by some subtle influence, whose nature is unknown to us, we may have a strange consciousness of the presence or the approach of some people, conveyed to us by neither the hearing nor the sight, but rather as if we *felt* that they were near?"

"*You* believe this possible, madame, or you would not ask the question."

"Perhaps. I have sometimes thought that I had this consciousness; but it related to a person who is dead——"

"Yes, madame."

"And—you will think me mad; Heaven knows, I think myself so—I feel as if that person were near me to-night."

The chemist rises, and, going over to her, feels her pulse. It is rapid and intermittent. She is evidently violently agitated, though she is trying with her utmost power to control herself.

"But you say that this person is dead?" he asks.

"Yes; he died some months since."

"You know that there are no such things as ghosts?"

"I am perfectly convinced of that!"

"And yet—?" he asks.

"And yet I feel as though the dead were near me to-night. Tell me—there is no one in this room but ourselves?"

"No one."

"And that door—it leads——"

"Into the room in which I sleep."

"And there is no one there?" she asks.

"No one. Let me give you a sedative, madame: you are certainly ill."

"No, no, monsieur; you are very good. I am still weak from the effects of a long illness. That weakness may be the cause of my silly fancies of to-night. To-morrow I leave France, perhaps for ever."

She leaves him; but on the steep dark staircase she pauses for a moment, and seems irresolute, as if half determined to return: then she hurries on, and in a minute is in the street.

She takes a circuitous route towards the house in which she lives. So plainly dressed, and thickly veiled, no one stops to notice her as she walks along.

Her husband, Monsieur Marolles, is engaged at a dinner given by a distinguished member of the chamber of peers. Decidedly he has held winning cards in the game of life. And she, for ever haunted by the past, with weary step goes onward to a dark and un-known future.

BOOK THE FOURTH

NAPOLEON THE GREAT

THE BOY FROM SLOPPERTON

Eight years have passed since the trial of Richard Marwood. How have those eight years been spent by "Daredevil Dick"?

In a small room a few feet square, in the County Lunatic Asylum, fourteen miles from the town of Slopperton, with no human being's companionship but that of a grumpy old deaf keeper, and a boy, his assistant—for eight monotonous years this man's existence has crept slowly on; always the same: the same food, the same hours at which that food must be eaten, the same rules and regulations for every action of his inactive life. Think of this, and pity the man surnamed "Daredevil Dick," and once the maddest and merriest creature in a mad and merry circle. Think of the daily walk in a great square flagged yard—the solitary walk, for he is not allowed even the fellowship of the other lunatics, lest the madness which led him to commit an awful crime should again break out, and endanger the lives of those about him. During eight long years he has counted every stone in the flooring, every flaw and every crack in each of those stones. He knows the shape of every shadow that falls upon the whitewashed wall, and can, at all seasons of the year, tell the hour by the falling of it. He knows that at such a time on a summer's evening the shadows of the iron bars of the window will make long black lines across the ground, and mount and mount, dividing the wall as if it were in panels, till they meet, and absorbing altogether the declining light, surround and absorb him too, till he is once more alone in the darkness. He knows, too, that at such a time on the grey winter's morning these same shadows will be the first indications of the coming light; that, from the thick gloom of the dead night they will break out upon the wall, with strips of glimmering day between, only enough like light to show the blackness of the shade. He has sometimes been mad enough and wretched enough to pray that these shadows might fall differently, that the very order of nature might be reversed, to break this bitter and deadly monotony. He has sometimes prayed that, looking up, he might see a great fire in the sky, and know that the world was at an end. How often he has prayed to die, it would be difficult to say. At one time it was his only prayer; at one time he did not pray at all. He has been permitted at intervals to see his mother; but her visits, though he has counted the days, hours, and even minutes between them, have only left him more despondent than ever. She brings so much with her into his lonely prison, so much memory of a joyous past, of freedom, of a happy home, whose happiness he did his best in his wild youth to destroy; the memory, too, of that careless youth, its boon companions, its devoted friends. She brings so much of all this back to him by the mere fact of her presence, that she leaves behind her the blackness of a despair far more terrible than the most terrible death. She represents to him the outer world; for she is the only creature belonging to it who ever crosses the threshold of his prison. The asylum chaplain, the asylum doctor, the keepers and the officials belonging to the asylum—all these are part and parcel of this great prison-house of stone, brick, and mortar, and seem to be about as capable of feeling for him, listening to him, or understanding him, as the stones, bricks, and mortar themselves. Routine is the ruler of this great prison; and if this wretched insane criminal cannot live by rules and regulations, he must die according to them, and be buried by them, and so be done with, out of the way; and his little room, No. 35, will be ready for some one else, as wicked, as dangerous, and as unfortunate as he.

During the earlier part of his imprisonment the idea had pervaded the asylum that as he had been found guilty of committing one murder, he might, very likely, find it necessary to his peculiar state of mind to commit more murders, and would probably find it soothing to his feelings to assassinate anybody who might come in his way any morning before breakfast. The watch kept upon him was therefore for some time very strict. He was rather popular at first in the asylum, as a distinguished public character; and the keepers, though a little shy of attending upon him in their proper persons, were extremely fond of peering in at him through a little oval opening in the upper panel of the door of his cell. They also brought such visitors as came to improve their minds by going over the hospital for the insane to have a special and private view of this maniacal murderer; and they generally received an extra donation from the sight-seers thus gratified. Even the lunatics themselves were interested in the supposed assassin. A gentleman, who claimed to be the Emperor of the German Ocean and the Chelsea Waterworks, was very anxious to see him, as he had received a despatch from his minister of police informing him that Richard Marwood had red hair, and he particularly wished to confirm this intelligence, or to give the minister his *congé*.[1]

Another highly-respectable person, whose case was before the House of Commons, and who took minutes of it every day on a slate, with a bit of slate pencil which he wore attached to his button-hole by a string, and which also served him as a toothpick—the slate being intrusted to a keeper who forwarded it to the electric tele-graph, to be laid on the table of the House, and brought home, washed clean, in half an hour, which was always done to the minute;—this gentleman also sighed for an introduction to poor Dick, for Maria Martin had come to him in a vision all the way from the Red Barn,[2] to tell him that the prisoner was his first cousin, through the marriage of his uncle with the third daughter of Henry the Eighth's seventh wife;[3] and he considered it only natural and proper that such near relations should become intimately ac-quainted with each other.

A lady, who pronounced herself to be the only child of the Pope of Rome, by a secret union with a highly-respectable youngperson, heiress to a gentleman connected with the muffin trade somewhere about Drury Lane, fell in love off-hand with Richard, from de-scription alone; and begged one of the keepers to let him know that she had a clue to a subterranean passage, which led straight from the asylum to a baker's shop in Little Russell Street, Covent Gar-den, a distance of some two hundred and fifty miles, and had been originally constructed by William the Conqueror[4] for the convenience of his visits to Fair Rosamond[5] when the weather was bad. The lady begged her messenger to inform Mr. Marwood that if he liked to unite his fortune with hers, they could escape by this passage, and set up in the muffin business—unless, indeed, his Holiness of the triple crown invited them over to the Vatican, which perhaps, under existing circumstances, was hardly likely.

But though a wonder, which elsewhere would only last nine days, may in the dreary monotony of such a place as this, endure for more than nine weeks, it must still die out at last. So at last Richard was forgotten by every one except his heartbroken mother, and the keeper and boy attending upon him.

His peculiar hallucination being his fancy that he was the Emperor Napoleon the First,[6] was, of course, little wonder in a place where every wretched creature fancied himself some one or something which he was not; where men and women walked about in long disjointed dreams, which had no waking but in death; where once bright and gifted human beings found a wild and imbecile happiness in crowns of straw, and decorations of paper and rags; which was more sad to see than the worst misery a consciousness of their state might have brought them. At first, Richard had talked wildly of his fancied greatness, had called his little room the rock of St. Helena,[7] and his keeper, Sir Hudson Lowe.[8] But he grew quieter day by day, and at last never spoke at all, except in answer to a question. And so on, for eight long years.

In the autumn of the eighth year he fell ill. A strange illness. Perhaps scarcely to be called an illness. Rather a dying out of the last light of hope, and an utter abandonment of himself to despair. Yes, that was the name of the disease under which the high and bold spirit of Daredevil Dick sank at last. Despair. A curious disease. Not to be cured by rules and regulations, however salutary those rules might be; not to be cured even by the Board, which was supposed to be in a manner omnipotent, and to be able to cure anything in one sitting; not to be cured certainly by the asylum doctor, who found Richard's case very difficult to deal with—more especially difficult since there was no positive physical malady to attack. There was a physical malady, because the patient grew every day weaker, lost appetite, and was compelled to take to his bed; but it was the malady of the mind acting on the body, and the cure of the last could only be effected by the cure of the first.

So Richard lay upon his narrow little couch, watching the shadows on the bare wall, and the clouds that passed across the patch of sky which he could see through the barred window opposite his bed, through long sunny days, and moonlight nights, throughout the month of September.

Thus it happened that one dull afternoon, on looking up, he saw a darker cloud than usual hurry by; and in its train another, darker still; then a black troop of ragged followers; and then such a shower of rain came down, as he could not remember having seen throughout the time of his captivity. But this heavy shower was only the beginning of three weeks' rainy weather; at the end of which time the country round was flooded in every direction, and Richard heard his keeper tell another man that the river outside the prison, which usually ran within twenty feet of the wall on one side of the great yard, was now swollen to such a degree as to wash the stonework of this wall for a considerable height.

The day Richard heard this he heard another dialogue, which took place in the passage outside his room. He was lying on his bed, thinking of the bitterness of his fate, as he had thought so many hundred times, through so many hundred days, till he had become, as it were, the slave of a dreadful habit of his mind, and was obliged to go over the same ground for ever and ever, whether he would or no—he was lying thus, when he heard his keeper say,—

"To think as how the discontented little beast should take and go and better hisself at such a time as this here, when there ain't a boy to be had for love or money—which three shillings a week is all the Board will give—as will come here to take care of him."

Richard knew himself to be the "him" alluded to. The doctor had ordered the boy to sit up with him at night during the latter part of his illness, and it had been something of a relief to him, in the blank monotony of his life, to watch this boy's attempts to keep awake, and his furtive games at marbles under the bed when he thought Richard was not looking, or to listen to his snoring when he slept.

"You see, boys as is as bold as brass many ways—as would run under 'osses' heads, and like it; as thinks it fun to run across the railroad when there's a *h*express *h*engine a-comin', and as will amuse theirselves for the hour together with twopen'orth of gunpowder and a lighted candle—still feels timersome about sittin' up alone of nights with him," said the keeper.

"But he's harmless enough, ain't he?" asked the other.

"Harmless! Lord bless his poor hinnercent 'art! there ain't no more harm in him nor a baby. But it's no use a sayin' that, for there ain't a boy far or near what'll come and help to take care of him."

A minute or two after this, the keeper came into Richard's room with the regulation basin of broth—a panacea, as it was supposed, for all ills, from water on the brain[9] to rheumatism. As he put the basin down, and was about to go, Richard spoke to him,—

"The boy is going, then?"

"Yes, sir." The keeper treated him with great respect, for he had been handsomely feed by Mrs. Marwood on every visit throughout the eight years of her son's imprisonment. "Yes, he's a-goin', sir. The place ain't lively enough for him, if you please. I'd lively him, if I was the Board! Ain't he had the run of the passages, and half an hour every night to enjoy hisself in the yard! He's a-goin' into a doctor's service. He says it'll be jolly, carring out medicine for other people to take, and gloating over the thought of 'em a-taking it."

"And you can't get another boy to come here?"

"Well, you see, sir, the boys about here don't seem to take kindly to the place. So I've got orders from the Board to put an advertisement in one of the Slopperton papers; and I'm a-goin' to do it this afternoon. So you'll have a change in your attendance, maybe, sir, before the week's out."

Nothing could better prove the utter dreariness and desolation of Richard's life than that such a thing as the probable arrival of a strange boy to wait upon him seemed an event of importance. He could not help, though he despised himself for his folly, speculating upon the possible appearance of the new boy. Would he be big or little, stout or thin? What would be the colour of his eyes and hair? Would his voice be gruff or squeaky; or would it be that peculiar and uncertain voice, common to over-grown boys, which is gruff one minute and squeaky the next, and always is in one of these extremes when you most expect it to be in the other?

But these speculations were of course a part of his madness; for it is not to be supposed that a long course of solitary confinement could produce any dreadful change in the mind of a sane man; or surely no human justices or lawgivers would ever adjudge so terrible a punishment to any creature, human as themselves, and no more liable to error than themselves.

—

So Richard, lying on his little bed through the long rainy days, awaits the departure of his old attendant and the coming of a new one; and in the twilight of the third day he still lies looking up at the square grated window, and counting the drops falling from the eaves—for there is at last some cessation in the violence of the rain. He knows it is an autumn evening; but he has not seen the golden red of one fallen leaf, or the subdued colouring of one autumnal flower: he knows it is the end of September, because his keeper has told him so; and when his window is open, he can hear sometimes, far away, deadened by the rainy atmosphere as well as by the distance, the occasional report of some sportsman's gun. He thinks, as he hears this, of a September many years ago, when he and a scapegrace companion took a fortnight's shooting in a country where to brush against a bush, or to tread upon the long grass, was to send a feathered creature whirring up in the clear air. He remembers the merry pedestrian journey, the roadside inns, the pretty barmaids, the joint purse; the blue smoke from two short meerschaum[10] pipes curling up to the grey morning sky; the merry laughter from two happy hearts ringing out upon the chill morning air. He remembers encounters with savage gamekeepers, of such ferocious principle and tender consciences as even the administration of a half-crown could not lull to sleep; he remembers jovial evenings in the great kitchens of old inns, where unknown quantities of good old ale were drunk, and comic songs were sung, with such a chorus, that to join in it was to be overcome by such fatigue, or to be reduced from wildest mirth to such a pitch of sudden melancholy, as ultimately to lead to the finishing of the evening in tears, or else under the table. He remembers all these things, and he wonders—as, being a madman, it is natural he should—wonders whether it can be indeed himself, who once was that wittiest, handsomest, most generous, and best of fellows, baptised long ago in a river of sparkling hock, moselle, and burgundy, "Daredevil Dick."

But something more than these sad memories comes with the deepening twilight, for presently Richard hears the door of his room unlocked, and his keeper's voice, saying,—

"There, go in, and tell the gent you've come. I'm a-comin' in with his supper and his lamp presently, and then I'll tell you what you've got to do."

Naturally Richard looked round in the direction of the door, for he knew this must be the strange boy. Now, his late juvenile attendant had numbered some fifteen summers; to say nothing of the same number of winters, duly chronicled by chilblains and chapped hands. Richard's eyes therefore looked towards the open door at about that height from the ground which a lad of fifteen has commonly attained; and looking thus, Richard saw nothing. He therefore lowered his glance, and in about the neighbourhood of what would have been the lowest button of his last attendant's waistcoat, he beheld the small pale thin face of a very small and very thin boy.

This small boy was standing rubbing his right little foot against his left little wizen leg, and looking intently at Richard. To say that his tiny face had a great deal of character in it would not be to say much; what face he had was all character.

Determination, concentration, energy, strength of will, and brightness of intellect, were all written in unmistakable lines upon that pale pinched face. The boy's features were wonderfully regular, and had nothing in common with the ordinary features of a boy of his age and his class; the tiny nose was a perfect aquiline; the decided mouth might have belonged to a prime minister with the blood of the Plantagenets in his veins. The eyes, of a bluish grey, were small, and a little too near together, but the light in them was the light of an intelligence marvellous in one so young.

Richard, though a wild and reckless fellow, had never been devoid of thought, and in the good days past had dabbled in many a science, and had adopted and abandoned many a creed. He was something of a physiognomist, and he read enough in one glance at this boy's face to awaken both surprise and interest in him.

"So," said he, "you are the new boy! Sit down," he pointed to a little wooden stool near the bed as he spoke. "Sit down, and make yourself at home."

The boy obeyed, and seated himself firmly by the side of Richard's pillow; but the stool was so low, and he was so small, that Richard had to change his position to look over the edge of the bed at his new attendant. While Daredevil Dick contemplated him the boy's small grey eyes peered round the four whitewashed walls, and then fixed themselves upon the barred window with such a look of concentration, that it seemed to Richard as if the little lad must be calculating the thickness and power of resistance of each iron bar with the accuracy of a mathematician.

"What's your name, my lad?" asked Richard. He had been always beloved by all his inferiors for a manner combining the stately reserve of a great king with the friendly condescension of a popular prince.

"Slosh, sir," answered the boy, bringing his grey eyes with a great effort away from the iron bars and back to Richard.

"Slosh! A curious name. Your surname, I suppose?"

"Surname and christen name too, sir. Slosh—short for Sloshy."

"But have you no surname, then?"

"No, sir; *fondling*, sir."

"A foundling: dear me, and you are called Sloshy! Why, that is the name of the river that runs through Slopperton."

"Yes, sir, which I was found in the mud of the river, sir, when I was only three months old, sir."

"Found in the river—were you? Poor boy—and by whom?"

"By the gent what adopted me, sir."

"And he is——?" asked Richard.

"A gent connected with the police force, sir; detective——"

This one word worked a sudden change in Richard's manner. He raised himself on his elbow, looked intently at the boy, and asked, eagerly,—

"This detective, what is his name? But no," he muttered, "I did not even know the name of that man. Stay—tell me, you know perhaps some of the men in the Slopperton police force besides your adopted father?"

"I knows every man jack of 'em, sir; and a fine staff they is—a credit to their country and a happiness to theirselves."

"Do you happen to know amongst them a dumb man?" asked Richard.

"Lor', sir, that's him."

"Who?"

"Father, sir. The gent what found me and adopted me. I've got a message for you, sir, from father, and I was a-goin' to give it you, only I thought I'd look about me a little first; but stay—Oh, dear, the gentleman's took and fainted. Here," he said, running to the door and calling out in a shrill voice, "come and unlock this here place, will yer, and look alive with that lamp! The gentleman's gone off into a dead faint, and there ain't so much as a drop of water to chuck over his face."

The prisoner had indeed fallen back insensible on the bed. For eight long years he had nourished in his heart a glimmering though dying hope that he might one day receive some token of remembrance from the man who had taken a strange part in the eventful crisis of his life. This ray of light had lately died out, along with every other ray which had once illuminated his dreary life; but in the very moment when hope was abandoned, the token once eagerly looked for came upon him so suddenly, that the shock was too much for his shattered mind and feeble frame.

When Richard recovered from his swoon, he found himself alone with the boy from Slopperton. He was a little startled by the position of that young person, who had seated himself upon the small square deal table by the bed-side, commanding from this elevation a full view of Richard's face, whereon his two small grey eyes were intently fixed, with that same odd look of concentration with which he had regarded the iron bars.

"Come now," said he, with the consolatory tone of an experienced sick-nurse; "come now, we mustn't give way like this, just because we hears from our friends; because, you see, if we does, our friends can't be no good to us whichever way their intention may be."

"You said you had a message for me," said Richard, in feeble but anxious tones.

"Well, it ain't a long un, and here it is," answered the young gentleman from his extempore pulpit; and then he continued, with very much the air of giving out a text—"Keep up your pecker."

"Keep up what?" muttered Richard.

"Your pecker. 'Keep up your pecker,' them's his words; and as he never yet vos known to make a dirty dinner off his own syllables, it ain't likely as he'll take and eat 'em. He says to me—on his fingers, in course—'Tell the gent to keep up his pecker, and leave all the rest to you; for you're a pocket edition of all the sharpness as ever knives was nothing to, or else say I've brought you up for no good whatsomedever.' "

This was rather a vague speech; so perhaps it is scarcely strange that Richard did not derive much immediate comfort from it. But, in spite of himself, he did derive a great deal of comfort from the presence of this boy, though he almost despised himself for attaching the least importance to the words of an urchin of little better than eight years of age. Certainly this urchin of eight had a shrewdness of manner which would have been almost remarkable in a man of the world of fifty, and Richard could scarcely help fancying that he must have graduated in some other hemisphere, and been thrown, small as to size, but full grown as to acuteness, into this; or it seemed as if some great strong man had been reduced into the compass of a little boy, in order to make him sharper, as cooks boil down a gallon of gravy to a pint in the manufacture of strong soup.

But, however the boy came to be what he was, there he was, holding forth from his pulpit, and handing Richard the regulation basin of broth which composed his supper.

"Now, what you've got to do," said he, "is to get well; for until you are well, and strong too, there ain't the least probability of your bein' able to change your apartments, if you should feel so inclined, which perhaps ain't likely."

Richard looked at the diminutive speaker with a wonderment he could not repress.

"Starin' won't cure you," said his juvenile attendant, with friendly disrespect, "not if you took the pattern of my face till you could draw it in the dark. The best thing you can do is to eat your supper, and to-morrow we must try what we can do for you in the way of port wine; for if you ain't strong and well afore that ere river outside this ere vall goes down, it's a chance but vot it'll be a long time afore you sees the outside of the val in question."

Richard caught hold of the boy's small arm with a grasp which, in spite of his weakness, had a convulsive energy that nearly toppled his youthful attendant from his elevation.

"You never can think of anything so wild?" he said, in a tumult of agitation.

"Lor' bless yer 'art, no," said the boy; "we never thinks of anything vot's wild—our 'abits is business-like; but vot you've got to do is to go to sleep, and not to worrit yourself; and as I said before, I say again, when you're well and strong we'll think about changin' these apartments. We can make excuse that the look-out was too lively, or that the colour of the whitewash was a-*h*injurin' our eyesight."

For the first time for many nights Richard slept well; and opening his eyes the next morning, his first anxiety was to convince himself that the arrival of the boy from Slopperton was not some foolish dream engendered in his disordered brain. No, there the boy sat: whether he had been to sleep on the table, or whether he had never taken his eyes off Richard the whole night, there he was, with those eyes fixed, exactly as they had been the night before, on the prisoner's face.

"Why, I declare we're all the better for our good night's rest," he said, rubbing his hands, as he contemplated Richard; "and we're ready for our breakfast as soon as ever we can get it, which will be soon, judging by our keeper's hobnailed boots as is a-comin' down the passage with a tray in his hand."

This rather confused statement was confirmed by a noise in the stone corridor without, which sounded as if a pair of stout working men's bluchers[11] were walking in company with a basin and a tea-spoon.

"Hush!" said the boy, holding up a warning forefinger, "keep it dark!" Richard did not exactly know what he was to keep dark; but as he had, without one effort at resistance, surrendered himself, mentally and physically, to the direction of his small attendant, he lay perfectly still, and did not utter a word.

In obedience to this youthful director, he also took his breakfast, to the last mouthful of the regulation bread, and to the last spoonful of the regulation coffee—ay, even to the grounds (which, preponderating in that liquid, formed a species of stratum at the bottom of the basin, commonly known to the inmates of the asylum as "the thick")—for as the boy said, "grounds is strengthening." Breakfast finished, the asylum physician came, in the course of his rounds, for his matutinal visit to Richard's cell. His skill was entirely at a loss to find any cure for so strange a disease as that which affected the prisoner. One of the leading features, however, in this young man's sickness, had been an entire loss of appetite, and almost an entire inability to sleep. When, therefore, he heard that his patient had eaten a good supper, slept well all night, and had just finished the regulation breakfast, he said,—

"Come, come, we are getting better, then—our complaint is taking a turn. We are quiet in our mind, too, eh? Not fretting about Moscow, or making ourselves unhappy about Waterloo, I hope?"

The asylum doctor was a cheerful easy good-tempered fellow, who humoured the fancies of his patients, however wild they might be; and though half the kings in the history of England, and some sovereigns unchronicled in any history whatever were represented in the establishment, he was never known to forget the respect due to a monarch, however condescending that monarch might be. He was, therefore, a general favourite; and had received more orders of the Bath and the Garter,[12] in the shape of red tape and scraps of paper, and more title-deeds, in the way of old curl-papers and bits of newspaper, than would have served as the stock-in-trade of a marine storekeeper, with the addition of a few bottles and a black doll. He knew that one characteristic of Richard's madness was to fancy himself the chained eagle of the sea-bound rock, and he thought to humour the patient by humouring the hallucination.

Richard looked at this gentleman with a thoughtful glance in his dark eyes.

"I didn't mind Moscow, sir," he said, very gravely; "the elements beat me there—and they were stronger than Hannibal; but at Waterloo, what broke my heart was—not the defeat, but the disgrace!" He turned away his head as he spoke, and lay in silence, with his back turned to the good-natured physician.

"No complaints about Sir Hudson Lowe, I hope?" said the medical man. "They give you everything you want, general?"

The good doctor, being so much in the habit of humouring his patients, had their titles always at the tip of his tongue; and walked about in a perfect atmosphere of Pinnock's Goldsmith.[13]

As the general made no reply to his question, the doctor looked from him to the boy, who had, out of respect to the medical official, descended from his pulpit, and stood tugging at a very diminutive lock of hair, with an action which he intended to represent a bow.

"Does he ask for anything?" asked the doctor.

"Don't he, sir?" said the boy, answering one question with another. "He's been doing nothin' for ever so long but askin' for a drop o' wine. He says he feels a kind of sinkin' that nothin' but wine can cure."

"He shall have it, then," said the doctor. "A little port wine with a touch of iron in it would help to bring him round as soon as anything, and be sure you see that he takes it. I've been giving him quinine for some time past; but it has done so little towards making him stronger, that I sometimes doubt his having taken it. Has he complained of anything else?"

"Well, sir," said the boy, this time looking at his questioner very intently, and seeming to consider every word before he said it, "there is somethin' which I can make out from what he says when he talks to hisself—and he does talk to hisself awful—somethin' which preys upon his mind very much; but I don't suppose it's much good mentioning it either." Here he stopped, hesitating, and looking very earnestly at the doctor.

"Why not, my boy?"

"Because you see, sir, what he hankers after is agen the rules of the asylum—leastways, the rules the Board makes for such as him."

"But what is it, my good lad? Tell me what it is he wishes for?" said the medical man.

"Why, it's a singular wish, I dare say, sir; but he's allus a talkin' about the other lun——" he hesitated, as if out of delicacy towards Richard, and substituted the word "boarders" for that which he had been about to use—"and he says, if he could only be allowed to mix with 'em now and then he'd be as happy as a king. But, of course, as I was a-tellin' him when you come in, sir, that's agen the rules of the establishment, and in consequence is impossible—'cause why, these 'ere rules is like Swedes and Nasturtiums—[the boy from Slopperton may possibly have been thinking of the Medes and Persians][14]—and can't be gone agen."

"I don't know about that," said the good-natured doctor. "So, general," he added, turning to Richard, who had shifted his position, and now lay looking at his visitor rather anxiously, "so, general, you would like to mix with your friends out there?"

"Indeed I should, sir." Those deep and earnest dark eyes, with which Richard watched the doctor's face, were scarcely the eyes of a madman.

"Very well, then," said the medical man, "very well; we must see if it can't be managed. But I say, general, you'll find the Prince Regent among your fellow-boarders; and I wouldn't answer for your not meeting with Lord Castlereagh,[15] and that might cause unpleasantness—eh, general?"

"No, no, sir; there's no fear of that. Political differences should never——"

"Interfere with private friendship. A noble sentiment, general. Very well, you shall mix with the other boarders to-morrow. I'll speak to the Board about it this afternoon. This, luckily, is a Board-day. You'll find George the Fourth a very nice fellow. He came here because he would take everything of other people's that he could lay his hands on, and said he was only taking taxes from his subjects. Good-day. I'll send round some port wine immediately, and you shall have a couple of glasses a day given you; so keep up your spirits, general."

"Well," said the boy from Slopperton, as the doctor closed the door behind him, "that 'ere medical officer's a regular brick: and all I can say is to repeat his last words—which ought to be printed in gold letters a foot high—and those words is,—'Keep up your spirits, general.' "

CHAPTER II

MR. AUGUSTUS DARLEY AND MR. JOSEPH PETERS GO OUT FISHING

A long period of incessant rains had by no means improved the natural beauties of the Sloshy; nor had it in any manner enhanced the advantages attending a residence on the banks of that river. The occupants of the houses by the waterside were in the habit of going to sleep at night with the firm conviction that the lower portion of their tenement was a comfortable kitchen, and awakening in the morning were apt to find it a miniature lake.

Then, again, the river had a knack of dropping in at odd times, in a friendly way, when least expected—when Mrs. Jones was cooking the Sunday's dinner, or while Mrs. Brown was gone to market; and, as its manner of entering an apartment was, after the fashion of a ghost in a melodrama, to rise through the floor, the surprise occasioned by its appearance was not unalloyed by vexation.

It would intrude, an uninvited guest, at a social tea-party, and suddenly isolate every visitor on his or her chair as on an island.

There was not a mouse or a black-beetle in any of the kitchens by the Sloshy whose life was worth the holding, such an enemy was the swelling water to all domestic peace or comfort.

It is true that to some fresh and adventurous spirits the rising of the river afforded a kind of eccentric gratification. It gave a smack of the flavour of Venice to the dull insipidity of Slopperton life; and to an imaginative mind every coal-barge that went by became a gondola, and only wanted a cavalier, with a very short doublet, pointed shoes, and a guitar, to make it perfection.

Indeed, Miss Jones, milliner and dressmaker, had been heard to say, that when she saw the water coming up to the parlour-windows she could hardly believe she was not really in the city of the winged horses, round the corner out of the square of St. Mark's,[1] and three doors from the Bridge of Sighs.[2] Miss Jones was well up in Venetian topography, as she was engaged in the perusal of a powerful work in penny numbers,[3] detailing the adventures of a celebrated "Bravo"[4] of that city.

To the ardent minds of the juvenile denizens of the waterside the swollen river was a source of pure and unalloyed delight. To take a tour round one's own back kitchen in a washing-tub, with a duster for a sail, is perhaps, at the age of six, a more perfect species of enjoyment than that afforded by any Alpine glories or Highland scenery through which we may wander in after-years, when Reason has taught us her cold lesson, that, however bright the sun may shine on one side of the mountain, the shadows are awaiting us on the other.

There is a gentleman in a cutaway coat and a white hat, smoking a very short and black clay pipe, as he loiters on the bank of the Sloshy. I wonder what he thinks of the river?

It is eight years since this gentleman was last in Slopperton; then he came as a witness in the trial of Richard Marwood; then he had a black eye, and was out-at-elbows; now, his optics are surrounded with no dark shades which mar their natural colour—clear bright grey. Now, too, he is, to speak familiarly, in high feather. His cutaway coat of the newest fashion (for there is fashion even in cutaways); his plaid trousers, painfully tight at the knees, and admirably adapted to display the development of the calf, are still bright with the greens and blues of the Macdonald. His hat is not crushed or indented in above half-a-dozen directions—a sign that it is comparatively new, for the circle in which he moves considers bonneting a friendly demonstration, and to knock a man's hat off his head and into the gutter rather a polite attention.

Yes, during the last eight years the prospects of Mr. Augustus Darley—(that is the name of the witness)—have been decidedly looking up. Eight years ago he was a medical student, loose on wide London; eating bread-and-cheese and drinking bottled stout in dissecting-rooms, and chalking up alarming scores at the caravansary[5] round the corner of Goodge Street—when the proprietor of the caravansary *would* chalk up. There were days which that stern man refused to mark with a white stone.[6] Now, he has a dispensary of his own; a marvellous place, which would be entirely devoted to scientific pursuits if dominoes and racing calendars did not in some degree predominate therein. This dispensary is in a populous neighbourhood on the Surrey side of the water; and in the streets and squares—to say nothing of the court and mows—round this establishment the name of Augustus Darley is synonymous with everything which is popular and pleasant. His very presence is said to be as good as physic. Now, as physic in the abstract, and apart from its curative qualities, is scarcely a very pleasant thing, this may be considered rather a doubtful compliment; but for all that, it was meant in perfect good faith, and what's more, it meant a great deal.

When anybody felt ill, he sent for Gus Darley—(he had never been called Mr. but once in his life, and then by a sheriff's officer, who, arresting him for the first time, wasn't on familiar terms; all Cursitor Street knew him as "Gus, old fellow," and "Darley, my boy," before long). If the patient was very bad, Gus told him a good story. If the case seemed a serious one, he sang a comic song. If the patient felt, in popular parlance, "low," Darley would stop to supper; and if by that time the patient was not entirely restored, his medical adviser would send him a ha'porth of Epsom salts,[7] or three-farthings' worth[8] of rhubarb and magnesia,[9] jocosely labelled "The Mixture." It was a comforting delusion, laboured under by every patient of Gus Darley's, that the young surgeon prescribed for him a very mysterious and peculiar amalgamation of drugs, which, though certain death to any other man, was the only preparation in the whole pharmacopœia that could possibly keep him alive.

There was a saying current in the neighbourhood of the dispensary, to the effect that Gus Darley's description of the Derby Day was the best Epsom salts ever invented for the cure of man's diseases; and he has been known to come home from the races at ten o'clock at night, and assist at a sick-bed (successfully), with a wet towel round his head, and a painful conviction that he was prescribing for two patients at once.

But all this time he is strolling by the swollen Sloshy, with his pipe in his mouth and a contemplative face, which ever and anon looks earnestly up the river. Presently he stops by a boat-builder's yard, and speaks to a man at work.

"Well," he says, "is that boat finished yet?"

"Yes, sir," says the man, "quite finished, and uncommon well she looks too; you might eat your dinner off her; the paint's as dry as a bone."

"How about the false bottom I spoke of?" he asks.

"Oh, that's all right, sir, two feet and a half deep, and six feet and a half long. I'll tell you what, sir,—no offence—but you must catch a precious sight more eels than I think you will catch, if you mean to fill the bottom of that 'ere punt."

As the man speaks, he points to where the boat lies high and dry in the builder's yard. A great awkward flat-bottomed punt, big enough to hold half-a-dozen people.

Gus strolls up to look at it. The man follows him.

He lifts up the bottom of the boat with a great thick loop of rope. It is made like a trap-door, two feet and a half above the keel.

"Why," said Gus, "a man could lie down in the keel of the boat, with that main deck over him."

"To be sure he could, sir, and a pretty long un, too; though I don't say much for its being a over-comfortable berth. He might feel himself rather cramped if he was of a restless disposition."

Gus laughed, and said,—"You're right, he might, certainly, poor fellow! Come, now, you're rather a tall chap, I should like to see if you could lie down there comfortably for a minute or so. We'll talk about some beer when you come out."

The man looked at Mr. Darley with rather a puzzled glance. He had heard the legend of the mistletoe bough.[10] He had helped to build the boat, but for all that there might be a hidden spring somewhere about it, and Gus's request might conceal some sinister intent; but no one who had once looked our medical friend in the face ever doubted him; so the man laughed and said,—

"Well, you're a rum un, whoever the other is" (people were rarely very deferential in their manner of addressing Gus Darley); "howsomedever, here's to oblige you." And the man got into the boat, and lying down, suffered Gus to lower the false bottom of it over him.

"How do you feel?" asks Gus. "Can you breathe?—have you plenty of air?"

"All right, sir," says the man through a hole in the plank. "It's quite a extensive berth, when you've once settled yourself, only it ain't much calculated for active exercise."

"Do you think you could stand it for half an hour?" Gus inquires.

"Lor, bless you, sir! for half-a-dozen hours, if I was paid accordin'."

"Should you think half-a-crown enough for twenty minutes?"

"Well, I don't know, sir; suppose you made it three shillings?"

"Very good," said Gus; "three shillings it shall be. It's now half-past twelve;" he looks at his watch as he speaks. "I'll sit here and smoke a pipe; and if you lie quiet till ten minutes to one, you'll have earned the three bob."

Gus steps into the boat, and seats himself at the prow; the man's head lies at the stern.

"Can you see me?" Gus inquires.

"Yes, sir, when I squints."

"Very well, then, you can see I don't make a bolt of it. Make your mind easy: there's five minutes gone already."

Gus finishes his pipe, looks at his watch again—a quarter to one. He whistles a scena from an opera, and then jumps out of the boat and pulls up the false bottom.

"All's right," he says; "time's up."

The man gets out and stretches his legs and arms, as if to convince himself that those members are unimpaired.

"Well, was it pretty comfortable?" Gus asks.

"Lor' love you, sir! regular jolly, with the exception of bein' rather warm, and makin' a cove precious dry."

Gus gives the man wherewith to assuage this drought, and says,—

"You may shove the boat down to the water, then. My friend will be here in a minute with the tackle, and we can then see about making a start."

The boat is launched, and the man amuses himself with rowing a few yards up the river, while Gus waits for his friend.

In about ten minutes his friend arrives, in the person of Mr. Joseph Peters, of the police force, with a couple of eel-spears[11] over his shoulder (which give him somewhat the appearance of a dry-land Neptune), and a good-sized carpet-bag, which he carries in his hand.

Gus and he exchange a few remarks in the silent alphabet, in which Gus is almost as great an adept as the dumb detective, and they step into the punt.

The boat-builder's man is sent for a gallon of beer in a stone bottle, a half-quartern loaf, and a piece of cheese. These provisions being shipped, Darley and Peters each take an oar, and they pull away from the bank and strike out into the middle of the river.

CHAPTER III

THE EMPEROR BIDS ADIEU TO ELBA

On this same day, but at a later hour in the afternoon, Richard Marwood, better known as the Emperor Napoleon, joined the inmates of the county asylum in their daily exercise in the grounds allotted for that purpose. These grounds consisted of prim grass-plots, adorned with here and there a bed in which some dismal shrubs, or a few sickly chrysanthemums held up their gloomy heads, beaten and shattered by the recent heavy rains. These grass-plots were surrounded by stiff straight gravel-walks; and the whole was shut in by a high wall, surmounted by a *chevaux-de-frise.*[1] The iron spikes composing this adornment had been added of late years; for, in spite of the comforts and attractions of the establishment, some foolish inhabitants thereof, languishing for gayer and more dazzling scenes, had been known to attempt, if not to effect, an escape from the numerous advantages of their home. I cannot venture to say whether or not the vegetable creation may have some mysterious sympathy with animated nature; but certainly no trees, shrubs, flowers, grass, or weeds ever grew like the trees, shrubs, flowers, grass, and weeds in the grounds of the county lunatic asylum. From the gaunt elm, which stretched out two great rugged arms, as if in a wild imprecation, such as might come from the lips of some human victim of the worst form of insanity, to the frivolous chickweed in a corner of a gravel-walk, which grew as if not a root, or leaf, or fibre but had a different purpose to its fellow, and flew off at its own peculiar tangent, with an infantine and kittenish madness, such as might have afflicted a love-sick miss of seventeen; from the great melancholy mad laurel-bushes that rocked themselves to and fro in the wind with a restlessness known only to the insane, to the eccentric dandelions that reared their disordered heads from amidst the troubled and dishevelled grass—every green thing in that great place seemed more or less a victim to that terrible disease whose influence is of so subtle a nature, that it infects the very stones of the dark walls which shut in shattered minds that once were strong and whole, and fallen intellects that once were bright and lofty.

But as a stranger to this place, looking for the first time at the groups of men and women lounging slowly up and down these gravel-walks, perhaps what most startles you, perhaps even what most distresses you, is, that these wretched people scarcely seem unhappy. Oh, merciful and wondrous wise dispensation from Him who fits the back to bear the burden! He so appoints it. The man, whose doubts or fears, or wild aspirings to the misty far-away, all the world's wisdom could not yesterday appease, is to-day made happy by a scrap of paper or a shred of ribbon. We who, standing in the blessed light, look in upon this piteous mental darkness, are perhaps most unhappy, because we cannot tell how much or how little sorrow this death-in-life may shroud. They have passed away from us; their language is not our language, nor their world our world. I think some one has asked a strange question—Who can tell whether their folly may not perhaps be better than our wisdom? He only, from whose mighty hand comes the music of every soul, can tell which is the discord and which the harmony. We look at them as we look at all else—through the darkened glass[2] of earth's uncertainty.

No, they do not seem unhappy. Queen Victoria is talking to Lady Jane Grey about to-day's dinner, and the reprehensible superabundance of fat in a leg-of-mutton served up thereat. Chronology never disturbs these good people; nobody thinks it any disgrace to be an anachronism. Lord Brougham will divide an unripe apple with Cicero, and William the Conqueror will walk arm-in-arm with Pius the Ninth, without the least uneasiness on the score of probability; and when, on one occasion, a gentleman, who for three years had enjoyed considerable popularity as Cardinal Wolsey, all of a sudden recovered, and confessed to being plain John Thomson, the inmates of the asylum were unanimous in feeling and expressing the most profound contempt for his unhappy state.

To-day, however, Richard is the hero. He is surrounded immediately on his appearance by all the celebrities and a great many of the non-celebrities of the establishment. The Emperor of the German Ocean and the Chelsea Waterworks in particular has so much to say to him, that he does not know how to begin; and when he does begin, has to go back and begin again, in a manner both affable and bewildering.

Why did not Richard join them before, he asks—they are so very pleasant, they are so very social; why, in goodness-gracious' name (he opens his eyes very wide as he utters the name of goodness-gracious, and looks back over his shoulder rather as if he thinks he may have invoked some fiend), why did not Richard join them?

Richard tells him he was not allowed to do so.

On this, the potentate looks intensely mysterious. He is rather stout, and wears a head-dress of his own manufacture—a species of coronet, constructed of a newspaper and a blue-and-white bird's-eye pocket-handkerchief. He puts his hands to the very furthest extent that he can push them into his trousers-pockets; plants himself right before Richard on the gravel-walk, and says, with a wink of intense significance, "Was it the Khan?"

Richard says, he thinks not.

"Not the Khan!" he mutters thoughtfully. "You really are of opinion that it was not the Khan?"

"I really am," Richard replies.

"Then it lies between the last Duke of Devonshire but sixteen and Abd-el-Kader: I do hope it wasn't Abd-el-Kader; I had a better opinion of Abd-el-Kader[3]—I had indeed."

Richard looks rather puzzled, but says nothing.

"There has evidently," continued his friend, "been some malignant influence at work to prevent your appearing amongst us before this. You have been a member of this society for, let me see, three hundred and sixty-three years—be kind enough to set me right if I make a mis-statement—three hundred and—did I say seventy-twelve years?—and you have never yet joined us! Now, there is something radically wrong here; to use the language of the ancients in their religious festivals, there is 'a screw loose.' You ought to have joined us, you really ought! We are very social; we are positively buoyant; we have a ball every evening. Well, no, perhaps it is not every evening. My ideas as to time, I am told, are vague; but I know it is either every ten years, or every other week. I incline to thinking it must be every other week. On these occasions we dance. Are you a votary of Terp—what-you-may-call-her, the lady who had so many unmarried sisters?[4] Do you incline to the light fantastic?" By way of illustration, the Emperor of the Waterworks executed a caper, which would have done honour to an elderly elephant taking his first lesson in the polka.

There was one advantage in conversing with this gentleman. If his questions were sometimes of rather a difficult and puzzling nature, he never did anything so under-bred as to wait for an answer.

It now appeared for the first time to strike him, that perhaps the laws of exclusiveness had in some manner been violated, by a person of his distinction having talked so familiarly to an entire stranger; he therefore suddenly skipped a pace or two backwards, leaving a track of small open graves in the damp gravel made by the impression of his feet, and said, in a tone of voice so dignified as to be almost freezing—

"Pray, to whom have I the honour to make these observations?"

Richard regretted to say he had not a card about him, but added—"You may have heard of the Emperor Napoleon?"

"Buonaparte? Oh, certainly; very frequently, very frequently: and you are that worthy person? Dear me! this is very sad. Not at your charming summer residence at Moscow, or your pleasant winter retreat on the field of Waterloo: this is really distressing, very."

His pity for Richard was so intense, that he was moved to tears, and picked a dandelion with which to wipe his eyes.

"My Chelsea property," he said presently, "is fluctuating—very. I find a tendency in householders to submit to having their water cut off, rather than pay the rate. Our only plan is to empty every cistern half an hour before tea-time. Persevered in for a week or so, we find that course has a harassing effect, and they pay. But all this is wearing for the nerves—very."

He shook his head solemnly, rubbed his eyes very hard with the dandelion, and then ate that exotic blossom.

"An agreeable tonic," he said; "known to be conducive to digestion. My German Ocean I find more profitable, on account of the sea-bathing."

Richard expressed himself very much interested in the commercial prospects of his distinguished friend; but at this moment they were interrupted by the approach of a lady, who, with a peculiar hop, skip, and jump entirely her own, came up to the Emperor of the Waterworks and took hold of his arm.

She was a gushing thing of some forty-odd summers, and wore a bonnet, the very purchase of which would have stamped her as of unsound intellect, without need of any further proof whatever. To say that it was like a coal-scuttle was nothing; to say that it resembled a coal-scuttle which had suffered from an aggravated attack of water on the brain, and gone mad, would be perhaps a little nearer the mark. Imagine such a bonnet adorned with a green veil, rather bigger than an ordinary table cloth, and three quill pens tastefully inserted in the direction in which Parisian milliners are wont to place the plumage of foreign birds—and you may form some idea of the lady's head-gear. Her robes were short and scanty, but plentifully embellished with a species of trimming, which to an ordinary mind suggested strips of calico, but which amongst the inmates passed current as Valenciennes lace. Below these robes appeared a pair of apple-green boots—boots of a pattern such as no shoemaker of sound mind ever in his wildest dreams could have originated, but which in this establishment were voted rather recherché than otherwise. This lady was no other than the damsel who had suggested an elopement with Richard some eight years ago, and who claimed for her distinguished connections the Pope and the muffin-man.

"Well," she said to the Emperor of the Waterworks, with a voice and manner which would have been rather absurdly juvenile in a girl of fifteen,—"and where has its precious one been hiding since dinner? Was it the fat mutton which rendered the most brilliant of mankind unfit for general society; or was it that it 'had a heart for falsehood framed?' I hope it was the fat mutton."

"Its precious one" looked from the charmer at his side to Richard, with rather an apologetic shrug.

"The sex is weak," he said, "conqueror of Agincourt—I beg pardon, Waterloo. The sex is weak: it is a fact established alike by medical science and political economy. Poor thing! she loves me."

The lady, for the first time, became aware of the presence of Richard. She dropped a very low curtsey, in the performance of which one of the green boots described a complete circle, and said,

"From Gloucestershire, sir?" interrogatively.

"The Emperor Napoleon Buonaparte," said the proprietor of the German Ocean. "My dear, you ought to know him."

"The Emperor Nap-o-le-on Bu-o-na-parte," she said very slowly, checking off the syllables on her fingers, "and from Gloucestershire? How gratifying! All our great men come from Gloucester-shire. It is a well-known fact—from Gloucestershire? muffins[5] were invented in Gloucestershire by Alfred the Great.[6] Did you know our dear Alfred? You are perhaps too young—a great loss, my dear sir, a great loss; conglomerated essence of toothache on the cerebral nerves took him off in fourteen days, three weeks, and one month. We tried everything, from dandelions"—(her eyes wandered as if searching the grounds for information as to what they had tried)— from dandelions to chevaux-de-frise—"

She stopped abruptly, staring Richard full in the face, as if she expected him to say something; but as he said nothing, she became suddenly interested in the contemplation of the green boots, look-ing first at one and then at the other, as if revolving in her mind the probability of their wanting mending.

Presently she looked up, and said with great solemnity—

"Do you know the muffin-man?"

Richard shook his head.

"He lives in Drury Lane,"[7] she added, looking at him rather sternly, as much as to say, "Come, no nonsense! you know him well enough!"

"No," said Richard, "I don't remember having met him."

"There are seventy-nine of us who know the muffin-man in this establishment, sir—seventy-nine; and do you dare to stand there and tell me that you——"

"I assure you, madam, I have not the honour of his acquaintance."

"Not know the muffin-man!—you don't know the muffin-man! Why, you contemptible stuck-up jackanapes——"

What the lady might have gone on to say, it would be difficult to guess. She was not celebrated for the refinement of her vocabulary when much provoked; but at this moment a great stout man, one of the keepers, came up, and cried out—

"Holloa! what's all this!"

"He says he doesn't know the muffin-man!" exclaimed the lady, her veil flying in the wind like a pennant, her arms akimbo, and the apple-green boots planted in a defiant manner on the gravel-walk.

"Oh, we know him well enough," said the man, with a wink at Richard, "and very slack he bakes his muffins." Having uttered which piece of information connected with the gentleman in question, the keeper strolled off, giving just one steady look straight into the eyes of the lively damsel, which seemed to have an instantaneous and most soothing effect upon her nerves.

As all the lunatics allowed to disport themselves for an hour in the gardens of the establishment were considered to be, upon the whole, pretty safe, the keepers were not in the habit of taking much notice of them. Those officials would congregate in little groups here and there, talking among themselves, and apparently utterly regardless of the unhappy beings over whom it was their duty to watch. But let Queen Victoria or the Emperor Nero, Lady Jane Grey or Lord John Russell, suffer themselves to be led away by their respective hobbies, or to ride those animals at too outrageous and dangerous a pace, and a strong hand would be laid upon the rider's shoulder, accompanied by a recommendation to "go indoors," which was very seldom disregarded.

As Richard was this afternoon permitted to mix with his fellow-prisoners for the first time, the boy from Slopperton was ordered to keep an eye upon him; and a very sharp eye the boy kept, never for one moment allowing a look, word, or action of the prisoner to escape him.

The keepers this afternoon were assembled near the portico, before which the gardens extended to the high outer wall. The ground between the portico and the wall was a little less than a quarter of a mile in length, and at the bottom was the grand entrance and the porter's lodge. The gardens surrounded the house on three sides, and on the left side the wall ran parallel with the river Sloshy. This river was now so much swollen by the late heavy rains that the waters washed the wall to the height of four feet, entirely covering the towing-path, which lay ordinarily between the wall and the waterside.

Now Richard and the Emperor of the Waterworks, accompanied by the gushing charmer in the green boots, being all three engaged in friendly though rather erratic conversation, happened to stroll in the direction of the grounds on this side, and consequently out of sight of the keepers.

The boy from Slopperton was, however, close upon their heels. This young gentleman had his hands in his pockets, and was loitering and lounging along with an air which seemed to say, that neither man nor woman gave him any more delight than they had afforded the Danish prince of used-up memory. Perhaps it was in utter weariness of life that he was, as if unconsciously, employed in whistling the melody of a song, supposed to relate to a passage in the life of a young lady of the name of Gray, christian name Alice, whose heart it was another's, and consequently, by pure logic, never could belong to the singer.

Now there may be something infectious in this melody; for no sooner had the boy from Slopperton whistled the first few bars, than some person in the distance outside the walls of the asylum gardens took up the air and finished it. A trifling circumstance this in itself; but it appeared to afford the boy considerable gratification; and he presently came suddenly upon Richard in the middle of a very interesting conversation, and whispered in his ear, or rather at his elbow, "All right, general!" Now as Richard, the Emperor of the Waterworks, and the only daughter of the Pope all talked at once, and all talked of entirely different subjects, their conversation might, perhaps, have been just a little distracting to a short-hand reporter; but as a conversation, it was really charming.

Richard—still musing on the wild idea which was known in the asylum to have possessed his disordered brain ever since the day of his trial—was giving his companions an account of his escape from Elba.

"I was determined," he said, taking the Emperor of the Waterworks by the button, "I was determined to make one desperate effort to return to my friends in France——"

"Very creditable, to be sure," said the damsel of the green boots; "your sentiments did you honour."

"But to escape from the island was an enterprise of considerable difficulty," continued Richard.

"Of course," said the damsel, "considering the price of flour. Flour rose a halfpenny in the bushel in the neighbourhood of Drury Lane, which, of course, reduced the size of muffins——"

"And had a depressing effect upon the water-rates," interrupted the gentleman.

"Now," continued Richard, "the island of Elba was surrounded by a high wall——"

"A very convenient arrangement; of course facilitating the process of cutting off the water from the inhabitants," muttered the Emperor of the German Ocean.

The boy Slosh again expressed his feelings with reference to Alice Gray, and some one on the other side of the wall coincided with him.

"And," said Richard, "on the top of this wall was a chevaux-de-frise."

"Dear me," exclaimed the Emperor, "quite a what-you-may-call-it. I mean an extraordinary coincidence; we too have a chevaux-de-thing-a-me, for the purpose, I believe, of keeping out the cats. Cats are unpleasant; especially," he added, thoughtfully, "especially the Tom-sex—I mean the sterner sex."

"To surmount this wall was my great difficulty."

"Naturally, naturally," said the damsel, "a great undertaking, considering the fall in muffins—a dangerous undertaking."

"There was a boat waiting to receive me on the other side," said Richard, glancing at the wall, which was about a hundred yards distant from him.

Some person on the other side of the wall had got a good deal nearer by this time; and, dear me, how very much excited he was about Alice Gray.

"But the question," Richard continued, "was how to climb the wall,"—still looking up at the chevaux-de-frise.

"I should have tried muffins," said the lady.

"I should have cut off the water," remarked the gentleman.

"I did neither," said Richard; "I tried a rope."

At this very moment, by some invisible agency, a thickly-knotted rope was thrown across the chevaux-de-frise, and the end fell within about four feet of the ground.

"But her heart it is another's, and it never can be mine."

The gentleman who couldn't succeed in winning the affections of Miss Gray was evidently close to the wall now.

In a much shorter time than the very greatest master in the art of stenography could possibly have reported the occurrence, Richard threw the Emperor of the Waterworks half-a-dozen yards from him, with such violence as to cause that gentleman to trip-up the heels of the only daughter of the Pope, and fall in a heap upon that lady as on a feather bed; and then, with the activity of a cat or a sailor, clambered up the rope, and disappeared over the chevaux-de-frise.

The gentleman outside was now growing indifferent to the loss of Miss Gray, for he whistled the melody in a most triumphant manner, keeping time with the sharp plash of his oars in the water.

It took the Emperor and his female friend some little time to recover from the effects of the concussion they had experienced, each from each; and when they had done so, they stood for a few moments looking at one another in mute amazement.

"The gentleman has left the establishment," at last said the lady.

"And a bruise on my elbow," muttered the gentleman, rubbing the locality in question.

"Such a very unpolite manner of leaving too," said the lady. "His muffins—I mean his manners—have evidently been very much neglected."

"He must be a Chelsea householder," said the Emperor. "The householders of Chelsea are proverbial for bad manners. They are in the habit of slamming the door in the face of the tax-gatherer, with a view to injuring the tip of his nose; and I'm sure Lord Chesterfield never advised his son to do that."[8]

It may be as well here to state that the Emperor of the Waterworks had in early life been collector of the water-rate in the neighbourhood of Chelsea; but having unfortunately given his manly intellect to drinking, and being further troubled with a propensity for speculation (some people pronounced the word without the first letter), which involved the advantageous laying-out of his sovereign's money for his own benefit, he had first lost his situation and ultimately his senses.

His lady friend had once kept a baker's shop in the vicinity of Drury Lane, and happening, in an evil hour, at the ripe age of forty, to place her affections on a young man of nineteen, the bent of whose genius was muffins, and being slighted by the youth in question, she had retired into the gin-bottle, and thence had been passed to the asylum of her native country.

Perhaps the inquiring reader will ask what the juvenile guardian of Richard is doing all this time? He has been told to keep an eye upon him; and how has he kept his trust?

He is standing, very coolly, staring at the lady and gentleman before him, and is apparently much interested in their conversation.

"I shall certainly go," said the Emperor of the Waterworks, after a pause, "and inform the superintendent of this proceeding—the superintendent ought really to know of it."

"Superintendent" was, in the asylum, the polite name given the keepers. But just as the Emperor began to shamble off in the direction of the front of the house, the boy called Slosh flew past him and ran on before, and by the time the elderly gentleman reached the porch, the boy had told the astonished keepers the whole story of the escape.

The keepers ran down to the gate, called to the porter to have it opened, and in a few minutes were in the road in front of it. They hurried thence to the river-side. There was not a sign of any human being on the swollen waters, except two men in a punt close to the opposite shore, who appeared to be eel-spearing.

"There's no boat nearer than that," said one of the men; he never could have reached that in this time if he had been the best swimmer in England."

The men took it for granted that they had been informed of his escape the moment it occurred.

"He must have jumped slap into the water," said another; "perhaps he's about somewhere, contriving to keep his head under."

"He couldn't do it," said the first man who had spoken; "it's my opinion the poor chap's drowned. They will try these escapes, though no one ever succeeded yet."

There was a boat moored at the angle of the asylum wall, and one of the men sprang into it.

"Show me the place where he jumped over the wall," he called to the boy, who pointed out the spot at his direction.

The man rowed up to it.

"Not a sign of him anywhere about here!" he cried.

"Hadn't you better call to those men?" asked his comrade; "they must have seen him jump."

The man in the boat nodded assent, and rowed across the river to the two fishermen.

"Holloa!" he said, "have you seen any one get over that wall?"

One of the men, who had just impaled a fine eel, looked up with a surprised expression, and asked—

"Which wall?"

"Why the asylum, yonder, straight before you."

"The asylum! Now, you don't mean to say that that's the asylum; and I've been taking it for a gentleman's mansion and grounds all the time," said the angler (who was no other than Mr. Augustus Darley), taking his pipe out of his mouth.

"I wish you'd give a straight answer to my question," said the man; "have you seen any one jump over that wall; yes, or no?"

"Then, no!" said Gus; "if I had, I should have gone over and picked him up, shouldn't I, stupid?"

The other fisherman, Mr. Peters, here looked up, and laying down his eel-spear, spelt out some words on his fingers.

"Stop a bit," cried Gus to the man, who was rowing off, "here's my friend says he heard a splash in the water ten minutes ago, and thought it was some rubbish shot over the wall."

"Then he did jump! Poor chap, I'm afraid he must be drowned."

"Drowned?"

"Yes; don't I tell you one of the lunatics has been trying to escape over that wall, and must have fallen into the river?"

"Why didn't you say so before, then?" said Gus. "What's to be done? Where are there any drags?"

"Why, half a mile off, worse luck, at a public-house down the river, the 'Jolly Life-boat.'"

"Then I'll tell you what," said Gus, "my friend and I will row down and fetch the drags, while you chaps keep a look-out about here."

"You're very good, sir," said the man; "dragging the river's about all we can do now, for it strikes me we've seen the last of the Emperor Napoleon. My eyes! won't there be a row about it with the Board!"

"Here we go," says Gus; "keep a good heart; he may turn up yet;" with which encouraging remarks Messrs. Darley and Peters struck off at a rate which promised the speedy arrival of the drags.

CHAPTER IV

Joy and Happiness for Everybody

Whether the drags reached the county asylum in time to be of any service is still a mystery; but Mr. Joseph Peters arrived with the punt at the boat-builder's yard in the dusk of the autumn evening. He was alone, and he left his boat, his tridents, and other fishing-tackle in the care of the men belonging to the yard, and then putting his hands in his pockets, trudged off in the direction of Little Gulliver Street.

If ever Mr. Peters had looked triumphant in his life, he looked triumphant this evening: if ever his mouth had been on one side, it was on one side this evening; but it was the twist of a conqueror which distorted that feature.

Eight years, too, have done something for Kuppins. Time hasn't forgotten Kuppins, though she is a humble individual. Time has touched up Kuppins; adding a little bit here, and taking away a little bit there, and altogether producing something rather imposing. Kuppins has grown. When that young lady had attained her tenth year, there was a legend current in Little Gulliver Street and its vicinity, that in consequence of a fatal predilection for gin-and-bitters[1] evinced by her mother during the infancy of Kuppins, that diminutive person would never grow any more: but she gave the lie both to the legend and the gin-and-bitters by outgrowing her frocks at the advanced age of seventeen; and now she was rather a bouncing young woman than otherwise, and had a pair of such rosy cheeks as would have done honour to healthier breezes than those of Slopperton-on-the-Sloshy.

Time had done something, too, for Kuppins's shock of hair, for it was now brushed, and combed, and dragged, and tortured into a state not so very far from smoothness; and it was furthermore turned up;[2] an achievement in the hair-dressing line which it had taken her some years to effect, and which, when effected, was perhaps a little calculated to remind the admiring beholder of a good-sized ball of black cotton with a hair-pin stuck through it.

What made Kuppins in such a state of excitement on this particular evening, who shall say? Certain it is that she was excited. At the first sound of the click of Mr. Peters's latchkey in the door of No. 5, Little Gulliver Street, Kuppins, with a lighted candle, flew to open it. How she threw her arms round Mr. Peters's neck and kissed him—how she left a lump of tallow in his hair, and a smell of burning in his whiskers—how, in her excitement she blew the candle out—and how, by a feat of leger-de-main,[3] or leger-de-lungs, she blew it in again, must have been seen to be sufficiently appreciated. Her next proceeding was to drag Mr. Peters upstairs into the indoor Eden, which bore the very same appearance it had done eight years ago. One almost expected to find the red baby grown up—but it wasn't; and that dreadful attack of the mumps from which the infant had suffered when Mr. Peters first became acquainted with it did not appear to have abated in the least. Kuppins thrust the detective into his own particular chair, planted herself in an opposite seat, put the candlestick on the table, snuffed the candle, and then, with her eyes opened to the widest extent, evidently awaited his saying something.

He did say something—in his own way, of course; the fingers went to work. "I've d——" said the fingers.

"*'One* it," cried Kuppins, dreadfully excited by this time, "done it! you've done it! Didn't I always say you would? Didn't I know you would? Didn't I always dream you would, three times running, and a house on fire?—that meant the river; and an army of soldiers—that meant the boat; and everybody in black clothes—meaning joy and happiness. It's come true; it's all come out. Oh, I'm so happy!" In proof of which Kuppins immediately commenced a series of evolutions of the limbs and exercises of the human voice, popularly known in the neighbourhood as strong hysterics—so strong, in fact, that Mr. Peters couldn't have held her still if he had tried. Perhaps that's why he didn't try; but he looked about in every direction for something cold to put down her back, and finding nothing handy but the poker, he stirred her up with that in the neighbourhood of the spinal marrow, as if she had been a bad fire; whereon she came to.

"And where's the blessed boy?" she asked, presently.

Mr. Peters signified upon his fingers that the blessed boy was still at the asylum, and that there he must remain till such time as he should be able to leave without raising suspicion.

"And to think," said Kuppins, "that we should have seen the advertisement for a boy to wait upon poor Mr. Marwood; and to think that we should have thought of sending our Slosh to take the situation; and to think that he should have been so clever in helping you through with it! Oh my!" As Kuppins here evinced a desire for a second edition of the hysterics, Mr. Peters changed the conversation by looking inquiringly towards a couple of saucepans on the fire.

"Tripe,"[4] said Kuppins, answering the look, "and taters,[5] floury ones;" whereon she began to lay the supper-table. Kuppins was almost mistress of the house now, for the elderly proprietress was a sufferer from rheumatism, and kept to her room, enlivened by the society of a large black cat, and such gossip as Kuppins collected about the neighbourhood in the course of the day and retailed to her mistress in the evening. So we leave Mr. Peters smoking his pipe and roasting his legs at his own hearth, while Kuppins dishes the tripe and onions, and strips the floury potatoes of their russet jackets.

Where all this time is the Emperor Napoleon?

There are two gentlemen pacing up and down the platform of the Birmingham station, waiting for the 10 p.m. London express. One of them is Mr. Augustus Darley; the other is a man wrapped in a greatcoat, who has red hair and whiskers, and wears a pair of spectacles; but behind these spectacles there are dark brown eyes, which scarcely match the red hair, any better than the pale dark complexion agrees with the very roseate hue of the whiskers. These two gentlemen have come across the country from a little station a few miles from Slopperton-on-the-Sloshy.

———

"Well, Dick," said Darley, "doesn't this bring back old times, my boy?"

The red-haired gentleman, who was smoking a cigar, took it from his mouth and clasped his companion by the hand, and said—

"It does, Gus, old fellow; and when I forget the share you've had in to-day's work, may I——may I go back to that place and eat out my own heart, as I have done for eight years!"

There was something so very like a mist behind his spectacles, and such an ominous thickness in his voice, as the red-haired gentleman said this, that Gus proposed a glass of brandy before the train started.

"Come, Dick, old fellow, you're quite womanish to-night, I declare. This won't do, you know. I shall have to knock up some of our old pals and make a jolly night of it, when we get to London; though it will be to-morrow morning if you go on in this way."

"I'll tell you what it is, Gus," replied the red-haired gentleman, "nobody who hadn't gone through what I've gone through could tell what I feel to-night. I think, Gus, I shall end by being mad in real earnest; and that my release will do what my imprisonment even couldn't effect—turn my brain. But I say, Gus, tell me, tell me the truth; did any of the old fellows—did they ever think me guilty?"

"Not one of them, Dick, not one; and I know if one of them had so much as hinted at such a thought, the others would have throttled him before he could have said the words. Have another drop of brandy," he said hastily, thrusting the glass into his hand; "you've no more pluck than a kitten or a woman, Dick."

"I had pluck enough to bear eight years of that," said the young man, pointing in the direction of Slopperton, "but this does rather knock me over. My mother, you'll write to her, Gus—the sight of my hand might upset her, without a word of warning—you'll write and tell her that I've got a chance of escaping; and then you'll write and say that I have escaped. We must guard against a shock, Gus; she has suffered too much already on my account."

At this moment the bell rang for the train's starting: the young men took their seats in a second-class carriage; and away sped the engine, out through the dingy manufacturing town, into the open moonlit country.

Gus and Richard light their cigars, and wrap themselves in their railway rugs. Gus throws himself back and drops off to sleep (he can almost smoke in his sleep), and in a quarter of an hour he is dreaming of a fidgety patient who doesn't like comic songs, and who can never see the point of a joke; but who has three pretty daughters, and who pays his bill every Christmas without even looking at the items.

But Richard Marwood doesn't go to sleep. Will he ever sleep again? Will his nerves ever regain their tranquillity, after the intense excitement of the last three or four days? He looks back—looks back at that hideous time, and wonders at its hopeless suffering—wonders till he is obliged to wrench his mind away from the subject, for fear he should go mad. How did he ever endure it? How did he ever live through it? He had no means of suicide? Pshaw! he might have dashed out his brains against the wall. He might have resolutely refused food, and so have starved himself to death. How did he endure it? Eight years! Eight centuries! and every hour a fresh age of anguish! Looking back now, he knows, what then he did not know, that at the worst—that in his bitterest despair, there was a vague undefined something, so vague and undefined that he did not recognise it for itself—a glimmering ray of hope, by the aid of which alone he bore the dreadful burden of his days; and with clasped hands and bent head he renders up to that God from whose pity came this distant light a thanksgiving, which perhaps is not the less sincere and heartfelt for a hundred reckless words, said long ago, which rise up now in his mind a shame and a reproach.

Perhaps it was such a trial as this that Richard Marwood wanted, to make him a good and earnest man. Something to awaken dormant energies; something to arouse the better feelings of a noble soul, to stimulate to action an intellect hitherto wasted; something to throw him back upon the God he had forgotten, and to make him ultimately that which God, in creating such a man, meant him to become.

Away flies the engine. Was there ever such an open country? Was there ever such a moonlight night? Was earth ever so fair, or the heavens ever so bright, since man's universe was created? Not for Richard! He is free; free to breathe that blessed air; to walk that glorious earth; free to track to his doom the murderer of his uncle.

In the dead of the night the express train rattles into the Euston Square station; Richard and Gus spring out, and jump into a cab. Even smoky London, asleep under the moonlight, is beautiful in the eyes of Daredevil Dick, as they rattle through the deserted streets on the way to their destination.

CHAPTER V

THE CHEROKEES TAKE AN OATH

The cab stops in a narrow street in the neighbourhood of Drury Lane, before the door of a small public-house, which announces itself, in tarnished gilt letters on a dirty board, as "The Cherokee, by Jim Stilson." Jim Stilson is a very distinguished professor of the noble art of self-defence; and (in consequence of a peculiar playful knack he has with his dexter fist) is better known to his friends and the general public as the Left-handed Smasher.[1]

Of course, at this hour of the night, the respectable hostelry is wrapped in that repose which befits the house of a landlord who puts up his shutters and locks his door as punctually as the clocks of St. Mary-le-Strand and St. Clement Danes strike the midnight hour. There is not so much as the faintest glimmer of a rushlight in one of the upper windows; but for all that, Richard and Darley alight, and having dismissed the cab, Gus looks up and down the street to see that it is clear, puts his lips to the keyhole of the door of Mr. Stilson's hostelry, and gives an excellent imitation of the feeble miauw of an invalid member of the feline species.

Perhaps the Left-handed Smasher is tender-hearted, and nourishes an affection for distressed grimalkins;[2] for the door is softly opened—just wide enough to admit Richard and his friend.

The person who opens the door is a young lady, who has apparently been surprised in the act of putting her hair in curl-papers, as she hurriedly thrusts her brush and comb in among the biscuits and meat-pies in a corner of the bar. She is evidently very sleepy, and rather inclined to yawn in Mr. Augustus Darley's face; but as soon as they are safe inside, she fastens the door and resumes her station behind the bar. There is only one gas-lamp alight, and it is rather difficult to believe that the gentleman seated in the easy-chair before an expiring fire in the bar-parlour, his noble head covered with a red cotton bandanna, is neither more nor less than the immortal Left-handed one; but he snores loud enough for the whole prize-ring, and the nervous listener is inclined to wish that he had made a point of clearing his head before he went to sleep.

"Well, Sophia Maria," says Mr. Darley, "are they all up there?" pointing in the direction of a door that leads to the stairs.

"Most every one of 'em, sir; there's no getting 'em to break up, nohow. Mr. Splitters has been and wrote a drama for the Victoria Theayter, and they've been a-chaffing of him awful because there's fifteen murders, and four low-comedy servants that all say, 'No you don't,' in it. The guv'nor had to go up just now, and talk to 'em, for they was a throwin' quart pots at each other, playful."

"Then I'll run up, and speak to them for a minute," said Gus. "Come along, Dick."

"How about your friend, sir," remonstrated the Smasher's Hebe; "he isn't a Cheerful, is he, sir?"

"Oh, I'll answer for him," said Gus. "It's all right, Sophia Maria; bring us a couple of glasses of brandy-and-water hot, and tell the Smasher to step up, when I ring the bell."

Sophia Maria looked doubtfully from Gus to the slumbering host, and said—

"He'll wake up savage if I disturb him. He's off for his first sleep now, and he'll go to bed as soon as the place is clear."

"Never mind, Sophia; wake him up when I ring, and send him upstairs; he'll find something there to put him in a good temper. Come, Dick, tumble up. You know the way."

The Cheerful Cherokees made their proximity known by such a stifling atmosphere of tobacco about the staircase as would have certainly suffocated anyone not initiated in their mysteries. Gus opened the door of a back room on the first floor, of a much larger size than the general appearance of the house would have promised. This room was full of gentlemen, who, in age, size, costume, and personal advantages, varied as much as it is possible for any one roomful of gentlemen to do. Some of them were playing billiards; some of them were looking on, betting on the players; or more often upbraiding them for such play as, in the Cheerful dialect, came under the sweeping denunciation of the Cherokee adjective "dufling." Some of them were eating a peculiar compound entitled "Welsh rarebit"[3]—a pleasant preparation, if it had not painfully reminded the casual observer of mustard-poultices, or yellow soap in a state of solution—while lively friends knocked the ashes of their pipes into their plates, abstracted their porter just as they were about to imbibe that beverage, and in like fascinating manner beguiled the festive hour. One gentleman, a young Cherokee, had had a rarebit, and had gone to sleep with his head in his plate and his eyebrows in his mustard. Some were playing cards; some were playing dominoes; one gentleman was in tears, because the double-six he wished to play had fallen into a neighbouring spittoon, and he lacked either the moral courage or the physical energy requisite for picking it up; but as, with the exception of the sleepy gentleman, everybody was talking very loud and on an entirely different subject, the effect was lively, not to say distracting.

"Gentlemen," said Gus, "I have the honour of bringing a friend, whom I wish to introduce to you."

"All right, Gus!" said the gentleman engaged at dominoes, "that's the cove I ought to play," and fixing one half-open eye on the spotted ivory, he lapsed into a series of imbecile imprecations on everybody in general, and the domino in particular.

Richard took a seat at a little distance from this gentleman, and at the bottom of the long table—a seat sacred on grand occasions to the vice-chairman. Some rather noisy lookers-on at the billiards were a little inclined to resent this, and muttered something about Dick's red wig and whiskers, in connection with the popular accompaniments to a boiled round of beef.

"I say, Darley," cried a gentleman, who held a billiard-cue in his hand, and had been for some time impotently endeavouring to smooth his hair with the same. "I say, old fellow, I hope your friend's committed a murder or two, because then Splitters can put him in a new piece."

Splitters, who had for four hours been in a state of abject misery, from the unmerciful allusions to his last *chef d'œuvre*, gave a growl from a distant corner of the table, where he was seeking consolation in everybody else's glass; and as everybody drank a different beverage, was not improving his state of mind thereby.

"My friend never committed a murder in his life, Splitters, so he won't dramatize on that score; but he's been accused of one; and he's as innocent as you are, who never murdered any thing in your life but Lindley Murray[4] and the language of your country."

"Who's been murdering somebody?" said the domino-player, passing his left hand through his hair, till his chevelure resembled a turk's-head broom. "Who's murdered? I wish everybody was; and that I could dance my favourite dance upon their graves. Blow that double-six; he's the fellow I ought to play."

"Perhaps you'll give us your auburn-haired friend's name, Darley," said a gentleman with his mouth full of Welsh rarebit; "he doesn't seem too brilliant to live; he'd better have gone to the 'Deadly Livelies,' in the other street." The "Deadly Livelies" was the sobriquet of a rival club, which plumed itself on being a cut above the Cherokees. "Who's dead?" muttered the domino-player. "I wish everybody was, and that I was contracted with to bury 'em cheap. I should have won the game," he added plaintively, "if I could have picked up that double-six."

"I suppose your friend wants to be Vice at our next meeting," said the gentleman with the billiard-cue; who, in default of a row, always complained that the assembly was too quiet for him.

"It wouldn't be the first time if he were Vice, and it wouldn't be the first time if you made him Chair," said Gus. "Come, old fellow, tell them you're come back, and ask them if they're glad to see you?"

The red-haired gentleman at this sprang to his feet, threw off the rosy locks and the ferocious whiskers, and looked round at the Cherokees with his hands in his pockets.

"Daredevil Dick!" A shout arose—one brief wild huzza, such as had not been heard in that room—which, as we know, was none of the quietest—within the memory of the oldest Cherokee. Daredevil Dick—escaped—come back—as handsome as ever—as jolly as ever—as glorious a fellow—as thoroughgoing a brick—as noble-hearted a trump as eight years ago, when he had been the life and soul of all of them! such shaking of hands; everybody shaking hands with him again and again, and then everybody shaking hands with everybody else; and the billiard-player wiping his eyes with his cue; and the sleepy gentleman waking up and rubbing the mustard into his drowsy optics; and the domino-player, who, though he execrates all mankind, wouldn't hurt the tiniest wing of the tiniest fly, even he makes a miraculous effort, picks up the double-six, and magnanimously presents it to Richard.

"Take it—take it, old fellow, and may it make you happy! If I'd played that domino, I should have won the game." Upon which he executed two or three steps of a Cherokee dance, and relapsed into the aforesaid imbecile imprecations, in mixed French and English, on the inhabitants of a world not capable of appreciating him.

It was a long time before anything like quiet could be restored; but when it was, Richard addressed the meeting.

"Gentlemen, before the unfortunate circumstance which has so long separated us, you knew me, I believe, well, and I am proud to think you esteemed and trusted me."

Did they? Oh, *rather.* They jingled all the glasses, and broke three in the enthusiastic protestation of an affirmative.

"I need not allude to the unhappy accusation of which I have been the victim. You are, I understand, acquainted with the full particulars of my miserable story, and you render me happy by thinking me to be innocent."

By thinking him to be innocent? By knowing him to be innocent! They are so indignant at the bare thought of anybody believing otherwise, that somebody in the doorway, the Smasher himself, growls out something about a—forcible adjective—noise, and the police.

"Gentlemen, I have this day regained my liberty; thanks to the exertions of a person to whom I am also indebted for my life, and thanks also to the assistance of my old friend Gus Darley."

Everybody here insisted on shaking hands over again with Gus, which was rather a hindrance to the speaker's progress; but at last Richard went on,—

"Now, gentlemen, relying on your friendship" (hear, hear! and another glass broken), "I am about to appeal to you to assist me in the future object of my life. That object will be to discover the real murderer of my uncle, Montague Harding. In what manner, when, or where you may be able to assist me in this, I cannot at present say, but you are all, gentlemen, men of talent." (More glasses broken, and a good deal of beer spilt into everybody's boots.) "You are all men of varied experience, of inexhaustible knowledge of the world, and of the life of London. Strange things happen every day of our lives. Who shall say that some one amongst you may not fall, by some strange accident, or let me say rather by the handiwork of Providence, across a clue to this at present entirely unravelled mystery? Promise me, therefore, gentlemen, to give me the benefit of your experience; and whenever that experience throws you into the haunts of bad men, remember that the man I seek may, by some remote chance, be amongst them; and that to find him is the one object of my life. I cannot give you the faintest index to what he may be, or who he may be. He may be dead, and beyond the reach of justice—but he may live! and if he does, Heaven grant that the man who has suffered the stigma of his guilt may track him to his doom. Gentlemen, tell me that your hearts go with me."

They told him so, not once, but a dozen times; shaking hands with him, and pushing divers liquors into his hand every time. But they got over it at last, and the gentleman with the billiard-cue rapped their heads with that instrument to tranquillize them, and then rose as president, and said,—

"Richard Marwood, our hearts go with you, thoroughly and entirely, and we swear to give you the best powers of our intellects and the utmost strength of our abilities to aid you in your search. Gentlemen, are you prepared to subscribe to this oath?"

They were prepared to subscribe to it, and they did subscribe to it, every one of them—rather noisily, but very heartily.

When they had done so, a gentleman emerges from the shadow of the doorway, who is no other than the illustrious Left-handed one, who had come upstairs in answer to Darley's summons, just before Richard addressed the Cherokees. The Smasher was not a handsome man. His nose had been broken a good many times, and that hadn't improved him; he had a considerable number of scars about his face, including almost every known variety of cut, and they didn't improve him. His complexion, again, bore perhaps too close a resemblance to mottled soap to come within the region of the beautiful; but he had a fine and manly expression of countenance, which, in his amiable moments, reminded the beholder of a benevolent bulldog.

He came up to Richard, and took him by the hand. It was no small ordeal of courage to shake hands with the Left-handed Smasher, but Daredevil Dick stood it like a man.

"Mr. Richard Marwood," said he, "you've been a good friend to me, ever since you was old enough—" he stopped here, and cast about in his mind for the fitting pursuits of early youth—"ever since you was old enough to give a cove a black eye, or knock your friend's teeth down his throat with a light backhander. I've known you down stairs, a-swearin' at the barmaid, and holdin' your own agin the whole lot of the Cheerfuls, when other young gents of your age was a-makin' themselves bad with sweetstuffs and green apples, and callin' it life. I've known you help that gent yonder," he gave a jerk with his thumb in the direction of the domino-player, "to wrench off his own pa's knocker, and send it to him by two-penny post next mornin', seventeen and sixpence to pay postage; but I never know'd you to do a bad action, or to hit out upon a cove as was down."

Richard thanked the Smasher for his good opinion, and they shook hands again.

"I'll tell you what it is," continued the host, "I'm a man of few words. If a cove offends me, I give him my left between his eyes, playful; if he does it agen, I give him my left agen, with a meanin', and he don't repeat it. If a gent as I like does me proud, I feels grateful, and when I has a chance I shows him my gratitude. Mr. Richard Marwood, I'm your friend to the last spoonful of my claret; and let the man as murdered your uncle keep clear of my left mawley,[5] if he wants to preserve his beauty."

CHAPTER VI

Mr. Peters Relates How He Thought He Had a Clue, and How He Lost It

A week after the meeting of the Cherokees Richard Marwood received his mother, in a small furnished house he had taken in Spring Gardens. Mrs. Marwood, possessed of the entire fortune of her murdered brother, was a very rich woman. Of her large income she had, during the eight years of her son's imprisonment, spent scarcely anything; as, encouraged by Mr. Joseph Peters's mysterious hints and vague promises, she had looked forward to the deliverance of her beloved and only child. The hour had come. She held him in her arms again, free.

"No, mother, no," he says, "not free. Free from the prison walls, but not free from the stain of the false accusation. Not till the hour when all England declares my innocence shall I be indeed a free man. Why, look you, mother, I cannot go out of this room into yonder street without such a disguise as a murderer himself might wear, for fear some Slopperton official should recognise the features of the lunatic criminal, and send me back to my cell at the asylum."

"My darling boy," she lays her hands upon his shoulders, and looks proudly into his handsome face, "my darling boy, these people at Slopperton think you dead. See," she touched her black dress as she spoke, "it is for you I wear this. A painful deception, Richard, even for such an object. I cannot bear to think of that river, and of what might have been."

"Dear mother, I have been saved, perhaps, that I may make some atonement for that reckless, wicked past."

"Only reckless, Richard; never wicked. You had always the same noble heart, always the same generous soul; you were always my dear and only son."

"You remember what the young man says in the play, mother, when he gets into a scrape through neglecting his garden and making love to his master's daughter—'You shall be proud of your son yet.' "

"I *shall* be proud of you, Richard. I am proud of you. We are rich; and wealth is power. Justice shall be done you yet, my darling boy. You have friends——"

"Yes, mother, good and true ones. Peters—you brought him with you?"

"Yes; I persuaded him to resign his situation. I have settled a hundred a year on him for life—a poor return for what he has done, Richard; but it was all I could induce him to accept, and he only agreed to take that on condition that every moment of his life should be devoted to your service."

"Is he in the house now, mother?"

"Yes, he is below; I will ring for him."

"Do, mother. I must go over to Darley, and take him with me. You must not think me an inattentive or neglectful son; but remember that my life has but one business till that man is found."

He wrung her hand, and left her standing at the window watching his receding figure through the quiet dusky street.

Her gratitude to Heaven for his restoration is deep and heartfelt; but there is a shade of sadness in her face as she looks out into the twilight after him, and thinks of the eight wasted years of his youth, and of his bright manhood now spent on a chimera; for she thinks he will never find the murderer of his uncle. How, after eight years, without one clue by which to trace him, how can he hope to track the real criminal?

But Heaven is above us all, Agnes Marwood; and in the dark and winding paths of life light sometimes comes when and whence we least expect it.

If you go straight across Blackfriars Bridge, and do not suffer yourself to be beguiled either by the attractions of that fashionable transpontine[1] lounge, the "New Cut," or by the eloquence of the last celebrity at that circular chapel some time sacred to Rowland Hill[2]—if you are not a man to be led away by whelks and other piscatorial delicacies, second-hand furniture, birds and bird-cages, or easy shaving, you may ultimately reach, at the inland end of the road, a locality known to the inhabitants of the district of Friar Street. Whether, in any dark period of our ecclesiastical history, the members of the mother church were ever reduced to the necessity of living in this neighbourhood I am not prepared to say. But if ever any of the magnates of the Catholic faith did hang out in this direction, it is to be hoped that the odours from the soap-boiler's round the corner, the rich essences from the tallow manufactory over the way, the varied perfumes from the establishment of the gentleman who does a thousand pounds a week in size, to say nothing of such minor and domestic effluvia as are represented by an amalgamation of red herrings, damp corduroy, old boots, onions, washing, a chimney on fire, dead cats, bad eggs, and an open drain or two—it is to be hoped, I say, that these conflicting scents did not pervade the breezes of Friar Street so strongly in the good old times as they do in these our later days of luxury and refinement.

Mr. Darley's establishment, ordinarily spoken of as *the* surgery *par excellence*, was perhaps one of the most pretending features of the street. It asserted itself, in fact, with such a redundancy of gilt letters and gas burners, that it seemed to say, "Really now, you must be ill; or if you're not, you ought to be." It was not a very large house, this establishment of Mr. Darley's, but there were at least half-a-dozen bells on the doorpost. There was Surgery; then there was Day and Night (Gus wanted to have Morning and Afternoon, but somebody told him it wasn't professional); then there was besides surgery, day, and night bells, another brilliant brass knob, inscribed "Visitors," and a ditto ditto, whereon was engraved "Shop." Though, as there was only one small back-parlour beyond the shop into which visitors ever penetrated, and as it was the custom for all such visitors to walk straight through the aforesaid shop into the aforesaid parlour without availing themselves of any bell whatever, the brass knobs were looked upon rather in the light of a conventionality than a convenience.

But Gus said they looked like business, especially when they were clean, which wasn't always, as a couple of American gentlemen, friends of Darley's, were in the habit of squirting tobacco-juice at them from the other side of the way, in the dusky twilight; the man who hit the brass oftenest out of six times to be the winner, and the loser to stand beer all the evening—that is to say, until some indefinite time on the following morning, for Darley's parties seldom broke up very early; and to let the visitors out and take the morning milk in was often a simultaneous proceeding in the household of our young surgeon.

If he had been a surgeon only, he would surely have been a Sir Benjamin Brodie;[3] for when it is taken into account that he could play the piano, organ, guitar, and violoncello, without having learned any of those instruments; that he could write a song, and compose the melody to it; that he could draw horses and dogs after Herring[4] and Landseer;[5] make more puns in one sentence than any burlesque writer living; make love to half-a-dozen women at once, and be believed by every one of them; sing a comic song, or tell a funny story; name the winner of the Derby safer than any prophet on that side of the water; and make his book for the Leger with one hand while he wrote a prescription with the other; the discriminating reader will allow that there was a good deal of some sort of talent or other in the composition of Mr. Augustus Darley.

In the twilight of this particular autumn evening he is busily engaged putting up a heap of little packets labelled "Best Epsom Salts," while his assistant, a very small youth, of a far more elderly appearance than his master, lights the gas. The half-glass door that communicates with the little back-parlour is ajar, and Gus is talking to some one within.

"If I go over the water to-night, Bell—" he says.

A feminine voice from within interrupts him—"But you won't go to-night, Gus; the last time you went to that horrid Smasher's, Mrs. Tompkins's little boy was ill, and they sent into the London Road for Mr. Parker. And you are such a favourite with everybody, dear, that they say if you'd only stay at home always, you'd have the best practice in the neighbourhood."

"But, Bell, how can a fellow stay at home night after night, and perhaps half his time only sell a penn'orth of salts or a poor man's plaster? If they'd be ill," he added, almost savagely, "I wouldn't mind stopping in; there's some interest in that. Or if they'd come and have their teeth drawn; but they never will: and I'm sure I sell 'em our Infallible Anti-toothache Tincture; and if that don't make 'em have their teeth out, nothing will."

"Come and have your tea, Gus; and tell Snix to bring his basin."

Snix was the boy, who forthwith drew from a cupboard under the counter the identical basin into which, when a drunken man was brought into the shop, Gus usually bled him, with a double view of obtaining practice in his art and bringing the patient back to consciousness.

The feminine occupant of the parlour is a young lady with dark hair and grey eyes, and something under twenty years of age. She is Augustus Darley's only sister; she keeps his house, and in an emergency she can make up a prescription—nay, has been known to draw a juvenile patient's first tooth, and give him his money back after the operation for the purchase of consolatory sweetstuffs.

Perhaps Isabel Darley is just a little what very prim young ladies, who have never passed the confines of the boarding-school or the drawing-room, might call "fast." But when it is taken into consideration that she was left an orphan at an early age, that she never went to school in her life, and that she has for a very considerable period been in the habit of associating with her brother's friends, chiefly members of the Cherokee Society, it is not so much to be wondered at that she is a little more masculine in her attainments, and "go-ahead" in her opinions, than some others of her sex.

The parlour is small, as has before been stated. One of the Cherokees has been known to suggest, when there were several visitors present and the time arrived for their departure, that they should be taken out singly with a corkscrew. Other Cherokees, arriving after the room had been filled with visitors, had been heard to advise that somebody should go in first with a candle, to ascertain whether vitality could be sustained in the atmosphere. Perhaps the accommodation was not extended by the character of the furniture, which consisted of a cottage piano, a chair for the purposes of dental surgery, a small Corinthian column supporting a basin with a metal plug and chain useful for like purposes; also a violoncello in the corner, a hanging bookshelf—(which was a torture to tall Cherokees, as one touch from a manly head would tilt down the shelves and shower the contents of Mr. Darley's library on the head in question, like a literary waterfall)—and a good-sized sofa, with that unmistakable well, and hard back and arms, which distinguish the genus sofa-bedstead. Of course tables, chairs, china ornaments, a plaster-of-Paris bust here and there, caricatures on the walls, a lamp that wouldn't burn, and a patent arrangement for the manufacture of toasted cheese, are trifles in the way of furniture not worth naming. Miss Darley's birds, again, though they did spill seed and water into the eyes of unoffending visitors, and drop lumps of dirty sugar sharply down upon the noses of the same, could not of course be considered a nuisance; but certainly the compound surgery and back-parlour in the mansion of Augustus Darley was, to say the least, a little too full of furniture.

While Isabel is pouring out the tea, two gentlemen open the shop door, and the bell attached thereto, which should ring but doesn't, catching in the foremost visitor's foot, nearly precipitates him headlong into the emporium of the disciple of Esculapius. This foremost visitor is no other than Mr. Peters, and the tall figure behind him, wrapped in a greatcoat, is Daredevil Dick.

"Here I am, Gus!" he cries out, in his own bold hearty voice; "here I am; found your place at last, in spite of the fascinations of half the stale shell-fish in the United Kingdom. Here I am; and here's the best friend I have in the world, not even excepting yourself, old fellow."

Gus introduces Richard to his sister Isabel, who has been taught from her childhood to look upon the young man shut up in a lunatic asylum down at Slopperton as the greatest hero, next to Napoleon Buonaparte, that ever the world had boasted. She was a little girl of eleven years old at the time of Dick's trial, and had never seen her wild brother's wilder companion; and she looks up now at the dark handsome face with a glance of almost reverence in her deep gray eyes. But Bell is by no means a heroine; and she has a dozen unheroine-like occupations. She has the tea to pour out, and in her nervous excitement she scalds Richard's fingers, drops the sugar into the slop-basin, and pours all the milk into one cup of tea. What she would have done without the assistance of Mr. Peters, it is impossible to say; for that gentleman showed himself the very genius of order; cut thin bread-and-butter enough for half-a-dozen, which not one of the party touched; re-filled the teapot before it was empty; lit the gas-lamp which hung from the ceiling; shut the door which communicated with the shop and the other door which led on to the staircase; and did all so quietly that nobody knew he was doing anything.

Poor Richard! In spite of the gratitude and happiness he feels in his release, there is a gloom upon his brow and an abstraction in his manner, which he tries in vain to shake off.

A small, round, chubby individual, who might be twelve or twenty, according to the notions of the person estimating her age, removed the tea-tray, and in so doing broke a saucer. Gus looked up. "She always does it," he said, mildly. "We're getting quite accustomed to the sound. It rather reduces our stock of china, and we sometimes are obliged to send out to buy tea-things before we can have any breakfast; but she's a good girl, and she doesn't steal the honey, or the jujubes,[6] or the tartaric acid[7] out of the seidlitz-powders,[8] as the other one did; not that I minded that much," he continued; "but she couldn't read, and she sometimes filled up the papers with arsenic for fear of being found out; and that might have been inconvenient, if we'd ever happened to sell them."

"Now, Gus," said Richard, as he drew his chair up to the fire-place and lit his pipe—permission being awarded by Bell, who lived in one perpetual atmosphere of tobacco-smoke—"now, Gus, I want Peters to tell you all about this affair; how it was he thought me innocent; how he hit upon the plan he formed for saving my neck; how he tried to cast about and find a clue to the real mur-derer; how he thought he had found a clue, and how he lost it."

"Shall my sister stop while he tells the story?" asked Gus.

"She *is* your sister, Gus," answered Richard. "She cannot be so un-like you as not to be a true and pitying friend to me. Miss Darley," he continued, turning towards her as he spoke, "you do not think me quite so bad a fellow as the world has made me out; you would like to see me righted, and my name freed from the stain of a vile crime?"

"Mr. Marwood," the girl answered, in an earnest voice, "I have heard your sad story again and again from my brother's lips. Had you too been my brother, I could not, believe me, have felt a deeper interest in your fate, or a truer sorrow for your misfortunes. It needs but to look into your face, or hear your voice, to know how little you deserve the imputation that has been cast upon you."

Richard rises and gives her his hand. No languid and lady-like pressure, such as would not brush the down off a butterfly's wing, but an honest hearty grasp, that comes straight from the heart.

"And now for Mr. Peters's story," said Gus, "while I brew a jugful of whisky-punch."

"You can follow his hands, Gus?" asks Richard.

"Every twist and turn of them. He and I had many a confab about you, old fellow, before we went out fishing," said Gus, look-ing up from the pleasing occupation of peeling a lemon.

"Now for it, then," said Richard; and Mr. Peters accordingly began.

Perhaps, considering his retiring from the Slopperton police force a great event, not to say a crisis, in his life, Mr. Peters had celebrated it by another event; and, taking the tide of his affairs at the flood, had availed himself of the water to wash his hands with. At any rate, the digital alphabet was a great deal cleaner than when, eight years ago, he spelt out the two words, "Not guilty," in the railway carriage.

There was something very strange to a looker-on in the little party, Gus, Richard, and Bell, all with earnest eyes fixed on the active fingers of the detective—the silence only broken by some exclamation at intervals from one of the three.

"When first I see this young gent," say the fingers, as Mr. Peters designates Richard with a jerk of his elbow, "I was a-standin' on the other side of the way, a-waitin' till my superior, Jinks, as was as much up to his business as a kitting,"—(Mr. Peters has rather what we may call a fancy style of orthography, and takes the final *g* off some words to clap it on to others, as his taste dictates)—"a-waitin,' I say, till Jinks should want my assistance. Well, gents all—beggin' the lady's parding, as sits up so manly, with none of yer faintin' nor 'steriky⁹ games, as I a'most forgot she was a lady—no sooner did I clap eyes upon Mr. Marwood here, a-smokin' his pipe, in Jinks's face, and a-answerin' him sharp, and a-behavin' what you may call altogether cocky, than I says to myself, 'They've got the wrong un. My fust words and my last about this 'ere gent, was, 'They've got the wrong un.' "

Mr. Peters looked round at the attentive party with a glance of triumph, rubbed his hands by way of a full-stop, and went on with his manual recital.

"For why?" said the fingers, interrogatively, "for why did I think as this 'ere gent was no good for this 'ere murder; for why did I think them chaps at Slopperton had got on the wrong scent? Because he was cheeky? Lor' bless your precious eyes, miss" (by way of gallantry he addresses himself here to Isabel), "not a bit of it! When a cove goes and cuts another cove's throat off-hand, it ain't likely he ain't prepared to cheek a police-officer. But when I reckoned up this young gent's face, what was it I see? Why, as plain as I see his nose and his moustachios—and he ain't bad off for neither of them," said the fingers, parenthetically—"I see that he hadn't done it. Now, a cove what's screwed up to face a judge and jury, maybe can face 'em, and never change a line of his mug; but there isn't a cove as lives as can stand that first tap of a detective's hand upon his shoulder as tells him, plain as words, 'The game is up.' The best of 'em, and the pluckiest of 'em, drops under that. If they keeps the colour in their face—which some of 'em has got the power to do, and none as never tried it on can guess the pain—if they can do that 'ere, the perspiration breaks out wet and cold upon their for'eds, and that blows 'em. But this young gent—he was took aback, he was surprised, and he was riled, and used bad language; but his colour never changed, and he wasn't once knocked over till Jinks, unbusiness-like, told him of his uncle's murder, when he turned as white as that 'ere 'ed of Bon-*er*-part." Mr. Peters, for want of a better comparison, glanced in the direction of a bust of the victor of Marengo,[10] which, what with tobacco-smoke and a ferocious pair of burnt cork moustachios, was by no means the whitest object in creation.

"Now, what a detective officer's good at, if he's worth his salt, is this 'ere: when he sees two here and another two there, he can put 'em together, though they might be a mile apart to anybody not up to the trade, and make 'em into four. So, thinks I, the gent isn't took aback at bein' arrested; but he *is* took aback when he hears as how his uncle's murdered. Now, if he'd committed the murder, he'd know of it; and he might sham surprise, but he wouldn't be surprised; and this young gent was knocked all of a heap as genuine as—" Mr. Peters's ideas still revert to the bust of Napoleon— "as ever that 'ere forring cove was, when he sees his old guard scrunched up small at the battle of Waterloo."

"Heaven knows, Peters," said Richard, taking his pipe out of his mouth, and looking up from his stooping position over the fire, "Heaven knows you were right; I did feel my heart turn cold when I heard of that good man's death."

"Well, that they'd got the wrong un I saw was as clear as daylight—but where was the right un? That was the question. Whoever committed the murder did it for the money in that 'ere cabinet: and sold agen they was, whoever they was, and didn't get the money. Who was in the house? This young gent's mother and the servant. I was nobody in the Gardenford force, and I was less than nobody at Slopperton; so get into that house at the Black Mill I couldn't. This young gent was walked off to jail and I was sent about my business—my orders bein' to be back in Gardenford that evenin', leavin' Slopperton by the three-thirty train. Well, I was a little cut up about this young gent; for I seed that the case was dead agen him; the money in his pocket—the blood on his sleeve—a cock-and-a-bull story of a letter of introduction, and a very evident attempt at a bolt—only enough to hang him, that's all; and, for all that, I had a inward conwiction that he was as hinnercent of the murder as that 'ere plaster-of-Paris stattur." Mr. Peters goes regularly to the bust for comparisons, by way of saving time and trouble in casting about for fresh ones.

"But my orders," continued the fingers, "was positive, so I goes down to the station to start by the three-thirty; and as I walks into the station-yard, I hears the whistle, and sees the train go. I was too late; and as the next train didn't start for near upon three hours, I thought I'd take a stroll and 'av a look at the beauties of Slopperton. Well, I strolls on, promiscuous like, till I comes to the side of a jolly dirty-looking river; and as by this time I feels a little dry, I walks on, lookin' about for a public; but ne'er a one do I see, till I almost tumbles into a dingy little place, as looked as if it did about half-a-pint a-day reg'lar, when business was brisk. But in I walks, past the bar; and straight afore me I sees a door as leads into the parlour. The passage was jolly dark; and this 'ere door was ajar; and inside I hears voices. Well, you see, business is business, and pleasure is pleasure; but when a cove takes a pleasure in his business, he gets a way of lettin' his business habits come out unbeknownst when he's takin' his pleasure: so I listens. Now, the voice I heerd fust was a man's voice; and, though the place was a sort of crib such as nobody but navvies or such-like would be in the habit of going to, this 'ere was the voice of a gentleman. I can't say as I ever paid much attention to grammar myself, though I daresay it's very pleasant and amusin' when you enter into it; but, for all that, I'd knocked about in the world long enough to know a gent's way of speakin' from a navvy's, as well as I know'd one tune on the accordion from another tune. It was a nice, soft-spoken voice too, and quite melodious and pleasant to listen to; but it was a-sayin' some of the cruelest and hardest words as ever was spoke to a woman yet by any creature with the cheek to call hisself a man. You're not much good, my friend, says I, with your lardy-dardy ways and your cold-blooded words, whoever you are. You're a thin chap, with light hair and white hands, I know, though I've never seen you; and there's very little in the way of wickedness that you wouldn't be up to on a push. Now, just as I was a-thinkin' this, he said somethin' that sent the blood up into my face as hot as fire—'I expected a sum of money, and I've been disappointed of it,' he said; and before the girl he was a-talkin' to could open her lips, he caught her up sudden—'Never you mind how,' he says, 'never you mind how.'

"He expected a sum of money, and he'd been disappointed of it! So had the man who had murdered this young gent's uncle.

"Not much in this, perhaps. But why was he so frightened at the thoughts of her asking him how he expected the money, and how he'd bin disappointed? There it got fishy. At any rate, says I to myself, I'll have a look at you, my friend; so in I walks, very quiet and quite unbeknownst. He was a-sittin' with his back to the door, and the young woman he was a-talkin' to was standin' lookin' out of the winder; so neither of 'em saw me. He was buildin' up some cards into a 'ouse, and had got 'em up very high, when I laid my hand upon his shoulder sudden. He turned round and looked at me." Mr. Peters here paused, and looked round at the little group, who sat watching his fingers with breathless attention. He had evidently come to a point in his narrative.

"Now, what did I see in his face when he looked at me? Why, the very same look that I *missed* in the face of this young gent when Jinks took him in the mornin'. The very same look that I'd seen in a many faces, and never know'd it differ, whether it came one way or another, always bein' the same look at bottom—the look of a man as is guilty of what will hang him and thinks that he's found out. But as you can't give looks in as evidence, this wasn't no good in a practical way; but I says to myself, if ever there was anything certain in this world since it was begun, I've come across the right un: so I sits down and takes up a newspaper. I signified to him that I was dumb, and he took it for granted that I was deaf as well—which was one of those stupid mistakes your clever chaps sometimes fall into—so he went on a-talking to the girl.

"Well, it was a old story enough, what him and the girl was talkin' of; but every word he said made him out a more cold-blooded villain than the last.

"Presently he offered her some money—four sovereigns. She served him as he ought to have been served, and threw them every one slap in his face. One cut him over the eye; and I was glad of it. 'You're marked, my man,' thinks I, 'and nothin' could be handier agen I want you.' He picked up three of the sovereigns, but for all he could do he couldn't find the fourth. So he had the cut (which was a jolly deep un) plastered up, and he went away. She stared at the river uncommon hard, and then she went away. Now I didn't much like the look she gave the river, so as I had about half an hour to spare before the train started, I followed her. I think she knew it; for presently she turned short off into a little street, and when I turned into it after her she wasn't to be seen right or left.

"Well, I had but half an hour, so I thought it was no use chasin' this unfortunate young creature through all the twistings and turnings of the back slums of Slopperton; so after a few minutes' consideration, I walked straight to the station. Hang me if I wasn't too late for the train again. I don't know how it was, but I couldn't keep my mind off the young woman, nor keep myself from wonderin' what she was a-goin' to do with herself, and what she was a-goin' to do with that 'ere baby. So I walks back agen down by the water, and as I'd a good hour and a half to spare, I walks a good way, thinking of the young man, and the cut on his forehead. It was nigh upon dark by this time, and foggy into the bargain. Maybe I'd gone a mile or more, when I comes up to a barge what lay at anchor quite solitary. It was a collier, and there was a chap on board, sittin' in the stern, smokin', and lookin' at the water. There was no one else in sight but him and me; and no sooner does he spy me comin' along the bank than he sings out,

" 'Hulloa! Have you met a young woman down that way?'

"His words struck me all of a heap somehow, comin' so near upon what I was a-thinkin' of myself. I shook my head; and he said,

" 'There's been some unfort'nate young girl down here tryin' to dround her baby. I see the little chap in the water, and fished him out with my boat-hook. I'd seen the girl hangin' about here, just as it was a-gettin' dark, and then I heard the splash when she threw the child in; but the fog was too thick for me to see anything ashore by that time.'

"The barge was just alongside the bank, and I stepped on board. Not bein' so fortunate as to have a voice, you know, it comes awkward with strangers, and I was rather put to it to get on with the young man. And didn't he sing out loud when he came to understand I was dumb; he couldn't have spoke in a higher key if I'd been a forriner.

"He told me he should take the baby round to the Union; all he hoped he said, was, that the mother wasn't a-goin' to do anything bad with herself.

"I hoped not too; but I remembered that look of hers when she stood at the window staring out at the river, and I didn't feel very easy in my mind about her.

"I took the poor little wet thing up in my arms. The young man had wrapped it in an old jacket, and it was a-cryin' piteous, and lookin', oh, so scared and miserable.

"Well, it may seem a queer whim, but I'm rather soft-hearted on the subject of babies, and often had a thought that I should like to try the power of cultivation in the way of business, and bring a child up from the very cradle to the police detective line, to see whether I couldn't make that 'ere child a ornament to the force. I wasn't a marryin' man, and by no means likely ever to 'av a family of my own; so when I took up that 'ere baby in my arms, somehow or other the thought came into my 'ed of adoptin' him, and bringin' of him up. So I rolled him up in my greatcoat, and took him with me to Gardenford."

"And a wonderful boy he is," said Richard; "we'll educate him, Peters, and make a gentleman of him."

"Wait a bit," said the fingers very quickly; "thank you kindly, sir; but if the police force of this 'ere country was robbed of that 'ere boy, it would be robbed of a gem as it couldn't afford to lose."

"Go on, Peters; tell them the rest of your story."

"Well, though I felt in my own mind that by one of those strange chances which does happen in life, maybe as often as they happen in story-books, I had fallen across the man who had committed the murder, yet for all that I hadn't evidence enough to get a hearin'. I got transferred from Gardenford to Slopperton, and every leisure minute I had I tried to come across the man I'd marked; but nowhere could I see him, or hear of any one answering his description. I went to the churches; for I thought him capable of anything, even to shammin' pious. I went to the theayter, and I see a young woman accused of poisonin' a fam'ly, and proved innocent by a police cove as didn't know his business any more than a fly. I went anywhere and everywhere, but I never see that man; and it was gettin' uncommon near the trial of this young gent, and nothin' done. How was he to be saved? I thought of it by night and thought of it by day; but work it out I couldn't nohow. One day I hears of an old friend of the pris'ner's being sup-boned-aed[11] as witness for the crown. This friend I determined to see; for two 'eds"—Mr. Peters looked round, as though he defied contradiction—"shall be better than one."

"And this friend," said Gus, "was your humble servant; who was only too glad to find that poor Dick had one sincere friend in the world who believed in his innocence, besides myself."

"Well, Mr. Darley and me," resumed Mr. Peters, "put our 'eds together, and we came to this conclusion, that if this young gent was mad when he committed the murder, they couldn't hang him, but would shut him in a asylum for the rest of his nat'ral life—which mayn't be pleasant in the habstract, but which is better than hangin', any day."

"So you determined on proving me mad," said Richard.

"We hadn't such very bad grounds to go upon, perhaps, old fellow," replied Mr. Darley; "that brain-fever, which we thought such a misfortune when it laid you up for three dreary weeks, stood us in good stead; we had something to go upon, for we knew we could get you off by no other means. But to get you off this way we wanted your assistance, and we didn't hit upon the plan till it was too late to get at you and tell you our scheme; we didn't hit upon it till twelve o'clock on the night before your trial. We tried to see your counsel; but he had that morning left the town, and wasn't to return till the trial came on. Peters hung about the court all the morning, but couldn't see him; and nothing was done when the judge and jury took their seats. You know the rest; how Peters caught your eye—"

"Yes," said Dick, "and how seven letters upon his fingers told me the whole scheme, and gave me my cue; those letters formed these two words, 'Sham mad.' "

"And very well you did it at the short notice, Dick," said Gus; "upon my word, for the moment I was almost staggered, and thought, suppose in getting up this dodge we are only hitting upon the truth, and the poor fellow really has been driven out of his wits by this frightful accusation?"

"A scrap of paper," said Mr. Peters, on his active fingers, "gave the hint to your counsel—a sharp chap enough, though a young un."

"I can afford to reward him now for his exertions," said Richard, "and I must find him for that purpose. But Peters, for heaven's sake tell us about this young man whom you suspect to be the murderer. If I go to the end of the world in search of him, I'll find him, and drag him and his villany to light, that my name may be cleared from the foul stain it wears."

Mr. Peters looked very grave. "You must go a little further than the end of this world to find him, I'm afraid, sir," said the fingers. "What do you say to looking for him in the next? for that's the station he'd started for when I last saw him; and I believe that on that line, with the exception of now and then a cock-and-a-bull-lane ghost, they don't give no return tickets."

"Dead?" said Richard. "Dead, and escaped from justice?"

"That's about the size of it, sir," replied Mr. Peters. "Whether he thought as how something was up, and he was blown, or whether he was riled past bearin' at findin' no money in that 'ere cabinet, I can't take upon myself to say; but I found him six months after the murder out upon a heath, dead, with a laudanum-bottle a-lying by his side."

"And did you ever find out who he was?" asked Gus.

"He was a usher, sir, at a 'cademy for young gents, and a very pious young man he was too, I've heard; but for all that he murdered this young gent's uncle, or my name isn't Peters."

"Beyond the reach of justice," said Richard; "then the truth can never be brought to light, and to the end of my days I must bear the stigma of a crime of which I am innocent."

BOOK THE FIFTH

THE DUMB DETECTIVE

CHAPTER I

The Count de Marolles at Home

The denizens of Friar Street and such localities, being in the habit of waking in the morning to the odour of melted tallow[1] and boiling soap, and of going to sleep at night with the smell of burning bones under their noses, can of course have nothing of an external nature in common with the inhabitants of Park Lane[2] and its vicinity; for the gratification of whose olfactory nerves exotics live short and unnatural lives, on staircases, in boudoirs, and in conservatories of rich plate-glass and fairy architecture, where perfumed waters play in gilded fountains through the long summer days.

It might be imagined, then, that the common griefs and vulgar sorrows—such as hopeless love and torturing jealousy, sickness, or death, or madness, or despair—would be also banished from the regions of Park Lane, and entirely confined to the purlieus of Friar Street. Any person with a proper sense of the fitness of things would of course conclude this to be the case, and would as soon picture my lady the Duchess of Mayfair dining on red herrings and potatoes at the absurd hour of one o'clock p.m., or blackleading her own grate with her own alabaster fingers, as weeping over the death of her child, or breaking her heart for her faithless husband, just like Mrs. Stiggins, potato and coal merchant on a small scale, or Mrs. Higgins, whose sole revenues come from "Mangling[3] done here."

And it does seem hard, oh my brethren, that there should be any limit to the magic power of gold! It may exclude bad airs, foul scents, ugly sights, and jarring sounds; it may surround its possessors with beauty, grace, art, luxury, and so-called pleasure; but it cannot shut out death or care; for to these stern visitors Mayfair[4] and St. Giles's[5] must alike open their reluctant doors whenever the dreaded guests may be pleased to call.

You do not send cards for your morning concerts, or *fêtes cham-pêtres,*[6] or *thés dansantes,*[7] to Sorrow or Sadness, oh noble duchesses and countesses; but have you never seen their faces in the crowd when you least looked to meet them?

Through the foliage and rich blossoms in the conservatory, and through the white damask curtains of the long French window, the autumn sunshine comes with subdued light into a boudoir on the second floor of a large house in Park Lane. The velvet-pile carpets in this room and the bedchamber and dressing-room adjoining, are made in imitation of a mossy ground on which autumn leaves have fallen; so exquisite, indeed, is the design, that it is difficult to think that the light breeze which enters at the open window cannot sweep away the fragile leaf, which seems to flutter in the sun. The walls are of the palest cream-colour, embellished with enamelled portraits of Louis the Sixteenth, Marie Antoinette, Madame Eliza-beth, and the unfortunate boy prisoner of the Temple,[8] let into the oval panels on the four sides of the room. Everything in this apart-ment, though perfect in form and colour, is subdued and simple; there are none of the buhl and marqueterie cabinets, the artificial flowers, ormolu clocks, French prints, and musical boxes which might adorn the boudoir of an opera-dancer or the wife of a par-venu. The easy-chairs and luxurious sofas are made of a polished white wood, and are covered with white damask. On the marble mantelpiece there are two or three vases of the purest and most classical forms; and these, with Canovo's[9] bust of Napoleon, are the only ornaments in the room. Near the fireplace, in which burns a small fire, there is a table loaded with books, French, English, and German, the newest publications of the day; but they are tossed in a great heap, as if they had one by one been looked at and cast aside unread. By this table there is a lady seated, whose beautiful face is rendered still more striking by the simplicity of her black dress.

This lady is Valerie de Lancy, now Countess de Marolles; for Monsieur Marolles has expended some part of his wife's fortune upon certain estates in the south of France which give him the title of Count de Marolles.

A lucky man, this Raymond Marolles. A beautiful wife, a title, and an immense fortune are no such poor prizes in the lottery of life. But this Raymond is a man who likes to extend his possessions; and in South America he has established himself as a banker on a large scale, and he has lately come over to England with his wife and son, for the purpose of establishing a branch of this bank in London. Of course, a man with his aristocratic connections and enormous fortune is respected and trusted throughout the continent of South America.

Eight years have taken nothing from the beauty of Valerie de Marolles. The dark eyes have the same fire, the proud head the same haughty grace; but alone and in repose the face has a shadow of deep and settled sadness that is painful to look upon, for it is the gloomy sadness of despair. The world in which this woman lives, which knows her only as the brilliant, witty, vivacious, and sparkling Parisian, little dreams that she talks because she dare not think; that she is restless and vivacious because she dare not be still; that she hurries from place to place in pursuit of pleasure and excitement because only in excitement, and in a life which is as false and hollow as the mirth she assumes, can she fly from the phantom which pursues her. O shadow that will not be driven away! O pale and pensive ghost, that rises before us in every hour and in every scene, to mock the noisy and tumultuous revelry which, by the rule of opposites, we call Pleasure!—which of us is free from your haunting presence, O phantom, whose name is The Past?

Valerie is not alone; a little boy, between seven and eight years of age, is standing at her knee, reading aloud to her from a book of fables.

"A frog beheld an ox——" he began. But as he read the first words the door of the boudoir opened, and a gentleman entered, whose pale fair face, blue eyes, light eyelashes, and dark hair and eyebrows proclaimed him to be the husband of Valerie.

"Ah," he said, glancing with a sneer at the boy, who lifted his dark eyes for a moment, and then dropped them on his book with an indifference that bespoke little love for the new-comer, "you are teaching your child, madame. Teaching him to read? Is not that an innovation? The boy has a fine voice, and the ear of a maestro. Let him learn the solfeggi,[10] and very likely one of these days he will be as great a man as——"

Valerie looks at him with the old contempt, the old icy coldness in her face. "Do you want anything of me this morning, monsieur?" she asked.

"No, madame. Having the entire command of your fortune, what can I ask? A smile? Nay, madame; you keep your smiles for your son; and again, they are so cheap in London, the smiles of beauty."

"Then, monsieur, since you require nothing at my hands, may I ask why you insult me with your presence?"

"You teach your son to respect—his father, madame," said Raymond with a sneer, throwing himself into an easy-chair opposite Valerie. "You set the future Count de Marolles a good example. He will be a model of filial piety, as you are of——"

"Do not fear, Monsieur de Marolles, but that one day I shall teach my son to respect his father; fear rather lest I teach him to avenge——"

"Nay, madame, it is for you to fear that."

During the whole of this brief dialogue, the little boy has held his mother's hand, looking with his serious eyes anxiously in her face. Young as he is, there is a courage in his glance and a look of firmness in his determined under-lip that promises well for the future. Valerie turns from the cynical face of her husband, and lays a caressing hand on the boy's dark ringlets. Do those ringlets remind her of any other dark hair? Do any other eyes look out in the light of those she gazes at now?

"You were good enough to ask me just now, madame, the purport of my visit; your discrimination naturally suggesting to you that there is nothing so remarkably attractive in the society to be found in these apartments, infantine lectures in words of one syllable included"—he glances towards the boy as he speaks, and the cruel blue eyes are never so cruel as when they look that way—"as to induce me to enter them without some purpose or other."

"Perhaps monsieur will be so good as to be brief in stating that purpose? He may imagine, that being entirely devoted to my son, I do not choose to have his studies, or even his amusements, inter-rupted."

"You bring up young Count Almaviva like a prince, madame. It is something to have good blood in one's veins, even on one side——"

If she could have killed him with a look of those bright dark eyes, he would have fallen dead as he spoke the words that struck one by one at her broken heart. He knew his power; he knew wherein it lay, and how to use it—and he loved to wound her; because, though he had won wealth and rank from her, he had never conquered her, and he felt that even in her despair she defied him.

"You are irrelevant, monsieur. Pray be so kind as to say what brought you here, where I would not insult your good sense by say-ing you are a welcome visitor."

"Briefly then, madame. Our domestic arrangements do not please me. We are never known to quarrel, it is true; but we are rarely seen to address each other, and we are not often seen in public together. Very well this in South America, where we were king and queen of our circle—here it will not do. To say the least, it is mysterious. The fashionable world is scandalous. People draw inferences—monsieur does not love madame, and he married her for her money; or, on the other hand, madame does not love monsieur, but married him be-cause she had some powerful *motive* for so doing. This will not do, countess. A banker must be respectable, or people may be afraid to trust him. I must be, what I am now called, 'the eminent banker;' and I must be universally trusted."

"That you may the better betray, monsieur; that is the motive for winning people's confidence, in your code of moral economy, is it not?"

"Madame is becoming a logician; her argument by induction does her credit."

"But, your business, monsieur?"

"Was to signify my wish, madame, that we should be seen oftener together in public. The Italian Opera, now, madame, though you have so great a distaste for it—a distaste which, by-the-bye, you did not possess during the early period of your life—is a very popular resort. All the world will be there to-night, to witness the *début* of a singer of continental celebrity. Perhaps you will do me the honour to accompany me there?"

"I do not take any interest, monsieur——"

"In the fortunes of tenor singers. Ah, how completely we outlive the foolish fancies of our youth! But you will occupy the box on the grand tier of her Majesty's Theatre, which I have taken for the season. It is to your son's—to Cherubino's[11] interest, for you to comply with my request." He glances towards the boy once more, with a sneer on his thin lips, and then turns and bows to Valerie, as he says—

"*Au revoir*, madame. I shall order the carriage for eight o'clock."

A horse, which at a sale at Tattersall's had attracted the attention of all the votaries of the Corner, for the perfection of his points and the enormous price which he realized, caracoles before the door, under the skilful horsemanship of a well-trained and exquisitely-appointed groom. Another horse, equally high-bred, waits for his rider, the Count de Marolles. The groom dismounts, and holds the bridle, as the gentleman emerges from the door and springs into the saddle. A consummate horseman the Count de Marolles; a handsome man too, in spite of the restless and shifting blue eyes and the thin nervous lips. His dress is perfect, just keeping pace with the fashion sufficiently to denote high ton in the wearer, without outstripping it, so as to stamp him a parvenu. It has that elegant and studious grace which, to a casual observer, looks like carelessness, but which is in reality the perfection of the highest art of all—the art of concealing art.

It is only twelve o'clock, and there are not many people of any standing in Piccadilly this September morning; but of the few gentlemen on horseback who pass Monsieur de Marolles, the most aristocratic-looking bow to him. He is well known in the great world as the eminent banker, the owner of a superb house in Park Lane. He possesses a man cook of Parisian renown, who wears the cross of the Legion of Honour, given him by the first Napoleon on the occasion of a dinner at Talleyrand's. He has estates in South

America and in France; a fortune, said to be boundless; and a lovely wife. For the rest, if his own patent of nobility is of rather fresh date, and if, as impertinent people say, he never had a grandfather, or indeed anything in the way of a father to speak of, it must be remembered that great men, since the days of mythic history, have been celebrated for being born in rather an accidental manner.

But why a banker? Why, possessed of an enormous fortune, try to extend that fortune by speculation? That question lies between Raymond de Marolles and his conscience. Perhaps there are no bounds to the ambition of this man, who entered Paris eight years ago an obscure adventurer, and who, according to some accounts, is now a millionaire.

CHAPTER II

MR. PETERS SEES A GHOST

Mr. Peters, pensioned off by Richard's mother with an income of a hundred pounds a year, has taken and furnished for himself a small house in a very small square not far from Mr. Darley's establishment, and rejoicing in the high-sounding address of Wellington Square, Waterloo Road. Having done this, he feels that he has nothing more to do in life than to retire upon his laurels, and enjoy the *otium cum dignitate*[1] which he has earned so well.

Of course Mr. Peters, as a single man, cannot by any possibility *do for*[2] himself; and as—having started an establishment of his own—he is no longer in a position to be taken in and done for, the best thing he can do is to send for Kuppins; accordingly he does send for Kuppins.

Kuppins is to be cook, housekeeper, laundress, and parlour-maid all in one; and she is to have ten pounds per annum, and her tea, sugar, and beer—wages only known in Slopperton in very high and aristocratic families where footmen are kept and no followers or Sundays out allowed.

So Kuppins comes to London, bringing the "fondling" with her;

and arriving at the Euston Square station at eight o'clock in the evening, is launched into the dazzlingly bewildering gaiety of the New Road.[3]

Well, it is not paved with gold certainly, this marvellous city; and it is, maybe, on the whole, just a little muddy. But oh, the shops— what emporiums of splendour! What delightful excitement in being nearly run over every minute!—to say nothing of that delicious chance of being knocked down by the crowd which is collected round a drunken woman expostulating with a policeman. Of course there must be a general election, or a great fire, or a man hanging, or a mad ox at large, or a murder just committed in the next street, or something wonderful going on, or there never could be such crowds of excited pedestrians, and such tearing and rushing, and smashing of cabs, carts, omnibuses, and parcel-delivery vans, all of them driven by charioteers in the last stage of insanity, and drawn by horses as wild as that time-honoured steed employed in the artistic and poetical punishment of our old friend Mazeppa.[4] Tottenham Court Road! What a magnificent promenade! Occupied, of course, by the houses of the nobility! And is that magnificent establishment with the iron shutters Buckingham Palace or the Tower of London? Kuppins inclines to thinking it must be the Tower of London, because the iron shutters look so warlike, and are evidently intended as a means of defence in case of an attack from the French.

Kuppins is told by her escort, Mr. Peters, that this is the emporium of Messrs. Shoolbred, haberdashers and linen-drapers. She thinks she must be dreaming, and wants to be pinched and awakened before she proceeds any further. It is rather a trying journey for Mr. Peters; for Kuppins wants to stop the cab every twenty yards or so, to get out and look at something in this wonderful Tottenham Court Road.

But the worst of Kuppins, perhaps, is, that she has almost an insane desire to see that Tottenham Court whence Tottenham Court Road derives its name; and when told that there is no such place, and never was—leastways, never as Mr. Peters heard of—she begins to think London, in spite of all its glories, rather a take-in. Then, again,

Kuppins is very much disappointed at not passing either Westminster Abbey or the Bank of England, which she had made up her mind were both situated at Charing Cross; and it was a little trying for Mr. Peters to be asked whether every moderate-sized church they passed was St. Paul's Cathedral, or every little bit of dead wall Newgate. To go over a bridge, and for it not to be London Bridge, but Waterloo Bridge, was in itself a mystery; but to be told that the Shot Tower on the Surrey side was not the Monument was too bewildering for endurance. As to the Victoria Theatre, which was illuminated to such a degree that the box-entrance seemed as a pathway to fairyland, Kuppins was so thoroughly assured in her own mind of its being Drury Lane and nothing else, unless, perhaps, the Houses of Parliament or Covent Garden—that no protestations on Mr. Peters's fingers could root out the fallacy.

But the journey came to an end at last; and Kuppins, safe with bag and baggage at No. 17, Wellington Square, partook of real London saveloys[5] and real London porter[6] with Mr. Peters and the "fondling," in an elegant front parlour, furnished with a brilliantly-polished but rather rickety Pembroke table, that was covered with a Royal Stuart plaid woollen cloth; half-a-dozen cane-seated chairs, so new and highly polished as to be apt to adhere to the garments of the person who so little understood their nature or properties as to attempt to sit upon them; a Kidderminster carpet,[7] the pattern of which was of the size adapted to the requirements of a town hall, but which looked a little disproportionate to Mr. Peters's apartment, two patterns and a quarter stretching the entire length of the room; and a mantelpiece ornamented with a looking-glass divided into three compartments by gilded Corinthian pillars, and further adorned with two black velvet kittens, one at each corner, and a parti-coloured velvet boy on a brown velvet donkey in the centre.

The next morning Mr. Peters announced his intention of taking the "fondling" into the city of London, for the purpose of showing him the outside of St. Paul's, the Monument, Punch and Judy, and other intellectual exhibitions adapted to his tender years. Kuppins was for starting then and there on a visit to the pig-faced lady, than which magnificent creature she could not picture any greater wonder in the whole metropolis; but Kuppins had to stay at home in her post of housekeeper, and to inspect and arrange the domestic machinery of No. 17, Wellington Square. So the "fondling," being magnificently arrayed in a clean collar and a pair of boots that were too small for him, took hold of his protector's hand, and they sallied forth.

If anything, Punch and Judy bore off the palm in this young gentleman's judgment of the miracles of the big village.

It was not so sublime a sight, perhaps, as the outside of St. Paul's; but, on the other hand, it was a great deal cleaner; and the "fondling" would have liked to have seen Sir Christopher Wren's masterpiece picked out with a little fresh paint before he was called upon to admire it. The Monument, no doubt, was very charming in the abstract; but unless he could have been perpetually on the top of it, and perpetually within a hair's breadth of precipitating himself on to the pavement below, it wasn't very much in his way. But Punch, with his delightfully original style of elocution, his overpoweringly comic domestic passages with Judy, and the dolefully funny dog with a frill round his neck and an evident dislike for his profession— this, indeed, was an exhibition to be seen continually, and to be more admired the more continually seen, as no doubt the "fondling" would have said had he been familiar with Dr. Johnson, which, it is to be hoped, for his own peace of mind, he wasn't.

It is rather a trying day for Mr. Peters, and he is not sorry when, at about four o'clock in the afternoon, he has taken the "fondling" all round the Bank of England—(that young gentleman insisting on peering in at the great massive windows, in the fond hope of seeing the money)—and has shown him the broad back of the Old Lady of Threadneedle Street,[8] and the Clearing-house, and they are going out of Lombard Street, on their way to an omnibus which will take them home. But just as they are leaving the street the "fondling" makes a dead stop, and constrains Mr. Peters to do the same.

Standing before the glass doors of a handsome building, which a brass plate announces to be the "Anglo-Spanish-American Bank," are two horses, and a groom in faultless buckskins and tops. He is evidently waiting for some one within the bank, and the "fondling" vehemently insists upon waiting too, to see the gentleman get on horseback. The good-natured detective consents; and they loiter about the pavement for some time before the glass doors are flung open by a white-neckclothed clerk, and a gentleman of rather foreign appearance emerges therefrom.

There is nothing particularly remarkable in this gentleman. The fit of his pale lavender gloves is certainly exquisite; the style of his dress is a recommendation to his tailor; but what there is in his appearance to occasion Mr. Peters's holding on to a lamp-post it is difficult to say. But Mr. Peters did certainly cling to the nearest lamp-post, and did certainly turn as white as the whitest sheet of paper that ever came out of a stationer's shop. The elegant-looking gentleman, who was no other than the Count de Marolles, had better occupation for his bright blue eyes than the observation of such small deer as Mr. Peters and the "fondling." He mounted his horse, and rode slowly away, quite unconscious of the emotion his appearance had occasioned in the breast of the detective. No sooner had he done so, than Mr. Peters, relinquishing the lamp-post and clutching the astonished "fondling," darted after him. In a moment he was in the crowded thoroughfare before Guildhall. An empty cab passed close to them. He hailed it with frantic gesticulations, and sprang in, still holding the "fondling." The Count de Marolles had to rein-in his horse for a moment from the press of cabs and omnibuses; and at Mr. Peters's direction the "fondling" pointed him out to the cabman, with the emphatic injunction to "follow that gent, and not to lose sight of him nohow." The charioteer gives a nod, cracks his whip, and drives slowly after the equestrian, who has some difficulty in making his way through Cheapside. The detective, whose complexion still wears a most striking affinity to writing-paper, looks out of the window, as if he thought the horseman they are following would melt into thin air, or go down a trap in St. Paul's Churchyard. The "fondling" follows his protector's eyes with his eyes, then looks back at Mr. Peters, and evidently does not know what to make of the business. At last his patron draws his head in at the window, and expresses himself upon his fingers thus—

"How can it be him, when he's dead?"

This is beyond the "fondling's" comprehension, who evidently doesn't understand the drift of the query, and as evidently doesn't altogether like it, for he says.

"Don't! Come, I say, don't, now."

"How can it be him," continues Mr. Peters, enlarging upon the question, "when I found him dead myself out upon that there heath, and took him back to the station, and afterwards see him buried, which would have been between four cross roads with a stake druv' through him if he'd poisoned himself fifty years ago?"[9]

This rather obscure speech is no more to the "fondling's" liking than the last, for he cries out more energetically than before,

"I say, now, I tell you I don't like it, father. Don't you try it on now, please. What does it mean? Who's been dead fifty years ago, with a stake druv' through 'em, and four cross roads on a heath? Who?"

Mr. Peters puts his head out of the window, and directing the attention of the "fondling" to the elegant equestrian they are following, says, emphatically, upon his fingers,

"Him!"

"Dead, is he?" said the "fondling," clinging very close to his adopted parent. "Dead! and very well he looks, considerin'; but," he continued, in an awful and anxious whisper, "where's the stake and the four cross roads as was druv' through him? Does he wear that 'ere loose coat to hide 'em?"

Mr. Peters didn't answer this inquiry, but seemed to be ruminating, and, if one may be allowed the expression, thought aloud upon his fingers, as it was his habit to do at times.

"There couldn't be two men so much alike, surely. That one I found dead was the one I saw at the public talkin' to the young woman; and if so, this is another one, for that one was dead as sure as eggs is eggs. When eggs ceases to be eggs, which," continued Mr. Peters, discoursively, "considerin' they're sellin' at twenty for a shilling, French, and dangerous, if you're not partial to young parboiled chickens, is not likely yet awhile, why, *then*, that one I found on the heath will come to life again."

The "fondling" was too busy stretching his neck out of the win-

dow of the cab, in his eagerness to keep his eye upon the Count de
Marolles, to pay any attention to Mr. Peters's fingers. The outside
of St. Pauls, and the performance of Punch and Judy, were very
well in their way, but they were mild dissipations indeed, compared
to the delight of following a ghost which had had a stake driven
through his phantasmal form and wore lavender kid gloves.

"There was one thing," continued the musing detective, "which
struck me as curious, when I found the body of that young gent.
Where was the scar from the sovering as that young woman throwed
at him? Why nowheres! Not a trace of it to be seen, which I looked
for it particular; and yet that cut wasn't one to leave a scar that
would wear out in six months, nor yet in six years either. I've had my
face scratched myself, though I'm a single man, and I know what
that is to last, and the awkwardness one has to go through in saying
one's been playing with spiteful kittens, and such-like. But what's
that to a cut half a inch deep from the sharp edge of a sovering? If I
could but get to see his forehead. The cut was just over his eyebrow,
and I could see the mark of it with his hat on."

While Mr. Peters abandons himself to such reflections as these,
the cab drives on and follows the Count de Marolles down Ludgate
Hill, through Fleet Street and the Strand, Charing Cross and Pall
Mall, St. James's Street and Piccadilly, till it comes up with him at
the corner of Park Lane.

"This," says Mr. Peters, "is where the swells live. Very likely he
hangs out here; he's a-ridin' as if he was goin' to stop presently, so
we'll get out." Whereupon the "fondling" interprets to the cabman
Mr. Peters's wish to that effect, and they alight from the vehicle.

The detective's surmise is correct. The Count stops, gets off his
horse, and throws the reins to the groom. It happens at this very moment that an open carriage, in which two ladies are seated, passes on
its way to the Grosvenor Gate. One of the ladies bows to the South-
American banker, and as he lifts his hat in returning her salute, Mr.
Peters, who is looking at nothing particular, sees very distinctly the
scar which is the sole memorial of that public-house encounter on
the banks of the Sloshy.

As Raymond throws the reins to the groom he says, "I shall not ride again to-day, Curtis. Tell Morgan to have the Countess's carriage at the door at eight for the opera."

Mr. Peters, who doesn't seem to be a person blest with the faculty of hearing, but who is, to all appearance, busily engaged in drawing the attention of the "fondling" to the architectural beauties of Grosvenor Gate, may nevertheless take due note of this remark.

The elegant banker ascends the steps of his house, at the hall-door of which stand gorgeous and obsequious flunkeys, whose liveries and legs alike fill with admiration the juvenile mind of the "fondling."

Mr. Peters is very grave for some time, as they walk away; but at last, when they have got halfway down Piccadilly, he has recourse once more to his fingers, and addresses his young friend thus:

"What did you think of him, Slosh?"

"Which," says the "fondling;" "the cove in the red velvet breeches as opened the door, or the swell ghost?"

"The swell."

"Well, I think he's uncommon handsome, and very easy in his manners, all things taken into consideration," said that elderly juvenile with deliberation.

"Oh, you do, do you, Slosh?"

Slosh repeats that he does.

Mr. Peters's gravity increases every moment. "Oh, you do, do you, Slosh?" he asks again, and again the boy answers. At last, to the considerable inconvenience of the passers-by, the detective makes a dead stop, and says, "I'm glad you think him han'some, Slosh; and I'm glad you thinks him easy, which, all things considered, he is, uncommon. In fact, I'm glad he meets your views as far as personal appearance goes, because, between you and me, Slosh, that man's your father."

It is the boy's turn to hold on to the lamp-post now. To have a ghost for a father, and, as Slosh afterwards remarked, "a ghost as wears polishy boots, and lives in Park Lane, too," was enough to take the breath out of any boy, however preternaturally elderly and superhumanly sharp his police-office experiences may have made him. On the whole, the "fondling" bears the shock very well, shakes off the effect of the information, and is ready for more in a minute.

"I wouldn't have you mention it just now, you know, Slosh," continues Mr. Peters, "because we don't know what he may turn out, and whether he may quite answer our purpose in the parental line. There's a little outstanding matter between me and him that I shall have to look him up for. I may want your help; and if I do, you'll give it faithful, won't you, Slosh?"

"Of course I will," said that young gentleman. "Is there any reward out for him, father?" He always called Mr. Peters father, and wasn't prepared to change his habit in deference to any ghostly phenomenon in the way of a parent suddenly turning up in Lombard Street. "Is there any reward out for him?" he asks, eagerly; "bankers is good for something in the levanting[10] line, I know, nowadays."

The detective looked at the boy's sharp thin features with a scrutinising glance common to men of his profession.

"Then you'll serve me faithful, if I want you, Slosh? I thought perhaps you might let family interests interfere with business, you know."

"Not a bit of it," said the youthful enthusiast. "I'd hang my grandmother for a sovering, and the pride of catching her, if she was a downy[11] one."

"Chips of old blocks is of the same wood, and it's only reasonable there should be a similarity in the grain," mused Mr. Peters, as he and the "fondling" rode home in an omnibus. "I thought I'd make him a genius, but I didn't know there was such a undercurrent of his father. It'll make him the glory of his profession. Softheartedness has been the ruin of many a detective as has had the brains to work out a deep-laid game, but not the heart to carry it through."

CHAPTER III

THE CHEROKEES MARK THEIR MAN

Her Majesty's Theatre is peculiarly brilliant this evening. Diamonds and beauty, in tier above tier, look out from the amber-curtained boxes. The stalls are full, and the pit is crammed. In fop's alley[1] there is scarcely standing room; indeed, one gentleman remarks to another, that if Pandemonium[2] is equally hot and crowded, he will turn Methodist parson in his old age, and give his mind to drinking at tea-meetings.

The gentleman who makes this remark is neither more nor less than a distinguished member of the "Cheerfuls," the domino-player alluded to some chapters back.

He is standing talking to Richard; and to see him now, with an opera-glass in his hand, his hair worn in a manner conforming with the usages of society, and only in a modified degree suggesting that celebrated hero of the Newgate calendar and modern romance, Mr. John Sheppard, a dress-coat, patent leather boots, and the regulation white waistcoat, you would think he had never been tipsy or riotous in his life.

This gentleman is Mr. Percy Cordonner. All the Cherokees are more or less literary, and all the Cherokees have, more or less, admission to every place of entertainment, from Her Majesty's Theatre to the meetings of the members of the "P.R." But what brings Richard to the Opera to-night? and who is that not very musical-looking little gentleman at his elbow?

"Will they all be here?" asked Dick of Mr. Cordonner.

"Every one of them; unless Splitters is unable to tear himself away from his nightly feast of blood and blue fire at the Vic. His piece has been performed fourteen times, and it's my belief he's been at every representation; and that he tears his hair when the actors leave out the gems of the dialogue and drop their h's. They *do* drop their h's over the water," he continues, lapsing into a reverie;

"when our compositors are short of type, they go over and sweep them up."

"You're sure they'll be here, then, Percy?"

"Every one of them, I tell you. I'm whipper-in. They're to meet at the oyster shop in the Haymarket; you know the place, where there's a pretty girl and fresh Colchesters,³ don't charge you anything extra for the lemon, and you can squeeze her hand when she gives you the change. They're sure to come in here two at a time, and put their mark upon the gentleman in question. Is he in the house yet, old fellow?"

Richard turns to the quiet little man at his elbow, who is our old friend Mr. Peters, and asks him a question: he only shakes his head in reply.

"No, he's not here yet," says Dick; "let's have a look at the stage, and see what sort of stuff this Signor Mosquetti is made of."

"I shall cut him up, on principle," says Percy; "and the better he is, the more I shall cut him up, on another principle."

There is a great deal of curiosity about this new tenor of continental celebrity. The opera is the *Lucia*,⁴ and the appearance of Edgardo⁵ is looked forward to with anxiety. Presently the hero of the square-cut coat and jack-boots enters. He is a handsome fellow, with a dark southern face, and an easy insouciant manner. His voice is melody itself; the rich notes roll out in a flood of sweetness, without the faintest indication or effort. Though Richard pretends to look at the stage, though perhaps he does try to direct his attention that way, his pale face, his wandering glance, and his restless underlip, show him to be greatly agitated. He is waiting for that moment when the detective shall say to him, "There is the murderer of your uncle. There is the man for whose guilt you have suffered, and must suffer, till he is brought to justice." The first act of the opera seemed endless to Daredevil Dick; while his philosophical friend, Mr. Cordonner, looked on as coolly as he would have done at an earthquake, or the end of the world, or any other trifling event of that nature.

The curtain has fallen upon the first act, when Mr. Peters lays his hand on Richard's arm and points to a box on the grand tier.

A gentleman and lady, and a little boy, have just taken their seats. The gentleman, as becomes him, sits with his back to the stage and faces the house. He lifts his opera-glass to take a leisurely survey of the audience. Percy puts his glass into Richard's hand, and with a hearty "Courage, old boy!" watches him as he looks for the first time at his deadliest enemy.

And is that calm, aristocratic, and serene face the face of a murderer? The shifting blue eyes and the thin arched lips are not discernible from this distance; but through the glass the general effect of the face is very plainly seen, and there is no fear that Richard will fail to know its owner again, whenever and wherever he may meet him.

Mr. Cordonner, after a deliberate inspection of the personal attractions of the Count de Marolles, remarks, with less respect than indifference,

"Well, the beggar is by no means bad-looking, but he looks a determined scoundrel. He'd make a first-rate light-comedy villain for a Porte-St.-Martin[6] drama. I can imagine him in Hessian boots[7] poisoning all his relations, and laughing at the police when they come to arrest him."

"Shall you know him again, Percy?" asks Richard.

"Among an army of soldiers, every one of them dressed in the same uniform," replies his friend. "There's something unmistakable about that pale thin face. I'll go and bring the other fellows in, that they may all be able to swear to him when they see him."

In groups of two and three the Cherokees strolled into the pit, and were conducted by Mr. Cordonner—who, to serve a friend, could, on a push, be almost active—to the spot where Richard and the detective stood. One after another they took a long look, through the most powerful glass they could select, at the tranquil features of Victor de Marolles.

Little did that gentleman dream of this amateur band of police, formed for the special purpose of the detection of the crime he was supposed to have committed.

One by one the "Cheerfuls" register the Count's handsome face upon their memories, and with a hearty shake of the hand each man declares his willingness to serve Richard whenever and wherever he may see a chance, however faint or distant, of so doing. And all this time the Count is utterly unmoved. Not quite so unmoved though, when, in the second act, he recognizes in the Edgardo—the new tenor, the hero of the night—his old acquaintance of the Parisian Italian Opera, the chorus-singer and mimic, Monsieur Paul Moucée. This skilful workman does not care about meeting with a tool which, once used, were better thrown aside and for ever done away with. But this Signor Paolo Mosquetti is neither more nor less than the slovenly, petit-verre-drinking, domino-playing chorus-singer, at a salary of thirty francs a-week. His genius, which enabled him to sing an aria in perfect imitation of the fashionable tenor of the day, has also enabled him, with a little industry, and a little less wine-drinking and gambling, to become a fashionable tenor himself, and Milan, Naples, Vienna, and Paris testify to his triumphs.

And all this time Valerie de Marolles looks on a stage such as that on which, years ago, she so often saw the form she loved. That faint resemblance, that likeness in his walk, voice, and manner, which Moucée has to Gaston de Lancy strikes her very forcibly. It is no great likeness, except when the mimic is bent on representing the man he resembles; then, indeed, as we know, it is remarkable. But at any time it is enough to strike a bitter pang to this bereaved and remorseful heart, which in every dream and every shadow is only too apt to recall that unforgotten past.

The Cherokees meanwhile express their sentiments pretty freely about Monsieur Raymond de Marolles, and discuss divers schemes for the bringing of him to justice. Splitters, whose experiences as a dramatic writer suggested to him every possible kind of mode but a natural one, proposed that Richard should wait upon the Count, when convenient, at the hour of midnight, disguised as his uncle's ghost, and confound the villain in the stronghold of his crime— meaning Park Lane. This sentence was verbatim from a playbill, as well as the whole very available idea; Mr. Splitters's notions of justice being entirely confined to the retributive or poetical, in the person of a gentleman with a very long speech and two pistols.

"The Smasher's outside," said Percy Cordonner. "He wants to have a look at our friend as he goes out, that he may reckon him up. You'd better let him go into the Count's peepers with his left, Dick, and damage his beauty; it's the best chance you'll get."

"No, no; I tell you, Percy, that man shall stand where I stood. That man shall drink to the dregs the cup I drank, when I stood in the criminal dock at Slopperton and saw every eye turned towards me with execration and horror, and knew that my innocence was of no avail to sustain me in the good opinion of one creature who had known me from my very boyhood."

"Except the 'Cheerfuls,' " said Percy. "Don't forget the 'Cheerfuls.' "

"When I do, I shall have forgotten all on this side of the grave, you may depend, Percy. No; I have some firm friends on earth, and here is one;" and he laid his hand on the shoulder of Mr. Peters, who still stood at his elbow.

The opera was concluded, and the Count de Marolles and his lovely wife rose to leave their box. Richard, Percy, Splitters, two or three more of the Cherokees, and Mr. Peters left the pit at the same time, and contrived to be at the box-entrance before Raymond's party came out.

At last the Count de Marolles's carriage was called; and as it drew up, Raymond descended the steps with his wife on his arm, her little boy clinging to her left hand.

"She's a splendid creature," said Percy; "but there's a spice of devilry in those glorious dark eyes. I wouldn't be her husband for a trifle, if I happened to offend her."

As the Count and Countess crossed from the doors of the opera-house to their carriage, a drunken man came reeling past, and before the servants or policemen standing by could interfere, stumbled against Raymond de Marolles, and in so doing knocked his hat off. He picked it up immediately, and, muttering some unintelligible apology, returned it to Raymond, looking, as he did so, very steadily in the face of M. de Marolles. The occurrence did not occupy a moment, and the Count was too finished a gentleman to make any disturbance. This man was the Smasher.

As the carriage drove off, he joined the group under the colonnade, perfectly sober by this time.

"I've had a jolly good look at him, Mr. Marwood," he said, "and I'd swear to him after forty rounds in the ring, which is apt sometimes to take a little of the Cupid out of a gent. He's not a bad-looking cove on the whole, and looks game. He's rather slight built, but he might make that up in science, and dance a pretty tidy quadrille[8] round the chap he was put up agin, bein' active and lissom. I see the cut upon his forehead, Mr. Peters, as you told me to take notice of," he said, addressing the detective. "He didn't get that in a fair stand-up fight, leastways not from an Englishman. When you cross the water for your antagonist, you don't know what you may get."

"He got it from an Englishwoman, though," said Richard.

"Did he, now? Ah, that's the worst of the softer sect; you see, sir, you never know where they'll have you. They're awful deficient in science, to be sure; but, Lord bless you, they make it up with the will," and the Left-handed one rubbed his nose. He had been married during his early career, and was in the habit of saying that ten rounds inside the ropes was a trifle compared with one round in your own back-parlour, when your missus had got your knowledge-box[9] in chancery against the corner of the mantelpiece, and was marking a dozen different editions of the ten commandments on your complexion with her bunch of fives.[10]

"Come, gentlemen," said the hospitable Smasher, "what do you say to a Welsh rarebit and a bottle of bitter at my place? We're as full as we can hold down stairs, for the Finsbury Fizzer's trainer has come up from Newmarket;[11] and his backers is hearin' anecdotes of his doings for the last interesting week. They talk of dropping down the river on Tuesday for the great event between him and the Atlantic Alligator, and the excitement's tremenjous; our barmaid's hands is blistered with working at the engines. So come round and see the game, gentlemen; and if you've any loose cash you'd like to put upon the Fizzer I can get you decent odds, considerin' he's the favourite."

Richard shook his head. He would go home to his mother, he

said; he wanted to talk to Peters about the day's work. He shook hands heartily with his friends, and as they strolled off to the Smasher's, walked with them as far as Charing Cross, and left them at the corner that led into quiet Spring Gardens.

In the club-room of the Cherokees that night the members renewed the oath they had taken on the night of Richard's arrival, and formally inaugurated themselves as "Daredevil Dick's secret police."

CHAPTER IV

THE CAPTAIN, THE CHEMIST, AND THE LASCAR

In the drawing-room of a house in a small street leading out of Regent Street are assembled, the morning after this opera-house recontre, three people. It is almost difficult to imagine three persons more dissimilar than those who compose this little group. On a sofa near the open window, at which the autumn breeze comes blowing in over boxes of dusty London flowers, reclines a gentleman, whose bronzed and bearded face, and the military style even of the loose morning undress which he wears, proclaim him to be a soldier. A very handsome face it is, this soldier's, although darkened not a little by a tropical sun, and a good deal shrouded by the thick black moustache and beard which conceal the expression of the mouth, and detract from the individuality of the face. He is smoking a long cherry-stemmed pipe, the bowl of which rests on the floor. A short distance from the sofa on which he is lying, an Indian servant is seated on the carpet, who watches the bowl of the pipe, ready to replenish it the moment it fails, and every now and then glances upward to the grave face of the officer with a look of unmistakable affection in his soft black eyes.

The third occupant of the little drawing-room is a pale, thin, studious-looking man, who is seated at a cabinet in a corner away from the window, amongst papers and books, which are heaped in a chaotic pile on the floor about him. Strange books and papers these are. Mathematical charts, inscribed with figures such as perhaps neither Newton[1] or Leplace[2] ever dreamed of. Volumes in old worm-eaten bindings, and written in strange languages long since dead and forgotten upon this earth; but they all seem familiar to this pale student, whose blue spectacles bend over pages of crabbed Arabic as intently as the eyes of a boarding-school miss who devours the last volume of the last new novel. Now and then he scratches a few figures, or a sign in algebra, or a sentence in Arabic, on the paper before him, and then goes back to the book again, never looking up towards the smoker or his Hindoo attendant. Presently the soldier, as he relinquishes his pipe to the Indian to be replenished, breaks the silence.

"So the great people of London, as well as of Paris, are beginning to believe in you, Laurent?" he says.

The student lifts his head from his work, and turning the blue spectacles towards the smoker, says in his old unimpassioned manner—

"How can they do otherwise, when I tell them the truth? These," he points to the pile of books and papers at his side, "do not err: they only want to be interpreted rightly. I may have been sometimes mistaken—I have never been deceived."

"You draw nice distinctions, Blurosset."

"Not at all. If I have made mistakes in the course of my career, it has been from my own ignorance, my own powerlessness to read these aright; not from any shortcoming in the things themselves. I tell you, they do not deceive."

"But will you ever read them aright? Will you ever fathom to the very bottom this dark gulf of forgotten science?"

"Yes, I am on the right road. I only pray to live long enough to reach the end."

"And then——?"

"Then it will be within the compass of my own will to live for ever."

"Pshaw! The old story—the old delusion. How strange that the wisest on this earth should have been fooled by it!"

"Make sure that it is a delusion, before you say they were fooled by it, Captain."

"Well, my dear Blurosset, Heaven forbid that I should dispute with one so learned as you upon so obscure a subject. I am more at home holding a fort against the Indians than holding an argument against Albertus Magnus.[3] You still, however, persist that this faithful Mujeebez here is in some manner or other linked with my destiny?"

"I do."

"And yet it is very singular! What can connect two men whose experiences in every way are so dissimilar?"

"I tell you again that he will be instrumental in confounding your enemies."

"You know who they are—or rather, who he is. I have but one."

"Not two, Captain?"

"Not two. No, Blurosset. There is but one on whom I would wreak a deep and deadly vengeance."

"And for the other?"

"Pity and forgiveness. Do not speak of that. There are some things which even now I am not strong enough to hear spoken of. That is one of them."

"The history of your faithful Mujeebez there is a singular one, is it not?" asks the student, rising from his books, and advancing to the window.

"A very singular one. His master, an Englishman, with whom he came from Calcutta, and to whom he was devotedly attached——"

"I was indeed, sahib," said the Indian, in very good English, but with a strong foreign accent.

"This master, a rich nabob, was murdered, in the house of his sister, by his own nephew."

"Very horrible, and very unnatural! Was the nephew hung?"

"No. The jury brought in a verdict of insanity: he was sent to a madhouse, where no doubt he still remains confined. Mujeebez was not present at the trial; he had escaped by a miracle with his own life; for the murderer, coming into the little room in which he slept, and finding him stirring, gave him a blow on the head, which placed him for some time in a very precarious state."

"And did you see the murderer's face, Mujeebez?" asks Monsieur Blurosset.

"No, sahib. It was dark, I could see nothing. The blow stunned me: when I recovered my senses, I was in the hospital, where I lay for months. The shock had brought on what the doctors called a nervous fever. For a long time I was utterly incapable of work; when I left the hospital I had not a friend in the world; but the good lady, the sister of my poor murdered master, gave me money to return to India, where I was kitmutghar[+] for some time to an English colonel, in whose household I learned the language, and whom I did not leave till I entered the service of the good Captain."

The "good Captain" laid his hand affectionately on his follower's white-turbaned head, something with the protecting gesture with which he might caress a favourite and faithful dog.

"After you had saved my life, Mujeebez," he said.

"I would have died to save it, sahib," answered the Hindoo. "A kind word sinks deep in the heart of the Indian."

"And there was no doubt of the guilt of this nephew?" asks Blurosset.

"I cannot say, sahib. I did not know the English language then; I could understand nothing told me, except my poor master's nephew was not hung, but put in a madhouse."

"Did you see him—this nephew?"

"Yes, sahib, the night before the murder. He came into the room with my master when he retired to rest. I saw him only for a minute, for I left the room as they entered."

"Should you know him again?" inquired the student.

"Anywhere, sahib. He was a handsome young man, with dark hazel eyes and a bright smile. He did not look like a murderer."

"That is scarcely a sure rule to go by, is it, Laurent?" asks the Captain, with a bitter smile.

"I don't know. A black heart will make strange lines in the handsomest face, which are translatable to the close observer."

"Now," says the officer, rising, and surrendering his pipe to the hands of his watchful attendant—"now for my morning's ride, and you will have the place to yourself for your scientific visitors, Laurent."

"You will not go where you are likely to meet——"

"Anyone I know? No, Blurosset. The lonelier the road the better I like it. I miss the deep jungle and the tiger-hunt, eh, Mujeebez?—we miss them, do we not?"

The Hindoo's eyes brightened, as he answered eagerly, "Yes, indeed, sahib."

Captain Lansdown (that is the name of the officer) is of French extraction; he speaks English perfectly, but still with a slightly foreign accent. He has distinguished himself by his marvellous courage and military genius in the Punjaub,[5] and is over in England on leave of absence. It is singular that so great a friendship should exist between this impetuous, danger-loving soldier, and the studious French chemist and pseudo-magician, Laurent Blurosset; but that a very firm friendship does exist between them is evident. They live in the same house; are both waited upon by Egerton Lansdown's Indian servant, and are constantly together.

Laurent Blurosset, after becoming the fashion in Paris, is now the rage in London. But he rarely stirs beyond the threshold of his own door, though his presence is eagerly sought for in scientific coteries, where opinion is still, however, divided as to whether he is a charlatan or a great man. The materialists sneer—the spiritualists believe. His disinterestedness, at any rate, speaks in favour of his truth. He will receive no money from any of his numerous visitors. He will serve them, he says, if he can, but he will not sell the wisdom of the mighty dead; for that is something too grand and solemn to be made a thing of barter. His discoveries in chemistry have made him sufficiently rich; and he can afford to devote himself to science, in the hope of finding truth for his reward. He asks no better recompense than the glory of the light he seeks. We leave him, then, to his eager and inquisitive visitors, while the Captain rides slowly through Oxford Street, on his way to the Edgware Road, through which he emerges into the country.

CHAPTER V

THE NEW MILKMAN IN PARK LANE

The post of kitchenmaid in the household of the Count de Marolles is no unimportant one, and Mrs. Moper is accounted a person of some consequence in the servants' hall. The French *chef,* who has his private sitting-room, wherein he works elaborate and scientific culinary combinations, which, when he condescends to talk English, he designates "plates," has of course very little communication with the household. Mrs. Moper is his prime minister; he gives his orders to her for execution, and throws himself back in his easy-chair to *think out* a dish, while his handmaiden collects for him the vulgar elements of his noble art. Mrs. Moper is a very good cook herself; and when she leaves the Count de Marolles she will go into a family where there is no foreigner kept, and will have forty pounds per annum and a still-room of her own. She is in the caterpillar stage now, Mrs. Sarah Moper, and is content to write herself down kitchenmaid *ad interim.*

The servants'-hall dinner and the housekeeper's repast are both over; but the preparations for *the* dinner have not yet begun, and Mrs. Moper and Liza, the scullerymaid, snatch half-an-hour's calm before the coming storm, and sit down to darn stockings,—

"Which," Mrs. Moper says, "my toes is through and my heels is out, and never can I get the time to set a stitch. For time there isn't any in this house for a under-servant, which under-servant I will be no more than one year longer; or say my name's not Sarah Moper."

Liza, who is mending a black stocking with white thread (and a very fanciful effect it has too), evidently has no wish to dispute such a proposition.

"Indeed, Mrs. Moper," she said, "that's the truest word as ever you've spoke. It's well for them as takes their wages for wearin' silk gowns, and oilin' of their hair, and lookin' out of winder to watch the carriages go in at Grosvenor Gate; which, don't tell me as Life Guardsmen would look up imperdent, if they hadn't been looked down to likewise." Eliza gets rather obscure here. "This 'ouse, Mrs.

M., for upper-servants may be 'eaven, but for unders it's more like the place as is pronounced like a letter of the alphabet, and isn't to be named by me."

There is no knowing how far this rather revolutionary style of conversation might have gone, for at this moment there came that familiar sound of the clink of milk-pails on the pavement above, and the London cry of milk.

"It's Bugden with the milk, Liza; there was a pint of cream wrong in the last bill, Mrs. Melliflower says. Ask him to come down and correctify it, will you, Liza?"

Liza ascends the area steps and parleys with the milkman; presently he comes jingling down, with his pails swinging against the railings; he is rather awkward with his pails, this milkman, and I'm afraid he must spill more milk than he sells, as the Park Lane pavements testify.

"It isn't Bugden," says Liza, explanatory, as she ushers him into the kitchen. "Bugden 'as 'urt his leg, a-milkin' a cow wot kicks when the flies worrits, and 'as sent this young man, as is rather new to the business, but is anxious to do his best."

The new milkman enters the kitchen as she concludes her speech, and releasing himself from the pails, expresses his readiness to settle any mistake in the weekly bill.

He is rather a good-looking fellow, this milkman, and he has a very curly head of flaxen hair, preposterously light eyebrows, and dark hazel eyes, which form rather a piquant contrast. I don't suppose Mrs. Moper and Liza think him bad-looking, for they beg him to sit down, and the scullerymaid thrusts the black stocking, on which she was heretofore engaged, into a table-drawer, and gives her hair a rapid extemporary smoothing with the palms of her hands. Mr. Bugden's man seems by no means disinclined for a little friendly chat: he tells them how new he is to the business; how he thinks he should scarcely have chosen cowkeeping for his way of life, if he'd known as much about it as he does now; how there's many things in the milk business, such as horses' brains, warm water and treacle, and such-like, as goes against his conscience; how he's quite new to London and London ways, having come up only lately from the country.

"Whereabouts in the country?" Mrs. Moper asks.

"Berkshire," the young man replies.

"Lor'," Mrs. Moper says, "never was any thing so remarkable. Poor Moper come from Berkshire, and knowed every inch of the country, and so I think do I, pretty well. What part of Berkshire, Mr.—Mr.——?"

"Volpes," suggested the young man.

"What part of Berkshire, Mr. Volpes?"

Mr. Volpes looks, strange to say, rather at a loss to answer this very natural and simple inquiry. He looks at Mrs. Moper, then at Liza, and lastly at the pails. The pails seem to assist his memory, for he says, very distinctly, "Burley Scuffers."

It is Mrs. Moper's turn to look puzzled now, and she exclaims "Burley——"

"Scuffers," replies the young man. "Burley Scuffers, market town, fourteen miles on this side of Reading. The 'Chicories,' Sir Yorrick Tristram's place, is a mile and a half out of the town."

There's no disputing such an accurate and detailed description as this. Mrs. Moper says it's odd, all the times she's been to Reading— "which I wish I had as many sovereigns," she mutters in parenthesis—never did she remember passing through "Burley Scuffers."

"It's a pretty little town, too," says the milkman; "there's a lime-tree avenue just out of the High Street, called Pork-butchers' Walk, as is crowded with young people of a Sunday evening after church."

Mrs. Moper is quite taken with this description; and says, the very next time she goes to Reading to see poor Moper's old mother, she will make a point of going to Burley Scuffers during her stay.

Mr. Volpes says, he would if he were she, and that she couldn't employ her leisure time better.

They talk a good deal about Berkshire; and then Mrs. Moper relates some very interesting facts relative to the late Mr. Moper, and her determination, "which upon his dying bed it was his comfort so to think," never to marry again; at which the milkman looks grieved, and says the gentlemen will be very blind indeed to their own interests if they don't make her change her mind some day; and somehow or other (I don't suppose servants often do such things), they get to talking about their master and their mistress. The milkman seems quite interested in this subject, and, forgetting in how many houses the innocent liquid he dispenses may be required, he sits with his elbows on the kitchen-table, listening to Mrs. Moper's remarks, and now and then, when she wanders from her subject, drawing her back to it with an adroit question. She didn't know much about the Count, she said, for the servants was most all of 'em new; they only brought two people with them from South America, which was Monsieur St. Mirotaine, the *chef*, and the Countess's French maid, Mademoiselle Finette. But she thought Monsieur de Marolles very 'aughty, and as proud as he was 'igh, and that madame was very unhappy, "though it's hard to know with them furriners, Mr. Volpes, what is what," she continues; "and madame's gloomy ways may be French for happiness, for all I knows."

"He's an Englishman, the Count, isn't he?" asks Mr. Volpes.

"A Englishman! Lor' bless your heart, no. They're both French; she's of Spanish igstraction, I believe, and they lived since their marriage mostly in Spanish America. But they always speaks to each other in French, when they do speak; which them as waits upon them says isn't often."

"He's very rich, I suppose," says the milkman.

"Rich!" cries Mrs. Moper, "the money as that man has got they say is fabellous; and he's a regular business man too, down at his bank every day, rides off to the City as punctual as the clock strikes ten. Lor', by the bye, Mr. Volpes," says Mrs. Moper suddenly, "you don't happen to know of a tempory tiger,[1] do you?"

"A temporary tiger!" Mr. Volpes looks considerably puzzled.

"Why, you see, the Count's tiger, as wasn't higher than the kitchen table I do believe, broke his arm the other day. He was a-hangin' on to the strap behind the cab, a-standin' upon nothing, as them boys will, when the vehicle was knocked agen an omnibus, and his arm bein' wrenched sudden out of the strap, snapped like a bit of sealing-wax; and they've took him to the hospital, and he's to come back as soon as ever he's well; for he's a deal thought on, bein' a'most the smallest tiger at the West-end. So, if you happen to know of a boy as would come temporary, we should be obliged by your sending him round."

"Did he know of a boy as would come temporary?" Mr. Budgen's young man appeared so much impressed by this question, that for a minute or two he was quite incapable of answering it. He leaned his elbows on the kitchen-table, with his face buried in his hands and his fingers twisted in his flaxen hair, and when he looked up there was, strange to say, a warm flush over his pale complexion, and something like a triumphant sparkle in his dark brown eyes.

"Nothing could fall out better," he said; "nothing, nothing!"

"What, the poor lad breaking his arm?" asked Mrs. Moper, in a tone of surprise.

"No, no, not that," said Mr. Budgen's young man, just a little confused; "what I mean is, that I know the very boy to suit you—the very boy, the very boy of all others to undertake the business. Ah," he continued in a lower voice, "and to go through with it, too, to the end."

"Why, as to the business," replied Mrs. Moper, "it ain't overmuch, hangin' on behind, and lookin' knowin', and givin' other tigers as good as they bring, when waitin' outside the *Calting* or the *Anthinium;*[2] which tigers as is used to the highest names in the peerage familiar as their meat and drink, will go on contemptuous about our fambly, callin' the bank 'the shop,' and a-askin', till they got our lad's blood up (which he had had his guinea lessons from the May Fair Mawler, and were better left alone), when the smash was a-comin', or whether we meant to give out three-and-sixpence in the pound like a honest house, or do the shabby thing and clear ourselves by a compensation with our creditors of fourpence-farthing? Ah," continued Mrs. Moper, gravely, "many's the time that child have come home with his nose as big as the 'ead of a six-week old baby, and no eyes at all as any one could discover, which he'd been that knocked about in a stand-up fight with a lad three times his weight and size."

"Then I can send the boy, and you'll get him the situation?" said Mr. Budgen's young man, who did not seem particularly interested in the rather elaborate recital of the exploits of the invalid tiger.

"He can have a character, I suppose?" inquired the lady.

"Oh, ah, to be sure. Budgen will give him a character."

"You will impress upon the youth," said Mrs. Moper, with great dignity, "that he will not be able to make this his permanence 'ome. The pay is good, and the meals is reg'lar, but the situation is tempory."

"All right," said Mr. Budgen's assistant; "he doesn't want a situation for long. I'll bring him round myself this evening—good afternoon;" with which very brief farewell, the flaxen-haired, dark-eyed milkman strode out of the kitchen.

"Hum!" muttered the cook, "his manners has not the London polish: I meant to have ast him to tea."

"Why, I'm blest," exclaimed the scullerymaid suddenly, "if he haven't been and gone and left his yoke and pails behind him! Well, of all the strange milkmen I ever come a-nigh, if he ain't the strangest!"

She might have thought him stranger still, perhaps, this light-haired milkman, had she seen him hail a stray cab in Brook Street, spring into it, snatch off his flaxen locks, whose hyacinthine waves were in the convenient form known by that most disagreeable of words, a wig; snatch off also the holland blouse common to the purveyors of milk, and rolling the two into a bundle, stuff them into the pocket of his shooting-jacket, before throwing himself back into the corner of the vehicle, to enjoy a meditative cigar, as his charioteer drives his best pace in the direction of that transpontine temple of Esculapius, Mr. Darley's surgery. Daredevil Dick has made the first move in that fearful game of chess which is to be played between him and the Count de Marolles.

CHAPTER VI

SIGNOR MOSQUETTI RELATES AN ADVENTURE

On the evening which follows the very afternoon during which Richard Marwood made his first and only essay in the milk-trade, the

Count and Countess de Marolles attend a musical party—I beg pardon, I should, gentle reader, as you know, have said a *soirée musicale*—at the house of a lady of high rank in Belgrave Square. London was almost empty, and this was one of the last parties of the season; but it is a goodly and an impressive sight to see—even when London is, according to every fashionable authority, a perfect Sahara—how many splendid carriages will draw up to the awning my Lady erects over the pavement before her door, when she announces herself "at home;" how many gorgeously dressed and lovely women will descend therefrom, scenting the night air of Belgravia with the fragrance wafted from their waving tresses and point-d'Alençon[1]-bordered handkerchiefs; lending a perfume to the autumn violets struggling out a fading existence in Dresden boxes on the drawing-room balconies; lending the light of their diamonds to the gas-lamps before the door, and the light of their eyes to help out the aforesaid diamonds; sweeping the autumn dust and evening dews with the borders of costly silks, and marvels of Lyons and Spitalfields,[2] and altogether glorifying the ground over which they walk.

On this evening one range of windows, at least, in Belgrave Square is brilliantly illuminated. Lady Londersdon's Musical Wednesday, the last of the season, has been inaugurated with *éclat* by a scena from Signora Scorici, of Her Majesty's Theatre and the Nobility's Concerts; and Mr. Argyle Fitz-Bertram, the great English basso-baritono, and the handsomest man in England, has just shaken the square with the buffo duet[3] from the Cenerentola[4]—in which performance he, Argyle, has so entirely swamped that amiable tenor Signor Maretti, that the latter gentleman has serious thoughts of calling him out tomorrow morning; which idea he would carry into execution if Argyle Fitz-Bertram were not a crack shot, and a pet pupil of Mr. Angelo's into the bargain.

But even the great Argyle finds himself—with the exception of being up to his eyes in a slough of despond, in the way of platonic flirtation with a fat duchess of fifty—comparatively nowhere. The star of the evening is the new tenor, Signor Mosquetti, who has condescended to attend Lady Londersdon's Wednesday. Argyle, who is the best-natured fellow as well as the most generous, and whose great rich voice wells up from a heart as sound as his lungs, throws himself back into a low easy-chair—it creaks a little under his weight, by the bye—and allows the duchess to flirt with him, while a buzz goes round the room; Mosquetti is going to sing. Argyle looks lazily out of his half-closed dark eyes, with that peculiar expression which seems to say—"Sing your best, old fellow! My *g* in the bass clef would crush your half-octave or so of falsetto before you knew where you were, or your 'Pretty Jane' either. Sing away, my boy! we'll have 'Scots wha hae' by-and-by. I've some friends down in Essex who want to hear it, and the wind's in the right quarter for the voice to travel. They won't hear *you* five doors off. Sing your best."

Just as Signor Mosquetti is about to take his place at the piano, the Count and Countess de Marolles advance through the crowd about the doorway.

Valerie, beautiful, pale, calm as ever, is received with considerable *empressement* by her hostess. She is the heiress of one of the most ancient and aristocratic families in France, and is moreover the wife of one of the richest men in London, so is sure of a welcome throughout Belgravia.

"Mosquetti is going to sing," murmurs Lady Londersdon; "you were charmed with him in the Lucia, of course? You have lost Fitz-Bertram's duet. It was charming; all the chandeliers were shaken by his lower notes; charming, I assure you. He'll sing again after Mosquetti: the Duchess of C. is *éprise,* as you see. I believe she is perpetually sending him diamond rings and studs; and the Duke, they do say, has refused to be responsible for her account at Storr's."

Valerie's interest in Mr. Fitz-Bertram's conduct is not very intense; she bends her haughty head, just slightly elevating her arched eyebrows with the faintest indication of well-bred surprise; but she *is* interested in Signor Mosquetti, and avails herself of the seat her hostess offers to her near Erard's[5] grand piano. The song concludes very soon after she is seated; but Mosquetti remains near the piano, talking to an elderly gentleman, who is evidently a connoisseur.

"I have never heard but one man, Signor Mosquetti," says this gentleman, "whose voice resembled yours."

There is nothing very particular in the words, but Valerie's attention is apparently arrested by them, for she fixes her eyes intently on Signor Mosquetti, as though awaiting his reply.

"And he, my lord?" says Mosquetti, interrogatively.

"He, poor fellow, is dead." Now indeed Valerie, pale with a pallor greater than usual, listens as though her whole soul hung on the words she heard.

"He is dead," continued the gentleman. "He died young, in the zenith of his reputation. His name was—let me see—I heard him in Paris last; his name was——"

"De Lancy, perhaps, my lord?" says Mosquetti.

"It was De Lancy; yes. He had some most peculiar and at the same time most beautiful tones in his voice, and you appear to me to have the very same."

Mosquetti bowed at the compliment. "It is singular, my lord," he said; "but I doubt if those tones are quite natural to me. I am a little of a mimic, and at one period of my life I was in the habit of imitating poor De Lancy, whose singing I very much admired."

Valerie grasps the delicate fan in her nervous hand so tightly that the group of courtiers and fair ladies, of the time of Louis Quatorze, dancing nothing particular on a blue cloud, are crushed out of all symmetry as she listens to this conversation.

"I was, at the time I knew De Lancy, merely a chorus-singer at the Italian Opera, Paris."

The listeners draw nearer, and form quite a circle round Mosquetti, who is the lion of the night; even Argyle Fitz-Bertram pricks up his ears, and deserts the Duchess in order to hear this conversation.

"A low chorus-singer," he mutters to himself. "So help me, Jupiter, I knew he was a nobody."

"This passion for mimicry," said Mosquetti, "was so great that I acquired a sort of celebrity throughout the Opera House, and even beyond its walls. I could imitate De Lancy better, perhaps, than any one else; for in height, figure, and general appearance I was said to resemble him."

"You do," said the gentleman; "you do very much resemble the poor fellow."

"This resemblance one day gave rise to quite an adventure, which, if I shall not bore you——" he glanced round.

There is a general murmur. "Bore us! No! Delighted, enraptured, charmed above all things!" Fitz-Bertram is quite energetic in this *omnes* business, and says, "No, no!"—muttering to himself afterwards, "So help me, Jupiter, I knew the fellow was a nuisance!"

"But the adventure! Pray let us hear it!" cried eager voices.

"Well, ladies and gentlemen, I was a careless reckless fellow; quite content to put on a pair of russet boots which half swallowed me, and a green cotton-velvet tunic short in the sleeves and tight across the chest, and to go on the stage and sing in a chorus with fifty others, as idle as myself, in other russet boots and cotton-velvet tunics, which, as you know, is the court costume of a chorus-singer from the time of Charlemagne[6] to the reign of Louis XV.[7] I was quite happy, I say, to lounge on to the stage, unknown, unnoticed, badly paid and worse dressed, provided when the chorus was finished I had my cigarette, dominoes, and my glass of cognac in a third-rate café. I was playing one morning at those eternal dominoes—(and never, I think," said Mosquetti, parenthetically, "had a poor fellow so many double-sixes in his hand)—when I was told a gentleman wanted to see me. This seemed too good a joke— a gentleman for me! It couldn't be a limb of the law, as I didn't owe a farthing—no Parisian tradesman being quite so demented as to give me credit. It was a gentleman—a very aristocratic-looking fellow; handsome—but I didn't like his face; affable—and yet I didn't like his manner."

Ah, Valerie! you may well listen now!

"He wanted me, he said," continued Mosquetti, "to decide a little wager. Some foolish girl, who had seen De Lancy on the stage, and who believed him the ideal hero of romance, and was only in too much danger of throwing her heart and fortune at his feet, was to be disenchanted by any stratagem that could be devised. Her parents had intrusted the management of the affair to him, a relation of the lady's. Would I assist him? Would I represent De Lancy, and play a little scene in the Bois de Boulogne, to open the eyes of this silly boarding-school miss—would I, for a consideration? It was only to act a little stage play off the stage, and was for a good cause. I consented; and that evening, at half-past ten o'clock, under the shadow of the winter night and the leafless trees, I——"

"Stop, stop! Signor Mosquetti!" cry the bystanders. "Madame! Madame de Marolles! Water! Smelling-salts! Your *flacon*, Lady Emily: she has fainted!"

No; she has not fainted; this is something worse than fainting, this convulsive agony, in which the proud form writhes, while the white and livid lips murmur strange and dreadful words.

"Murdered, murdered and innocent! while I, vile dupe, pitiful fool, was only a puppet in the hands of a demon!"

At this very moment Monsieur de Marolles, who has been summoned from the adjoining apartment, where he has been discussing a financial measure with some members of the lower House,[8] enters hurriedly.

"Valerie, Valerie, what is the matter?" he says, approaching his wife.

She rises—rises with a terrible effort, and looks him full in the face.

"I thought, monsieur, that I knew the hideous abyss of your black soul to its lowest depths. I was wrong; I never knew you till to-night."

Imagine such strong language as this in a Belgravian drawing-room, and then you can imagine the astonishment of the bystanders.

"Good heavens!" exclaimed Signor Mosquetti hurriedly.

"What?" cried they eagerly.

"That is the very man I have been speaking of."

"That? The Count de Marolles?"

"The man bending over the lady who has fainted."

Petrified Belgravians experience a new sensation—surprise—and rather like it.

Argyle Fitz-Bertram twists his black moustachios reflectively, and mutters—

"So help me, Jupiter, I knew there'd be a row! I shan't have to sing 'Scots wha hae,' and shall be just in time for that little supper at the Café de l'Europe."

CHAPTER VII

THE GOLDEN SECRET IS TOLD, AND THE GOLDEN BOWL IS BROKEN[1]

The new tiger, or, as he is called in the kitchen, the "tempory tiger," takes his place, on the morning after Lady Londersdon's Wednesday, behind the Count de Marolles's cab, as that gentleman drives into the City.

There is little augury to be drawn from the pale smooth face of Raymond de Marolles, though Signor Mosquetti's revelation has made his position rather a critical one. Till now he has ruled Valerie with a high hand; and though never conquering the indomitable spirit of the proud Spanish woman, he has at least forced that spirit to do the will of his. But *now,* now that she knows the trick put upon her—now that she knows that the man she so deeply adored did not betray her, but died the victim of another's treachery—that the blood in which she has steeped her soul was the blood of the innocent,—what if now, in her desperation and despair, she dares all, and reveals all; what then?

"Why, then," says Raymond de Marolles, cutting his horse over the ears with a delicate touch of the whip, which stings home, though, for all its delicacy; "why then, never shall it be said that Raymond Marolles found himself in a dilemma, without finding within himself the power to extricate himself. We are not conquered yet, and we have seen a good deal of life in thirty years—and not a little danger. Play your best card, Valerie; I've a trump in my own hand to play when the time comes. Till then, keep dark. I tell you, my good woman, I have hothouses of my own, and don't want your Covent-Garden exotics at twopence a bunch!"

This last sentence is addressed to a woman, who pleads earnestly for the purchase of a wretched bunch of violets, which she holds up to tempt the man of fashion as she runs by the wheels of his cab, driving very slowly through the Strand.

"Fresh violets, sir. Do, sir, please. Only twopence, just twopence, sir, for the love of charity. I've a poor old woman at home, not related to me, sir, but I keep her. She's dying—starving, sir, and dying of old age."

"Bah! I tell you, my good woman, I'm not Lawrence Sterne on a sentimental journey,[2] but a practical man of business. I don't give macaroons to donkeys, or save mythic old women from starvation. You'd better keep out of the way of the wheels—they'll be over your feet presently, and if you suffer from corns they may probably hurt you," says the philanthropic banker, in his politest tones.

"Stop, stop!" suddenly exclaims the woman, with an energy that almost startles even Raymond. "It's you, is it—Jim? No, not Jim; he's dead and gone, I know; but you, you, the fine gentleman, the other brother. Stop, stop, I tell you, if you want to know a secret that's in the keeping of one who may die while I am talking here! Stop, if you want to know who you are and what you are! Stop!"

Raymond does pull up at this last sentence.

"My good woman, do not be so energetic. Every eye in the Strand is on us; we shall have a crowd presently. Stay, wait for me in Essex Street; I'll get out at the corner; that's a quiet street, and we shall not be observed. Anything you have to tell me you can tell me there."

The woman obeys him, and draws back to the pavement, where she keeps pace with the cab.

"A pretty time this for discoveries!" mutters the Count. "Who I am, and what I am! It's the secret, I suppose, that the twaddling old maniac in Blind Peter made such a row about. Who I am, and what I am! Oh, I dare say I shall turn out to be somebody great, as the hero does in a lady's novel. It's a pity I haven't the mark of a coronet behind my ear, or a bloody hand on my wrist. Who I am, and what I am! The son of a journeyman tailor perhaps, or a chemist's apprentice, whose aristocratic connections prevented his acknowledging my mother."

He is at the corner of Essex Street by this time, and springs out of the cab, throwing the reins to the temporary tiger, whose sharp face we need scarcely inform the reader discloses the features of the boy Slosh.

The woman is waiting for him; and after a few moments' earnest conversation, Raymond emerges from the street, and orders the boy to drive the cab home immediately: he is not going to the City, but is going on particular business elsewhere.

Whether the "temporary tiger" proves himself worthy of the responsible situation he holds, and does drive the cab home, I cannot say; but I only know that a very small boy, in a ragged coat a great deal too large for him, and a battered hat so slouched over his eyes as quite to conceal his face from the casual observer, creeps cautiously, now a few paces behind, now a hundred yards on the other side of the way, now disappearing in the shadow of a doorway, now reappearing at the corner of the street, but never losing sight of the Count de Marolles and the purveyor of violets, as they bend their steps in the direction of Seven Dials.[3]

Heaven forbid that we should follow them through all the turnings and twistings of that odoriferous neighbourhood, where foul scents, foul sights, and fouler language abound; whence May Fair and Belgravia shrink shuddering, as from an ill it is well for them to let alone, and a wrong that he may mend who will: not they who have been born for better things than to set disjointed times aright, or play the revolutionist to the dethronement of the legitimate monarchy of Queen Starvation and King Fever, to say nothing of the princes of the blood—Dirt, Drunkenness, Theft, and Murder. When John Jones, tired of the monotonous pastime of beating his wife's skull with a poker, comes to Lambeth and murders an Archbishop of Canterbury[4] for the sake of the spoons, it will be time, in the eyes of Belgravia, to reform John Jones. In the meanwhile we of the upper ten thousand have Tattersall's and Her Majesty's

Theatre, and John Jones (who, low republican, says he must have his amusements too) has such little diversions as wife-murder and cholera to break the monotony of his existence.

The Count and the violet-seller at last come to a pause. They had walked very quickly through the pestiferous streets, Raymond holding his aristocratic breath and shutting his patrician ears to the scents and the sounds around him. They come to a stand at last, in a dark court, before a tall lopsided house, with irresolute chimney-pots, which looked as if the only thing that kept them erect was the want of unanimity as to which way they should fall.

Raymond, when invited by the woman to enter, looks suspiciously at the dingy staircase, as if wondering whether it would last his time, but at the request of his companion ascends it.

The boy in the large coat and slouched hat is playing marbles with another boy on the second-floor landing, and has evidently lived there all his life: and yet I'm puzzled as to who drove that cab home to the stables at the back of Park Lane. I fear it was not the "temporary tiger."

The Count de Marolles and his guide pass the youthful gamester, who has just lost his second halfpenny, and ascend to the very top of the rickety house, the garrets of which are afflicted with intermittent ague whenever there is a high wind.

Into one of these garrets the woman conducts Raymond, and on a bed—or its apology, a thing of shreds and patches, straw and dirt, which goes by the name of a bed at this end of the town—lies the old woman we last saw in Blind Peter.

Eight years, more or less, have not certainly had the effect of enhancing the charms of this lady; and there is something in her face to-day more terrible even than wicked old age or feminine drunkenness. It is death that lends those livid hues to her complexion, which all the cosmetics from Atkinson's[5] or the Burlington Arcade,[6] were she minded to use them, would never serve to conceal. Raymond has not come too soon if he is to hear any secret from those ghastly lips. It is some time before the woman, whom she still calls Sillikens, can make the dying hag understand who this fine gentleman is, and what it is he wants with her; and even when she does succeed in making her comprehend all this, the old woman's speech is very obscure, and calculated to try the patience of a more amiable man than the Count de Marolles.

"Yes, it was a golden secret—a golden secret, eh, my dear? It was something to have a marquis for a son-in-law, wasn't it, my dear, eh?" mumbled the dying old hag.

"A marquis for a son-in-law! What does the jibbering old idiot mean?" muttered Raymond, whose reverence for his grandmother was not one of the strongest points in his composition. "A marquis! I dare say my respected progenitor kept a public-house, or something of that sort. A marquis! The 'Marquis of Granby,'[7] most likely!"

"Yes, a marquis," continued the old woman, "eh, dear! And he married your mother—married her at the parish church, one cold dark November morning; and I've got the c'tificate. Yes," she mumbled, in answer to Raymond's eager gesture, "I've got it; but I'm not going to tell you where;—no, not till I'm paid. I must be paid for that secret in gold—yes, in gold. They say that we don't rest any easier in our coffins for the money that's buried with us; but I should like to lie up to neck in golden sovereigns new from the Mint, and not one light one amongst 'em."

"Well," said Raymond, impatiently, "your secret! I'm rich, and can pay for it. Your secret—quick!"

"Well, he hadn't been married to her long before a change came, in his native country, over the sea yonder," said the old woman, pointing in the direction of St. Martin's Lane, as if she thought the British Channel flowed somewhere behind that thoroughfare. "A change came, and he got his rights again. One king was put down and another king was set up, and everybody else was massacred in the streets; it was—a—I don't know what they call it; but they're always a-doin' it. So he got his rights, and he was a rich man again, and a great man; and then his first thought was to keep his marriage with my girl a secret. All very well, you know, my girl for a wife while he was giving lessons at a shilling a-piece, in *Parlez-vous Français,* and all that; but now he was a marquis, and it was quite another thing."

Raymond by this time gets quite interested; so does the boy in the big coat and the slouched hat, who has transferred the field of his gambling operations in the marble line to the landing outside the garret door.

"He wanted the secret kept, and I kept it for gold. I kept it even from her, your mother, my own ill-used girl, for gold. She never knew who he was; she thought he'd deserted her, and she took to drinking; she and I threw you into the river when we were mad drunk, and couldn't stand your squalling. She died—don't you ask me how. I told you before not to ask me how my girl died—I'm mad enough without that question; she died, and I kept the secret. For a long time it was gold to me, and he used to send me money regular to keep it dark; but by-and-by the money stopped from coming. I got savage, but still I kept the secret; because, you see, it was nothing when it was told, and there was no one rich enough to pay me to tell it. I didn't know where to find the marquis; I only knew he was somewhere in France."

"France?" exclaims Raymond.

"Yes; didn't I tell you France? He was a French marquis—a refugee they called him when he first made acquaintance with my girl—a teacher of French and mathematics."

"And his name—his name?" asks Raymond, eagerly. "His name, woman, if you don't want to drive me mad."

"He called himself Smith, when he was a-teachin', my dear," said the old woman with a ghastly leer; "what are you going to pay me for the secret?"

"Whatever you like, only tell me—tell me before you——"

"Die. Yes, deary; there ain't any time to waste, is there? I don't want to make a hard bargain. Will you bury me up to my neck in gold?"

"Yes, yes; speak!" He is almost beside himself, and raises a threatening hand. The old woman grins.

"I told you before *that* wasn't the way, deary. Wait a bit. Sillikens, give me that 'ere old shoe, will you? Look you here! It's a double sole, and the marriage certificate is between the two leathers. I've walked on it this thirty years and more."

"And the name—the name?"

"The name of the Marquis was De—de——"

"She's dying! Give me some water!" cried Raymond.

"De Ce—Ce——" the syllables come in fitful gasps. Raymond throws some water over her face.

"De Cevennes, my deary!—and the golden secret is told."

And the golden bowl is broken!

Lay the ragged sheet over the ghastly face, Sillikens, and kneel down and pray for help in your utter loneliness; for the guilty being whose soul has gone forth to meet its Maker was your only companion and stay, however frail that stay might be.

Go out into the sunshine, Monsieur de Marolles; that which you leave behind in the tottering garret, shaken by an ague-paroxysm with the fitful autumn wind, is nothing so terrible to your eyes.

You have accustomed yourself to the face of Death before now; you have met that grim potentate on his own ground, and done with him what it is your policy to do with everything on earth—you have made him useful to you.

CHAPTER VIII

ONE STEP FURTHER ON THE RIGHT TRACK

It is not a very romantic locality to which we must now conduct the reader, being neither more nor less than the shop and surgery of Mr. Augustus Darley; which temple of the healing god is scented, this autumn afternoon, with the mingled perfumes of Cavendish and bird's-eye tobacco, Turkey rhubarb, whiskey-punch, otto of roses,[1] and muffins; conflicting odours, which form, or rather object to form, an amalgamation, each particular effluvium asserting its individuality.

In the surgery Gus is seated, playing the intellectual and intensely exciting game of dominoes with our acquaintance of the Cheerful Cherokee Society, Mr. Percy Cordonner. A small jug, without either of those earthenware conventionalities, spout or handle, and with Mr. Cordonner's bandanna stuffed into the top to imprison the subtle essences of the mixture within, stands between the two gentlemen; while Percy, as a guest, is accommodated with a real tumbler, having only three triangular bits chipped out of the edge. Gus imbibes the exciting fluid from a cracked custard-cup, with paper wafered round it to keep the parts from separating, two of which cups are supposed to be equal (by just measurement) to Mr. P. C.'s tumbler. Before the small fire kneels the juvenile domestic of the young surgeon, toasting muffins, and presenting to the two gentlemen a pleasing study in anatomical perspective and the mysteries of foreshortening; to which, however, they are singularly inattentive, devoting their entire energies to the pieces of spotted ivory in their hands, and the consumption, by equitable division, of the whiskey-punch.

"I say, Gus," said Mr. Cordonner, stopping in the middle of a gulp of his favourite liquid, at the risk of strangulation, with as much alarm in his face as his placid features were capable of exhibiting— "I say, this isn't the professional tumbler, is it?"

"Why, of course it is," said his friend. "We have only had that one since midsummer. The patients don't like it because it's chipped; but I always tell them, that after having gone through having a tooth out—particularly," he added parenthetically, "as I take 'em out (plenty of lancet, forceps, and key, for their eighteen-pence)— they needn't grumble about having to rinse their mouths out of a cracked tumbler."

Mr. Cordonner turned pale.

"Do they do that?" he said, and deliberately shot his last sip of the delicious beverage over the head of the kneeling damsel, with so good an aim that it in a manner grazed her curl-papers. "It isn't friendly of you, Gus," he said, with mild reproachfulness, "to treat a fellow like this."

"It's all right, old boy," said Gus, laughing. "Sarah Jane washes it, you know. You wash the tumbler and things, don't you, Sarah Jane?"

"Wash 'em?" answered the youthful domestic; "I should think so, sir, indeed. Why, I wipes 'em round reg'lar with my apron, and breathes on 'em to make 'em bright."

"Oh, that'll do!" said Mr. Cordonner, piteously. "Don't investigate, Gus; you'll only make matters worse. Oh, why, why did I ask that question? Why didn't I remember 'it's folly to be otherwise?' That punch was delicious—and now——" He leant his head upon his hand, buried his face in his pocket-handkerchief, pondered in his heart, and was still.

In the mean time the shop is not empty. Isabella is standing behind the counter, very busy with several bottles, a glass measure, and a pestle and mortar, making up a prescription, a cough mixture, from her brother's Latin. Rather a puzzling document, this prescription, to any one but Bell; for there are calculations about next year's Derby scribbled on the margin, and rough sketches of the Smasher, and a more youthful votary of the Smasher's art, surnamed "Whooping William," pencilled on the back thereof; but to Bell it seems straightforward enough. At any rate, she dashes away with the bottles, the measure, and the pestle and mortar, as if she knew perfectly well what she was about.

She is not alone in the shop. A gentleman is leaning on the counter, watching the busy white hands very intently, and apparently deeply interested in the progress of the cough-mixture. This gentleman is her brother's old friend, "Daredevil Dick."

Richard Marwood has been a great deal at the surgery since the night on which he first set foot in his old haunts; he has brought his mother over, and introduced that lady to Miss Darley. Mrs. Marwood was delighted with Isabella's frank manners and handsome face, and insisted on carrying her back to dine in Spring Gardens. Quite a sociable little dinner they had too, Richard being—for a man who had been condemned for a murder, and had escaped from a lunatic asylum—very cheerful indeed. The young man told Isabella all his adventures, till that young lady alternately laughed and cried—thereby affording Richard's fond mother most convincing proof of the goodness of her heart—and was altogether so very brilliant and amusing, that when at eleven o'clock Gus came round from a very critical case (viz., a quarrel of the Cheerfuls as to whether Gustavus Ponsonby, novelist and satirist, magazine-writer and poet, deserved the trouncing he had received in the "Friday Pillory") to take Bell home in a cab, the little trio simultaneously declared that the evening had gone as if by magic! As if by magic! What if to two out of those three the evening did really go by magic? There is a certain pink-legged little gentleman, with wings, and a bandage round his eyes, who, some people say, is as great a magician in his way as Albertus Magnus or Doctor Dee,[2] and who has done as much mischief and worked as much ruin in his own manner as all the villainous saltpetre ever dug out of the bosom of the peaceful, corn-growing, flower-bearing earth. That gentleman, I have no doubt, presided on the occasion.

Thus the acquaintance of Richard and Isabella had ripened into something very much like friendship; and here he is, watching her employed in the rather unromantic business of making up a cough-mixture for an elderly washerwoman of methodistical persuasions. But it is one of the fancies of the pink-legged gentleman aforesaid to lend his bandage to his victims; and there is nothing that John, William, George, Henry, James, or Alfred can do, in which Jane, Eliza, Susan, or Sarah will not see a dignity and a charm, or *vice versâ*. Pshaw! It is not Mokannah who wears the silver veil; it is we who are in love with Mokannah[3] who put on the glittering, blinding medium; and, looking at that gentleman through the dazzle and the glitter, insist on thinking him a very handsome man, till some one takes the veil off our eyes, and we straightway fall to and abuse poor Mokannah, because he is not what we chose to fancy him. It is very hard upon poor tobacco-smoking, beer-imbibing, card-playing, latch-key-loving Tom Jones, that Sophia will insist on elevating him into a god, and then being angry with him because he is Tom Jones and fond of bitter ale and bird's-eye. But come what may, the pink-legged gentleman must have his diversion, and no doubt his eyes twinkle merrily behind that bandage of his, to see the fools this wise world of ours is made up of.

"You could trust me, Isabella, then," said Richard; "you could trust me, in spite of all—in spite of my wasted youth and the blight upon my name?"

"Do we not all trust you, Mr. Marwood, with our entire hearts?" answered the young lady, taking shelter under cover of a very wide generality.

"Not 'Mr. Marwood,' Bell; it sounds very cold from the lips of my old friend's sister. Every one calls me Richard, and I, without once asking permission, have called you Bell. Call me Richard, Bell, if you trust me."

She looks him in the face, and is silent for a moment; her heart beats a great deal faster—so fast that her lips can scarcely shape the words she speaks.

"I do trust you, Richard; I believe your heart to be goodness and truth itself."

"Is it worth having, then, Bell? I wouldn't ask you that question if I had not a hope now—ay, and not such a feeble one either—to see my name cleared from the stain that rests upon it. If there is any truth in my heart, Isabella, that truth is yours alone. Can you trust me, as the woman who loves trusts—through life and till death, under every shadow and through every cloud?"

I don't know whether essence of peppermint, tincture of myrrh, and hair-oil, are the proper ingredients in a cough-mixture; but I know that Isabella poured them into the glass measure very liberally.

"You do not answer me, Isabella. Ah, you cannot trust the branded criminal—the escaped lunatic—the man the world calls a murderer!"

"Not trust you, Richard?" Only four words, and only one glance from the grey eyes into the brown, and so much told! So much more than I could tell in a dozen chapters, told in those four words and that one look!

Gus opens the half-glass door at this very moment. "Are you coming to tea?" he asks; "here's Sarah Jane up to her eyes in grease and muffins."

"Yes, Gus, dear old friend," said Richard, laying his hand on Darley's shoulder; "we're coming in to tea immediately, *brother!*"

Gus looked at him with a glance of considerable astonishment, shook him heartily by the hand, and gave a long whistle; after which he walked up to the counter and examined the cough-mixture.

"Oh!" he said, "I suppose that's why you've put enough laudanum into this to poison a small regiment, eh, Bell? Perhaps we may as well throw it out of the window; for if it goes out of the door I shall be hung for wholesale murder."

They were a very merry party over the little tea-table; and if nobody ate any of the muffins, which Mr. Cordonner called "embodied indigestions," they laughed a great deal, and talked still more—so much so, that Percy declared his reasoning faculties to be quite overpowered, and wanted to be distinctly informed whether it was Richard who was going to marry Gus, or Gus about to unite himself to the juvenile domestic, or he himself who was to be married against his inclination—which, seeing he was of a yielding and peace-loving disposition, was not so unlikely—or, in short, to use his own expressive language, "what the row was all about?".

Nobody, however, took the trouble to set Mr. P. C.'s doubts at rest, and he drank his tea with perfect contentment, but without sugar, and in a dense intellectual fog. "It doesn't matter," he murmured; "perhaps Richard will turn again and be Lord Mayor of London town, and then my children will read his adventures in a future Pinnock,[4] and they may understand it. It's a great thing to be a child, and to understand those sort of things. When I was six years old I knew who William Rufus married, and how many people died in the Plague of London. I can't say it made me any happier or better, but I dare say it was a great advantage."

At this moment the bell hung at the shop-door (a noisy preventive of petty larceny, giving the alarm if any juvenile delinquent had a desire to abstract a bottle of castor-oil, or a camomile-pill or so, for his peculiar benefit) rang violently, and our old friend Mr. Peters burst into the shop, and through the shop into the parlour, in a state of such excitement that his very fingers seemed out of breath.

"Back again?" cried Richard, starting up with surprise; for be it known to the reader that Mr. Peters had only the day before started for Slopperton-on-the-Sloshy to hunt up evidence about this man, whose very image lay buried outside that town.

Before the fingers of Mr. Peters, which quite shook with excitement, could shape an answer to Richard's exclamation of surprise, a very dignified elderly gentleman, whose appearance was almost clerical, followed the detective into the room, and bowed politely to the assembled party.

"I will take upon myself to be my own sponsor," said that gentleman. "If, as I believe, I am speaking to Mr. Marwood," he added, looking at Richard, who bowed affirmatively, "it is to the interest of both of us—of you, sir, more especially—that we should become acquainted. I am Dr. Tappenden, of Slopperton."

Mr. Cordonner, having politely withdrawn himself from the group so as not to interfere with any confidential communication, was here imprudent enough to attempt to select a book from the young surgeon's hanging-library, and, in endeavouring to take down the third volume of *Bragelonne,*[5] brought down, as usual, the entire literary shower-bath on his devoted head, and sat quietly snowed up, as it were, in loose leaves of Michel Lévy's[6] shilling edition, and fragments of illustrations by Tony Johannot.[7]

Richard looked a little puzzled at Dr. Tappenden's introduction; but Mr. Peters threw in upon his fingers this piece of information,— "He knows *him!*" and Richard was immediately interested.

"We are all friends here, I believe?" said the schoolmaster, glancing round interrogatively.

"Oh, decidedly, Monsieur d'Artagnan,"[8] replied Percy, absently looking up from one of the loose leaves he had selected for perusal from those scattered around him.

"Monsieur d'Artagnan! Your friend is pleased to be facetious," said the Doctor, with some indignation.

"Oh, pray excuse him, sir. He is only absent-minded," replied Richard. "My friend Peters informs me that you know this man— this singular, this incomprehensible villain, whose supposed death is so extraordinary."

"He—either the man who died, or this man who is now occupying a high position in London—was for some years in my employ; but in spite of what our worthy friend the detective says, I am inclined to think that Jabez North, my tutor, did actually die, and that it was his body which I saw at the police-station."

"Not a bit of it, sir," said the detective on his rapid fingers, "not a bit of it! That death was a do—a do, out and out. It was too system-atic to be anything else, and I was a fool not to see there was some-thing black at the bottom of it at the time. People don't go and lay themselves out high and dry upon a heath, with clean soles to their shoes, on a stormy night, and the bottle in their hand—not took hold of, neither, but lying loose, you understand; *put there*—not clutched as a dying man clutches what his hand closes upon. I say this ain't how people make away with themselves when they can't stand life any longer. It was a do—a plant, such as very few but that man could be capable of; and that man's your tutor, and the death was meant to put a stop to all suspicion; and while you was a-sighin' and a-groanin' over that poor young innocent, Mr. Jabez North was a-cuttin' a fine figure, and a-captivatin' a furrin heiress, with your money, or your banker's money, as had to bear the loss of them forged cheques."

"But the likeness?" said Dr. Tappenden. "That dead man was the very image of Jabez North."

"Very likely, sir. There's mysterious goin's on, and some coinci-dences in this life, as well as in your story-books that's lent out at three half-pence a volume, keep 'em three days and return 'em clean."

"Well," continued the schoolmaster, "the moment I see this man I shall know whether he is indeed the person we want to find. If he should be the man who was my usher, I can prove a circumstance which will go a great way, Mr. Marwood, towards fixing your uncle's murder upon him."

"And that is——?" asked Richard, eagerly.

But there is no occasion for the reader to know what it is just yet; so we will leave the little party in the Friar Street surgery to talk this business over, which they do with such intense interest that the small hours catch them still talking of the same subject, and Mr. Percy Cor-donner still snowed up in his corner, reading from the loose leaves the most fascinating *olla pòdrida*[9] of literature, wherein the writings of Charles Dickens, George Sand, Harrison Ainsworth, and Alexandre Dumas are blended together in the most delicious and exciting con-fusion.

CHAPTER IX

CAPTAIN LANSDOWN OVERHEARS A CONVERSATION
WHICH APPEARS TO INTEREST HIM

Laurent Blurosset was a sort of rage at the West-end of London. What did they seek, these weary denizens of the West-end, but excitement? Excitement! No matter how obtained. If Laurent Blurosset were a magician, so much the better; if he had sold himself to the devil, so much the better again, and so much the more exciting. There was something almost approaching to a sensation in making a morning call upon a gentleman who had possibly entered into a contract with Sathanas, or put his name on the back of a bit of stamped paper payable at sight to Lucifer himself. And then there was the slightest chance, the faintest shadow of a probability, of meeting the proprietor of the gentleman they called upon; and what could be more delightful than that? How did he visit Marlborough Street—the proprietor? Had he a pass-key to the hall-door? or did he leave his card with the servant, like any other of the gentlemen his pupils and allies? Or did he rise through a trap in the Brussels carpet in the drawing-room? or slide through one of the sham Wouvermanns[1] that adorned the walls? At any rate, a visit to the mysterious chemist of Marlborough Street was about the best thing to do at this fag-end of the worn-out London season; and Monsieur Laurent Blurosset was considered a great deal better than the Opera.

It was growing dusk on the evening on which there was so much excitement in the little surgery in Friar Street, when a plain close carriage stopped at Monsieur Blurosset's door, and a lady alighted thickly veiled. The graceful but haughty head is one we know. It is Valerie, who, in the depth of her misery, comes to this man, who is in part the author of that misery.

She is ushered into a small apartment at the back of the house, half study, half laboratory, littered with books, manuscripts, crucibles, and mathematical instruments. On a little table, near a fire that burns low in the grate, are thrown in a careless heap the well-remembered cards—the cards which eight years ago foretold the death of the king of spades.

The room is empty when she enters it, and she seats herself in the depth of the shadow; for there is no light but the flickering flame of the low fire.

What does she think of, as she sits in the gloom of that silent apartment? Who shall say? What forest deep, what lonely ocean strand, what desert island, is more dismal than the backroom of a London house, at the window of which looks in a high black wall, or a dreary, smoke-dried, weird, vegetable phenomenon which nobody on earth but the landlord ever called a tree?

What does she think of in this dreary room? What *can* she think of? What has she ever thought for eight years past but of the man she loved and murdered? And he was innocent! As long as she had been convinced of his guilt, of his cruel and bitter treachery, it had been a sacrifice, that ordeal of the November night. Now it took another colour; it was a murder—and she a pitiful puppet in the hands of a master-fiend!

Monsieur Blurosset enters the room, and finds her alone with these thoughts.

"Madame," he says, "I have perhaps the honour of knowing you?" He has so many fair visitors that he thinks this one, whose face he cannot see, may be one of his old clients.

"It is eight years since you have seen me, monsieur," she replies. "You have most likely forgotten me?"

"Forgotten you, madame, perhaps, but not your voice. That is not to be forgotten."

"Indeed, monsieur—and why not?"

"Because, madame, it has a peculiarity of its own, which, as a physiologist, I cannot mistake. It is the voice of one who has suffered?"

"It is!—it is!"

"Of one who has suffered more than it is the common lot of woman to suffer."

"You are right, monsieur."

"And now, madame, what can I do for you?"

"Nothing, monsieur. You can do nothing for me but that which the commonest apothecary in this city who will sell me an ounce of laudanum can do as well as you."

"Oh, has it come to that again?" he says, with a shade of sarcasm in his tone. "I remember, eight years ago——"

"I asked you for the means of death. I did not say I wished to die then, at that moment. I did not. I had a purpose in life. I have still."

As she said these words the fellow-lodger of Blurosset—the Indian soldier, Captain Lansdown, who had let himself in with his latch-key—crossed the hall, and was arrested at the half-open door of the study by the sound of voices within. I don't know how to account for conduct so unworthy of an officer and a gentleman, but the captain stopped in the shadow of the dark hall and listened—as if life and death were on the words—to the voice of the speaker.

"I have, I say, still a purpose in life—a solemn and a sacred one—to protect the innocent. However guilty I may be, thank Heaven I have still the power to protect my son."

"You are married, madame?"

"I am married. You know it as well as I, Monsieur Laurent Blurosset. The man who first brought me to your apartment must have been, if not your accomplice, at least your colleague. He revealed to you his scheme, no doubt, in order to secure your assistance in that scheme. I am married to a villain—such a villain as I think Heaven never before looked down upon."

"And you would protect your son, madame, from his father?"

Captain Lansdown's face gleams through the shadow as white as the face of Valerie herself, as she stands looking full at Monsieur Blurosset in the flickering fire-light.

"And you would protect your son from his father, madame?" repeats the chemist.

"The man to whom I am at present married is not the father of my son," says Valerie, in a cold calm voice.

"How, madame?"

"I was married before," she continued. "The son I so dearly love is the son of my first husband. My second marriage has been a marriage only in name.[2] All your worthy colleague, Monsieur Raymond Marolles, stained his hands in innocent blood to obtain was a large fortune. He has that, and is content; but he shall not hold it long."

"And your purpose in coming to me, madame——?"

"Is to accuse you—yes, Monsieur Laurent Blurosset, to accuse you—as an accomplice in the murder of Gaston de Lancy."

"An accomplice in a murder!"

"Yes; you sold me a poison—you knew for what that poison was to be used; you were in the plot, the vile and demoniac plot, that was to steep my soul in guilt. You prophesied the death of the man I was intended to murder; you put the thought into my distracted brain—the weapon into my guilty hand; and while I suffer all the tortures which Heaven inflicts on those who break its laws, are you to go free? No, monsieur, you shall not go free. Either join with me in accusing this man, and help me to drag him to justice, or by the light in the sky, by the life-blood of my broken heart—by the life of my only child, I swear to denounce you! Gaston de Lancy shall not go unavenged by the woman who loved and murdered him."

The mention of the name of Gaston de Lancy, the man she so dearly and devotedly loved, has a power that nothing else on earth has over Valerie, and she breaks into a passionate torrent of tears.

Laurent Blurosset looks on silently at this burst of anguish; perhaps he regards it as a man of science, and can calculate to a moment how long it will last.

The Indian officer, in the shadow of the doorway, is more affected than the chemist and philosopher, for he falls on his knees by the threshold and hides his pale face in his hands.

There is a silence of perhaps five minutes—a terrible silence it seems, only broken by the heartrending sobs of this despairing woman. At last Laurent Blurosset speaks—speaks in a tone in which she has never heard him speak before—in a tone in which, probably, very few have heard him speak—in a tone so strange to him and his ordinary habits that it in a manner transforms him into a new man.

"You say, madame, I was an accomplice of this man's. How if he did not condescend to make me an accomplice? How, if this gentleman, who, owing all his success in life to his unassisted villany, has considerable confidence in his own talents, did not think me worthy of the honour of being his accomplice?"

"How, monsieur?"

"No, madame; Laurent Blurosset was not a man for the brilliant Parisian adventurer Raymond Marolles to enlist as a colleague. No, Laurent Blurosset was merely a philosopher, a physiologist, a dreamer, a little bit of a madman, and but a poor puppet in the hands of the man of the world, the chevalier of fortune, the unscrupulous and designing Englishman."

"An Englishman?"

"Yes, madame; that is one of your husband's secrets: he is an Englishman. I was not clever enough to be the accomplice of Monsieur Marolles; in his opinion I was not too clever to become his dupe."

"His dupe?"

"Yes, madame, his dupe. His contempt for the man of science was most supreme: I was a useful automaton—nothing more. The chemist, the physiologist, the man whose head had grown gray in the pursuit of an inductive science—whose nights and days had been given to the study of the great laws of cause and effect—was a puppet in the hands of the chevalier of fortune, and as little likely to fathom his motives as the wooden doll is likely to guess those of the showman who pulls the strings that make it dance. So thought Raymond Marolles, the adventurer, the fortune-hunter, the thief, the murderer!"

"What, monsieur, you knew him, then?"

"To the very bottom of his black heart, madame. Science would indeed have been a lie, wisdom would indeed have been a chimera, if I could not have read through the low cunning of the superficial showy adventurer, as well as I can read the words written in yonder book through the thin veil of a foreign character. I, his dupe, as he thought—the learned fool at whose labours he laughed, even while he sought to avail himself of their help—I laughed at him in turn, read every motive; but let him laugh on, lie on, till the time at which it should be my pleasure to lift the mask, and say to him—'Raymond Marolles, charlatan! liar! fool! dupe! in the battle between Wisdom and Cunning the grey-eyed goddess is the conqueror.'"

"What, monsieur? Then you are doubly a murderer. You knew this man, and yet abetted him in the vilest plot by which a wretched woman was ever made to destroy the man she loved a thousand times better than her worthless self!"

Laurent Blurosset smiled a most impenetrable smile.

"I acted for a purpose, madame. I wished to test the effects of a new poison. Yours the murder—if there was a murder; not mine. You asked me for a weapon; I put it into your hands; I did not compel you to use it."

"No, monsieur; but you prompted me. If there is justice on earth, you shall suffer for that act as well as Monsieur Marolles; if not, there is justice in heaven! God's punishments are more terrible than those of men, and you have all the more cause to tremble, you and the wretch whose accomplice you were—whose willing accomplice, by your own admission, you were."

"And yourself, madame? In dragging us to justice, may you not yourself suffer?"

"Suffer!" She laughs a hollow bitter peal of mocking laughter, painful to hear; very painful to the ears of the listener in the shadow, whose face is still buried in his hands. "Suffer! No, Monsieur Blurosset, for me on earth there is no more suffering. If in hell the wretches doomed to eternal punishment suffer as I have suffered for the last eight years, as I suffered on that winter's night when the man I loved died, then, indeed, God is an avenging Deity. Do you think the worst the law can inflict upon me for that guilty deed is by one thousandth degree equal to the anguish of my own mind, every day and every hour? Do you think I fear disgrace? Disgrace! Bah! What is it? There never was but one being on earth whose good opinion I valued, or whose bad opinion I feared. That man I murdered. You think I fear the world? The world to me was him; and he is dead. If you do not wish to be denounced as the accomplice of a murderess and *her* accomplice, do not let me quit this room; for, by the heaven above me, so surely as I quit this room alive I go to deliver you, Raymond Marolles, and myself into the hands of justice!"

"And your son, madame—what of him?"

"I have made arrangements for his future happiness, monsieur. He will return to France, and be placed under the care of my uncle."

For a few moments there is silence. Laurent Blurosset seems lost in thought. Valerie sits with her bright hollow eyes fixed on the flickering flame of the low fire. Blurosset is the first to speak.

"You say, madame, that if I do not wish to be given up to justice as the accomplice of a murderer, I shall not suffer you to leave this room, but sacrifice you to the preservation of my own safety. Nothing more easy, madame; I have only to raise my hand—to wave a handkerchief, medicated in the manner of those the Borgias and Medicis used of old, before your face; to scatter a few grains of powder into that fire at your feet; to give you a book to read, a flower to smell; and you do not leave this room alive. And this is how I should act, if I were, what you say I am, the accomplice of a murderer."

"How, monsieur!—you had no part in the murder of my husband?—you, who gave me the drug which killed him?"

"You jump at conclusions, madame. How do you know that the drug which I gave you killed Gaston de Lancy?"

"Oh, for pity's sake, do not juggle with me, Monsieur. Speak! What do you mean?"

"Simply this, madame. That the death of your husband on the evening of the day on which you gave him the drugged wine may have been—a coincidence."

"Oh, monsieur! in mercy——"

"Nay, madame, it was a coincidence. The drug I gave you was not a poison. You are guiltless of your husband's death."

"Oh, heaven be praised! Merciful heaven be praised!" She falls on her knees, and buries her head in her hands in a wild burst of tearful thanksgiving.

While her face is thus hidden, Blurosset takes from a little cabinet on one side of the fireplace a handful of a light-coloured powder, which he throws upon the expiring cinders in the grate. A lurid flame blazes up, illuminating the room with a strange unnatural glare.

"Valerie, Countess de Marolles," he says, in a tone of solemn earnestness, "men say I am a magician—a sorcerer—a disciple of the angel of darkness! Nay, some more foolish than the rest have been so blasphemous as to declare that I have power to raise the dead. Yours is no mind to be fooled by such shallow lies as these. The dead never rise again in answer to the will of mortal man. Lift your head, Valerie—not Countess de Marolles. I no longer call you by that name, which is in itself a falsehood. Valerie de Lancy, look yonder!"

He points in the direction of the open door. She rises, looks towards the threshold, staggers a step forward, utters one long wild shriek, and falls senseless to the floor.

In all the agonies she has endured, in all the horrors through which she has passed, she has never before lost her senses. The cause must indeed be a powerful one.

BOOK THE SIXTH

ON THE TRACK

FATHER AND SON

Three days have passed since the interview of Valerie with Laurent Blurosset, and Raymond de Marolles paces up and down his study in Park Lane. He is not going to the bank to-day. The autumn rains beat in against the double windows of the apartment, which is situated at the back of the house, looking out upon a small square patch of so-called garden. This garden is shut in by a wall, over which a weak-minded and erratic-looking creeper sprawls and straggles; and there is a little green door in this wall, which communicates with a mews.

A hopelessly wet day. Twelve by the clock, and not enough blue in the gloomy sky to make the smallest article of wearing apparel— no, not so much as a pair of wrist-bands for an unhappy seaman.[1] Well to be the Count de Marolles, and to have no occasion to extend one's walk beyond the purple-and-crimson border of that Turkey carpet on such a day as this! The London sparrows, transformed for the time being into a species of water-fowl, flutter dismally about the small swamp of grass-plot, flanked here and there by a superannuated clump of withered geraniums which have evidently seen better days. The sparrows seem to look enviously at the bright blaze reflected on the double windows of the Count's apartment, and would like, perhaps, to go in and sit on the hob; and I dare say they twitter to each other, in confidence, "A fine thing to be the Count de Marolles, with a fortune which it would take the lifetime of an Old Parr[2] to calculate, and a good fire in wet weather."

Yet, for all this, Raymond de Marolles does not look the most enviable object in creation on this particular rainy morning. His pale fair face is paler than ever; there are dark circles round the blue eyes, and a nervous and incessant twitching of the thin lower lip—

signs which never were, and never will be, indications of a peaceful mind. He has not seen Valerie since the night on which Monsieur Paul Moucée, *alias* Signor Mosquetti, told his story. She has remained secluded in her own apartments; and even Raymond de Marolles has scarce cared to break upon the solitude of this woman, in whom grief is so near akin to desperation.

"What will she do, now she knows all? Will she denounce me? If she does, I am prepared. If Blurosset, poor scientific fool, only plays his part faithfully, I am safe. But she will hardly reveal the truth. For her son's sake she will be silent. Oh, strange, inexplicable, and mysterious chance, that this fortune for which I have so deeply schemed, for which I have hazarded so much and worked so hard, should be my own—my own!—this woman a mere usurper, and I the rightful heir to the wealth of the De Cevennes! What is to be done? For the first time in my life I am at fault. Should I fly to the Marquis—tell him I am his son?—difficult to prove, now that old hag is dead; and even if I prove it—as I would move heaven and earth to do—what if she denounce me to her uncle, and he refuse to acknowledge the adventurer, the poisoner? I could soon silence her. But unfortunately she has been behind the scenes, and I fear she would scarcely accept a drop of water from the hands of her devoted husband. If I had any one to help me! But I have no one; no one that I can trust—no one in my power. Oh, Laurent Blurosset, for some of your mighty secrets, so that the very autumn wind blowing in at her window might seal the lips of my beautiful cousin for ever!"

Pleasant thoughts to be busy with this rainy autumn day; but such thoughts are by no means unfamiliar to the heart of Raymond de Marolles.

It is from a reverie such as this that he is aroused by the sound of carriage-wheels, and a loud knocking and ringing at the hall door. "Too early for morning callers. Who can it be at such an hour? Some one from the bank, perhaps?" He paces up and down the room rather anxiously, wondering who this unexpected visitor might be, when the groom of the chambers opens the door and announces, "The Marquis de Cevennes!"

"So, then," mutters Raymond, "she has played her first card—she has sent for her uncle. We shall have need of all our brains to-day. Now then, to meet my father face to face."

As he speaks, the Marquis enters.

Face to face—father and son. Sixty years of age—fair and pale, blue eyes, aquiline nose, and thin lips. Thirty years of age—fair and pale, blue eyes, aquiline nose, and thin lips again; and neither of the two faces to be trusted; not one look of truth, not one glance of benevolence, not one noble expression in either. Truly father and son—all the world over, father and son.

"Monsieur le Marquis affords me an unexpected honour and pleasure," said Raymond Marolles, as he advanced to receive his visitor.

"Nay, Monsieur de Marolles, scarcely, I should imagine, unexpected; I come in accordance with the earnest request of my niece; though what that most erratic young lady can want with me in this abominable country of your adoption is quite beyond my poor comprehension."

Raymond draws a long breath. "So," he thinks, "he knows nothing *yet.* Good! You are slow to play your cards, Valerie. I will take the initiative; my leading trump shall commence the game."

"I repeat," said the Marquis, throwing himself into the easy-chair which Raymond had wheeled forward, and warming his delicate white hands before the blazing fire; "I repeat, that the urgent request of my very lovely but extremely erratic niece, that I should cross the Channel in the autumn of a very stormy year—I am not a good sailor—is quite beyond my comprehension." He wears a very magnificent emerald ring, which is too large for the slender third finger of his left hand, and he amuses himself by twisting it round and round, sometimes stopping to contemplate the effect of it with the plain gold outside, when it looks like a lady's wedding-ring. "It is, I positively assure you," he repeated, looking at the ring, and not at Raymond, "utterly beyond the limited powers of my humble comprehension."

Raymond looks very grave, and takes two or three turns up and down the room. The light-blue eyes of the Marquis follow him for a turn and a half—find the occupation monotonous, and go back to the ring and the white hand, always interesting objects for contemplation. Presently the Count de Marolles stops, leans on the easychair on the opposite side of the fireplace to that on which the Marquis is seated, and says, in a very serious tone of voice—

"Monsieur de Cevennes, I am about to allude to a subject of so truly painful and distressing a nature, both for you to hear and for me to speak of, that I almost fear adverting to it."

The Marquis has been so deeply interested in the ring, emerald outwards, that he has evidently heard the words of Raymond without comprehending their meaning; but he looks up reflectively for a moment, recalls them, glances over them afresh as it were, nods, and says—

"Oh, ah! Distressing nature; you fear adverting to it—eh! Pray don't agitate yourself, my good De Marolles. I don't think it likely you'll agitate me." He leaves the ring for a minute or two, and looks over the five nails on his left hand, evidently in search of the pinkest; finds it on the third finger, and caresses it tenderly, while awaiting Raymond's very painful communication.

"You said, Monsieur le Marquis, that you were utterly at a loss to comprehend my wife's motive in sending for you in this abrupt manner?"

"Utterly. And I assure you I am a bad sailor—a very bad sailor. When the weather's rough, I am positively compelled to—it is really so absurd," he says, with a light clear laugh—"I am obliged to—to go to the side of the vessel. Both undignified and disagreeable, I give you my word of honour. But you were saying——"

"I was about to say, monsieur, that it is my deep grief to have to state that the conduct of your niece has been for the last few months in every way inexplicable—so much so, that I have been led to fear——"

"What, monsieur?" The Marquis folds his white hands one over the other on his knee, leaves off the inspection of their beauties, and looks full in the face of his niece's husband.

"I have been led, with what grief I need scarcely say——"

"Oh, no, indeed; pray reserve the account of your grief—your grief must have been so very intense. You have been led to fear——"

"That my unhappy wife is out of her mind."

"Precisely. I thought that was to be the climax. My good Monsieur Raymond, Count de Marolles—my very worthy Monsieur Raymond Marolles—my most excellent whoever and whatever you may be—do you think that René Théodore Auguste Philippe Le Grange Martel, Marquis de Cevennes, is the sort of man to be twisted round your fingers, however clever, unscrupulous, and designing a villain you may be?"

"Monsieur le Marquis!"

"I have not the least wish to quarrel with you, my good friend. Nay, on the contrary, I will freely confess that I am not without a certain amount of respect for you. You are a thorough villain. Everything thorough is, in my mind, estimable. Virtue is said to lie in the golden mean—virtue is not in my way; I therefore do not dispute the question—but to me all mediums are contemptible. You are, in your way, thorough; and, on the whole, I respect you."

He goes back to the contemplation of his hands and his rings, and concentrates all his attention on a cameo head of Mark Antony, which he wears on his little finger.

"A villain, Monsieur le Marquis!"

"And a clever villain, Monsieur de Marolles—a clever villain! Witness your success. But you are not quite clever enough to hoodwink me—not quite clever enough to hoodwink any one blest with a moderate amount of brains!"

"Monsieur!"

"Because you have one fault. Yes, really,"—he flicks a grain of dust out of Mark Antony's eye with his little finger—"yes, you have one fault. You are too smooth. Nobody ever *was* so estimable as you *appear* to be—you over-do it. If you remember," continues the Marquis, addressing him in an easy, critical, and conversational tone, "the great merit in that Venetian villain in the tragedy of the worthy but very much over-rated person, William Shakespeare, is, that he is *not* smooth. Othello trusts Iago, not because he *is* smooth, but because he *isn't.* 'I know this fellow's of exceeding honesty,' says the Moor; as much as to say, 'He's a disagreeable beast, but I think trustworthy.' You are a very clever fellow, Monsieur Raymond de Marolles, but you would never have got Desdemona smothered. Othello would have seen through you—as I did!"

"Monsieur, I will not suffer——"

"You will be good enough to allow me to finish what I have to say. I dare say I am prosy, but I shall not detain you long. I repeat, that though you are a very clever fellow, you would never have got the bolster-and-pillow business accomplished, because Othello would have seen through you as I did. My niece insisted on marrying you. Why? It was not such a very difficult riddle to read, this marriage, apparently so mysterious. You, an enterprising person, with small capital, plenty of brains, and white hands quite unfit for rough work, naturally are on the look-out for some heiress whom you may entrap into marrying you."

"Monsieur de Cevennes!"

"My dear fellow, I am not quarrelling with you. In your position I should have done the same. That is the very clue by which I un- ravel the mystery. I say to myself, what should I have done if fate had been so remarkably shabby as to throw me into the position of that young man? Why, naturally I should have looked out for some woman foolish enough to be deceived by that legitimate and old- established sham—so useful to novelists and the melodramatic theatres—called 'Love.' Now, my niece is not a fool; ergo, she was not in love with you. You had then obtained some species of power over her. What that power was I did not ask; I do not ask now. Enough that it was necessary for her, for me, that this marriage should take place. She swore it on the crucifix. I am a Voltairean myself, but, poor girl, she derived those sort of ideas from her mother; so there was nothing for me but to consent to the marriage, and accept a gentleman of doubtful pedigree."

"Perhaps not so doubtful."

"Perhaps not so doubtful! There is a triumphant curl about your upper lip, my dear nephew-in-law. Has papa turned up lately?"

"Perhaps. I think I shall soon be able to lay my hand upon him."

He lays a light and delicate hand on the Marquis's shoulder as he says the words.

"No doubt; but if in the meantime you would kindly refrain from laying it on me, you would oblige—you would really oblige me. Though why," said the Marquis philosophically, addressing himself to Mark Antony, as if he would like to avail himself of that Roman's sagacity, "why we should object to a villain simply because he is a villain, I can't imagine. We may object to him if he is coarse, or dirty, or puts his knife in his mouth, or takes soup twice, or wears ill-made coats, because those things annoy *us;* but, object to him because he is a liar, or a hypocrite, or a coward? Perfectly absurd! I say, therefore, I consented to the marriage, asked no unnecessary or ill-bred questions, and resigned myself to the force of circumstances; and for some years affairs appeared to go on very smoothly, when suddenly I am startled by a most alarming letter from my niece. She implores me to come to England. She is alone, without a friend, an adviser, and she is determined to reveal all."

"To reveal all!" Raymond cannot repress a start. The *sang froid* of the Marquis had entirely deceived him whose chief weapon was that very *sang froid.*

"Yes. What then? You, being aware of this letter having been written—or, say, guessing that such a letter would be written—determine on your course. You will throw over your wife's evidence by declaring her to be mad. Eh? This is what you determine upon, isn't it?" It appears so good a joke to the Marquis, that he laughs and nods at Mark Antony, as if he would really like that respectable Roman to participate in the fun.

For the first time in his life Raymond Marolles has found his match. In the hands of this man he is utterly powerless.

"An excellent idea. Only, as I said before, too obvious—too transparently obvious. It is the only thing you can do. If I were looking for a man, and came to a part of the country where there was but one road, I should of course know that he must—if he went anywhere—go down that road. So with you, my dear Marolles, there was but one resource left you—to disprove the revelations of your wife by declaring them the hallucinations of a maniac. I take no credit to myself for seeing through you, I assure you. There is no talent whatever in finding out that two and two make four; the genius would be the man who made them into five. I do not think I have anything more to say. I have no wish to attack you, my dear nephew-in-law. I merely wanted to prove to you that I was not your dupe. I think you must be by this time sufficiently convinced of that fact. If you have any good Madeira in your cellars, I should like a glass or two, and the wing of a chicken, before I hear what my niece may have to say to me. I made a very poor breakfast some hours ago at the Lord Warden." Having expressed himself thus, the Marquis throws himself back in his easy-chair, yawns once or twice, and polishes Mark Antony with the corner of his handkerchief; he has evidently entirely dismissed the subject on which he has been speaking, and is ready for pleasant conversation.

At this moment the door is thrown open, and Valerie enters the room.

It is the first time Raymond has seen Valerie since the night of Mosquetti's story, and as his eyes meet hers he starts involuntarily.

What is it?—this change, this transformation, which has taken eight years off the age of this woman, and restored her as she was on that night when he first saw her at the Opera House in Paris. What is it? So great and marvellous an alteration, he might almost doubt if this indeed were she. And yet he can scarcely define the change. It seems a transformation, not of the face, but of the soul. A new soul looking out of the old beauty. A new soul? No, the old soul, which he thought dead. It is indeed a resurrection of the dead.

She advances to her uncle, who embraces her with a graceful and drawing-room species of tenderness, about as like real tenderness as ormolu is like rough Australian gold—as Lawrence Sterne's sentiment is like Oliver Goldsmith's[3] pathos.

"My dear uncle! You received my letter, then?"

"Yes, dear child. And what, in Heaven's name, can you have to tell me that would not admit of being delayed until the weather changed?—and I am such a bad sailor," he repeats plaintively. "What can you have to tell me?"

"Nothing yet, my dear uncle"—the bright dark eyes look with a steady gaze at Raymond as she speaks—"nothing yet; the hour has not yet come."

"For mercy's sake, my dear girl," says the Marquis, in a tone of horror, "don't be melodramatic. If you're going to act a Porte-St.-Martin drama, in thirteen acts and twenty-six tableaux, I'll go back to Paris. If you've nothing to say to me, why, in the name of all that's feminine, did you send for me?"

"When I wrote to you, I told you that I appealed to you because I had no other friend upon earth to whom, in the hour of my anguish, I could turn for help and advice."

"You did, you did. If you had not been my only brother's only child, I should have waited a change in the wind before I crossed the Channel—I am such a wretched sailor! But life, as the religious party asserts, is a long sacrifice—I came!"

"Suppose that, since writing that letter, I have found a friend, an adviser, a guiding hand and a supporting arm, and no longer need the help of any one on earth besides this new-found friend to revenge me upon my enemies?"

Raymond's bewilderment increases every moment. Has she indeed gone mad, and is this new light in her eyes the fire of insanity?

"I am sure, my dear Valerie, if you have met with such a very delightful person, I am extremely glad to hear it, as it relieves me from the trouble. It is melodramatic certainly, but excessively convenient. I have remarked, that in melodrama circumstances generally are convenient. I never alarm myself when everything is hopelessly wrong, and villany deliciously triumphant; for I know that somebody who died in the first act will come in at the centre doors, and make it all right before the curtain falls."

"Since Madame de Marolles will no doubt wish to be alone with her uncle, I may perhaps be permitted to go into the City till dinner, when I shall have the honour of meeting Monsieur le Marquis, I trust."

"Certainly, my good De Marolles; your chef, I believe, understands his profession. I shall have great pleasure in dining with you.

Au revoir, mon enfant; we shall go upon velvet, now we so thoroughly understand each other." He waves his white left hand to Raymond, as a graceful dismissal, and turns towards his niece.

"Adieu, madame," says the Count, as he passes his wife; then, in a lower tone, adds, "I do not ask you to be silent for my sake or your own; I merely recommend you to remember that you have a son, and that you will do well not to make me your enemy. When I strike, I strike home, and my policy has always been to strike in the weakest place. Do not forget poor little Cherubino!" He looks at her steadily with his cruel blue eyes, and then turns to leave the room.

As he opens the door, he almost knocks down an elderly gentleman dressed in a suit of clerical-looking black and a white neckcloth, and carrying an unpleasantly damp umbrella under his arm.

"Not yet, Mr. Jabez North," says the gentleman, who is neither more nor less than that respectable preceptor and guide to the youthful mind, Dr. Tappenden, of Slopperton—"not yet, Mr. North; I think your clerks in Lombard Street will be compelled to do without you to-day. You are wanted elsewhere at present."

Anything but this—anything but this, and he would have borne it, like—like himself! Thank Heaven there is no comparison for such as he. He was prepared for all but this. This early period of his life, which he thought blotted out and forgotten—this he is unprepared for; and he falls back with a ghastly face, and white lips that refuse to shape even one exclamation of horror or surprise.

"What is this?" murmurs the Marquis. "North—Jabez—Jabez North? Oh, I see, we have come upon the pre-Parisian formation, and that," he glances towards Dr. Tappenden, "is one of the vestiges."

At last Raymond's tremulous lips consent to form the words he struggles to utter.

"You are under some mistake, sir, whoever you may be. My name is not North, and I have not the honour of your acquaintance. I am a Frenchman; my name is De Marolles. I am not the person you seek."

A gentleman advances from the doorway—(there is quite a group of people in the hall)—and says—

"At least, sir, you are the person who presented, eight years ago, three forged cheques at my bank. I am ready, as well as two of my clerks, to swear to your identity. We have people here with a warrant to arrest you for that forgery."

The forgery, not the murder?—no one knows of that, then—that, at least, is buried in oblivion.

"There are two or three little things out against you, Mr. North," said the doctor; "but the forgery will serve our purpose very well for the present. It's the easiest charge to bring home as yet."

What do they mean? What other charges? Come what may, he will be firm to the last—to the last he will be himself. After all, it is but death they can threaten him with: and the best people have to die, as well as the worst.

"Only death, at most!" he mutters. "Courage, Raymond, and finish the game as a good player should, without throwing away a trick, even though beaten by better cards."

"I tell you, gentlemen, I know nothing of your forgery, or you either. I am a Frenchman, born at Bordeaux, and never in your very eccentric country before; and indeed, if this is the sort of thing a gentleman is liable to in his own study, I shall certainly, when I once return to France, never visit your shores again."

"*When* you do return to France, I think it very unlikely you will ever revisit England, as you say, sir. If, as you affirm, you are indeed a Frenchman—(what excellent English you speak, monsieur, and what trouble you must have taken to acquire so perfect an accent!)—you will, of course, have no difficulty in proving the fact; also that you were not in England eight years ago, and consequently were not for some years assistant in the academy of this gentleman at Slopperton. All this an enlightened British jury will have much pleasure in hearing. We have not, however, come to try you, but to arrest you. Johnson, call a cab for the Count de Marolles! If we are wrong, monsieur, you will have a magnificent case of false imprisonment, and I congratulate you on the immense damages which you will most likely obtain. Thomson, the handcuffs! I must trouble you for your wrists, Monsieur de Marolles."

The police officer politely awaits the pleasure of his prisoner. Raymond pauses for a moment; thinks deeply, with his head bent on his breast; lifts it suddenly with a glitter in his eyes, and his thin lips set firm as iron. He has arranged his game.

"As you say, sir, I shall have an excellent case of false imprisonment, and my accusers shall pay for their insolence, as well as for their mistake. In the meantime, I am ready to follow you; but, before I do so, I wish to have a moment's conversation with this gentleman, the uncle of my wife. You have, I suppose, no objection to leaving me alone with him for a few minutes. You can watch outside in the hall; I shall not attempt to escape. We have, unfortunately, no trap-doors in this room, and I believe they do not build the houses in Park Lane with such conveniences attached to them as sliding panels or secret staircases."

"Perhaps not, sir," replies the inflexible police officer; "but they do, I perceive, build them with gardens"—he walks to the window, and looks out—"a wall eight feet high—door leading into mews. Not by any means such a very inconvenient house, Monsieur de Marolles. Thomson, one of the servants will be so good as to show you the way into the garden below these windows, where you will amuse yourself till this gentleman has done talking with his uncle."

"One moment—one moment," says the Marquis, who, during the foregoing conversation has been entirely absorbed in the endeavour to extract a very obstinate speck of dust from Mark Antony's nostril. "One moment, I beg"—as the officer is about to withdraw—"why an interview? Why a police person in the garden— if you call that dreadful stone dungeon with the roof off a garden? I have nothing to say to this gentleman. Positively nothing. All I ever had to say to him I said ten minutes ago. We perfectly understand each other. He can have nothing to say to me, or I to him; and really, I think, under the circumstances, the very best thing you can do is to put on that unbecoming iron machinery—I never saw a thing of the kind before, and, as a novelty, it is actually quite interesting"—(he touches the handcuffs that are lying on the table with the extreme tip of his taper third finger, hastily withdrawing it, as if he thought they would bite)—"and to take him away immediately. If he has committed a forgery, you know," he adds, deprecatingly, "he is not the sort of thing one likes to see about one. He really is not."

Raymond de Marolles never had, perhaps, too much of that absurd weakness called love for one's fellow-creatures; but if ever he hated any man with the blackest and bitterest hate of his black and bitter heart, so did he hate the man standing now before him, twisting a ring round and round his delicate finger, and looking as entirely at his ease as if no point were in discussion of more importance than the wet weather and the cold autumn day.

"Stay, Monsieur le Marquis de Cevennes," he said, in a tone of suppressed passion, "you are too hasty in your conclusions. You have nothing to say to me. Granted! But I may have something to say to you—and I have a great deal to say to you, which must be said; if not in private, then in public—if not by word of mouth, I will print it in the public journals, till Paris and London shall ring with the sound of it on the lips of other men. You will scarcely care for this alternative, Monsieur de Cevennes, when you learn *what* it is I have to say. Your *sang froid* does you credit, monsieur; especially when, just now, though you could not repress a start of surprise at hearing that gentleman," he indicates Dr. Tappenden with a wave of his hand, "speak of a certain manufacturing town called Slopperton, you so rapidly regained your composure that only so close an observer as myself would have perceived your momentary agitation. You appear entirely to ignore, monsieur, the existence of a certain aristocratic emigrant's son, who thirty years ago taught French and mathematics in that very town of Slopperton. Nevertheless, there was such a person, and you knew him—although he was content to teach his native language for a shilling a lesson, and had at that period no cameo or emerald rings to twist round his fingers."

If the Marquis was ever to be admired in the whole course of his career, he was to be admired at this moment. He smiled a gentle and deprecating smile, and said, in his politest tone—

"Pardon me, he had eighteenpence a lesson—eighteenpence,

I assure you; and he was often invited to dinner at the houses where he taught. The women adored him—they are so simple, poor things. He might have married a manufacturer's daughter, with an immense fortune, thick ancles, and erratic h's."

"But he did not marry any one so distinguished. Monsieur de Cevennes, I see you understand me. I do not ask you to grant me this interview in the name of justice or humanity, because I do not wish to address you in a language which is a foreign one to me, and which you do not even comprehend; but in the name of that young Frenchman of noble family, who was so very weak and foolish, so entirely false to himself and to his own principles, as to marry a woman because he loved, or fancied that he loved her, I say to you, Monsieur le Marquis, you will find it to your interest to hear what I have to reveal."

The Marquis shrugs his shoulders slightly. "As you please," he says. "Gentlemen, be good enough to remain outside that door. My dear Valerie, you had better retire to your own apartments. My poor child, all this must be so extremely wearisome to you—almost as bad as the third volume of a fashionable novel. Monsieur de Marolles, I am prepared to hear what you may have to say— though"—he here addresses himself generally—"I beg to protest against this affair from first to last—I repeat, from first to last—it is so intolerably melodramatic."

CHAPTER II

RAYMOND DE MAROLLES SHOWS HIMSELF BETTER THAN ALL BOW STREET

"And so, Monsieur de Marolles," said the Marquis, as Raymond closed the door on the group in the hall, and the two gentlemen were left entirely alone, "and so you have—by what means I shall certainly not so far inconvenience myself as to endeavour to guess—contrived to become informed of some of the antecedents of your very humble servant?"

"Of some of the antecedents—why not say of all the antecedents, Monsieur de Cevennes?"

"Just as you like, my dear young friend," replies the Marquis. He really seems to get quite affectionate to Raymond, but in a far-off, patronizing, and superb manner—something that of a gentlemanly Mephistopheles to a promising Doctor Faustus;[1]—"and having possessed yourself of this information, may I ask what use you intend making of it? In this utilitarian age everything is put to a use, sooner or later. Do you purpose writing my biography? It will not be interesting. Not as you would have to write it to-day. Alas! we are not so fortunate as to live under the Regency, and there are not many interesting biographies nowadays."

"My dear Marquis, I really have no time to listen to what I have no doubt, amongst your own particular friends, is considered most brilliant wit; I have two or three things to say to you that must be said; and the sort of people who are now waiting outside the door are apt to be impatient."

"Ah, you are experienced; you know their manners and customs! And they are impatient," murmured the Marquis, thoughtfully; "and they put you in stone places as if you were coal, and behind bars as if you were zoological; and then they hang you. They call you up at an absurd hour in the morning, and they take you out into a high place, and drop you down through a hole as if you were a penny put into a savings box; and other people get up at an equally absurd hour of the morning, or stay up all night, in order to see it done. And yet there are persons who declare that the age of romance has passed away."

"Monsieur de Cevennes, that which I have to say to you relates to your marriage."

"My marriage. Suppose I say that I never was married, my amiable friend?"

"I shall then reply, monsieur, that I not only am informed of all the circumstances of your marriage, but what is more, I am possessed of a proof of that marriage."

"Supposing there was such a marriage, which I am prepared to deny, there could only be two proofs—the witnesses and the certificate."

"The witnesses, monsieur, are dead," said Raymond.

"Then that would reduce the possible proofs to one—the certificate."

"Nay, monsieur, there might be another evidence of the marriage."

"And that would be——?"

"The issue of it. You had two sons by that marriage, monsieur. One of those sons died eight years ago."

"And the other——?" asked the Marquis.

"Still lives. I shall have something to say about him by-and-by."

"It is a subject in which I take no sort of interest," said the Marquis, throwing himself back into his chair, and abandoning himself once more to Mark Antony. "I may have been married, or I may not have been married—it is not worth my while to deny that fact to you; because if I confess it to you, I can of course deny it the moment I cross the threshold of that door—I may have sons, or I may not have sons; in either case, I have no wish to hear of them, and anything you may have to say about them is, it appears to me, quite irrelevant to the matter in hand; which merely is your going to prison for forgery, or your *not* going to prison for forgery. But what I most earnestly recommend, my very dear young friend, is, that you take the cab and handcuffs quietly, and go! That will, at least, put an end to fuss and discussion; and oh, what an inexpressible relief there is in that! I always envy Noah, floundering about in that big boat of his: no new books; no houses of parliament; no poor relations; no *Times* newspaper; and no taxes—'universal as you were,' as Mr. Carlyle[2] says; plenty to eat, and everything come to an end; and that foolish Noah must needs send out the dove, and begin it all over again. Yes, he began it all over again, that preposterous Noah. Whereby, cab, handcuffs, forgery, long conversation, and police persons outside that door; all of which might have been prevented if Noah had kept the dove indoors, and had been unselfish enough to bore a hole in the bottom of his boat."

"If you will listen to me, Monsieur le Marquis, and keep your philosophical reflections for a more convenient season, there will be some chance of our coming to an understanding. One of these twin sons still lives."

"Now, really, that is the old ground again. We are not getting on——"

"Still lives, I say. Whatever he is, Monsieur de Cevennes—whatever his chequered life may have been, the guilt and the misery of that life rest alike on your head."

The Marquis gives the head alluded to an almost imperceptible jerk, as if he threw this moral burden off, and looks relieved by the proceeding. "Don't be melodramatic," he remarks, mildly; "this is not the Porte-St.-Martin, and there are no citizens in the gallery to applaud."

"That guilt and that misery, I say, rest upon your head. When you married the woman whom you abandoned to starvation and despair, you loved her, I suppose?"

"I dare say I did; I have no doubt I told her so, poor little thing!"

"And a few months after your marriage you wearied of her, as you would have done of any other plaything."

"As I should have done of any other plaything. Poor dear child, she was dreadfully wearisome. Her relations too. Heaven and earth, what relations! They were looked upon in the light of human beings at Slopperton: but they were wise to keep out of Paris, for they'd have been most decidedly put into the Jardin des Plantes;[3] and, really," said the Marquis, thoughtfully, "behind bars, and aggravated by fallacious offers of buns from small children, they would have been rather amusing."

"You were quite content that this unhappy girl should share your poverty, Monsieur le Marquis; but in the hour of your good fortune——"

"I left her. Decidedly. Look you, Monsieur de Marolles, when I married that young person, whom you insist on dragging out of her grave—poor girl, she is dead, no doubt, by this time—in this remarkably melodramatic manner, I was a young man, without a penny in the world, and with very slight expectations of ever becoming possessed of one. I am figurative, of course. I believe men of my temperament and complexion are not very subject to that popular epidemic, called love. But as much as it was in my power to love any one, I loved this little factory girl. I used to meet her going backwards and forwards to her work, as I went backwards and forwards to mine; and we became acquainted. She was gentle, innocent, pretty. I was very young, and, I need scarcely say, extremely stupid; and I married her. We had not been married six months before that dreadful Corsican person[4] took it into his head to abdicate, and I was summoned back to France, to make my appearance at the Tuileries as Marquis de Cevennes. Now, what I have to say is this: if you wish to quarrel with any one, quarrel with the Corsican person; for if he had never signed his abdication at Fontainebleau (which he did, by the bye, in a most melodramatic manner—I am acquainted with some weak-minded people who cannot read the description of that event without shedding tears), I should never have deserted my poor little English wife."

"The Marquis de Cevennes could not, then, ratify the marriage of the obscure teacher of French and mathematics?" asked Raymond.

"If the Marquis de Cevennes had been a rich man, he might have done so; but the Restoration, which gave me back my title, and the only château (my ancestors had three) which the Jacobins had not burned to the ground, did not restore me the fortune which the Revolution had devoured. I was a poor man. Only one course was open to me—a rich marriage. The wealthy widow of a Buonapartist general beheld and admired your humble servant, and the doom of my poor little wife was sealed. For many years I sent money regularly to her old mother—an awful woman, who knew my secret. She had, therefore, no occasion to starve, Monsieur de Marolles. And now, may I be permitted to ask what interest you have in this affair, that you should insist on recalling these very disagreeable circumstances at this particular moment?"

"There is one question you do not ask, Monsieur le Marquis."

"Indeed; and what is that?" asked the Marquis.

"You seem to have very little curiosity about the fate of your surviving son."

"I seem to have very little curiosity, my young friend; I have very little curiosity. I dare say he is a very worthy individual; but I have no anxiety whatever about his fate; for if he at all resembles his father, there is very little doubt that he has taken every care of himself. The De Cevennes have always taken care of themselves; it is a family trait."

"He has proved himself worthy of that family, then. He was thrown into a river, but he did not sink; he was put into a workhouse and brought up as a pauper, but by the force of his own will and the help of his own brain he extricated himself, and won his way in the world. He became, what his father was before him, a teacher in a school. He grew tired of that, as his father did, and left England for Paris. In Paris, like his father before him, he married a woman he did not love for the sake of her fortune. He became master of that fortune, and till this very day he has surmounted every obstacle and triumphed over every difficulty. Your only son, Monsieur de Cevennes—the son whose mother you deserted—the son whom you abandoned to starve, steal, drown, or hang, to beg in the streets, die in a gutter, a workhouse, or a prison—has lived through all, to stand face to face with you this day, and to tell you that for his own and for his mother's wrongs, with all the strength of a soul which those wrongs have steeped in wickedness—*he hates you!*"

"Don't be violent," said the Marquis, gently. "So, you are my son? Upon my word I thought all along you were something of that kind, for you are such a consummate villain."

For the first time in his life Raymond de Marolles feels what it is to be beaten by his own weapons. Against the *sang froid* of the Marquis the torrent of his passionate words dashes, as the sea dashes at the foot of a rock, and makes as little impression.

"And what then?" says the Marquis. "Since it appears you are my son, what then?"

"You must save me, monsieur," said Raymond, in a hoarse voice.

"Save you? But, my worthy friend, how save you? Save you from the cab and handcuffs? If I go out to those people and say, 'He is my son; be so good as to forego the cab and handcuffs,' they will laugh at me. They are so dreadfully matter-of-fact, that sort of people. What is to be done?"

"Only this, monsieur. I must make my escape from this apartment. That window looks into the garden, from the garden to the mews, through the mews into a retired street, and thence——"

"Never mind that, if you get there. I really doubt the possibility of your getting there. There is a policeman watching in that garden."

Raymond smiles. He is recovering his presence of mind in the necessity for action. He opens a drawer in the library table and takes out an air-pistol, which looks rather like some elegant toy than a deadly weapon.

"I must shoot that man," he says.

"Then I give the alarm. I will not be implicated in a murder. Good Heavens! the Marquis de Cevennes implicated in a murder! Why, it would be talked of in Paris for a month."

"There will be no murder, monsieur. I shall fire at that man from this window and hit him in the knee. He will fall, and most likely faint from the pain, and will not, therefore, know whether I pass through the garden or not. You will give the alarm, and tell the men without that I have escaped through this window and the door in the wall yonder. They will pursue me in that direction, while I——"

"You will do what?"

"Go out at the front door as a gentleman should. I was not unprepared for such an event as this. Every room in this house has a secret communication with the next room. There is only one door in this library, as it seems, and they are carefully watching that."

As he speaks he softly opens the window and fires at the man in the garden, who falls, only uttering a groan. As Raymond predicted, he faints with the pain.

With the rapidity of lightning he flings the window up violently, hurls the pistol to the farthest extremity of the garden, snatches the Marquis's hat from the chair on which it lies, presses one finger on the gilded back of a volume of Gibbon's *Rome,* a narrow slip of the bookcase opens inwards, and reveals a door leading into the next apartment, which is the dining-room. This door is made on a peculiar principle, and, as he pushes through, it closes behind him.

This is the work of a second; and as the officers, alarmed by the sound of the opening of the window, rush into the room, the Marquis gives the alarm. "He has escaped by the window!" he said. "He has wounded your assistant, and passed through that door. He cannot be twenty yards in advance; you will easily know him by his having no hat on."

"Stop!" cries the detective officer, "this may be a trap. He may have got round to the front door. Go and watch, Johnson."

A little too late this precaution. As the officers rushed into the library, Raymond passed from the dining-room door out of the open street-door, and jumped into the very cab which was waiting to take him to prison. "Five pounds, if you catch the Liverpool Express," he said to the cabman.

"All right, sir," replied that worthy citizen, with a wink. "I've druv a many gents like you, and very good fares they is too, and a godsend to a hard-working man, what old ladies with hand-bags and umbrellas grudges eightpence a mile to," mutters the charioteer, as he gallops down Upper Brook Street and across Hanover Square, while the gentlemen of the police force, aided by Dr. Tappenden and the obliging Marquis, search the mews and neighbourhood adjoining. Strange to say, they cannot obtain any information from the coachman and stable-boys concerning a gentleman without a hat, who must have passed through the mews about three minutes before.

CHAPTER III

THE LEFT-HANDED SMASHER MAKES HIS MARK

"It is a palpable and humiliating proof of the decadence of the glories of white-cliffed Albion[1] and her lion-hearted children," said the sporting correspondent of the *Liverpool Bold Speaker and Threepenny Aristides*—a gentleman who, by the bye, was very clever at naming—for half-a-dozen stamps—the horses that *didn't* win; and was, indeed, useful to fancy betters, as affording accurate information what to avoid; nothing being better policy than to give the odds against any horse named by him as a sure winner, or a safe second: for those gallant steeds were sure to be, whatever the fluctuating fortune of the race, ignominiously nowhere. "It is," continued the *Liverpool B. S.*, "a sign of the downfalling of the lion and unicorn— over which Britannia may shed tears and the inhabitants of Liverpool and its vicinity mourn in silent despair—that the freedom of England is no more! We repeat (the *Liverpool Aristides* here gets excited, and goes into small capitals)—BRITAIN is no longer FREE! Her freedom departed from her on that day on which the blue-coated British Sbirri of Sir Robert Peel[2] broke simultaneously into the liberties of the nation, the mightiest clauses of Magna Charta, and the Prize Ring, and stopped the operations of the Lancashire Daddy Longlegs and the celebrated Metropolitan favourite, the Left-handed Smasher, during the eighty-ninth round, and just as the real interest of the fight was about to begin. Under these humiliating circumstances, a meeting has been held by the referees and backers of the men, and it has been agreed between the latter and the stakeholder to draw the money. But, that the valiant and admired Smasher may have no occasion to complain of the inhospitality of the town of Liverpool, the patrons of the fancy have determined on giving him a dinner, at which his late opponent, our old favourite and honoured townsman, Daddy Longlegs, will be in the chair, having a distinguished gentleman of sporting celebrity as his vice. It is to be hoped that, as some proof that the noble art of self-defence is not entirely extinct in Liverpool, the friends of the Ring will muster pretty strong on this occasion. Tickets, at half-a-guinea, to be obtained at the Gloves Tavern, where the entertainment will take place."

On the very day on which the Count de Marolles left his establishment in Park Lane in so very abrupt a manner, the tributary banquet to the genius of the Ring, in the person of the Left-handed Smasher, came off in excellent style at the above-mentioned Gloves Tavern—a small hostelry, next door to one of the Liverpool minor theatres, and chiefly supported by the members of the Thespian and pugilistic arts. The dramatic element, perhaps, rather predominated in the small parlour behind the bar, where Brandolph of the

Burning Brand—after fighting sixteen terrific broadsword combats, and being left for dead behind the first grooves seven times in the course of three acts—would take his Welsh rarebit and his pint of half-and-half in company with the Lancashire Grinder and the Pottery Pet, and listen with due solemnity to the discourse of these two popular characters. The little parlour was so thickly hung with portraits of theatrical and sporting celebrities, that Œdipus himself—distinguished as he is for having guessed the dullest of conundrums—could never have discovered the pattern of the paper which adorned the walls. Here, Mr. Montmorency, the celebrated comedian, smirked—with that mild smirk only known in portraits—over the ample shoulders of his very much better half, at the Pet in fighting attitude. There, Mr. Marmaduke Montressor, the great tragedian, frowned, in the character of Richard the Third, at Pyrrhus the First, winner of the last Derby. Here, again, Mademoiselle Pasdebasque pointed her satin slipper side by side with the youthful Challoner of that day; and opposite Mademoiselle Pasdebasque, a gentleman in scarlet, whose name is unknown, tumbled off a burnt-sienna horse, in excellent condition, and a very high state of varnish, into a Prussian-blue ditch, thereby filling the spectator with apprehension lest he should be, not drowned, but dyed. As to Brandolph of the Brand, there were so many pictures of him, in so many different attitudes, and he was always looking so very handsome and doing something so very magnanimous, that perhaps, upon the whole, it was rather a disappointment to look from the pictures down to the original of them in the dingy costume of private life, seated at the shiny little mahogany table, partaking of refreshment.

The theatrical profession mustered pretty strongly to do honour to the sister art on this particular occasion. The theatre next door to the Gloves happened, fortunately, to be closed, on account of the extensive scale of preparations for a grand dramatic and spectacular performance, entitled, "The Sikh Victories; or, The Tyrant of the Ganges," which was to be brought out the ensuing Monday, with even more than usual magnificence. So the votaries of Thespis[3] were free to testify their admiration for the noble science of self-defence, by taking tickets for the dinner at ten-and-sixpence a-piece, the banquet being, as Mr. Montressor, the comedian above-mentioned, remarked, with more energy than elegance, a cheap blow-out, as the dinner would last the guests who partook of it two days, and the indigestion attendant thereon would carry them through the rest of the week.

I shall not enter into the details of the pugilistic dinner, but will introduce the reader into the banquet-hall at rather a late stage in the proceedings; in point of fact, just as the festival is about to break up. It is two o'clock in the morning; the table is strewn with the *débris* of a dessert, in which figs, almonds and raisins, mixed biscuits, grape-stalks, and apple and orange-peel seem rather to predominate. The table is a very field of Cressy or Waterloo, as to dead men in the way of empty bottles; good execution having evidently been done upon Mr. Hemmar's well-stocked cellar. From the tumblers and spoons before each guest, however, it is also evident that the festive throng has followed the example of Mr. Sala's renowned hero, and after having tried a "variety of foreign drains," has gone back to gin-and-water *pur et simple*. It is rather a peculiar and para-doxical quality of neat wines that they have, if anything, rather an untidy effect on those who drink them: certainly there is a loose-ness about the hair, a thickness and indecision in the speech, and an erratic and irrelevant energy and emphasis in the gestures of the friends of the Smasher, which is entirely at variance with our ordi-nary idea of the word "neat." Yet, why should we quarrel with them on that account? They are harmless, and they are happy. It is surely no crime to see two gas-burners where, to the normal eye, there is only one; neither is it criminal to try five distinct times to enunci-ate the two words, "slightest misunderstanding," and to fail igno-miniously every time. If anything, that must be an amiable feeling which inspires a person with a sudden wild and almost pathetic friendship for a man he never saw before; such a friendship, in short, as pants to go to the block for him, or to become his surety to a loan-office for five pounds. Is it any such terrible offence against society to begin a speech of a patriotic nature, full of allusions to John Bull, Queen Victoria, Wooden Walls, and the Prize Ring, and to burst into tears in the middle thereof? Is there no benevolence in the wish to see your friend home, on account of your strong impression that he has taken a little too much, and that he will tumble against the railings and impale his chin upon the spikes; which, of course, *you* are in no danger of doing? Are these things crimes? No! We answer boldly, No! Then, hurrah for neat wines and free trade![+] Open wide our harbours to the purple grapes that flourish in the vineyards of sunny Burgundy and Bordeaux; and welcome, thrice welcome, to the blushing tides which Horace sang so many hundred years ago, when our beautiful Earth was younger, and maybe fairer, and held its course, though it is hard to believe it, very well indeed, without the genius of modern civilization at the helm.

There had been a silver cup, with one of the labours of Hercules— poor Hercules, how hard they work him in the sporting world!— embossed thereon, presented to the Smasher, as a tribute of respect for those British qualities which had endeared him to his admirers; and the Smasher's health had been drunk with three-times-three, and a little one in; and then three more three-times-three, and another little one in; and the Smasher had returned thanks, and Brandolph of the Brand had proposed the Daddy Longlegs, and the Daddy Longlegs had made a very neat speech in the Lancashire dialect, which the gentlemen of the theatrical profession had pretended to understand, but had not understood; and a literary individual—being, in fact, the gentleman whose spirited writing we have quoted above, Mr. Jeffrey Hallam Jones, of the *Liverpool Aristides,* sporting and theatrical correspondent, and constant visitor at the Gloves—had proposed the Ring; and the Smasher had proposed the Press, for the liberties of which, as he said in noble language afterwards quoted in the *Aristides,* the gentlemen of the Prize Ring were prepared to fight as long as they had a bunch of fives to rattle upon the knowledge-box of the foe; and then the Daddy Longlegs had proposed the Stage, and its greatest glory, Brandolph of the Brand; and ultimately everybody had proposed everybody else—and then, some one suggesting a quiet song, everybody sang.

Now, as the demand for a song from each member of the festive band was of so noisy and imperative a nature that a refusal was not only a moral, but a physical impossibility, it would be unbecoming to remark that the melody and harmony of the evening were, at best, fluctuating. Annie Laurie was evidently a young lady of an undecided mind, and wandered in a pleasing manner from C into D, and from D into E, and then back again with laudable dexterity to C, for the finish. The gentleman whose heart was bowed down in the key of G might have rendered his performance more effective, had he given his statement of that affliction entirely in one key; and another gentleman, who sang a comic song of seventeen eight-line verses, with four lines of chorus to every verse, would have done better if he had confined himself to his original plan of singing super-humanly flat, instead of varying it, as he occasionally did, by singing preternaturally sharp. Of course it is an understood thing, that in a chorus, every singer should choose his own key, or where is the liberty of the subject?—so *that* need not be alluded to. But all this is over; and the guests of Mr. Hemmar have risen to depart, and have found the act of rising to depart by no means the trifle they thought it. It is very hard, of course, in such an atmosphere of tobacco, to find the door; and that, no doubt, is the reason why so many gentlemen seek for it in the wrong direction, and buffet insanely with their arms against the wall, in search of that orifice.

Now, there are two gentlemen in whom Mr. Hemmar's neat wines have developed a friendship of the warmest description. Those two gentlemen are none other than the two master-spirits of the evening, the Left-handed Smasher and Brandolph of the Brand—who, by the bye, in private life, is known as Augustus de Clifford. His name is not written thus in the register of his baptism. On that malicious document he is described as William Watson; but to his friends and the public he has for fifteen years been admired and beloved as the great De Clifford, although often familiarly called Brandolph, in delicate allusion to his greatest character.

Now, Brandolph is positively convinced that the Smasher is not in a fit state to go home alone, and the Smasher is equally assured that Brandolph will do himself a mischief unless he is watched; so Brandolph is going to see the Smasher home to his hotel, which is a considerable distance from the Gloves Tavern; and then the Smasher is coming back again to see Brandolph to his lodgings, which are next door but two to the Gloves Tavern. So, after having bade good night to every one else, in some instances with tears, and always with an affectionate pathos verging upon tears, Brandolph flings on his loose overcoat, just as Manfred might have flung on his cloak prior to making a morning call upon the witch of the Alps, and the Smasher twists about five yards of particoloured woollen raiment, which he calls a comforter, round his neck, and they sally forth.

A glorious autumn night; the full moon high in the heavens, with a tiny star following in her wake like a well-bred tuft-hunter,[5] and all the other stars keeping their distance, as if they had retired to their own "grounds," as the French say, and were at variance with their queen on some matter connected with taxes. A glorious night; as light as day—nay, almost lighter; for it is a light which will bear looking at, and which does not dazzle our eyes as the sun does, when we are presumptuous enough to elevate our absurdly infinitesimal optics to his sublimity. Not a speck on the Liverpool pavement, not a dog asleep on the doorstep, or a dissipated cat sneaking home down an area, but is as visible as in the broad glare of noon. "Such a night as this" was almost too much for Lara, and Brandolph of the Brand grows sentimental.

"You wouldn't think," he murmurs, abstractedly, gazing at the moon, as he and the Smasher meander arm-in-arm over the pavement; "you wouldn't think she hadn't an atmosphere, would you? A man might build a theatre there, and he might get his company up in balloons; but I question if it would pay, on account of that trivial want—she hasn't got an atmosphere."

"Hasn't she?" said the Smasher, who certainly, if anything, had, in the matter of sobriety, the advantage of the tragedian. "You'll have a black eye though, if you don't steer clear of that 'ere lamppost you're makin' for. I never did see such a cove," he added; "with his *h*atmospheres, and his moons, and his b'loons, one would think he'd never had a glass or two of wine before."

Now, to reach the hotel which the left-handed one honoured by his presence, it was necessary to pass the quay; and the sight of the water and the shipping reposing in the stillness under the light of the moon, again awakened all the poetry in the nature of the romantic Brandolph.

"It is beautiful!" he said, taking his pet position, and waving his arm in the orthodox circle, prior to pointing to the scene before him. "It is peaceful: it is we who are the blots upon the beauty of the earth. Oh, why—why are we false to the beautiful and heroic, as the author of the Lady of Lyons[6] would observe? Why are we false to the true? Why do we drink too much and see double? Standing amidst the supreme silences, with breathless creation listening to our words, we look up to the stars that looked down upon the philosopher of the cave; and we feel that we have retrograded." Here the eminent tragedian gave a lurch, and seated himself with some violence and precipitation on the kerbstone. "We feel," he repeated, "that we have retrograded. It is a pity!"

"Now, who's to pick him up?" inquired the Smasher, looking round in silent appeal to the lamp-posts about him. "Who's to pick him up? I can't; and if he sleeps here he'll very likely get cold. Get up, you snivelling fool, can't you?" he said, with some asperity, to the descendant of Thespis, who, after weeping piteously, was drying his eyes with an announce bill of the "Tyrant of the Ganges," and by no means improving his personal appearance with the red and black printer's ink thereof.

How mine host of the Cheerful Cherokee would ever have extricated his companion from this degraded position, without the timely intervention of others, is not to be said; for at this very moment the Smasher beheld a gentleman alight from a cab at a little distance from where he stood, ask two or three questions of the cabman, pay and dismiss him, and then walk on in the direction of some steps that led to the water. This gentleman wore his hat very much slouched over his face; he was wrapped in a heavy loose coat, that entirely concealed his figure, and evidently carried a parcel of some kind under his left arm.

"Hi!" said the Smasher, as the pedestrian approached; "Hi, you there! Give us a hand, will you?"

The gentleman addressed as "you there" took not the slightest notice of this appeal, except, indeed, that he quickened his pace considerably, and tried to pass the left-handed one.

"No, you don't," said our pugilistic friend; "the cove as refuses to pick up the man that's down is a blot upon the English character, and the sooner he's scratched out the better;" wherewith the Smasher squared his fists and placed himself directly in the path of the gentleman with the slouched hat.

"I tell you what it is, my good fellow," said this individual, "you may pick up your drunken friend yourself, or you may wait the advent of the next policeman, who will do the public a service by conveying you both to the station-house, where you may finish the evening in your own highly-intellectual manner. But perhaps you will be good enough to let me pass, for I'm in a hurry! You see that American vessel yonder—she's dropped down the river to wait for the wind: the breeze is springing up as fast as it can, and she may set sail as it is before I can reach her; so, if you want to earn a sovereign, come and see if you can help me in arousing a waterman and getting off to her?"

"Oh, you are off to America, are you?" said the Smasher, thoughtfully. "Blow that 'ere wine of Hemmar's! I ought to know the cut of your figure-head. I've seen you before—I've seen you somewheres before, though where that somewheres was, spiflicate me if I can call to mind! Come, lend a hand with this 'ere friend o' mine, and I'll lend you a hand with the boatman."

"D—n your friend," said the other, savagely; "let me pass, will you, you drunken fool?"

This was quite enough for the Smasher, who was just in that agreeable frame of mind attendant on the consumption of strong waters, in which the jaundiced eye is apt to behold an enemy even in a friend, and the equally prejudiced ear is ready to hear an insult in the most civil address.

"Come on, then," said he; and putting himself in a scientific attitude, he dodged from side to side two or three times, as if setting to his partner in a quadrille, and then, with a movement rapid as lightning, went in with his left fist, and planted a species of postman's knock exactly between the eyes of the stranger, who fell to the ground as an ox falls under the hand of an accomplished butcher. .

It is needless to say that, in falling, his hat fell off, and as he lay senseless on the pavement, the moonlight on his face revealed every feature as distinctly as in the broadest day.

The Smasher knelt down by his side, looked at him attentively for a few moments, and then gave a long, low whistle.

"Under the circumstances," he said, "perhaps I couldn't have done a better thing than this 'ere I've done promiscuous. He won't go to America by that vessel at any rate; so if I telegraph to the Cherokees, maybe they will be glad to hear what he's up to down here. Come along," continued the sobered Smasher, hauling up Mr. de Clifford by the collar, as ruthlessly as if he had been a sack of coal; "I think I hear the footsteps of a Bobby[7] a-coming this way, so we'd better make ourselves scarce before we're asked any questions."

"If," said the distinguished Brandolph, still shedding tears, "if the town of Liverpool was conducted after the manner of the Republic of Plato,[8] there wouldn't be any policemen. But, as I said before, we have retrograded. Take care of the posts," he added plaintively. "It is marvellous the effect a few glasses of light wine have upon some people's legs; while others, on the contrary——" here he slid again to the ground, and this time eluded all the Smasher's endeavours to pick him up.

"You had better let me be," he murmured. "It is hard, but it is clean and comfortable. Bring me my boots and hot water at nine o'clock; I've an early rehearsal of 'The Tyrant.' Go home quietly, my dear friend, and don't take anything more to drink, for your head is evidently not a strong one. Good night."

"Here's a situation!" said the Smasher. "I can't dance attendance on him any more, for I must run round to the telegraph office and see if it's open, that I may send Mr. Marwood word about this night's work. The Count de Marolles is safe enough for a day or two, anyhow; for I have set a mark upon him that he won't rub off just yet, clever as he is."

CHAPTER IV

What They Find in the Room in Which the Murder Was Committed

At the time that the arrest of the Count de Marolles was taking place, Mr. Joseph Peters was absent from London, being employed upon some mission of a delicate and secret nature in the town of Slopperton-on-the-Sloshy.

Slopperton is very little changed since the murder at the Black Mill set every tongue going upon its nine-days wonder. There may be a few more tall factory chimneys; a few more young factory ladies in cotton jackets and coral necklaces all the week, and in rustling silks and artificial flowers on Sunday; the new town—that dingy hanger-on of the old town—may have spread a little farther out towards the bright and breezy country; and the railway passenger may perhaps see a larger veil of black smoke hanging in the atmosphere as he approaches the Slopperton station than he saw eight years ago.

Mr. Peters, being no longer a householder in the town, takes up his abode at a hostelry, and, strange to say, selects the little riverside public-house in which he overheard that conversation between the usher and the country girl, the particulars of which are already known to the reader.

He is peculiar in his choice of an hotel, for "The Bargeman's Delight" certainly does not offer many attractions to any one not a bargeman. It is hard indeed to guess what the particular delight of the bargeman may be, which the members of that guild find provided for them in the waterside tavern alluded to. The bargeman's delight is evidently not cleanliness, or he would go elsewhere in search of that virtue; neither can the bargeman affect civility in his entertainers, for the host and that one slip-shod young person who is barmaid, barman, ostler, cook, chambermaid, and waiter all in one, are notoriously sulky in their conversation with their patrons, and have an aggrieved and injured bearing very unpleasant to the sensitive customer. But if, on the other hand, the bargeman's delight should happen to consist in dirt, and damp, and bad cooking, and worse attendance, and liquors on which the small glass brandy-balls peculiar to the publican float triumphantly, and pertinaciously refuse to go down to the bottom—if such things as these be the bargeman's delight, he has them handsomely provided for him at this establishment.

However this may be, to "The Bargeman's Delight" came Mr. Peters on the very day of the Count's arrest, with a carpet-bag in one hand and a fishing-rod in the other, and with no less a person than Mr. Augustus Darley for his companion. The customer, by the bye, was generally initiated into the pleasures of this hostelry by being tripped up or tripped down on the threshold, and saluting a species of thin soup of sawdust and porter, which formed the upper stratum of the floor, with his olfactory organ. The neophyte of the Rosicrucian[1] mysteries and of Freemasonry[2] has, I believe, something unpleasant done to him before he can be safely trusted with the secrets of the Temple; why, then, should not the guest of the Delight have *his* initiation? Mr. Darley, with some dexterity, however, escaped this danger; and, entering the bar safely, entreated with the slip-shod and defiant damsel aforesaid.

"Could we have a bed?" Mr. Darley asked; "in point of fact, two beds?"

The damsel glared at him for a few minutes without giving any answer at all. Gus repeated the question.

"We've got two beds," muttered the defiant damsel.

"All right, then," said Gus. "Come in, old fellow," he added to Mr. Peters, whose legs and bluchers were visible at the top of the steps, where he patiently awaited the result of his companion's entreaty with the priestess of the temple.

"But I don't know whether you can have 'em," said the girl, with a more injured air than usual. "We ain't in general asked for beds."

"Then why do you put up that?" asked Mr. Darley, pointing to a board on which, in letters that had once been gilt, was inscribed this legend, "Good Beds."

"Oh, as for that," said the girl, "that was wrote up before we took the place, and we had to pay for it in the fixtures, so of course we wasn't a-goin' to take it down! But I'll ask master." Whereon she disappeared into the damp and darkness, as if she had been the genius of that mixture; and presently reappeared, saying they could have beds, but that they couldn't have a private sitting-room because there wasn't one—which reason they accepted as unanswerable, and furthermore said they would content themselves with such accommodation as the bar-parlour afforded; whereon the slip-shod barmaid relaxed from her defiant mood, and told them that they would find it quite cheerful, as there was a nice look-out upon the river."

Mr. Darley ordered a bottle of wine—a tremendous order, rarely known to be issued in that establishment—and further remarked that he should be glad if the landlord would bring it in, as he would like five minutes' conversation with him. After having given this overwhelming order, Gus and Mr. Peters entered the parlour.

It was empty, the parlour; the bargeman was evidently taking his delight somewhere else that afternoon. There were the wet marks of the bargeman's porter-pots of the morning, and the dry marks of the bargeman's porter-pots of the day before, still on the table; there were the bargeman's broken tobacco-pipes, and the cards wherewith he had played all-fours—which cards he had evidently chewed at the corners in aggravation of spirit when his luck deserted him—strewn about in every direction. There were the muddy marks of the bargeman's feet on the sandy floor; there was a subtle effluvium of mingled corduroy, tobacco, onions, damp leather, and gin, which was the perfume of the bargeman himself; but the bargeman in person was not there.

Mr. Darley walked to the window, and looked out at the river. A cheerful sight, did you say, slip-shod Hebe?[3] Is it cheerful to look at that thick dingy water, remembering how many a wretched head its current has flowed over; how many a tired frame has lain down to find in death the rest life could not yield; how many a lost soul has found a road to another world in that black tide, and gone forth impenitent, from the shore of time to the ocean of eternity; how often the golden hair has come up in the fisherman's net; and how many a Mary, less happy, since less innocent than the heroine of Mr. Kingsley's melodious song, has gone out, never, never to return! Mr. Darley perhaps thinks this, for he turns his back to the window, calls out to the barmaid to come and light a fire, and proceeds to fill man's great consoler, his pipe.

I very much wonder, gentle readers of the fair sex, that you have never contrived somehow or other to pick a quarrel with the manes of good, cloak-spoiling, guinea-finding, chivalrous, mutineer-encountering, long-suffering, maid-of-honour-adoring Walter Raleigh—the importer of the greatest rival woman ever had in the affections of man, the tenth Muse, the fourth Grace, the uncanonized saint, Tobacco. You are angry with poor Tom, whom you henpeck so cruelly, Mrs. Jones, because he came home last night from that little business dinner at Greenwich slightly the worse for the salmon and the cucumber—not the iced punch!—oh, no! he scarcely touched that! You are angry with your better half, and you wish to give him, as you elegantly put it, a bit of your mind. My good soul, what does Tom care for you—behind his pipe? Do you think he is listening to *you*, or thinking of *you*, as he sits lazily watching with dreamy eyes the blue wreaths of smoke curling upwards from that honest meerschaum bowl? He is thinking of the girl he knew fourteen years ago, before ever he fell on his knees in the back parlour, and ricked his ankle in proposing to you; he is thinking of a picnic in Epping Forest, where he first met *her;* when coats were worn short-waisted, and Plancus[4] was consul; when there was scaffolding at Charing Cross, and stage-coaches between London and Brighton; when the wandering minstrel was to be found at Beulah Spa,[5] and there was no Mr. Robson at the Olympic.[6] He is looking full in your face, poor Tom! and attending to every word you say—as you think! Ah! my dear madam, believe me, he does not see one feature of your face, or hear one word of your peroration. He sees *her;* he sees her standing at the end of a green arcade, with the sunlight flickering between the restless leaves upon her bright brown curls, and making arabesques of light and shade on her innocent white dress; he sees the little coquettish glance she flings back at him, as he stands in an attitude he knows now was, if anything, spooney, all amongst the *débris* of the banquet—lobster-salads, veal-and-ham pies, empty champagne-bottles, strawberry-stalks, parasols, and bonnets and shawls. He hears the singing of the Essex birds, the rustling of the forest leaves, her ringing laugh, the wheels of a carriage, the tinkling of a sheep-bell, the roar of a blacksmith's forge, and the fall of waters in the distance. All those sweet rustic sounds, which make a music very different to the angry tones of your voice, are in his ears; and you, madam—you, for any impression you can make on him, might just as well be on the culminating point of Teneriffe, and would find quite as attentive a listener in the waste of ocean you might behold from that eminence!

And who is the fairy that works the spell? Her earthly name is Tobacco, *alias* Bird's-eye, *alias* Latakia, *alias* Cavendish; and the magician who raised her first in the British dominions was Walter Raleigh. Are you not glad now, gentle reader, that the sailors mutinied, that the dear son was killed in that far land, and that the mean-spirited Stuart rewarded the noblest and wisest of his age with a life in a dungeon and the death of a traitor?

I don't know whether Augustus Darley thought all this as he sat over the struggling smoke and damp in the parlour of "The Bargeman's Delight," which smoke and damp the defiant barmaid told him would soon develop into a good fire. Gus was not a married man; and, again, he and Mr. Peters had very particular business on their hands, and had very little time for sentimental or philosophical reflections.

The landlord of the "Delight" appeared presently, with what, he assured his guests, was such a bottle of port as they wouldn't often meet with. There was a degree of obscurity in this commendation which savoured of the inspired communications of the priestess of the oracle. Æacida might conquer the Romans, or the Romans might annihilate Æacida; the bottle of port might be unapproachable by its excellence, or so utterly execrable in quality as to be beyond the power of wine-merchant to imitate; and either way the landlord not forsworn. Gus looked at the bright side of the question, and requested his host to draw the cork and bring another glass—"that is," he said, "if you can spare half an hour or so for a friendly chat."

"Oh, as for that," said the landlord, "I can spare time enough, it isn't the business as'll keep me movin'; it's never brisk except on wet afternoons, when they comes in with their dirty boots, and makes more mess than they drinks beer. A 'found drowned' or a inquest enlivens us up now and then; but Lord, there's nothing doing nowadays, and even inquests and drownin' seems a-goin' out."

The landlord was essentially a melancholy and blighted creature; and he seated himself at his own table, wiped away yesterday's beer with his own coat-sleeve, and prepared himself to drink his own port, with a gloomy resignation sublime enough to have taken a whole band of conspirators to the scaffold in a most creditable manner.

"My friend," said Mr. Darley, introducing Mr. Peters by a wave of his hand, "is a foreigner, and hasn't got hold of our language yet; he finds it slippery, and hard to catch, on account of the construction of it, so you must excuse his not being lively."

The landlord nodded, and remarked, in a cheering manner, that he didn't see what there was for the liveliest cove goin' to be lively about nowadays.

After a good deal of desultory conversation, and a description of several very interesting inquests, Gus asked the landlord whether he remembered an affair that happened about eight or nine years ago, or thereabouts—a girl found drowned in the fall of the year.

"There's always bein' girls found drowned," said the landlord moodily; "it's my belief they likes it, especially when they've long hair. They takes off their bonnets, and they lets down their back hairs, and they puts a note in their pockets, wrote large, to say as they hopes as how he'll be sorry, and so on. I can't remember no girl in particular, eight years ago, at the back end of the year. I can call to mind a many promiscuous like, off and on, but not to say this was Jane, or that was Sarah."

"Do you remember a quarrel, then, between a man and a girl in this very room, and the man having his head cut by a sovereign she threw at him?"

"We never have no quarrels in this room," replied the landlord, with dignity. "The bargemen sometimes have a few words, and tramples upon each other with their hobnailed boots, and their iron heels and toes will dance again when their temper's up; but I don't allow no quarrels here. And yet," he added, after a few moments' reflection, "there was a sort of a row, I remember, a many years ago, between a girl as drowned herself that night down below, and a young gent, in this 'ere room; he a-sittin' just as you may be a-sittin' now, and she a-standin' over by that window, and throwin' four sovereigns at him spiteful, one of them a-catchin' him just over the eyebrow, and cuttin' of him to the bone—and he a-pickin' 'em up when his head was bound, and walkin' off with 'em as if nothin' had happened."

"Yes; but do you happen to remember," said Gus, "that he only found three out of the four sovereigns; and that he was obliged to give up looking for the last, and go away without it?"

The landlord of the "Delight" suddenly lapsed into most profound meditation; he rubbed his chin, making a rasping noise as he did so, as if going cautiously over a French roll, first with one hand and then with the other; he looked with an earnest gaze into the glass of puce-coloured liquid before him, took a sip of that liquid, smacked his lips after the manner of a connoisseur, and then said that he couldn't at the present moment call to mind the last circumstance alluded to.

"Shall I tell you," said Gus, "my motive in asking this question?"

The landlord said he might as well mention it as not.

"Then I will. I want that sovereign. I've a particular reason, which I don't want to stop to explain just now, for wanting that very coin of all others; and I don't mind giving a five-pound note to the man that'll put that twenty shillings worth of gold into my hand."

"You don't, don't you?" said the landlord, repeating the operations described above, and looking very hard at Gus all the time: after which he sat staring silently from Gus to Peters, and from Pe-

ters to the puce-coloured liquid, for some minutes: at last he said—
"It ain't a trap?"

"There's the note," replied Mr. Darley; "look at it, and see if it's
a good one. I'll lay it on this table, and when you lay down that
sovereign—*that* one, mind, and no other—it's yours."

"You think I've got it, then?" said the landlord, interrogatively.

"I know you've got it," said Gus, "unless you've spent it."

"Why, as to that," said the landlord, "when you first called to
mind the circumstance of the girl, and the gent, and the inquest,
and all that, I've a short memory, and couldn't quite recollect that
there sovereign; but now I *do* remember finding of that very coin a
year and a half afterwards, for the drains was bad that year, and the
Board of Health came a-chivying of us to take up our floorings, and
lime-wash ourselves inside; and in taking up the flooring of this
room what should we come across but that very bit of gold?"

"And you never changed it?"

"Shall I tell you why I never changed it? Sovereigns ain't so plen-
tiful in these parts that I should keep this one to look at. What do
you say to its not being a sovereign at all?"

"Not a sovereign?"

"Not; what do you say to its being a twopenny-halfpenny foreign
coin, with a lot of rum writin' about it—a coin as they has the
cheek to offer me four-and-sixpence for as old gold, and as I kep',
knowin' it was worth more for a curiosity—eh?"

"Why, all I can say is," said Gus, "that you did very wisely to
keep it; and here's five or perhaps ten times its value, and plenty of
interest for your money."

"Wait a bit," muttered the landlord; and disappearing into the
bar, he rummaged in some drawer in the interior of that sanctum,
and presently reappeared with a little parcel screwed carefully in
newspaper. "Here it is," he said, "and jolly glad I am to get rid of
the useless lumber, as wouldn't buy a loaf of bread if one was
a-starving; and thank you kindly, sir," he continued, as he pocketed
the note. "I should like to sell you half-a-dozen more of 'em at the
same price, that's all."

The coin was East Indian; worth perhaps six or seven rupees; in size and touch not at all unlike a sovereign, but about fifty years old.

"And now," said Gus, "my friend and I will take a stroll; you can cook us a steak for five o'clock, and in the meantime we can amuse ourselves about the town."

"The factories might be interesting to the foreigneering gent," said the landlord, whose spirits seemed very much improved by the possession of the five-pound note; "there's a factory hard by as employs a power of hands, and there's a wheel as killed a man only last week, and you could see it, I'm sure, gents, and welcome, by only mentioning my name. I serves the hands as lives round this way, which is a many."

Gus thanked him for his kind offer, and said they would make a point of availing themselves of it.

The landlord watched them as they walked along the bank in the direction of Slopperton. "I expect," he remarked to himself, "the lively one's mad, and the quiet one's his keeper. But five pounds is five pounds; and that's neither here nor there."

Instead of seeking both amusement and instruction, as they might have done from a careful investigation of the factory in question, Messrs. Darley and Peters walked at a pretty brisk rate, looking neither to the right nor to the left, choosing the most out-of-the-way and unfrequented streets, till they left the town of Slopperton and the waters of the Sloshy behind them, and emerged on to the high road, not so many hundred yards from the house in which Mr. Montague Harding met his death—the house of the Black Mill.

It had never been a lively-looking place at best; but now, with the association of a hideous murder belonging to it—and so much a part of it, that, to all who knew the dreadful story, death, like a black shadow, seemed to brood above the gloomy pile of building and warn the stranger from the infected spot—it was indeed a melancholy habitation. The shutters of all the windows but one were closed; the garden-paths were overgrown with weeds; the beds choked up; the trees had shot forth wild erratic branches that trailed across the path of the intruder, and entangling themselves about him, threw him down before he was aware. The house, however, was not uninhabited—Martha, the old servant, who had nursed Richard Marwood when a little child, had the entire care of it; and she was further provided with a comfortable income and a youthful domestic to attend upon her, the teaching, admonishing, scolding, and patronizing of whom made the delight of her quiet existence.

The bell which Mr. Darley rang at the gate went clanging down the walk, as if to be heard in the house were a small part of its mission, for its sonorous power was calculated to awaken all Slopperton in case of fire, flood, or invasion of the foreign foe.

Perhaps Gus thought just a little—as he stood at the broad white gate, overgrown now with damp and moss, but once so trim and bright—of the days when Richard and he had worn little cloth frocks, all ornamented with divers meandering braids and shining buttons, and had swung to and fro in the evening sunshine on that very gate.

He remembered Richard throwing him off, and hurting his nose upon the gravel. They had made mud-pies upon that very walk; they had set elaborate and most efficient traps for birds, and never caught any, in those very shrubberies; they had made a swing under the lime-trees yonder, and a fountain that would never work, but had to be ignominiously supplied with jugs of water, and stirred with spoons like a pudding, before the crystal shower would consent to mount. A thousand recollections of that childish time came back, and with them came the thought that the little boy in the braided frock was now an outcast from society, supposed to be dead, and his name branded as that of a madman and a murderer.

Martha's attendant, a rosy-cheeked country girl, came down the walk at the sound of the clanging bell, and stared aghast at the apparition of two gentlemen—one of them so brilliant in costume as our friend Mr. Darley.

Gus told the youthful domestic that he had a letter for Mrs. Jones. Martha's surname was Jones; the Mrs. was an honorary distinction, as the holy state of matrimony was one of the evils the worthy woman had escaped. Gus brought a note from Martha's mistress, which assured him a warm welcome. "Would the gentlemen have tea?" Martha said. "Sararanne—(the youthful domestic's name was Sarah Anne, pronounced, both for euphony and convenience, Sararanne)—Sararanne should get them anything they would please to like directly." Poor Martha was quite distressed, on being told that all they wanted was to look at the room in which the murder was committed.

"Was it in the same state as at the time of Mr. Harding's death?" asked Gus.

It had never been touched, Mrs. Jones assured them, since that dreadful time. Such was her mistress's wish; it had been kept clean and dry; but not a bit of furniture had been moved.

Mrs. Jones was rheumatic, and rarely stirred from her seat of honour by the fireside; so Sararanne was sent with a bunch of keys in her hand to conduct the gentlemen to the room in question.

Now there were two things self-evident in the manner of Sararanne; first, that she was pleased at the idea of a possible flirtation with the brilliant Mr. Darley; secondly, that she didn't at all like the ordeal of opening and entering the dreaded room in question; so, between her desire to be fascinating and her uncontrollable fear of the encounter before her, she endured a mental struggle painful to the beholder.

The shutters in the front of the house being, with one exception, all closed, the hall and staircase were wrapped in a shadowy gloom, far more alarming to the timid mind than complete darkness. In complete darkness, for instance, the eight-day clock in the corner would have been a clock, and not an elderly ghost with a broad white face and a brown greatcoat, as it seemed to be in the uncertain glimmer which crept through a distant skylight covered with ivy. Sararanne was evidently possessed with the idea that Mr. Darley and his friend would decoy her to the very threshold of the haunted chamber, and then fly ignominiously, leaving her to brave the perils of it by herself. Mr. Darley's repeated assurances that it was all right, and that on the whole it would be advisable to look alive, as life was short and time was long, etcetera, had the effect at last of inducing the damsel to ascend the stairs—looking behind her at every other step—and to conduct the visitors along a passage, at the end of which she stopped, selected with considerable celerity a key from the bunch, plunged it into the keyhole of the door before her, said, "That is the room, gentlemen, if you please," dropped a curtsey, and turned and fled.

The door opened with a scroop,[8] and Mr. Peters realized at last the darling wish of his heart, and stood in the very room in which the murder had been committed. Gus looked round, went to the window, opened the shutters to the widest extent, and the afternoon sunshine streamed full into the room, lighting every crevice, revealing every speck of dust on the moth-eaten damask[9] bed-curtains—every crack and stain on the worm-eaten flooring.

—

To see Mr. Darley look round the room, and to see Mr. Peters look round it, is to see two things as utterly wide apart as it is possible for one look to be from another. The young surgeon's eyes wander here and there, fix themselves nowhere, and rest two or three times upon the same object before they seem to take in the full meaning of that object. The eyes of Mr. Peters, on the contrary, take the circuit of the apartment with equal precision and rapidity—go from number one to number two, from number two to number three; and having given a careful inspection to every article of furniture in the room, fix at last in a gaze of concentrated intensity on the *tout ensemble* of the chamber.

"Can you make out anything?" at last asks Mr. Darley.

Mr. Peters nods his head, and in reply to this question drops on one knee, and falls to examining the flooring.

"Do you see anything in that?" asks Gus.

"Yes," replies Mr. Peters on his fingers; "look at this."

Gus does look at this. This is the flooring, which is in a very rotten and dilapidated state, by the bed-side. "Well, what then?" he asks.

"What then?" said Mr. Peters, on his fingers, with an expression of considerable contempt pervading his features; "what then? You're a very talented young gent, Mr. Darley, and if I wanted a prescription for the bile, which I'm troubled with sometimes, or a

tip for the Derby, which I don't, not being a sporting man, you're
the gent I'd come to; but for all that you ain't no police-officer, or
you'd never ask that question. What then? Do you remember as one
of the facts so hard agen Mr. Marwood was the blood-stains on his
sleeve? You see these here cracks and crevices in this here floorin'?
Very well, then; Mr. Marwood slept in the room under this. He was
tired, I've heard him say, and he threw himself down on the bed in
his coat. What more natural, then, than that there should be blood
upon his sleeve, and what more easy to guess than the way it came
there?"

"You think it dropped through, then?" asked Gus.

"I *think* it dropped through," said Mr. Peters, on his fingers, with
biting irony; "I know it dropped through. His counsel was a nice un,
not to bring this into court," he added, pointing to the boards on
which he knelt. "If I'd only seen this place before the trial——But
I was nobody, and it was like my precious impudence to ask to go
over the house, of course! Now then, for number two."

"And that is——?" asked Mr. Darley, who was quite in the dark
as to Mr. Peters's views; that functionary being implicitly believed
in by Richard and his friend, and allowed, therefore, to be just as
mysterious as he pleased.

"Number two's this here," answered the detective. "I wants to
find another or two of them rum Indian coins; for our young friend
Dead-and-Alive, as is here to-day and gone to-morrow, got that one
as he gave the girl from that cabinet, or my name's not Joseph Peters;" wherewith Mr. Peters, who had been entrusted by Mrs. Marwood with the keys of the cabinet in question, proceeded to open
the doors of it, and to carefully inspect that old-fashioned piece of
furniture.

There were a great many drawers, and boxes, and pigeon-holes,
and queer nooks and corners in this old cabinet, all smelling
equally of old age, damp, and cedar-wood. Mr. Peters pulled out
drawers and opened boxes, found secret drawers in the inside of
other drawers, and boxes hid in ambush in other boxes, all with so
little result, beyond the discovery of old papers, bundles of letters
tied with faded red tape, a simpering and neutral-tinted miniature

or two of the fashion of some fifty years gone by, when a bright blue coat and brass buttons was the correct thing for a dinner-party, and your man about town wore a watch in each of his breeches-pockets, and simpered at you behind a shirt-frill wide enough to separate him for ever from his friends and acquaintance. Besides these things, Mr. Peters found a Johnson's dictionary, a ready-reckoner, and a pair of boot-hooks; but as he found nothing else, Mr. Darley grew quite tired of watching his proceedings, and suggested that they should adjourn; for he remarked—"Is it likely that such a fellow as this North would leave anything behind him?"

"Wait a bit," said Mr. Peters, with an expressive jerk of his head. Gus shrugged his shoulders, took out his cigar-case, lighted a cheroot, and walked to the window, where he leaned with his elbows on the sill, puffing blue clouds of tobacco-smoke down among the straggling creepers that covered the walls and climbed round the casement, while the detective resumed his search among the old bundles of papers. He was nearly abandoning it, when, in one of the outer drawers, he took up an object he had passed over in his first inspection. It was a small canvas bag, such as is used to hold money, and was apparently empty; but while pondering on his futile search, Mr. Peters twisted this bag in a moment of absence of mind between his fingers, swinging it backwards and forwards in the air. In so doing, he knocked it against the side of the cabinet, and, to his surprise, it emitted a sharp metallic sound. It was not empty, then, although it appeared so. A moment's examination showed the detective that he had succeeded in obtaining the object of his search; the bag had been used for money, and a small coin had lodged in the seam at one corner of the bottom of it, and had stuck so firmly as not to be easily shaken out. This, in the murderer's hurried ransacking of the cabinet, in his blind fury at not finding the sum he expected to obtain, had naturally escaped him. The piece of money was a small gold coin, only half the value of the one found by the landlord, but of the same date and style.

Mr. Peters gave his fingers a triumphant snap, which aroused the attention of Mr. Darley; and, with a glance expressive of the pride in his art which is peculiar to your true genius, held up the little piece of dingy gold.

"By Jove!" exclaimed the admiring Gus, "you've got it, then! Egad, Peters, I think you'd make evidence, if there wasn't any."

"Eight years of that young man's life, sir," said the rapid fingers, "has been sacrificed to the stupidity of them as should have pulled him through."

CHAPTER V

MR. PETERS DECIDES ON A STRANGE STEP, AND ARRESTS THE DEAD

While Mr. Peters, assisted by Richard's sincere friend, the young surgeon, made the visit above described, Daredevil Dick counted the hours in London. It was essential to the success of his cause, Gus and Peters urged, that he should not show himself, or in any way reveal the fact of his existence, till the real murderer was arrested. Let the truth appear to all the world, and then time enough for Richard to come forth, with an unbranded forehead,[1] in the sight of his fellow-men. But when he heard that Raymond Marolles had given his pursuers the slip, and was off, no one knew where, it was all that his mother, his friend Percy Cordonner, Isabella Darley, and the lawyers to whom he had intrusted his cause, could do, to prevent his starting that instant on the track of the guilty man. It was a weary day, this day of the failure of the arrest, for all. Neither his mother's tender consolation, nor his solicitor's assurances that all was not yet lost, could moderate the young man's impatience. Neither Isabella's tearful prayers that he would leave the issue in the hands of Heaven, nor Mr. Cordonner's philosophical recommendation to take it quietly and let the "beggar" go, could keep him quiet. He felt like a caged lion, whose ignoble bonds kept him from the vile object of his rage. The day wore out, however, and no tidings came of the fugitive. Mr. Cordonner insisted on stopping with his friend till three o'clock in the morning, and at that very late hour set out, with the intention of going down to the Cherokees—it was a Cheerful night, and they would most likely be still assembled—to ascertain, as he popularly expressed it, whether anything had "turned up" there. The clock of St. Martin's struck three as he stood with Richard at the street-door in Spring Gardens, giving friendly consolation between the puffs of his cigar to the agitated young man.

"In the first place, my dear boy," he said, "if you can't catch the fellow, you can't catch the fellow—that's sound logic and a mathematical argument; then why make yourself unhappy about it? Why try to square the circle, only because the circle's round, and can't be squared? Let it alone. If this fellow turns up, hang him! I should glory in seeing him hung,[2] for he's an out-and-out scoundrel, and I should make a point of witnessing the performance, if the officials would do the thing at a reasonable hour, and not execute him in the middle of the night and swindle the respectable public. If he doesn't turn up, why, let the matter rest; marry that little girl in there, Darley's pretty sister—who seems, by the bye, to be absurdly fond of you—and let the question rest. That's my philosophy."

The young man turned away with an impatient sigh; then, laying his hand on Percy's shoulder, he said, "My dear old fellow, if everybody in the world were like you, Napoleon would have died a Corsican lawyer, or a lieutenant in the French army. Robespierre would have lived a petty barrister, with a penchant for getting up in the night to eat jam tarts and a mania for writing bad poetry. The third state[3] would have gone home quietly to its farmyards, and its merchants' offices; there would have been no Oath of the Tenis Court,[4] and no Battle of Waterloo."[5]

"And a very good thing, too," said his philosophical friend; "nobody would have been a loser but Astley's[6]—only think of that. If there had been no Napoleon, what a loss for image boys, Gomersal the Great, and Astley's. Forgive me, Dick, for laughing at you. I'll cut down to the Cheerfuls, and see if anything's up. The Smasher's away, or he might have given us his advice; the genius of the P.R. might have been of some service in this affair. Good night!" He gave Richard a languidly affectionate shake of the hand, and departed.

Now, when Mr. Cordonner said he would cut down to the Cherokees, let it not be thought by the simple-minded reader that the expression "cut down," from his lips, conveyed that degree of velocity which, though perhaps a sufficiently vague phrase in itself, it is calculated to carry to the ordinary mind. Percy Cordonner had never been seen by mortal man in a hurry. He had been known to be too late for a train, and had been beheld placidly lounging at a few paces from the departing engine, and mildly but rather reproachfully regarding that object. The prospects of his entire life may have hinged on his going by that particular train; but he would never be so false to his principles as to make himself unpleasantly warm, or in any way disturb the delicate organization with which nature had gifted him. He had been seen at the doors of the Opera-house when Jenny Lind[7] was going to appear in the *Figlia*,[8] and while those around him were afflicted with a temporary lunacy, and trampling one another wildly in the mud, he had been observed leaning against a couple of fat men as in an easy-chair, and standing high and dry upon somebody else's boots, breathing gentlemanly and polyglot execrations upon the surrounding crowd, when, in swaying to and fro, it disturbed or attempted to disturb his serenity. So, when he said he would cut down to the Cherokees, he of course meant that he would cut after his manner; and he accordingly rolled languidly along the deserted pavements of the Strand, with something of the insouciant and purposeless manner that Rasselas may have had in a walk through the arcades of his happy valley. He reached the well-known tavern at last, however, and stopping under the sign of the washed-out Indian desperately tomahawking nothing, in the direction of Covent Garden, with an arm more distinguished for muscular development than correct drawing, he gave the well-known signal of the club, and was admitted by the damsel before described, who appeared always to devote the watches of the night to the process of putting her hair in papers, that she might wear that becoming "head" for the admiration of the jug-and-bottle customers of the following day, and shine in a frame of very long and very greasy curls that were apt to sweep the heads off brown stouts,[9] and dip gently into "goes" of spirits upon the more brilliant company of the evening. This young lady, popularly known as 'Liza,[10] was well up in the sporting business of the house, read the *Life*[11] during church-time on Sundays, and was even believed to have communicated with that Rhadamanthine[12] journal, under the signature of L., in the answers to correspondents. She was understood to be engaged, or, as her friends and admirers expressed it, to be "keeping company"[13] with that luminary of the P.R., the Middlesex Mawler, whose head-quarters were at the Cherokee.

Mr. Cordonner found three Cheerfuls assembled in the bar, in a state of intense excitement and soda-water. A telegraphic message had just arrived from the Smasher. It was worthy, in economy of construction, of the Delphic oracle, and had the advantage of being easy to understand. It was as follows—"Tell R. M. *he's* here: had no orders, so went in with left: he won't be able to move for a day or two."

Mr. Cordonner was almost surprised, and was thus very nearly false, for once in his life, to the only art he knew. "This will be good news in Spring Gardens," he said; "but Peters won't be back till to-morrow night. Suppose," he added, musing, "we were to telegraph to him at Slopperton instanter? I know where he hangs out there. If anybody could find a cab and take the message it would be doing Marwood an inestimable service," added Mr. Cordonner, passing through the bar, and lazily seating himself on a green-and-gold Cream of the Valley cask, with his hat very much on the back of his head, and his hands in his pockets. "I'll write the message."

He scribbled upon a card—"Go across to Liverpool. He's given us the slip, and is there;" and handed it politely towards the three Cheerfuls who were leaning over the pewter counter.

Splitters, the dramatic author, clutched the document eagerly; to his poetic mind it suggested that best gift of inspiration, "a situation."

"I'll take it," he said; "what a fine line it would make in a bill! 'The intercepted telegram,' with a comic railway clerk, and the villain of the piece cutting the wires!"

"Away with you, Splitters," said Percy Cordonner. "Don't let the Strand become verdant beneath your airy tread. Don't stop to compose a five-act drama as you go, that's a good fellow. 'Liza, my dear girl, a pint of your creamiest Edinburgh, and let it be as mild as the disposition of your humble servant."

Three days after the above conversation, three gentlemen were assembled at breakfast in a small room in a tavern overlooking the quay at Liverpool. This triangular party consisted of the Smasher, in an elegant and simple morning costume, consisting of tight trousers of Stuart plaid, an orange-coloured necktie, a blue checked waistcoat, and shirt-sleeves. The Smasher looked upon a coat as an essentially outdoor garment, and would no more have invested himself in it to eat his breakfast than he would have partaken of that refreshment with his hat on, or an umbrella up. The two other gentlemen were Mr. Darley, and his chief, Mr. Peters, who had a little document in his pocket signed by a Lancashire magistrate, on which he set considerable value. They had come across to Liverpool as directed by the telegraph, and had there met with the Smasher, who had received letters for them from London with the details of the escape, and orders to be on the look-out for Peters and Gus. Since the arrival of these two, the trio had led a sufficiently idle and apparently purposeless life. They had engaged an apartment overlooking the quay, in the window of which they were seated for the best part of the day, playing the intellectual and exciting game of all-fours. There did not seem much in this to forward the cause of Richard Marwood. It is true that Mr. Peters was wont to vanish from the room every now and then, in order to speak to mysterious and grave-looking gentlemen, who commanded respect wherever they went, and before whom the most daring thief in Liverpool shrank as before Mr. Calcraft himself.[14] He held strange conferences with them in corners of the hostelry in which the trio had taken up their abode; he went out with them, and hovered about the quays and the shipping; he prowled about in the dusk of the evening, and meeting these gentlemen also prowling in the uncertain light, would sometimes salute them as friends and brothers, at other times be entirely unacquainted with them, and now and then interchange two or three hurried gestures with them, which the close observer would have perceived to mean a great deal. Beyond this, nothing had been done—and, in spite of all this, no tidings could be obtained of the Count de Marolles, except that no person answering to his description had left Liverpool either by land or water. Still, neither Mr. Peters's spirits nor patience failed him; and after every interview held upon the stairs or in the passage, after every excursion to the quays or the streets, he returned as briskly as on the first day, and re-seated himself at the little table by the window, at which his colleagues—or rather his companions, for neither Mr. Darley nor the Smasher were of the smallest use to him—played, and took it in turns to ruin each other from morning till night. The real truth of the matter was, that, if anything, the detective's so-called assistants were decidedly in his way; but Augustus Darley, having distinguished himself in the escape from the asylum, considered himself an amateur Vidocque;[15] and the Smasher, from the moment of putting in his left, and unconsciously advancing the cause of Richard and justice by extinguishing the Count de Marolles, had panted to write his name, or rather make his mark, upon the scroll of fame, by arresting that gentleman in his own proper person, and without any extraneous aid whatever. It was rather hard for him, then, to have to resign the prospect of such a glorious adventure to a man of Mr. Peters's inches; but he was of a calm and amiable disposition, and would floor his adversary with as much good temper as he would eat his favourite dinner; so, with a growl of resignation, he abandoned the reins to the steady hands so used to hold them, and seated himself down to the consumption of innumerable clay pipes and glasses of bitter ale with Gus, who, being one of the most ancient of the order of the Cherokees, was an especial favourite with him.

On this third morning, however, there is a decided tone of weariness pervading the minds of both Gus and the Smasher. Three-handed all-fours, though a delicious and exciting game, will pall upon the inconstant mind, especially when your third player is perpetually summoned from the table to take part in a mysterious dialogue with a person or persons unknown, the result of which he declines to communicate to you. The view from the bow-window of the blue parlour in the White Lion, Liverpool, is no doubt as animated as it is beautiful; but Rasselas, we know, got tired of some very pretty scenery, and there have been readers so inconstant as to grow weary of Dr. Johnson's book, and to go down peacefully to their graves unacquainted with the climax thereof. So it is scarcely perhaps to be wondered that the volatile Augustus thirsted for the waterworks of Blackfriars; while the Smasher, feeling himself to be blushing unseen, and wasting his stamina, if not his sweetness, on the desert air,[16] pined for the familiar shades of Bow Street and Vinegar Yard, and the home-sounds of the rumbling and jingling of the wagons, and the unpolite language of the drivers thereof, on market mornings in the adjacent market. Pleasures and palaces are all very well in their way, as the song says; but there is just one little spot on earth which, whether it be a garret in Petticoat Lane or a mansion in Belgrave Square, is apt to be dearer to us than the best of them; and the Smasher languishes for the friendly touch of the ebony handles of the porter-engine, and the scent of the Welsh rarebits of his youth. Perhaps I express myself in a more romantic manner on this subject, however, than I should do, for the remark of the Left-handed one, as he pours himself out a cup of tea from the top of the teapot—he despises the spout of that vessel as a modern innovation on ancient simplicity—is as simple as it is energetic. He merely observes that he is "jolly sick of this lot,"—this lot meaning Liverpool, the Count de Marolles, the White Lion, three-handed all-fours, and the detective police force.

"There was nobody ill in Friar Street when I left," said Gus mournfully; "but there had been a run upon Pimperneckel's Universal Regenerator Pills: and if that don't make business a little brisker, nothing will."

"It's my opinion," observed the Smasher doggedly, "that this 'ere forrin cove has give us the slip out and out; and the sooner we gets back to London the better. I never was much of a hand at chasing wild geese, and"—he added, with rather a spiteful glance at the mild countenance of the detective—"I don't see neither that standin' and makin' signs to parties unbeknown at street-corners and stair-heads is the quickest way to catch them sort of birds; leastways it's not the opinion held by the gents belongin' to the Ring as I've had the honour to make acquaintance with."

"Suppose——" said Mr. Peters, on his fingers.

"Oh!" muttered the Smasher, "blow them fingers of his. I can't understand 'em—there!" The left-handed Hercules knew that this was to attack the detective on his tenderest point. "Blest if I ever knows his *p*'s from his *b*'s, or his *w*'s from his *x*'s, let alone his vowels, and them would puzzle a conjuror."

Mr. Peters glanced at the prize-fighter more in sorrow than in anger, and taking out a greasy little pocket-book, and a greasier little pencil, considerably the worse for having been vehemently chewed in moments of preoccupation, he wrote upon a leaf of it thus—"Suppose we catch him to-day?"

"Ah, very true," said the Smasher sulkily, after he had examined the document in two or three different lights before he came upon its full bearings; "very true, indeed, suppose we do—and suppose we don't, on the other hand; and I know which is the likeliest. Suppose, Mr. Peters, we give up lookin' for a needle in a bundle of hay, which after a time gets tryin' to a lively disposition, and go back to our businesses. If you had a girl as didn't know British from best French a-servin' of *your* customers," he continued in an injured tone, "*you'd* be anxious to get home, and let your forrin counts go to the devil their own ways."

"Then go," Mr. Peters wrote, in large letters and no capitals.

"Oh, ah; yes, to be sure," replied the Smasher, who, I regret to say, felt painfully, in his absence from domestic pleasures, the want of somebody to quarrel with; "No, I thank you! Go the very day as you're going to catch him! Not if I'm in any manner aware of the circumstance. I'm obliged to you," he added, with satirical emphasis.

"Come, I say, old boy," interposed Gus, who had been quietly doing execution upon a plate of devilled kidneys[17] during this little friendly altercation, "come, I say, no snarling, Smasher, Peters isn't going to contest the belt with you, you know."

"You needn't be a-diggin' at me because I ain't champion," said the ornament of the P.R., who was inclined to find a malicous meaning in every word uttered that morning; "you needn't come any of your sneers because I ain't got the belt any longer."

The Smasher had been Champion of England in his youth, but had retired upon his laurels for many years, and only occasionally emerged from private life in a public-house to take a round or two with some old opponent.

"I tell you what it is, Smasher—it's my opinion the air of Liverpool don't suit your constitution," said Gus. "We've promised to stand by Peters here, and to go by his word in everything, for the sake of the man we want to serve; and, however trying it may be to our patience doing nothing, which perhaps is about as much as we can do and make no mistakes, the first that gets tired and deserts the ship will be no friend to Richard Marwood."

"I'm a bad lot, Mr. Darley, and that's the truth," said the mollified Smasher; "but the fact is, I'm used to a turn with the gloves every morning before breakfast with the barman, and when I don't get it, I dare say I ain't the pleasantest company goin'. I should think they've got gloves in the house: would you mind taking off your coat and having a turn—friendly like?"

Gus assured the Smasher that nothing would please him better than that trifling diversion; and in five minutes they had pushed Mr. Peters and the breakfast-table into a corner, and were hard at it, Mr. Darley's knowledge of the art being all required to keep the slightest pace with the scientific movements of the agile though elderly Smasher.

Mr. Peters did not stay at the breakfast-table long, but after having drunk a huge breakfast cupful of very opaque and substantial-looking coffee at a draught, just as if it had been half a pint of beer, he slid quietly out of the room.

"It's my opinion," said the Smasher, as he stood, or rather lounged, upon his guard, and warded off the most elaborate combinations of Mr. Darley's fists with as much ease as he would have brushed aside so many flies—"it's my opinion that chap ain't up to his business."

"Isn't he?" replied Gus, as he threw down the gloves in despair, after having been half an hour in a violent perspiration, without having succeeded in so much as rumpling the Smasher's hair. "Isn't he?" he said, choosing the interrogative as the most expressive form of speech. "That man's got head enough to be prime minister, and carry the House along with every twist of his fingers."

"He must make his *p*'s and *b*'s a little plainer afore he'll get a bill through the Commons though," muttered the Left-handed one, who couldn't quite get over his feelings of injury against the detective for the utter darkness in which he had been kept for the last three days as to the other's plans.

The Smasher and Mr. Darley passed the morning in that remarkably intellectual and praiseworthy manner peculiar to gentlemen who, being thrown out of their usual occupation, are cast upon their own resources for amusement and employment. There was the daily paper to be looked at, to begin with; but after Gus had glanced at the leading article, a *rifacimento*[18] of the *Times* leader of the day before, garnished with some local allusions, and highly spiced with satirical remarks *apropos* to our spirited contemporary the *Liverpool Aristides;* after the Smasher had looked at the racing fixtures for the coming week, and made rude observations on the editing of a journal which failed to describe the coming off of the event between Silver-polled Robert and the Chester Crusher— after, I say, the two gentlemen had each devoured his favourite page, the paper was an utter failure in the matter of excitement, and the window was the next best thing. Now to the peculiarly constituted mind of the Left-handed one, looking out of a window was in itself very slow work; and unless he was allowed to eject missiles of a trifling but annoying character—such as hot ashes out of his pipe, the last drop of his pint of beer, the dirty water out of the saucers belonging to the flower-pots on the window-sill, or lighted lucifer-matches—into the eyes of the unoffending passers-by, he didn't, to use his own forcible remark, "seem to see the fun of it." Harmless old gentlemen with umbrellas, mild elderly ladies with handbaskets and brass-handled green-silk parasols, and young ladies of from ten to twelve going to school in clean frocks, and on particularly good terms with themselves, the Smasher looked upon as his peculiar prey. To put his head out of the window and make tender and polite inquiries about their maternal parents; to go further still, and express an earnest wish to be informed of those parents' domestic arrangements, and whether they had been induced to part with a piece of machinery of some importance in the getting up of linen; to insinuate alarming suggestions of mad bulls in the next street, or a tiger just broke loose from the Zoological Gardens; to terrify the youthful scholar by asking him derisively whether he wouldn't "catch it when he got to school? Oh, no, not at all, neither!" and to draw his head away suddenly, and altogether disappear from public view; to act, in fact, after the manner of an accomplished clown in a Christmas pantomime, was the weak delight of his manly mind: and when prevented by Mr. Darley's friendly remonstrance from doing this, the Smasher abandoned the window altogether, and concentrated all the powers of his intellect on the pursuit of a lively young bluebottle, which eluded his bandanna at every turn, and bumped itself violently against the window-panes at the very moment its pursuer was looking for it up the chimney.

Time and the hour made very long work of this particular morning, and several glasses of bitter had been called for, and numerous games of cribbage had been played by the two companions, when Mr. Darley, looking at his watch for not more than the twenty-second time in the last hour, announced with some satisfaction that it was half-past two o'clock, and that it was consequently very near dinner-time.

"Peters is a long time gone," suggested the Smasher.

"Take my word for it," said Gus, "something has turned up; he has laid his hand upon De Marolles at last."

"I don't think it," replied his ally, obstinately refusing to believe in Mr. Peters's extra share of the divine afflatus;[19] "and if he did come across him, how's he to detain him, I'd like to know? *He* couldn't go in with *his* left," he muttered derisively, "and split his head open upon the pavement to keep him quiet for a day or two."

At this very moment there came a tap at the door, and a youthful person in corduroy and a perspiration entered the room, with a very small and very dirty piece of paper twisted up into a bad imitation of a three-cornered note.

"Please, you was to give me sixpence if I run all the way," remarked the youthful Mercury, "an' I 'ave: look at my forehead;" and, in proof of his fidelity, the messenger pointed to the waterdrops which chased each other down his open brow and ran a dead heat to the end of his nose.

The scrawl ran thus—"The *Washington* sails at three for New York: be on the quay and see the passengers embark: don't notice me unless I notice you. Yours truly ———"

"It was just give me by a gent in a hurry wot was dumb, and wrote upon a piece of paper to tell me to run my legs off so as you should have it quick—thank you kindly, sir, and good afternoon," said the messenger, all in one breath, as he bowed his gratitude for the shilling Gus tossed him as he dismissed him.

"I said so," cried the young surgeon, as the Smasher applied himself to the note with quite as much, nay, perhaps more earnestness and solemnity than Chevalier Bunsen[20] might have assumed when he deciphered a half-erased and illegible inscription, in a language which for some two thousand years has been unknown to mortal man. "I said so; Peters is on the scent, and this man will be taken yet. Put on your hat, Smasher, and let's lose no time; it only wants a quarter to three, and I wouldn't be out of this for a great deal."

"I shouldn't much relish being out of the fun either," replied his companion; "and if it comes to blows, perhaps it's just as well I haven't had my dinner."

There were a good many people going by the *Washington*, and the deck of the small steamer which was to convey them on board the great ship, where she lay in graceful majesty down the noble Mersey river, was crowded with every species of luggage it was possible to imagine as appertaining to the widest varieties of the genus traveller. There was the maiden lady, with a small income from the three-per-cents,[21] and a determination of blood to the tip of a sharp nose, going out to join a married brother in New York, and evidently intent upon importing a gigantic brass cage, containing a parrot in the last stage of bald-headedness—politely called moulting; and a limp and wandering-minded umbrella—weak in the ribs, and further afflicted with a painfully sharp ferrule,[22] which always appeared where it was not expected, and evidently hankered wildly after the bystanders' backbones—as favourable specimens of the progress of the fine arts in the mother country. There were several of those brilliant birds-of-passage popularly known as "travellers," whose heavy luggage consisted of a carpet-bag and walking-stick, and whose light ditto was composed of a pocket-book and a silver pencil-case of protean[23] construction, which was sometimes a pen, now and then a penknife, and very often a toothpick. These gentlemen came down to the steamer at the last moment, inspiring the minds of nervous passengers with supernatural and convulsive cheerfulness by the light and airy way in which they bade adieu to the comrades who had just looked round to see them start, and who made appointments with them for Christmas supper-parties, and booked bets with them for next year's Newmarket first spring—as if such things as shipwreck, peril by sea, heeling over *Royal Georges,* lost *Presidents,* with brilliant Irish comedians setting forth on their return to the land in which they had been so beloved and admired, never, never to reach the shore, were things that could not be. There were rosy-cheeked country lasses, going over to earn fabulous wages and marry impossibly rich husbands. There were the old people, who essayed this long journey on an element which they knew only by sight, in answer to the kind son's noble letter, inviting them to come and share the pleasant home his sturdy arm had won far away in the fertile West. There were stout Irish labourers armed with pickaxe and spade, as with the best sword wherewith to open the great oyster of the world in these latter degenerate days. There was the distinguished American family, with ever so many handsomely dressed, spoiled, affectionate children clustering round papa and mamma, and having their own way, after the manner of transatlantic youth. There were, in short, all the people who usually assemble when a good ship sets sail for the land of dear brother Jonathan; but the Count de Marolles there was not.

No, decidedly, no Count de Marolles! There was a very quiet-looking Irish labourer, keeping quite aloof from the rest of his kind, who were sufficiently noisy and more than sufficiently forcible in the idiomatic portions of their conversation. There was this very quiet Irishman, leaning on his spade and pickaxe, and evidently bent on not going on board till the very last moment; and there was an elderly gentleman in a black coat, who looked rather like a Methodist parson, and who held a very small carpet-bag in his hand; but there was no Count de Marolles; and what's more, there was no Mr. Peters.

This latter circumstance made Augustus Darley very uneasy; but I regret to say that the Smasher wore, if anything, a look of triumph as the hands of the clocks about the quay pointed to three o'clock, and no Peters appeared.

"I knowed," he said, with effusion—"I knowed that cove wasn't up to his business. I wouldn't mind bettin' the goodwill of my little crib in London agen sixpenn'orth of coppers, that he's a-standin' at this very individual moment of time at a street-corner a mile off, makin' signs to one of the Liverpool police-officers."

The gentleman in the black coat standing before them turned round on hearing this remark, and smiled—smiled very very faintly; but he certainly did smile. The Smasher's blood, which was something like that of Lancaster, and distinguished for its tendency to mount,[24] was up in a moment.

"I hope you find my conversation amusin', old gent," he said, with considerable asperity; "I came down here on purpose to put you in spirits, on account of bein' grieved to see you always a-lookin' as if you'd just come home from your own funeral, and the undertaker was a-dunnin' you for the burial-fees."

Gus trod heavily on his companion's foot as a friendly hint to him not to get up a demonstration; and addressing the gentleman, who appeared in no hurry to resent the Smasher's contemptuous animadversions,[25] asked him when he thought the boat would start.

"Not for five or ten minutes, I dare say," he answered. "Look there; is that a coffin they're bringing this way? I'm rather short-sighted; be good enough to tell me if it is a coffin?"

The Smasher, who had the glance of an eagle, replied that it decidedly was a coffin; adding, with a growl, that he knowed somebody as might be in it, and no harm done to society.

The elderly gentleman took not the slightest notice of this gratuitous piece of information on the part of the left-handed gladiator; but suddenly busied himself with his fingers in the neighbourhood of his limp white cravat.

"Why, I'm blest," cried the Smasher, "if the old baby ain't at Peters's game, a-talkin' to nobody upon his fingers!"

Nay, most distinguished professor of the noble art of self-defence, is not that assertion a little premature? Talking on his fingers, certainly—looking at nobody, certainly; but for all that, talking to somebody, and to a somebody who is looking at him; for, from the other side of the little crowd, the Irish labourer fixes his eyes intently on every movement of the grave elderly gentleman's fingers, as they run through four or five rapid words; and Gus Darley, perceiving this look, starts in amazement, for the eyes of the Irish labourer are the eyes of Mr. Peters of the detective police.

But neither the Smasher nor Gus is to notice Mr. Peters unless Mr. Peters notices them. It is so expressed in the note, which Mr. Darley has at that very moment in his waistcoat pocket. So Gus gives his companion a nudge, and directs his attention to the smock-frock and the slouched hat in which the detective has hidden himself, with a hurried injunction to him to keep quiet. We are human at the best; ay, even when we are celebrated for our genius in the muscular science, and our well-known blow of the left-handed postman's knock, or double auctioneer: and, if the sober truth must be told, the Smasher was sorry to recognize Mr. Peters in that borrowed garb. He didn't want the dumb detective to arrest the Count de Marolles. He had never read Coriolanus, neither had he seen *the* Roman, Mr. William Macready,[26] in that character; but, for all that, the Smasher wanted to go home to the dear purlieus of Drury Lane, and say to his astonished admirers, "Alone I did it!" And lo, here were Mr. Peters and the elderly stranger both entered for the same event.

While gloomy and vengeful thoughts, therefore, troubled the

manly breast of the Vinegar-Yard gladiator, four men approached, bearing on their shoulders the coffin which had so aroused the stranger's attention. They bore it on board the steamer, and a few moments after a gentlemanly and cheerful-looking man, of about forty, stepped across the narrow platform, and occupied himself with a crowd of packages, which stood in a heap, apart from the rest of the luggage on the crowded deck.

Again the elderly stranger's fingers were busy in the region of his cravat. The superficial observer would have merely thought him very fidgety about the limp bit of muslin; but this time the fingers of Mr. Peters telegraphed an answer.

"Gentlemen," said the stranger, addressing Mr. Darley and the Smasher in the most matter-of-fact manner, "you will be good enough to go on board that steamer with me? I am working with Mr. Peters in this affair. Remember, I am going to America by that vessel yonder, and you are my friends come with me to see me off. Now, gentlemen."

He has no time to say any more, for the bell rings; and the last stragglers, the people who will enjoy the latest available moment on *terra firma*, scramble on board; amongst them the Smasher, Gus, and the stranger, who stick very closely together.

The coffin has been placed in the centre of the vessel, on the top of a pile of chests, and its gloomy black outline is sharply defined against the clear blue autumn sky. Now there is a general feeling amongst the passengers that the presence of this coffin is a peculiar injury to them.

It is unpleasant, certainly. From the very moment of its appearance amongst them a change has come over the spirits of every one of the travellers. They try to keep away from it, but they try in vain; there is a dismal fascination in the defined and ghastly shape, which all the rough wrappers that can be thrown over it will not conceal. They find their eyes wandering to it, in preference even to watching receding Liverpool, whose steeples and tall chimneys are dipping down and down into the blue water, and will soon disappear altogether. They are interested in it in spite of themselves; they ask questions of one another; they ask questions of the engineer, and of the steward, and of the captain of the steamer, but can elicit nothing—except that lying in that coffin, so close to them, and yet so very very far away from them, there is an American gentleman of some distinction, who, having died suddenly in England, is being carried back to New York, to be buried amongst his friends in that city. The aggrieved passengers for the *Washington* think it very hard upon them that the American gentleman of distinction—they remember that he *is* a gentleman of distinction, and modify their tone accordingly—could not have been buried in England like a reasonable being. The British dominions were not good enough for *him*, they supposed. Other passengers, pushing the question still further, ask whether he couldn't have been taken home by some other vessel; nay, whether indeed he ought not to have had a ship all to himself, instead of harrowing the feelings and preying upon the spirits of first-class passengers. They look almost spitefully, as they make these remarks, towards the shrouded coffin, which, to their great aggravation, is not entirely shrouded by the wrappers about it. One corner has been left uncovered, revealing the stout rough oak; for it is only a temporary coffin, and the gentleman of distinction will be put into something better befitting his rank when he arrives at his destination. It is to be observed, and it is observed by many, that the cheerful passenger in fashionable mourning, and with the last greatcoat which the inspiration of Saville Row has given to the London world thrown over his arm, hovers in a protecting manner about the coffin, and evinces a fidelity which, but for his perfectly cheerful countenance and self-possessed manner, would be really touching, towards the late American gentleman of distinction, whom he has for his only travelling companion.

Now, though a great many questions had been asked on all sides, one question especially, namely, whether *it*—people always dropped their voices when they pronounced that small pronoun—whether *it* would not be put in the hold as soon as they got on board the *Washington*, the answer to which question was an affirmative, and gave considerable satisfaction—except indeed to one moody old gentleman, who asked, "How about getting any little thing one happened to want on the journey out of the hold?" and was very properly snubbed for the suggestion, and told that passengers had no business to want things out of the hold on the voyage; and furthermore insulted by the liveliest of the lively travellers, who suggested, in an audible aside, that perhaps the old gentleman had only one clean shirt, and had put that at the bottom of his travelling chest,—now, though, I say, so many questions had been asked, no one had as yet presumed to address the cheerful-looking gentleman convoying the American of distinction home to his friends, though this very gentleman might, after all, be naturally supposed to know more than anybody else about the subject. He was smoking a cigar, and though he kept very close to the coffin, he was about the only person on board who did not look at it, but kept his gaze fixed on the fading town of Liverpool. The Smasher, Gus, and Mr. Peters's unknown ally stood very close to this gentleman, while the detective himself leant over the side of the vessel, near to, though a little apart from, the Irish labourers and rosy-cheeked country girls, who, as steerage passengers, very properly herded together, and did not attempt to contaminate by their presence the minds or the garments of those superior beings who were to occupy state-cabins six feet long by three feet wide, and to have green peas and new milk from the cow all the way out. Presently, the elderly gentleman of rather shabby-genteel but clerical appearance, who had so briefly introduced himself to Gus and the Smasher, made some remarks about the town of Liverpool to the cheerful friend of the late distinguished American.

The cheerful friend took his cigar out of his mouth, smiled, and said, "Yes; it's a thriving town, a small London, really—the metropolis in miniature."

"You know Liverpool very well?" asked the Smasher's companion.

"No, not very well; in point of fact, I know very little of England at all. My visit has been a brief one."

He is evidently an American from this remark, though there is very little of brother Jonathan in his manner.

"Your visit has been a brief one? Indeed. And it has had a very melancholy termination, I regret to perceive," said the persevering stranger, on whose every word the Smasher and Mr. Darley hung respectfully.

"A very melancholy termination," replied the gentleman, with the sweetest smile. "My poor friend had hoped to return to the bosom of his family, and delight them many an evening round the cheerful hearth by the recital of his adventures in, and impressions of, the mother country. You cannot imagine," he continued, speaking very slowly, and as he spoke, allowing his eyes to wander from the stranger to the Smasher, and from the Smasher to Gus, with a glance which, if anything, had the slightest shade of anxiety in it; "you cannot imagine the interest we on the other side of the Atlantic take in everything that occurs in the mother country. We may be great over there—we may be rich over there—we may be universally beloved and respected over there,—but I doubt—I really, after all, doubt," he said sentimentally, "whether we are truly happy. We sigh for the wings of a dove, or to speak practically, for our travelling expenses, that we may come over here and be at rest."

"And yet I conclude it was the especial wish of your late friend to be buried over there?" asked the stranger.

"It was—his dying wish."

"And the melancholy duty of complying with that wish devolved on you?" said the stranger, with a degree of puerile curiosity and frivolous interest in an affair entirely irrelevant to the matter in hand which bewildered Gus, and at which the Smasher palpably turned up his nose; muttering to himself at the same time that the forrin swell would have time to get to America while they was a-palaverin' and a-jawin' this 'ere humbug.

"Yes, it devolved on me," replied the cheerful gentleman, offering his cigar-case to the three friends, who declined the proffered weeds. "We were connections; his mother's half-sister married my second cousin—not very nearly connected certainly, but extremely attached to each other. It will be a melancholy satisfaction to his poor widow to see his ashes entombed upon his native shore, and the thought of that repays me threefold for anything I may suffer."

He looked altogether far too airy and charming a creature to suffer very much; but the stranger bowed gravely, and Gus, looking towards the prow of the vessel, perceived the earnest eyes of Mr. Peters attentively fixed on the little group.

As to the Smasher, he was so utterly disgusted with the stranger's manner of doing business, that he abandoned himself to his own thoughts and hummed a tune—the tune appertaining to what is generally called a comic song, being the last passages in the life of a humble and unfortunate member of the working classes as related by himself.

While talking to the cheerful gentleman on this very melancholy subject, the stranger from Liverpool happened to get quite close to the coffin, and, with an admirable freedom from prejudice which astonished the other passengers standing near, rested his hand carelessly on the stout oaken lid, just at that corner where the canvas left it exposed. It was a most speaking proof of the almost overstrained feeling of devotion possessed by the cheerful gentleman towards his late friend that this trifling action seemed to disturb him; his eyes wandered uneasily towards the stranger's black-gloved hand, and at last, when, in absence of mind, the stranger actually drew the heavy covering completely over this corner of the coffin, his uneasiness reached a climax, and drawing the dingy drapery hurriedly back, he rearranged it in its old fashion.

"Don't you wish the coffin to be entirely covered?" asked the stranger quietly.

"Yes—no; that is," said the cheerful gentleman, with some embarrassment in his tone, "that is—I—you see there is something of profanity in a stranger's hand approaching the remains of those we love."

"Suppose, then," said his interlocutor, "we take a turn about the deck? This neighbourhood must be very painful to you."

"On the contrary," replied the cheerful gentleman, "you will think me, I dare say, a very singular person, but I prefer remaining by him to the last. The coffin will be put in the hold as soon as we get on board the *Washington;* then my duty will have been accomplished and my mind will be at rest. You go to New York with us?" he asked.

"I shall have that pleasure," replied the stranger.

"And your friend—your sporting friend?" asked the gentleman, with a rather supercilious glance at the many-coloured raiment and mottled-soap complexion of the Smasher, who was still singing *sotto voce*[27] the above-mentioned melody, with his arms folded on the rail of the bench on which he was seated, and his chin resting moodily on his coat-sleeves.

"No," replied the stranger; "my friends, I regret to say, leave me as soon as we get on board."

In a few minutes more they reached the side of the brave ship, which, from the Liverpool quay, had looked a white-winged speck not a bit too big for Queen Mab; but which was, oh, such a Leviathan of a vessel when you stood just under her, and had to go up her side by means of a ladder—which ladder seemed to be subject to shivering fits, and struck terror into the nervous lady and the bald-headed parrot.

All the passengers, except the cheerful gentleman with the coffin and the stranger—with Gus and the Smasher and Mr. Peters loitering in the background—seemed bent on getting up each before the other, and considerably increased the confusion by evincing this wish in a candid but not conciliating manner, showing a degree of ill-feeling which was much increased by the passengers that had not got on board looking daggers at the passengers that had got on board, and seemed settled quite comfortably high and dry upon the stately deck. At last, however, every one but the aforesaid group had ascended the ladder. Some stout sailors were preparing great ropes wherewith to haul up the coffin, and the cheerful gentleman was busily directing them, when the captain of the steamer said to the stranger from Liverpool, as he loitered at the bottom of the ladder, with Mr. Peters at his elbow,—"Now then, sir, if you're for the *Washington*, quick's the word. We're off as soon as ever they've got that job over," pointing to the coffin. The stranger from Liverpool, instead of complying with this very natural request, whispered a few words into the ear of the captain, who looked very grave on hearing them, and then, advancing to the cheerful gentleman, who was very anxious and very uneasy about the manner in which the coffin was to be hauled up the side of the vessel, he laid a heavy hand upon his shoulder, and said,—"I want the lid of that coffin taken off before those men haul it up."

Such a change came over the face of the cheerful gentleman as only comes over the face of a man who knows that he is playing a desperate game, and knows as surely that he has lost it. "My good sir," he said, "you're mad. Not for the Queen of England would I see that coffin-lid unscrewed."

"I don't think it will give us so much trouble as that," said the other quietly. "I very much doubt its being screwed down at all. You were greatly alarmed just now, lest the person within should be smothered. You were terribly frightened when I drew the heavy canvas over those incisions in the oak," he added, pointing to the lid, in the corner of which two or three cracks were apparent to the close observer.

"Good Heavens! the man is mad!" cried the gentleman, whose manner had entirely lost its airiness. "The man is evidently a maniac! This is too dreadful! Is the sanctity of death to be profaned in this manner? Are we to cross the Atlantic in the company of a madman?"

"You are not to cross the Atlantic at all just yet," said the Liverpool stranger. "The man is not mad, I assure you, but he is one of the principal members of the Liverpool detective police force, and is empowered to arrest a person who is supposed to be on board this boat. There is only one place in which that person can be concealed. Here is my warrant to arrest Jabez North, *alias* Raymond Marolles, *alias* the Count de Marolles. I know as certainly as that I myself stand here that he lies hidden in that coffin, and I desire that the lid may be removed. If I am mistaken, it can be immediately replaced, and I shall be ready to render you my most fervent apologies for having profaned the repose of the dead. Now, Peters!"

The dumb detective went to one end of the coffin, while his colleague stood at the other. The Liverpool officer was correct in his supposition. The lid was only secured by two or three long stout nails, and gave way in three minutes. The two detectives lifted it off the coffin—and there, hot, flushed, and panting, half-suffocated, with desperation in his wicked blue eyes, his teeth locked in furious rage at his utter powerlessness to escape from the grasp of his pursuers—there, run to earth at last, lay the accomplished Raymond, Count de Marolles!

They put the handcuffs on him before they lifted him out of the coffin, the Smasher assisting. Years after, when the Smasher grew to be an older and graver man, he used to tell to admiring and awe-stricken customers the story of this arrest. But it is to be observed that his memory on these occasions was wont to play him false, for he omitted to mention either the Liverpool detective or our good friend Mr. Peters as taking any part in the capture; but described the whole affair as conducted by himself alone, with an incalculable number of "I says," and "so then I thinks," and "well, what do I do next?" and other phrases of the same description.

The Count de Marolles, with tumbled hair, and a white face and blue lips, sitting handcuffed upon the bench of the steamer between the Liverpool detective and Mr. Peters, steaming back to Liverpool, was a sight not good to look upon. The cheerful gentleman sat with the Smasher and Mr. Darley, who had been told to keep an eye upon him, and who—the Smasher especially—kept both eyes upon him with a will.

Throughout the little voyage there were no words spoken but these from the Liverpool detective, as he first put the fetters on the white and slender wrists of his prisoner: "Monsieur de Marolles," he said, "you've tried this little game once before. This is the second occasion, I understand, on which you've done a sham die. I'd have you beware of the third time. According to superstitious people, it's generally fatal."

CHAPTER VI

THE END OF THE DARK ROAD

Once more Slopperton-on-the-Sloshy rang with a subject dismissed from the public mind eight years ago, and now revived with a great deal more excitement and discussion than ever. That subject was, the murder of Mr. Montague Harding. All Slopperton made itself into one voice, and spoke but upon one theme—the pending trial of another man for that very crime of which Richard Marwood had been found guilty years ago—Richard, who, according to report, had died in an attempt to escape from the county asylum.

Very little was known of the criminal, but a great deal was conjectured; a great deal more was invented; and ultimately, most conflicting reports were spread abroad by the citizens of Slopperton, every one of whom had his particular account of the seizure of De Marolles, and every one of whom stood to his view of the case with a pertinacity and fortitude worthy of a better cause. Thus, if you went into High Street, entering that thoroughfare from the Market-place, you would hear how this De Marolles was a French nobleman, who had crossed the Channel in an open boat on the night of the murder, walked from Dover to Slopperton—(not above two hundred miles by the shortest cut)—and gone back to Calais in the same manner. If, staggered by the slight discrepancies of time and place in this account of the transaction, you pursued your inquiries a little further down the same street, you would very likely be told that De Marolles was no Frenchman at all, but the son of a clergyman in the next county, whose unfortunate mother was at that moment on her knees in the throne-room at Buckingham Palace, soliciting his pardon on account of his connection with the clerical interest. If this story struck you as more romantic than probable, you had only to turn the corner into Little Market Street—(rather a low neighbourhood, and chiefly inhabited by butchers and the tripe and cow-heel trade)—and you might sup full of horrors, the denizens of this locality labouring under the fixed conviction that the prisoner then lying in Slopperton gaol was neither more nor less than a distinguished burglar, long the scourge of the united kingdoms of Great Britain and Ireland, and guilty of outrages and murders innumerable.

There were others who confined themselves to animated and detailed descriptions of the attempted escape and capture of the accused. These congregated at street-corners, and disputed and gesticulated in little groups, one man often dropping back from his companions, and taking a wide berth on the pavement, to give his particular story the benefit of illustrative action. Some stories told how the prisoner had got half-way to America concealed in the paddle wheel of a screw steamer; others gave an animated account of his having been found hidden in the corner of the engine-room, where he had lain concealed for fourteen days without either bite or sup. Others told you he had been furled up in the foretopsail of an American man-of-war; others related how he had made the passage in the main-top of the same vessel, only descending in the dead of the night for his meals, and paying the captain of the ship a quarter of a million of money for the accommodation. As to the sums of money he had embezzled in his capacity of banker, they grew with every hour; till at last Slopperton turned up its nose at anything under a billion for the sum total of his plunder.

The assizes were looked forward to with such eager expectation and interest as never had been felt about any other assizes within the memory of living Slopperton; and the judges and barristers on this circuit were the envy of judges and barristers on other circuits, who said bitterly, that no such case ever came across their way, and that it was like Prius Q.C.'s luck to be counsel for the prosecution in such a trial; and that if Nisi, whom the Count de Marolles had intrusted with his defence, didn't get him off, he, Nisi, deserved to be hung in lieu of his client.

It seemed a strange and awful instance of retributive justice that Raymond Marolles, having been taken in his endeavour to escape in the autumn of the year, had to await the spring assizes of the following year for his trial, and had, therefore, to drag out even a longer period in his solitary cell than Richard Marwood, the innocent victim of circumstantial evidence, had done years before.

Who shall dare to enter this man's cell? Who shall dare to look into this hardened heart? Who shall follow the dark and terrible speculations of this perverted intellect?

At last the time, so welcome to the free citizens of Slopperton, and so very unwelcome to some of the denizens in the gaol, who preferred awaiting their trial in that retreat to crossing the briny ocean for an unlimited period as the issue of that trial—at last, the assize time came round once more. Once more the tip-top Slopperton hotels were bewilderingly gay with elegant young barristers and grave grey-headed judges. Once more the criminal court was one vast sea of human heads, rising wave on wave to the very roof; and once more every eager eye was turned towards the dock in which stood the elegant and accomplished Raymond, Count de Marolles, *alias* Jabez North, sometime pauper of the Slopperton-on-the-Sloshy Union, afterwards usher in the academy of Dr. Tappenden, charged with the wilful murder of Montague Harding, also of Slopperton, eight years before.

The first point the counsel for the prosecution endeavoured to prove to the minds of the jury was the identity of Raymond de Marolles, the Parisian, with Jabez North, the pauper schoolboy. This hinged chiefly upon his power to disprove the supposed death of Jabez North, in which all Slopperton had hitherto firmly believed. Dr. Tappenden had stood by his usher's corpse. How, then, could that usher be alive and before the Slopperton jury to-day? But there were plenty to certify that here he was in the flesh—this very Jabez North, whom so many people remembered, and had been in the habit of seeing, eight years ago. They were ready to identify him, in spite of his dark hair and eyebrows. On the other hand, there were some who had seen the body of the suicide, found by Peters the detective, on the heath outside Slopperton; and these were as ready to declare that the afore-mentioned body was the body of Jabez North, the usher to Dr. Tappenden, and none other. But when a rough-looking man, with a mangy fur cap in his hand, and two greasy locks of hair carefully twisted into limp curls on either side of his swarthy face, which curls were known to his poetically and figuratively-disposed friends as Newgate knockers—when this man, who gave his name to the jury as Slithery Bill—or, seeing the jury didn't approve of this cognomen, Bill Withers, if they liked it better—was called into the witness-box, his evidence, sulkily and rather despondingly given, as from one who says, "It may be my turn next," threw quite a new light upon the subject.

Bill Withers was politely asked if he remembered the summer of

18——. Yes; Mr. Withers could remember the summer of 18——; was out of work that summer, and made the marginal remark that "them as couldn't live might starve or steal, for all Slopperton folks cared."

Was again politely asked if he remembered doing one particular job of work that summer.

Did remember it—made the marginal remark, "and it was a jolly queer dodge as ever a cove had a hand in."

Was asked to be good enough to state what the particular job was.

Assented to the request with a polite nod of the head, and proceeded to smooth his Newgate knockers, and fold his arms on the ledge of the witness-box prior to stating his case; then cleared his throat, and commenced discursively, thus,—

"Vy, it vas as this 'ere—I vas out of work. I does up small gent's gardens in the spring, and tidies and veeds and rakes and hoes 'em a bit, back and front, vhen I can get it to do, vich ain't often; and bein' out of vork, and old Mother Thingamy, down Blind Peter, she ses to me, vich she vas a vicked old 'ag, she ses to me, 'I've got a job for them as asks no questions, and don't vant to be told no lies;' by vich remark, and the vay of her altogether, I knowed she veren't up to no good; so I ses, 'You looks here, mother; if it's a job a respectable young man, vot's out o' vork, and ain't had a bite or sup since the day afore yesterday, can do vith a clear conscience, I'll do it—if it ain't, vy I von't. There!' " Having recorded which heroic declaration, Mr. William Withers wiped his mouth with the back of his hand, and looked round the court, as much as to say, "Let Slopperton be proud of such a citizen."

" 'Don't you go to flurry your tender constitution and do yourself a unrecoverable injury,' the old cat made reply; 'it's a job as the parson of the parish might do, if he'd got a truck.' 'A truck?' I ses; 'is it movin' boxes you're making this 'ere palaver about?' 'Never you mind vether it's boxes or vether it ain't; vill you do it?' she ses; 'vill you do it, and put a sovering in your pocket, and never go for to split, unless you vant that precious throat of yours slit some fine evenin'?' "

"And you consented to do what she required of you?" suggested the counsel.

"Vell, I don't know about that," replied Mr. Withers, "but I un-dertook the job. 'So,' ses she, that's the old 'un, she ses, 'you bring a truck down by that there broken buildin' ground at the back of Blind Peter at ten o'clock to-night, and you keep yourself quiet till you hears a vhistle; ven you hears a vhistle,' she ses, 'bring your truck around agin our front door. This here's all *you've* got to do,' she ses, 'besides keepin' your tongue between your teeth.' 'All right,' I ses, and off I goes to see if there was any cove as would trust me with a truck agen the evenin'. Vell, I finds the cove, vich, seein' I wanted it bad, he stood out for a bob[1] and a tanner[2] for the loan of it."

"Perhaps the jury would wish to be told what sum of money—I conclude it is money—a bob and a tanner represent?" said the counsel.

"They must be a jolly ignorant lot, then, anyways," replied Mr. Withers, with more candour than circumlocution. "Any infant knows eighteenpence ven it's showed him."

"Oh, a bob and a tanner are eighteenpence? Very good," said the counsel, encouragingly; "pray go on, Mr. Withers."

"Vell, ten o'clock come, and veren't it a precious stormy night, that's all; and there I was a-vaitin' a-sittin' on this blessed truck at the back of Blind Peter, vich vos my directions. At last the vhistle come, and a precious cautious vhistle it vas too, as soft as a niteingel vot's payin' its addresses to another niteingel; and round I goes to the front, as vos my directions. There, agen' her door, stands the old 'ag, and agen her stands a young man in an old ragged pair of trousis an' a shirt. Lookin' him hard in the face, who does I see but Jim, the old un's grandson; so I ses, 'Jim!' friendly like, but he makes no reply; and then the old un ses, 'Lend this young gent a 'and 'ere, vill yer?' So in I goes, and there on the bed I sees something rolled up very careful in a old counterpane. It giv' me a turn like, and I didn't much like the looks of it; but I ses nothink; and then the young man, Jim, as I thinks, ses, 'Lend us a hand with this 'ere, vill yer?' and it giv'd me another turn like, for though it's Jim's face, somehow it ain't quite Jim's voice—more genteel and fine like; but I goes up to the bed, and I takes hold of von end of vot lays there;

and then I gets turn number three—for I find my suspicions was correct—it was a dead body!"

"A dead body?"

"Yes; but whose it vos there vos no knowin', it vos wrapped up in that manner. But I feels myself turn dreadful vhite, and I ses, 'If this ere's anythink wrong, I vashes my hands ov it, and you may do your dirty vork yourself.' I hadn't got the vords out afore this 'ere young man, as I thought at first vos Jim, caught me by the throat sudden, and threw me down on my knee. I ain't a baby; but, lor', I vos nothink in his grasp, though his hand vos as vite and as deliket as a young lady's. 'Now, you just look 'ere,' he says; and I looked, as vell as I could, vith my eyes a-startin' out ov my head in cosekence of bein' just upon the choke, 'you see vot this is,' and vith his left hand he takes a pistol out ov his pocket; 'you refuse to do vot ve vant done, or you go for to be noisy or in any vay ill-conwenient, and it's the last time as ever you'll have the chance ov so doing. Get up,' he says, as if I vos a dog; and I gets up, and I agrees to do vot he vants, for there vas that there devil in that young man's hye, that I began to think it vos best not to go agen him."

Here Mr. Withers paused for refreshment after his exertion and blew his nose very deliberately on a handkerchief which, from its dilapidated condition, resembled a red cotton cabbage-net.[3] Silence reigned throughout the crowded court, broken only by the scratching of the pen with which the counsel for the defence was taking notes of the evidence, and the fluttering of the leaves of the reporters' pocket-books, as they threw off page after page of flimsy paper.

The prisoner at the bar looked straight before him; the firmly-compressed lips had never once quivered, the golden fringed eye-lashes had never drooped.

"Can you tell me," said the counsel for the prosecution, "whether you have ever, since that night, seen this young man, who so closely resembled your old friend, Jim?"

"Never seen him since, to my knowledge"—there was a flutter in the crowded court, as if every spectator had simultaneously drawn a long breath—"till to-day."

"Till to-day?" said the counsel. This time it was more than a flutter, it was a subdued murmur that ran through the listening crowd.

"Be good enough to say if you can see him at this present moment."

"I can," replied Mr. Withers. "That's him! or my name ain't vot I've been led to believe it is." And he pointed with a dirty but decided finger at the prisoner at the bar.

The prisoner slightly elevated his arched eyebrows superciliously, as if he would say, "This is a pretty sort of witness to hang a man of my standing."

"Be so good as to continue your story," said the counsel.

"Vell, I does vot he tells me, and I lays the body, vith his 'elp, on the truck. 'Now,' he ses, 'follow this 'ere old voman and do everythink vot she tells you, or you'll find it considerably vorse for your future 'appiness;' vith vich he slams the door upon me, the old un, and the truck, and I sees no more of 'im. Vell, I follows the old un through a lot o' lanes and back slums, till ve leaves the town behind, and gets right out upon the 'eath; and ve crosses over the 'eath, till ve comes to vere it's precious lonely, yet the hedge of the pathway like; and 'ere she tells me as ve're to leave the body, and 'ere ve shifts it off the truck and lays it down upon the grass, vich it vas a-rainin' 'eavens 'ard, and a-thunderin' and a-lightnin' like von o'clock. 'And now,' she ses, 'vot you've got to do is to go back from vheres you come from, and lose no time about it; and take notice,' she ses, 'if ever you speaks or jabbers about this 'ere business, it'll be the end of your jabberin' in this world,' vith vitch she looks at me like a old vitch as she vos, and points vith her skinny arm down the road. So I valks my chalks, but I doesn't valk 'em very far, and presently I sees the old 'ag a-runnin' back tovards the town as fast as ever she could tear. 'Ho!' I ses, 'you are a nice lot, you are; but I'll see who's dead, in spite of you.' So I crawls up to vere ve'd left the body, and there it vos sure enuff, but all uncovered now, the face a-starin' up at the black sky, and it vos dressed, as far as I could make out, quite like a gentleman, all in black, but it vos so jolly dark I couldn't see the face, vhen all of a sudden, vhile I vos a-kneelin' down and lookin' at it, there comes von of the longest flashes of lightnin' as I ever remember, and in the blue light I sees the face plainer than I could have seen it in the day. I thought I should have fell down all of a-heap. It vos Jim! Jim hisself, as I knowed as well as I ever knowed myself, dead at my feet! My first thought vos as how that young man as vos so like Jim had murdered him; but there vorn't no marks of wiolence novheres about the body. Now, I hadn't in my own mind any doubts as how it vos Jim; but still, I ses to myself, I ses, 'Everythink seems topsy-turvy like this night, so I'll be sure;' so I takes up his arm, and turns up his coat-sleeve. Now, vy I does this is this 'ere: there vos a young voman Jim vos uncommon fond ov, vhich her name vos Bess, though he and many more called her, for short, Sillikens: and von day vhen me and Jim vos at a public, ve happened to fall in vith a sailor, vot ve'd both knowed afore he vent to sea. So he vos a-tellin' of us his adventures and such-like, and then he said promiscus, 'I'll show you somethin' pretty;' and sure enuff, he slipped up the sleeve ov his Garnsey, and there, all over his arm, vos all manner ov sort ov picters done vith gunpowder, such as ankers, and Rule Britannias, and ships in full sail on the backs of flyin' alligators. So Jim takes quite a fancy to this 'ere, and he ses, 'I vish, Joe (the sailor's name bein' Joe), I vish, Joe, as how you'd do me my young voman's name and a wreath of roses on my arm, like that there.' Joe ses, 'And so I vill, and velcome.' And sure enuff, a veek or two artervards, Jim comes to me vith his arm like a picter-book, and Bess as large as life just above the elber-joint. So I turns up his coat-sleeve, and vaits for a flash ov lightnin'. I hasn't to vait long, and there I reads, 'B.E.S.S.' 'There ain't no doubt now,' I ses, 'this 'ere's Jim, and there's some willany or other in it, vot I ain't up to.' "

"Very good," said the counsel; "we may want you again by-and-by, I think, Mr. Withers; but for the present you may retire."

The next witness called was Dr. Tappenden, who related the circumstances of the admission of Jabez North into his household, the high character he had from the Board of the Slopperton Union, and the confidence reposed in him.

"You placed great trust, then, in this person?" asked the counsel for the prosecution.

"The most implicit trust," replied the schoolmaster; "so much so, that he was frequently employed by me to collect subscriptions for a public charity of which I was the treasurer—the Slopperton Orphan Asylum. I think it only right to mention this, as on one occasion it was the cause of his calling upon the unfortunate gentleman who was murdered."

"Indeed! Will you be so good as to relate the circumstance?"

"I think it was about three days before the murder, when, one morning, at a little before twelve o'clock—that being the time at which my pupils are dismissed from their studies for an hour's recreation—I said to him, 'Mr. North, I should like you to call upon this Indian gentleman, who is staying with Mrs. Marwood, and whose wealth is so much talked of——"

"Pardon me. You said, 'whose wealth is so much talked of.' Can you swear to having made that remark?"

"I can."

"Pray continue," said the counsel.

" 'I should like you,' I said, 'to call upon this Mr. Harding, and solicit his aid for the Orphan Asylum; we are sadly in want of funds. I know, North, your heart is in the work, and you will plead the cause of the orphans successfully. You have an hour before dinner; it is some distance to the Black Mill, but you can walk fast there and back.' He went accordingly, and on his return brought a five-pound note, which Mr. Harding had given him."

Dr. Tappenden proceeded to describe the circumstance of the death of the little boy in the usher's apartment, on the very night of the murder. One of the servants was examined, who slept on the same floor as North, and who said she had heard strange noises in his room that night, but had attributed the noises to the fact of the usher sitting up to attend upon the invalid. She was asked what were the noises she had heard.

"I heard some one open the window, and shut it a long while after."

"How long do you imagine the interval to have been between the opening and shutting of the window?" asked the counsel.

"About two hours," she replied, "as far as I could guess."

The next witness for the prosecution was the old servant, Martha.

"Can you remember ever having seen the prisoner at the bar?"

The old woman put on her spectacles, and steadfastly regarded the elegant Monsieur de Marolles, or Jabez North, as his enemies insisted on calling him. After a very deliberate inspection of that gentleman's personal advantages, rather trying to the feelings of the spectators, Mrs. Martha Jones said, rather obscurely—

"He had light hair then."

" 'He had light hair then.' You mean, I conclude," said the counsel, "that at the time of your first seeing the prisoner, his hair was of a different colour from what it is now. Supposing that he had dyed his hair, as is not an uncommon practice, can you swear that you have seen him before to-day?"

"I can."

"On what occasion?" asked the counsel.

"Three days before the murder of my mistress's poor brother. I opened the gate for him. He was very civil-spoken, and admired the garden very much, and asked me if he might look about it a little."

"He asked you to allow him to look about the garden? Pray was this as he went in, or as he went out?"

"It was when I let him out."

"And how long did he stay with Mr. Harding?"

"Not more than ten minutes. Mr. Harding was in his bedroom; he had a cabinet in his bedroom in which he kept papers and money, and he used to transact all his business there, and sometimes would be there till dinner-time."

"Did the prisoner see him in his bedroom?"

"He did. I showed him upstairs myself."

"Was anybody in the bedroom with Mr. Harding when he saw the prisoner?"

"Only his coloured servant: he was always with him."

"And when you showed the prisoner out, he asked to be allowed to look at the garden? Was he long looking about?"

"Not more than five minutes. He looked more at the house than the garden. I noticed him looking at Mr. Harding's window, which is on the first floor; he took particular notice of a very fine creeper that grows under the window."

"Was the window, on the night of the murder, fastened, or not?"

"It never was fastened. Mr. Harding always slept with his window a little way open."

After Martha had been dismissed from the witness-box, the old servant of Mr. Harding, the Lascar, who had been found living with a gentleman in London, was duly sworn, prior to being examined.

He remembered the prisoner at the bar, but made the same remark as Martha had done, about the change in colour of his hair.

"You were in the room with your late master when the prisoner called upon him?" asked the counsel.

"I was."

"Will you state what passed between the prisoner and your master?"

"It is scarcely in my power to do so. At that time I understood no English. My master was seated at his cabinet, looking over papers and accounts. I fancy the prisoner asked him for money. He showed him papers both printed and written. My master opened a pocket-book filled with notes, the pocket-book afterwards found on his nephew, and gave the prisoner a bank note. The prisoner appeared to make a good impression on my late master, who talked to him in a very cordial manner. As he was leaving the room, the prisoner made some remark about me, and I thought from the tone of his voice, he was asking a question."

"You thought he was asking a question?"

"Yes. In the Hindostanee language we have no interrogative form of speech, we depend entirely on the inflexion of the voice; our ears are therefore more acute than an Englishman's. I am certain he asked my master some questions about me."

"And your master——?"

"After replying to him, turned to me, and said, 'I am telling this gentleman what a faithful fellow you are, Mujeebez, and how you always sleep in my dressing-room.'"

"You remember nothing more?"

"Nothing more."

The Indian's deposition, taken in the hospital at the time of the trial of Richard Marwood, was then read over to him. He certified to the truth of this deposition, and left the witness-box.

The landlord of the Bargeman's Delight, Mr. Darley, and Mr. Peters (the latter by an interpreter), were examined, and the story of the quarrel and the lost Indian coin was elicited, making considerable impression on the jury.

There was only one more witness for the crown, and this was a young man, a chemist, who had been an apprentice at the time of the supposed death of Jabez North, and who had sold to him a few days before that supposed suicide the materials for a hair-dye.

The counsel for the prosecution then summed up.

It is not for us to follow him through the twistings and windings of a very complicated mass of evidence; he had to prove the identity of Jabez North with the prisoner at the bar, and he had to prove that Jabez North was the murderer of Mr. Montague Harding. To the mind of every spectator in that crowded court he succeeded in proving both.

In vain the prisoner's counsel examined and cross-examined the witnesses.

The witnesses for the defence were few. A Frenchman, who represented himself as a Chevalier of the Legion of Honour, failed signally in an endeavour to prove an *alibi,* and considerably damaged the defence. Other witnesses appeared, who swore to having known the prisoner in Paris the year of the murder. They could not say they had seen him during the November of that year—it might have been earlier, it might have been later. On being cross-examined, they broke down ignominiously, and acknowledged that it might not have been that year at all. But they *had* known him in Paris *about* that period. They had always believed him to be a Frenchman. They had always understood that his father fell at Waterloo, in the ranks of the Old Guard. On cross-examination they all owned to having heard him at divers periods speak English. He had, in fact, spoken it fluently, yes, even like an Englishman. On further cross-examination it also appeared that he did not like being thought an Englishman; that he would insist vehemently upon his

French extraction; that nobody knew who he was, or whence he came; and that all any one did know of him was what he himself had chosen to state.

The defence was long and laboured. The prisoner's counsel did not enter into the question of the murder having been committed by Jabez North, or not having been committed by Jabez North. What he endeavoured to show was, that the prisoner at the bar was not Jabez North; but that he was a victim to one of those cases of mistaken identity of which there are so many on record both in English and foreign criminal archives. He cited the execution of the Frenchman Joseph Lesurges, for the murder of the Courier of Lyons.[4] He spoke of the case of Elizabeth Canning,[5] in which a crowd of witnesses on either side persisted in supporting entirely conflicting statements, without any evident motive whatsoever. He endeavoured to dissect the evidence of Mr. William Withers; he sneered at that worthy citizen's wholesale slaughter of the English of her most gracious Majesty and subjects. He tried to overthrow that gentleman by ten minutes on the wrong side of the Slopperton clocks; he did his best to damage him by puzzling him as to whether the truck he spoke of had two legs and one wheel, or two wheels and one leg: but he tried in vain. Mr. Withers was not to be damaged; he stood as firm as a rock, and still swore that he carried the dead body of Jim Lomax out of Blind Peter and on to the heath, and that the man who commanded him so to do was the prisoner at the bar. Neither was Mr. Augustus Darley to be damaged; nor yet the landlord of the Bargeman's Delight, who, in spite of all cross-examination, preserved a gloomy and resolute attitude, and declared that "that young man at the bar, which his hair was then light, had a row with a young woman in the tap-room, and throwed that there gold coin to her, which she chucked it back savage." In short, the defence, though it lasted two hours and a half, was a very lame one; and a close observer might have seen one flash from the blue eyes of the man standing at the bar, which glanced in the direction of the eloquent Mr. Prius, Q.C., as he uttered the last words of his peroration, revengeful and murderous enough, brief though it was, to give to the spectator some idea that the Count de Marolles, in-

nocent and injured victim of circumstantial evidence as he might
be, was not the safest person in the world to offend.

The judge delivered his charge to the jury, and they retired.

There was breathless impatience in the court for three-quarters
of an hour; such impatience that the three-quarters seemed to be
three entire hours, and some of the spectators would have it that
the clock had stopped. Once more the jury took their places.

"Guilty!" A recommendation to mercy? No! Mercy was not for
such as he. Not man's mercy. Oh, Heaven be praised that there is
One whose mercy is as far above the mercy of the tenderest of
earth's creatures as heaven is above that earth. Who shall say where
is the man so wicked he may not hope for compassion *there?*

The judge put on the black cap and delivered the sentence.

"To be hanged by the neck!"

The Count de Marolles looked round at the crowd. It was beginning to disperse, when he lifted his slender ringed white hand. He
was about to speak. The crowd, swaying hither and thither before,
stopped as one man. As one man, nay, as one surging wave of the
ocean, changed, in a breath, to stone. He smiled a bitter mocking
defiant smile.

"Worthy citizens of Slopperton," he said, his clear enunciation
ringing through the building distinct and musical, "I thank you for
the trouble you have taken this day on my account. I have played a
great game, and I have lost a great stake; but, remember, I first won
that stake, and for eight years held it and enjoyed it. I have been the
husband of one of the most beautiful and richest women in France.
I have been a millionaire, and one of the wealthiest merchant
princes of the wealthy south. I started from the workhouse of this
town; I never in my life had a friend to help me or a relation to advise me. To man I owe nothing. To God I owe only this, a will as indomitable as the stars He made, which have held their course
through all time. Unloved, unaided, unprayed for, unwept; motherless, fatherless, sisterless, brotherless, friendless; I have taken my
own road, and have kept to it; defying the earth on which I have
lived, and the unknown Powers above my head. That road has come
to an end, and brought me—here! So be it! I suppose, after all, the

unknown Powers are strongest! Gentlemen, I am ready." He bowed and followed the officials who led him from the dock to a coach waiting for him at the entrance to the court. The crowd gathered round him with scared faces and eager eyes.

The last Slopperton saw of the Count de Marolles was a pale handsome face, a sardonic smile, and the delicate white hand which rested upon the door of the hackney-coach.

Next morning, very early, men with grave faces congregated at street-corners, and talked together earnestly. Through Slopperton like wildfire spread the rumour of something, which had only been darkly hinted at the gaol.

The prisoner had destroyed himself!

Later in the afternoon it was known that he had bled himself to death by means of a lancet not bigger than a pin, which he had worn for years concealed in a chased gold ring of massive form and exquisite workmanship.

The gaoler had found him, at six o'clock on the morning after his trial, seated, with his bloodless face lying on the little table of his cell, white, tranquil, and dead.

The agents from an exhibition of wax-works, and several phre-nologists, came to look at and to take casts of his head, and masks of the handsome and aristocratic face. One of the phrenologists, who had given an opinion on his cerebral development ten years before, when Mr. Jabez North was considered a model of all Sloppertonian virtues and graces, and who had been treated with ignominy for that very opinion, was now in the highest spirits, and introduced the whole story into a series of lectures, which were afterwards very popular. The Count de Marolles, with very long eyelashes, very small feet, and patent-leather boots, a faultless Stultsian[6] evening costume, a white waistcoat, and any number of rings, was much admired in the Chamber of Horrors at the eminent wax-work exhibition above mentioned, and was considered well worth the extra sixpence for admission. Young ladies fell in love with him, and vowed that a being—they called him a being—with such dear blue glass eyes, with beautiful curly eyelashes, and specks of lovely vermilion in each corner, could never have committed a horrid murder, but was, no doubt, the innocent victim of that cruel circumstantial evidence. Mr. Splitters put the Count into a melodrama in four periods—not acts, but periods: 1. Boyhood—the Workhouse. 2. Youth—the School. 3. Manhood—the Palace. 4. Death—the Dungeon. This piece was very popular, and as Mr. Percy Cordonner had prophesied, the Count was represented as living *en permanence* in Hessian boots with gold tassels; and as always appearing, with a spirited disregard for the unities of time and space,[7] two or three hundred miles distant from the spot in which he had appeared five minutes before, and performing in scene four the very action which his foes had described as being already done in scene three. But the transpontine audiences to whom the piece was represented were not in the habit of asking questions, and as long as you gave them plenty of Hessian boots and pistol-shots for their money, you might snap your fingers at Aristotle's ethics,[8] and all the Greek dramatists into the bargain. What would they have cared for the classic school? Would they have given a thank-you for "Zaire, vous pleurez!"[9] or "Qu'il mourut!"[10] No; give them enough blue fire[11] and honest British sentiment, with plenty of chintz waistcoats and top-boots, and you might laugh Corneille[12] and Voltaire to scorn, and be sure of a long run on the Surrey side of the water.

So the race was run, and, after all, the cleverest horse was not the winner. Where was the Countess de Marolles during her husband's trial? Alas! Valerie, thine has been a troubled youth, but it may be that a brighter fate is yet in store for thee!

CHAPTER THE LAST

FAREWELL TO ENGLAND

Scarcely had Slopperton subsided in some degree from the excitement into which it had been thrown by the trial and suicide of Raymond de Marolles, when it was again astir with news, which was, if anything, more exciting. It is needless to say that after the trial and condemnation of De Marolles, there was not a little regretful sympathy felt by the good citizens of Slopperton for their unfortunate townsman, Richard Marwood, who, after having been found guilty of a murder he had never committed, had perished, as the story went, in a futile attempt to escape from the asylum in which he had been confined. What, then, were the feelings of Slopperton when, about a month after the suicide of the murderer of Montague Harding, a paragraph appeared in one of the local papers which stated positively that Mr. Richard Marwood was still alive, he having succeeded in escaping from the county asylum?

This was enough. Here was a hero of romance indeed; here was innocence triumphant for once in real life, as on the mimic scene. Slopperton was wild with one universal desire to embrace so distinguished a citizen. The local papers of the following week were full of the subject, and Richard Marwood was earnestly solicited to appear once more in his native town, that every inhabitant thereof, from the highest to the lowest, might be enabled to testify heartfelt sympathy for his undeserved misfortunes, and sincere delight in his happy restoration to name and fame.

The hero was not long in replying to the friendly petition of the inhabitants of his native place. A letter from Richard appeared in one of the papers, in which he stated that as he was about to leave England for a considerable period, perhaps for ever, he should do himself the honour of responding to the kind wishes of his friends, and once more shake hands with the acquaintance of his youth before he left his native country.

The Sloppertonian Jack-in-the-green,[1] assisted by the rather stalwart damsels in dirty pink gauze and crumpled blue-and-yellow artificial flowers, had scarcely ushered in the sweet spring month of the year, when Slopperton arose simultaneously and hurried as one man to the railway-station, to welcome the hero of the day. The report has spread—no one ever knows how these reports arise—that Mr. Richard Marwood is to arrive this day. Slopperton must be at hand to bid him welcome to his native town, to repair the wrong it has so long done him in holding him up to universal detestation as the George Barnwell[2] of modern times.

Which train will he come by? There is a whisper of the three o'clock express; and at three o'clock in the afternoon, therefore, the station and station-yard are crowded.

The Slopperton station, like most other stations, is built at a little distance from the town, so that the humble traveller who arrives by the parliamentary train,[3] with all his earthly possessions in a red cotton pocket-handkerchief or a brown-paper parcel, and to whom such things as cabs are unknown luxuries, is often disappointed to find that when he gets to Slopperton station he is not in Slopperton proper. There is a great Sahara of building-ground and incomplete brick-and-mortar, very much to let, to be crossed before the traveller finds himself in High Street, or South Street, or East Street, or any of the populous neighbourhoods of this magnificent city.

Every disadvantage, however, is generally counterbalanced by some advantage, and nothing could be more suitable than this grand Sahara of broken ground and unfinished neighbourhood for the purposes of a triumphal entry into Slopperton.

There is a great deal of animated conversation going on upon the platform inside the station. It is a noticeable fact that everybody present—and there are some hundreds—appears to have been intimately acquainted with Richard from his very babyhood. This one remembers many a game at cricket with him on those very fields yonder; another would be a rich man if he had only a sovereign for every cigar he has smoked in the society of Mr. Marwood. That old gentleman yonder taught our hero his declensions, and always had a difficulty with him about the ablative[4] case. The elderly female with the dropsical[5] umbrella had nursed him as a baby; "and the finest baby he was as ever I saw," she adds enthusiastically. Those two gentlemen who came down to the station in their own brougham are the kind doctors who carried him through that terrible brain-fever of his early youth, and whose evidence was of some service to him at his trial. Everywhere along the crowded platform there are friends; noisy excited gesticulating friends, who have started a hero on their own account, and who wouldn't turn aside to-day to get a bow from majesty itself.

Five minutes to three. From the doctor's fifty-guinea chronometer, by Benson, to the silver turnip from the wide buff waistcoat of the farmer, everybody's watch is out, and nobody will believe but that his particular time is the right time, and every other watch, and the station clock into the bargain, wrong.

Two minutes to three. Clang goes the great bell. The station-master clears the line. Here it comes, only a speck of dull red fire as yet, and a slender column of curling smoke; but the London express for all that. Here it comes, wildly tearing up the tender green country, rushing headlong through the smoky suburbs; it comes within a few hundred yards of the station; and there, amidst a labyrinth of straggling lines and a chaos of empty carriages and disabled engines, it stops deliberately for the ticket-collectors to go their accustomed round.

Good gracious me, how badly those ticket-collectors do their duty!—how slow they are!—what a time the elderly females in the second class appear to be fumbling in their reticules before they produce the required document!—what an age, in short, it is before the train puffs lazily up to the platform; and yet, only two minutes by the station-clock.

Which is he? There is a long line of carriages. The eager eyes look into each. There is a fat dark man with large whiskers reading the paper. Is that Richard? He may be altered, you know, they say; but surely eight years could never have changed him into that. No! there he is! There is no mistaking him this time. The handsome dark face, with the thick black moustache, and the clustering frame of waving raven hair, looks out of a first-class carriage. In another moment he is on the platform, a lady by his side, young and pretty, who bursts into tears as the crowd press around him, and hides her face on an elderly lady's shoulder. That elderly lady is his mother. How eagerly the Sloppertonians gather round him! He does not speak, but stretches out both his hands, which are nearly shaken off his wrists before he knows where he is.

Why doesn't he speak? Is it because he cannot? Is it because there is a choking sensation in his throat, and his lips refuse to articulate the words that are trembling upon them? Is it because he remembers the last time he alighted on this very platform—the time when he wore handcuffs on his wrists and walked guarded between two men; that bitter time when the crowd held aloof from him, and pointed him out as a murderer and a villain? There is a mist over his dark eyes as he looks round at those eager friendly faces, and he is glad to slouch his hat over his forehead, and to walk quickly through the crowd to the carriage waiting for him in the station-yard. He has his mother on one arm and the young lady on the other; his old friend Gus Darley is with him too; and the four step into the carriage.

Then, how the cheers and the huzzas burst forth, in one great hoarse shout! Three cheers for Richard, for his mother, for his faithful friend Gus Darley, who assisted him to escape from the lunatic asylum, for the young lady—but who is the young lady? Everybody is so anxious to know who the young lady is, that when Richard introduces her to the doctors, the crowd presses round, and putting aside ceremony, openly and deliberately listens. Good Heavens! the young lady is his wife, the sister of his friend Mr. Darley, "who wasn't afraid to trust me," the crowd heard him say, "when the world was against me, and who in adversity or prosperity alike was ready to bless me with her devoted love." Good gracious me! More cheers for the young lady. The young lady is Mrs. Marwood. Three cheers for Mrs. Marwood! Three cheers for Mr. and Mrs. Marwood! Three cheers for the happy pair!

At length the cheering is over—or, at least, over for the moment. Slopperton is in such an excited state that it is easy to see it will break out again by-and-by. The coachman gives a preliminary flourish of his whip as a signal to his fiery steeds. Fiery steeds, indeed! "Nothing so common as a horse shall carry Richard Marwood into Slopperton," cry the excited townspeople. We ourselves will draw the carriage—we, the respectable tradespeople—we, the tag-rag and bob-tail, anybody and everybody—will make ourselves for the nonce beasts of burden, and think it no disgrace to draw the triumphal car of this our townsman. In vain Richard remonstrates. His handsome face—his radiant smiles, only rekindle the citizens' enthusiasm. They think of the bright young scapegrace whom they all knew years ago. They think of his very faults—which were virtues in the eyes of the populace. They remember the day he caned a policeman who had laid violent hands on a helpless little boy for begging in the streets—the night he wrenched off the knocker of an unpopular magistrate who had been hard upon a poacher. They recalled a hundred escapades for which those even who reproved him had admired him; and they gather round the carriage in which he stands with his hat off, the May sunlight in his bright hazel eyes, his dark hair waving in the spring breeze around his wide candid brow, and one slender hand stretched out to restrain, if he can, this tempest of enthusiasm. Restrain it?—No! that is not to be done. You can go and stand upon the shore and address yourselves to the waves of the sea; you can mildly remonstrate with the wolf as to his intentions with regard to the innocent lamb; but you *cannot* check the enthusiasm of a hearty British crowd when its feelings are excited in a good cause.

Away the carriage goes! with the noisy populace about the wheels. What is this?—music? Yes; two opposition bands. One is playing "See, the conquering hero comes!" while the other exhausts itself, and gets black in the face, with the exertion necessary in doing justice to "Rule Britannia." At last, however, the hotel is reached. But the triumph of Richard is not yet finished. He must make a speech. He does, ultimately, consent to say a few words in answer to the earnest entreaties of that clamorous crowd. He tells his friends, in a very few simple sentences, how this hour, of all others, is the hour for which he has prayed for nearly nine long years; and how he sees, in the most trifling circumstances which have aided, however remotely, in bringing this hour to pass, the hand of an all-powerful Providence. He tells them how he sees in these years of sorrow through which he has passed a punishment for the careless sins of his youth, for the unhappiness he has caused his devoted mother, and for his indifference to the blessings Heaven has bestowed on him; how he now prays to be more worthy of the bright future which lies so fair before him; how he means the rest of his life to be an earnest and a useful one; and how, to the last hour of that life, he will retain the memory of their generous and enthusiastic reception of him this day. It is doubtful how much more he might have said; but just at this point his eyes became pe-

culiarly affected—perhaps by the dust, perhaps by the sunshine—
and he was forced once more to have recourse to his hat, which he
pulled fairly over those optics prior to springing out of the carriage
and hurrying into the hotel, amidst the frantic cheers of the sterner
sex, and the audible sobs of the fairer portion of the community.

His visit was but a flying one. The night train was to take him
across country to Liverpool, whence he was to start the following
day for South America. This was kept, however, a profound secret
from the crowd, which might else have insisted on giving him a second ovation. It was not very quickly dispersed, this enthusiastic
throng. It lingered for a long time under the windows of the hotel.
It drank a great deal of bottled ale and London porter in the bar
round the corner by the stable-yard; and it steadfastly refused to go
away until it had had Richard out upon the balcony several times,
and had given him a great many more tumultuous greetings. When
it had quite exhausted Richard (our hero looking pale from over-
excitement) it took to Mr. Darley as vice-hero, and would have carried him round the town with one of the bands of music, had he not
prudently declined that offer. It was so bent on doing something,
that at last, when it did consent to go away, it went into the Market-
place and had a fight—not from any pugilistic or vindictive feeling,
but from the simple necessity of finishing the evening somehow.

There is no possibility of sitting down to dinner till after dark.
But at last the shutters are closed and the curtains are drawn by the
obsequious waiters; the dinner-table is spread with glittering plate
and snowy linen; the landlord himself brings in the soup and un-
corks the sherry, and the little party draws round the social board.
Why should we break in upon that happy group? With the wife he
loves, the mother whose devotion has survived every trial, the
friend whose aid has brought about his restoration to freedom and
society, with ample wealth wherefrom to reward all who have
served him in his adversity, what more has Richard to wish for?

A close carriage conveys the little party to the station; and by the
twelve o'clock train they leave Slopperton, some of them perhaps
never to visit it again.

The next day a much larger party is assembled on board the

Oronoko, a vessel lying off Liverpool, and about to sail for South America. Richard is there, his wife and mother still by his side; and there are several others whom we know grouped about the deck. Mr. Peters is there. He has come to bid farewell to the young man in whose fortunes and misfortunes he has taken so warm and unfailing an interest. He is a man of independent property now, thanks to Richard, who thinks the hundred-a-year settled on him a very small reward for his devotion—but he is very melancholy at parting with the master he has so loved.

"I think, sir," he says on his fingers, "I shall marry Kuppins, and give my mind to the education of the 'fondling.' He'll be a great man, sir, if he lives; for his heart, boy as he is, is all in his profession. Would you believe it, sir, that child bellowed for three mortal hours because his father committed suicide, and disappointed the boy of seein' him hung? That's what I calls a love of business, and no mistake."

On the other side of the deck there is a little group which Richard presently joins. A lady and gentleman and a little boy are standing there; and, at a short distance from them, a grave-looking man with dark-blue spectacles, and a servant—a Lascar.

There is a peculiar style about the gentleman, on whose arm the lady leans, that bespeaks him to the most casual observer to be a military man, in spite of his plain dress and loose greatcoat. And the lady on his arm, that dark classic face, is not one to be easily forgotten. It is Valerie de Cevennes, who leans on the arm of her first and beloved husband, Gaston de Lancy. If I have said little of this meeting—of this restoration of the only man she ever loved, which has been to her as a resurrection of the dead—it is because there are some joys which, from their very intensity, are too painful and too sacred for many words. He was restored to her. She had never murdered him. The potion given her by Blurosset was a very powerful opiate, which had produced a sleep resembling death in all its outward symptoms. Through the influence of the chemist the report of the death was spread abroad. The truth, except to Gaston's most devoted friends, had never been revealed. But the blow had been too much for him; and when he was told by whom his death had been attempted, he fell into a fever, which lasted for many months, during which period his reason was entirely lost, and from which he was only rescued by the devotion of the chemist—a devotion on Blurosset's part which, perhaps, had proceeded as much from love of the science he studied as of the man he saved. Recovering at last, Gaston de Lancy found that the glorious voice which had been his fortune was entirely gone. What was there for him to do? He enlisted in the East India Company's[6] service; rose through the Sikh campaign[7] with a rapidity which astonished the bravest of his compeers. There was a romance about his story that made him a hero in his regiment. He was known to have plenty of money—to have had no earthly reason for enlisting; but he told them he would rise, as his father had done before him, in the wars of the Empire, by merit alone, and he had kept his word. The French ensign, the lieutenant, the captain—in each rising grade he had been alike beloved, alike admired, as a shining example of reckless courage and military genius.

The arrest of the *soi-disant*[8] Count de Marolles had brought Richard Marwood and Gaston de Lancy into contact. Both sufferers from the consummate perfidy of one man, they became acquainted, and, ere long, friends. Some part of Gaston's story was told to Richard and his young wife, Isabella; but it is needless to say, that the dark past in which Valerie was concerned remained a secret in the breast of her husband, of Laurent Blurosset, and herself. The father clasped his son to his heart, and opened his arms to receive the wife whom he had pardoned long ago, and whose years of terrible agony had atoned for the wildly-attempted crime of her youth.

On Richard and Gaston becoming fast friends, it had been agreed between them that Richard should join De Lancy and his wife in South America; where, far from the scenes which association had made painful to both, they might commence a new existence. Valerie, once more mistress of that immense fortune of which De Marolles had so long had the command, was enabled to bestow it on the husband of her choice. The bank was closed in a manner satisfactory to all whose interests had been connected with it. The cashier, who was no other than the lively gentleman who had assisted in De Marolles's attempted escape, was arrested on a charge of embezzlement, and made to disgorge the money he had abstracted.

The Marquis de Cevennes elevated his delicately-arched eyebrows on reading an abridged account of the trial of his son, and his subsequent suicide; but the elegant Parisian did not go into mourning for this unfortunate scion of his aristocratic house; and indeed, it is doubtful if five minutes after he had thrown aside the journal he had any sensation whatever about the painful circumstances therein related. He expressed the same gentlemanly surprise upon being informed of the marriage of his niece with Captain Lansdown, late of the East India Company's service, and of her approaching departure with her husband for her South American estates. He sent her his blessing and a breakfast-service; with the portraits of Louis the Well-beloved, Madame du Barry,[9] Choiseul,[10] and D'Aiguillon,[11] painted on the cups, in oval medallions, on a background of turquoise, packed in a casket of buhl lined with white velvet; and, I dare say, he dismissed his niece and her troubles from his recollection quite as easily as he despatched this elegant present to the railway which was to convey it to its destination.

The bell rings; the friends of the passengers drop down the side of the vessel into the little Liverpool steamer. There are Mr. Peters and Gus Darley waving their hats in the distance. Farewell, old and faithful friends, farewell; but surely not for ever. Isabella sinks sobbing on her husband's shoulder. Valerie looks with those deep unfathomable eyes out towards the blue horizon-line that bounds the far-away to which they go.

"There, Gaston, we shall forget——"

"Never your long sufferings, my Valerie," he murmurs, as he presses the little hand resting on his arm; "those shall never be forgotten."

"And the horror of that dreadful night, Gaston——"

"Was the madness of a love which thought itself wronged, Valerie; we can forgive every wrong which springs from the depth of such a love."

Spread thy white wings, oh, ship! The shadows melt away into that purple distance. I see in that far South two happy homes; glistening white-walled villas, half buried in the luxuriant verdure of that lovely climate. I hear the voices of the children in the dark orange-groves, where the scented blossoms fall into the marble basin of the fountain. I see Richard reclining in an easy-chair, under the veranda, half hidden by the trailing jasmines that shroud it from the evening sunshine, smoking the long cherry-stemmed pipe which his wife has filled for him. Gaston paces, with his sharp military step, up and down the terrace at their feet, stopping as he passes by to lay a caressing hand on the dark curls of the son he loves. And Valerie—she leans against the slender pillar of the porch, round which the scented yellow roses are twined, and watches, with earnest eyes, the husband of her earliest choice. Oh, happy shadows! Few in this work-a-day world so fortunate as you who win in your prime of life the fulfilment of the dear dream of your youth!

AFTERWORD

Chris Willis

The Trail of the Serpent is probably the first British detective novel. When Mary Elizabeth Braddon wrote it in 1860, detective fiction barely existed. There were many novels and stage melodramas about crime, but these usually focused on the exploits of the criminal rather than the process of detection.[1] In America, Edgar Allan Poe's short stories "The Murders in the Rue Morgue" (1841), "The Mystery of Marie Rogêt" (1842), "The Gold Bug" (1843), and "The Purloined Letter" (1845) laid down many of the conventions of the detective genre, but few British writers followed Poe's example. Dickens's *Bleak House* (1853) included a police detective, Inspector Bucket, who solves a murder, but this is a minor part of a complex story.[2] Wilkie Collins's short story "The Diary of Anne Rodway" (1859) featured English fiction's first female detective—a milliner who investigates the death of her friend and brings the killer to justice. But there were no detective novels as such. The nearest thing was the semiautobiographical "casebook" genre, such as the bestselling fictionalized memoirs of French police chief Eugène Vidocq, published in 1828–29.[3] Vidocq's work was an influence on Poe[4] as well as on Braddon, who mentions him in *The Trail of the Serpent* (p. 364). English equivalents included *Scenes in the Life of a*

Bow Street Runner (1827) by "Richmond" and *Recollections of a Detective Police Officer* (c. 1856) by "Waters" (a pseudonym of journalist William Russell), both of which recounted cases investigated by official detectives.

Braddon's achievement was to take the conventions of popular novels, casebooks, and stage melodrama and fuse them into a detective novel. Working-class policeman Peters has strong similarities with the hard-working detectives of the casebooks. Jabez North was modeled on the type of criminal featured in melodrama—an evil mastermind with no redeeming features. The plot of *The Trail of the Serpent* has strong similarities with popular melodramas such as Charles Reade's adaptation of the French drama *The Courier of Lyons,* which Braddon mentions on p. 394. In both texts, a man is wrongly convicted of murder, and his friends work to clear him. This has been one of the staple plots of detective fiction ever since. In *The Trail of the Serpent,* this plot has two parallel threads: North's criminal career and Peters's detective work. As North rises higher in the world, the pursuit intensifies and the reader becomes aware that Peters will inevitably track him down. Unlike many later detective stories, *The Trail of the Serpent* is not so much a whodunnit as a "howdunnit." The murderer's identity is clear from the start. The interest lies in the process of detection: How will enough evidence be found to convince the police to bring North to justice?

The growth of detective fiction in the U.K. has strong links with the development of the detective police force. Until the 1840s, there were no police detectives in Britain. The Detective Branch of London's Metropolitan Police was established on August 15, 1842. This was a plainclothes force of permanent official police detectives, based at Scotland Yard and headed by Inspector Nicholas Pearce. For many years the Metropolitan Police remained the only force with a specialist detective branch, hence the custom of "calling in Scotland Yard" to investigate murders that baffled the local police. After a series of high-profile mid-century murder cases, the public gradually became more interested in the work of the detectives, creating a market for detective fiction.

When *The Trail of the Serpent* was released in book form in 1861, it became a bestseller, and other authors soon realized that detective fiction was a highly marketable commodity. Twentieth-century critic R. F. Stewart credits "Miss Braddon and her monstrous regiment of imitators" with inventing a genre in which crime is "at the heart of a story."[5] The most successful of these novels was Wilkie Collins's *The Moonstone*. Like *The Trail of the Serpent*, it features a police detective and is centered on a crime. Collins borrowed one of Braddon's cleverest character inventions—the juvenile detective. Braddon's "Sloshy" is a forerunner of *The Moonstone*'s boy detective "Gooseberry," and both can be seen as influences on Conan Doyle, who famously equipped Holmes with a whole set of juvenile colleagues known as the "Baker Street Irregulars" in *The Sign of Four* (1890). By the mid-1860s, the crime fiction genre was becoming well established, largely thanks to Braddon and Collins. In 1864, the *Westminster Review* commented that "If it be good to stimulate our predatory instincts... while we trace the dodgings and doublings of an accomplished scoundrel matched with an adroit detective, then let all praise be given to Miss Braddon."[6]

However, the term "detective fiction" was not used until the 1880s.[7] Novels such as Braddon's and Collins's were usually described as "sensation novels." Not all of these involved detection, although their plots often centered on unsolved crimes. Struggling to find a suitable term to describe Braddon's crime fiction, the *Eclectic Review* of 1868 described Braddon's novels as "Works answering all the purposes of lengthened Police Reports."[8] In 1862, Braddon's contemporary, the novelist Mrs. Oliphant, bemoaned the introduction of a detective element into fiction:

> "We have already had specimens, as many as are desirable, of what the detective policeman can do for the enlivenment of literature; and it is into the hands of the literary detective that this school of story-telling must fall at last. He is not a collaborator whom we welcome with any pleasure into the republic of letters. His appearance is neither favourable to taste nor morals."[9]

But the "literary detective" was here to stay. Readers of twentieth-century detective fiction will find many familiar elements in *The Trail of the Serpent*. North builds card houses as a form of stress relief, as does Agatha Christie's Hercule Poirot.[10] The poisoned book mentioned on p. 152 foreshadows a similar device in Umberto Eco's *The Name of the Rose* (1983). North hides in a coffin as does the hero of Michael Crichton's Victorian pastiche *The Great Train Robbery* (1975). Peters's convincing disguise as an Irish laborer and Dick's disguise as a milkman foreshadow Sherlock Holmes's use of disguise. North plants clues on a corpse to ensure that it will be wrongly identified, a device later used by Agatha Christie in *Why Didn't They Ask Evans?* (1933) and Dorothy L. Sayers in *Whose Body?* (1923). Both Christie and Sayers read Braddon. Sayers mentions her in her introduction to *The Moonstone* and Christie's short story "Greenshaw's Folly" features an old woman hiding her will in a copy of Braddon's *Lady Audley's Secret*, which, she acidly comments, is far more readable than many modern novels.

One of the greatest strengths of *The Trail of the Serpent* is the figure of the detective. Peters is a rare creation. Even nowadays, few novels feature detectives with physical disabilities.[11] In Peters, Braddon gives what is arguably one of the most positive portrayals of a disabled person in Victorian fiction. Peters is unable to speak because of a childhood illness but, paradoxically, this supposed disability gives him an extra level of ability. His use of sign language is vital to the plot, enabling him to communicate secretly with his colleagues, and to "speak" to Richard Marwood in court without the judge realizing what is going on. His enforced silence makes him all the more effective at surveillance because people wrongly assume that he is deaf, and speak unguardedly in front of him. A similar device was used by a later crime writer, Richard Marsh (who also wrote as Bernard Heldmann), in *Judith Lee* (1912). The eponymous heroine is a teacher of deaf children, who solves several crimes purely because of her ability to lip-read.

Braddon's fiction features an interesting range of detectives. In *The Black Band* (1861–62) police detectives and a disreputable-looking lawyer's clerk combine to defeat the machinations of a criminal gang. In this book, Braddon refers to police work as "that wonderful science which tracks the dark pathway of crime with such marvellous success, that we come at last to look upon the detective officer as the magician of modern life."[12] *Eleanor's Victory* (1863) features one of fiction's first (and least efficient) female detectives. Eleanor Vane haphazardly blunders her way from clue to clue, losing vital evidence on the way, and becoming so obsessed with the suspect that her long-suffering husband begins to wonder whether she is having an affair with him. A more efficient female detective is Margaret Wilmot, heroine of *Henry Dunbar* (1864), who proves herself more efficient than a professional male detective investigating the same crime. In the short story "George Caulfield's Journey" (1879), a vicar turns detective when his curate is arrested for murder. To his own surprise, the vicar turns out to be what another character describes as "a genius in the art of hunting a criminal."[13] *Wyllard's Weird* (1888) is a railway mystery in which a woman is killed by being thrown from a moving train. *Rough Justice* (1898) and *His Darling Sin* (1899) are detective novels featuring retired police detective John Faunce.

Braddon was at her best when writing about crime. Henry James compared her understanding of the criminal mind and the workings of conscience to that of Shakespeare, most notably *Macbeth*, commenting that in her and Wilkie Collins's fiction "an admirable organization of police detectives" had replaced the "avenging deity" of Fate. He felt that the only thing which marred her work was commercialism: she sought "at any hazard to make a hit, to catch the public ear."[14] Braddon herself was well aware of this, and understood the commercial appeal of crime fiction. Fifty years after writing *The Trail of the Serpent*, she wrote that:

> There is nothing that English men and women enjoy more than the crime which they call "a really good murder." ... every man is at heart a Sherlock Holmes while every woman thinks herself a criminal investigator by instinct.[15]

It is Braddon's understanding of this perennial appeal of detection that makes *The Trail of the Serpent* so compulsively readable over 140 years since it was written.

NOTES

1. William Godwin's *Caleb Williams* (1794) is sometimes said to be the first British detective novel, but its plot bears little resemblance to detective fiction as we now know it. For details, see Ousby, Ian, *Bloodhounds of Heaven* (London: Harvard University Press, 1976), pp. 19–42, and Symons, Julian, *Bloody Murder* (1975; revised and reprinted, London: Pan, 1992), pp. 31–36.

2. Dickens fictionalized the exploits of two real-life London police detectives, Inspectors Wicher and Field, in journal articles entitled "Three Detective Anecdotes" and "On Duty with Inspector Field," both of which were reprinted in *Reprinted Pieces* in 1861.

3. For further details of Vidocq, see endnote 15 on page 456.

4. See, for example, Herbert, Rosemary (ed.), *The Oxford Companion to Crime and Mystery Writing* (Oxford: Oxford University Press, 1999), p. 479.

5. Stewart, R. F., ... *And Always a Detective: Chapters in the History of Detective Fiction* (London: David & Charles, 1980), p. 34.

6. "Contemporary Literature," *Westminster Review*, 1864, cited Stewart pp. 220–21.

7. According to Braddon's biographer, Jennifer Carnell, the term "detective fiction" was first used in the *Morning Post* in 1888, in a review of H. F. Wood's *The Passenger from Scotland Yard*. See Carnell, Jennifer, *The Literary Lives of Mary Elizabeth Braddon* (Hastings: Sensation Press, 2000), p. 244.

8. Quoted in Carnell, *Literary Lives*, p. 236.

9. Mrs. Oliphant, "Sensation Novels," *Blackwood's Edinburgh Magazine*, Volume XCI (May 1862), p. 568.

10. See, for example, Christie, Agatha, *The Mysterious Affair at Styles* (1920), *Peril at End House* (1932), and *Three Act Tragedy* (1934).

11. Among the other rare examples are the hero of Edwin Balmer and William B. MacHarg's *The Blind Man's Eyes* (1916), Ernest Bramah's blind detective Max Carrados, and the wheelchair-bound hero of the 1960s detective TV series *Ironside*.

12. Braddon, Mary Elizabeth, *The Black Band* (1861–62; reprinted Hastings: Sensation Press, 1999), p. 219.

13. Braddon, Mary Elizabeth, "George Caulfield's Journey" (1879), reprinted in *Flower and Weed* (1882; reprinted London: Maxwell, c. 1884), p. 156.

14. James, Henry, review of Braddon's *Aurora Floyd* in *The Nation*, Nov. 9, 1865.

15. Braddon, Mary Elizabeth, *Beyond These Voices* (London: Hutchinson, 1910), p. 185.

APPENDIX

MY FIRST NOVEL

Mary Elizabeth Braddon

My first novel! Far back in the distinctness of childish memories I
see a little girl who has lately learnt to write, who has lately been
given a beautiful brand new mahogany desk, with a red velvet
slope, and a glass ink bottle, such a desk as might now be bought for
three and sixpence, but which in the forties cost at least half-a-
guinea. Very proud is the little girl, with the Kenwigs pigtails, and

Lichfield House, Richmond

the Kenwigs frills, of that mahogany desk, and its infinite capacities for literary labour, above all, gem of gems, its stick of variegated sealing-wax, brown, speckled with gold, and its little glass seal with an intaglio representing two doves—Pliny's doves perhaps, famous in mosaic, only the little girl had never heard of Pliny, or his Laurentine Villa.

Armed with that desk and its supply of stationery, Mary Elizabeth Braddon—very fond of writing her name at full-length, and her address also at full-length, though the word "Middlesex" offered difficulties—began that pilgrimage on the broad high road of fiction, which was destined to be a longish one. So much for the little girl of eight years old, in the third person, and now to become strictly autobiographical.

My first story was based on those fairy tales which first opened to me the world of imaginative literature. My first attempt in fiction, and in round-hand, on carefully pencilled double lines, was a

The Hall

story of two sisters, a good sister and a wicked, and I fear adhered more faithfully to the lines of the archetypal story than the writer's pen kept to the double fence which should have ensured neatness.

The interval between the ages of eight and twelve was a prolific period, fertile in unfinished MSS., among which I can now trace a historical novel on the Siege of Calais— an Eastern story, suggested by a passionate love of Miss Pardoe's Turkish tales, and Byron's "Bride of Abydos," which my mother, a devoted Byron worshipper, allowed me to read aloud to her—and doubtless murder in the reading—a story of the Hartz Mountains, with audacious flights in German diablerie; and lastly, very seriously undertaken, and very perseveringly worked upon, a domestic story, the outline of which was suggested by the same dear and sympathetic mother.

Now it is a curious fact, which may or may not be common to other story-spinners, that I have never been able to take kindly to a plot—or the suggestion of a plot—offered to me by anybody else. The moment a friend tells me that he or she is desirous of imparting a series of facts—strictly true—as if truth in fiction mattered one jot!—which in his or her opinion would make the ground plan of an admirable, startling, and altogether original three-volume novel, I know in advance that my imagination will never grapple with those startling circumstances—that my thoughts will begin to wander before my friend has got half through the remarkable chain of events, and that if the obliging purveyor of romantic incidents were to examine me at the end of the story, I should be spun ignominiously. For the most part, such subjects as have been proposed to me by friends have been hopelessly unfit for the circulating library; or, where not immoral, have been utterly dull; but it is, I believe, a fixed idea in the novel-reader's mind that any combination of events out of the beaten way of life will make an admirable subject for the novelist's art.

My dear mother, taking into consideration my tender years, and perhaps influenced in somewise by her own love of picking up odd bits of Sheraton or Chippendale furniture in the storehouses of the less ambitious second-hand dealers of those simpler days, offered me the following *scenario* for a domestic story. It was an incident which, I doubt not, she had often read at the tail of a newspaper column, and which certainly savours of the gigantic goose-berry, the sea-serpent, and the agricultural labourer who unexpectedly inherits half-a-million. It was eminently a Simple Story, and far more worthy of that title than Mrs. Inchbald's long and involved romance.

An honest couple, in humble circumstances, possess among their small household gear a good old easy chair, which has been the pride of a former generation, and is the choicest of their household gods. A comfortable cushioned chair, snug and restful, albeit the chintz covering, though clean and tidy, as virtuous people's furniture always is in fiction, is worn thin by long service, while the dear chair itself is no longer the chair it once was as to legs and framework.

Evil days come upon the praiseworthy couple and their dependent brood, among whom I faintly remember the love interest of the story to have lain; and that direful day arrives when the average landlord of juvenile fiction, whose heart is of adamant and brain of brass, distrains for the rent. The rude broker swoops upon the humble dovecot; a cart or hand-barrow waits on the carefully hearth-stoned door-step for the household gods; the family gather round the cherished chair, on which the rude broker has already laid his grimy fingers; they hang over the back and fondle the padded arms; and the old grandmother, with clasped hands, entreats that, if able to raise the money in a few days,

The Staircase

they may be allowed to buy back that loved heirloom.

The broker laughs the plea to scorn; they might have their chair, and cheap enough, he had no doubt. The cover was darned and patched—as only the virtuous poor of fiction do darn and do patch—and he made no doubt the stuffing was nothing better than brown wool; and with that coarse taunt the coarser broker dug his clasp-knife into the cushion against which grandfatherly backs had leaned in happier days, and lo! an avalanche of banknotes fell out of the much-maligned horsehair, and the family was lifted from penury to wealth. Nothing more simple—or more natural. A prudent but eccentric ancestor had chosen this mode of putting by his savings, assured that, whenever discovered, the money would be useful to—somebody.

The Dining Room

So ran the *scenario:* but I fancy my juvenile pen hardly held on to the climax. My brief experience of boarding school occurred at this time, and I well remember writing "The Old Arm Chair" in a penny account book, in the schoolroom of Cresswell Lodge, and that I was both surprised and offended at the laughter of the kindly music-teacher who, coming into the room to summon a pupil, and seeing me gravely occupied, enquired what I was doing, and was intensely amused at my stolid method of composition, plodding on undisturbed by the voices and occupations of the older girls around me. "The Old Arm Chair" was certainly my first serious, painstaking effort in fiction, but as it was abandoned unfinished before my eleventh birthday, and as no line thereof ever achieved the distinction of type, it can hardly rank as my first novel.

There came a very few years later the sentimental period, in which my unfinished novels assumed a more ambitious form, and were modelled chiefly upon Jane Eyre, with occasional tentative imitations of Thackeray. Stories of gentle hearts that loved in vain, always ending in renunciation. One romance there was, I well remember, begun with resolute purpose, after the first reading of Esmond, and in the endeavour to give life and local colour to a story of the Restoration period, a brilliantly wicked interval in the social history of England, which, after the lapse of thirty years, I am still as bent upon taking for the background of a love story as I was when I began "Master Anthony's Record" in Esmondese, and made my girlish acquaintance with the Reading-room of the British Museum, where I went in quest of local colour, and where much kindness was shown to my youth and inexperience of the book world. Poring over a folio edition of the State Trials at my uncle's quiet rectory in sleepy Sandwich, I had discovered the passionate romantic story of Lord Grey's elopement with his sister-in-law, next in sequence to the trial of Lawrence Braddon and Hugh Speke for conspiracy. At the risk of seeming disloyal to my own race, I must add that it seemed to me a very tinpot order of plot to which these two learned gentlemen bent their legal minds, and which cost the Braddon family a heavy fine in land near Camelford—confiscation which I have heard my father complain of as especially unfair,

Lawrence being a younger son. The romantic story of Lord Grey was to be the subject of "Master Anthony's Record," but Master Anthony's sentimental autobiography went the way of all my earlier efforts. It was but a year or so after the collapse of Master Anthony, that a blindly-enterprising printer of Beverley, who had seen my poor little verses in the *Beverley Recorder,* made me the spirited offer of ten pounds for a serial story, to be set up and printed at

The Drawing-Room

Beverley, and published on commission by a London firm in Warwick Lane. I cannot picture to myself, in my after-knowledge of the bookselling trade, any enterprise more futile in its inception or more feeble in its execution; but to my youthful ambition the actual commission to write a novel, with an advance payment of fifty shillings to show good faith on the part of my Yorkshire speculator, seemed like the opening of that pen-and-ink paradise which I had sighed for ever since I could hold a pen. I had, previously to this date, found a Mæcenas in Beverley, in the person of a learned gentleman who volunteered to foster my love of the Muses by buying the copyright of a volume of poems and publishing the same at his own expense—which he did, poor man, without stint, and by which noble patronage of Poet's Corner verse, he must have lost money. He had, however, the privilege of dictating the subject of the principal poem, which was to sing—however feebly—Garibaldi's Sicilian campaign.

The Beverley printer suggested that my Warwick Lane serial should combine, as far as my powers allowed, the human interest and genial humour of Dickens with the plot-weaving of G. W. R. Reynolds; and, furnished with these broad instructions, I filled my ink bottle, spread out my fools-cap, and, on a hopelessly wet afternoon, began my first novel—now known as "The Trail of the Serpent"—but published in Warwick Lane, and later in the stirring High Street of Beverley, as "Three Times Dead." In "Three Times Dead" I gave loose to all my leanings to the violent in melodrama. Death stalked in ghastliest form across my pages; and villainy reigned triumphant till the Nemesis of the last chapter. I wrote with all the freedom of one who feared not the face of a critic; and, indeed, thanks to the obscurity of its original production, and its re-issue as the ordinary two-shilling railway novel, this first novel of mine has almost entirely escaped the critical lash, and has pursued its way as a chartered libertine. People buy it and read it, and its faults and follies are forgiven as the exuberances of a pen unchastened by experience; but faster and more facile at that initial stage than it ever became after long practice.

I dashed headlong at my work, conjured up my images of horror or of mirth, and boldly built the framework of my story, and set my puppets moving. To me, at least, they were living creatures, who seemed to follow impulses of their own, to be impelled by their own passions, to love and hate, and plot and scheme of their own accord. There was unalloyed pleasure in the composition of that first story, and the knowledge that it was to be actually printed and published, and not to be declined with thanks by adamantine magazine editors, like a certain short story which I had lately written, and which contained the germ of "Lady Audley's Secret." Indeed, at this period of my life, the postman's knock had become associated in my mind with the sharp sound of a rejected MS. dropping through the open letterbox on to the floor of the hall, while my heart seemed to drop in sympathy with that book-post packet.

The Library

Short of never being printed at all, my Beverley-born novel could have hardly entered upon the world of books in a more profound obscurity. That one living creature ever bought a number of "Three Times Dead" I greatly doubt. I can recall the thrill of emotion with which I tore open the envelope that contained my complimentary copy of the first number, folded across, and in aspect inferior to a gratis pamphlet about a patent medicine. The miserable little wood block which illustrated that first number would have disgraced a baker's whitey-brown bag, would have been unworthy to illustrate a penny bun. My spirits were certainly dashed at the technical shortcomings of that first serial, and I was hardly surprised when I was informed a few weeks later, that although my admirers at Beverley were deeply interested in the story, it was not a financial success, and that it would be only obliging on my part, and in accordance with my known kindness of heart, if I were to restrict the development of the romance to half its intended length, and to accept five pounds in lieu of ten as my reward. Having no desire that the rash Beverley printer should squander his own or his children's fortune in the obscurity of Warwick Lane, I immediately acceded to his request, shortened sail, and went on with my story, perhaps with a shade less enthusiasm, having seen the shabby figure it was to make in the book world. I may add that the Beverley publisher's payments began and ended with his noble advance of fifty shillings. The balance was never paid; and it was rather hard lines that, on his becoming bankrupt in his poor little way a few years later, a judge in the Bankruptcy Court remarked that, as Miss Braddon was now making a good deal of money by her pen, she ought to "come to the relief" of her first publisher.

And now my volume of verses being well under weigh, I went with my mother to farm-house lodgings in the neighbourhood of that very Beverley, where I spent, perhaps, the happiest half-year of my life—half a year of tranquil, studious days, far from the madding crowd, with the mother whose society was always all sufficient for me—half a year among level pastures, with unlimited books from the library in Hull, an old farm-horse to ride about the green lanes, the breath of summer, with all its sweet odours of flower and herb, around and about us: half a year of unalloyed bliss, had it not been for one dark shadow, the heroic figure of Garibaldi, the sailor-soldier, looming large upon the foreground of my literary labours, as the hero of a lengthy narrative poem in the Spenserian metre.

My chief business at Beverley was to complete the volume of verse commissioned by my Yorkshire Mæcenas, at that time a very rich man, who paid me a much better price for my literary work than his townsman, the enterprising printer, and who had the first claim on my thought and time.

With the business-like punctuality of a salaried clerk, I went every morning to my file of the *Times,* and pored and puzzled over Neapolitan revolution and Sicilian campaign, and I can only say that if Emile Zola has suffered as much over Sedan as I suffered in the freshness of my youth, when flowery meadows and the old chestnut mare invited to summer idlesse, over the fighting in Sicily, his dogged perseverance in uncongenial labour should place him among the Immortal Forty. How I hated the great Joseph G. and the Spenserian metre, with its exacting demands upon the rhyming faculty. How I hated my own ignorance of modern Italian history, and my own eyes for never having looked upon Italian landscape, whereby historical allusion and local colour were both wanting to that dry-as-dust record of heroic endeavour. I had only the *Times* correspondent; where he was picturesque I could be picturesque—allowing always for the Spenserian straining—

Miss Braddon's Favourite Mare

where he was rich in local colour I did my utmost to reproduce his colouring, stretched always on the Spenserian rack, and lengthened out by the bitter necessity of finding triple rhymes. Next to Guiseppe Garibaldi I hated Edmund Spenser, and it may be from a vengeful remembrance of those early struggles with a difficult form of versification, that, although throughout my literary life I have been a lover of England's earlier poet, and have delighted in the quaintness and *naïveté* of Chaucer, I have refrained from reading more than a casual stanza or two of the "Faëry Queen." When I lived at Beverley, Spenser was to me but a name, and Byron's "Childe Harold" was my

only model for that exacting verse. I should add that the Beverley
Mæcenas, when commissioning this volume of verse, was less superb
in his ideas than the literary patron of the past. He looked at the matter from a purely commercial standpoint, and believed that a volume
of verse, such as I could produce, would pay—a delusion on his part
which I honestly strove to combat before accepting his handsome
offer of remuneration for my time and labour. It was with this idea in
his mind that he chose and insisted upon the Sicilian Campaign as a
subject for my muse, and thus started me heavily handicapped on the
racecourse of Parnassus.

Miss Braddon's Cottage at Lyndhurst

The weekly number of "Three Times Dead" was "thrown off"
in brief intervals of rest from my *magnum opus,* and it was an infinite
relief to turn from Garibaldi and his brothers in arms to the angels
and the monsters which my own brain had engendered, and which
to me seemed more alive than the good great man whose arms I so
laboriously sang. My rustic pipe far better loved to sing of melodramatic poisoners and ubiquitous detectives; of fine houses in the
West of London, and dark dens in the East. So the weekly chapter
of my first novel ran merrily off my pen while the printer's boy
waited in the farm-house kitchen.

Happy, happy days, so near to memory, and yet so far. In that
peaceful summer I finished my first novel, knocked Garibaldi on
the head with a closing rhapsody, saw the York spring and summer
races in hopelessly wet weather, learnt to love the Yorkshire people,

and left Yorkshire almost broken-heartedly on a dull gray October morning, to travel Londonwards through a landscape that was mostly under water.

And, behold, since that October morning I have written fifty-three novels; I have lost dear old friends and found new friends, who are also dear, but I have never looked on a Yorkshire landscape since I turned my reluctant eyes from those level meadows and green lanes where the old chestnut mare used to carry me ploddingly to and fro between tall, tangled hedges of eglantine and honeysuckle.

Illustrations by Miss F. L. Fuller

NOTES

I would like to acknowledge my debt to Jennifer Carnell's The Literary Lives of Mary Elizabeth Braddon *(Hastings: Sensation Press, 2000) and Robert Lee Wolff's* Sensational Victorian: The Life and Fiction of Mary Elizabeth Braddon *(New York: Garland, 1979). I would also like to acknowledge the help of Jennifer Carnell, Stuart Egan, Jane Ennis, Wendy Hall, Rose Johnston, Les Kirkham, J. P. Lodge, Charlotte Mitchell, Ros Tatham, Ernest C. Willis, Peter Wood, the members of the Victoria List and Braddon List, and the staff of the Rare Books and Music Reading Room at the British Library.* —Chris Willis

EPIGRAPH

1. The quotation is from "Paradise and the Peri" by the Irish poet Thomas Moore (1779–1852). "Paradise and the Peri" is the second of four "poetical tales" in Thomas Moore's book-length poem *Lalla Rookh* (1817). It is about a "peri," or spirit, who tries to gain admission to heaven. Braddon also cites "The Veiled Prophet of Khorassan," the first "poetical tale," which is about Mokanna, on p. 299 of the novel *(see also note 3 on p. 451).* Braddon herself appeared as Lalla Rookh in a musical burlesque by Robert Brough, which was performed at the Theatre Royal, Brighton, in August 1858. (For details see Jennifer Carnell, *The Literary Lives of Mary Elizabeth Braddon* [Hastings: Sensation Press, 2000], 56, 339–40.)

BOOK THE FIRST. A RESPECTABLE YOUNG MAN
CHAPTER I. THE GOOD SCHOOLMASTER

1. *laudanum:* a mixture of opium and alcohol, used as a sedative.
2. *Police Reports:* reports of criminal activity circulated by the police or printed in the popular press.
3. *thank Heaven that they are not as other men:* a reference to the biblical parable of the publican and the Pharisee (Luke 18:10–14), which

warns against arrogance. "Two men went up into the temple to pray; the one a Pharisee, and the other a publican. The Pharisee stood and prayed thus with himself, 'God, I thank thee that I am not as other men are, extortionists, unjust, adulterers, or even as this publican. I fast twice a week, I give tithes of all that I possess.' And the publican standing afar off, would not lift up so much as his eyes to heaven, but smote upon his breast, saying, 'God be merciful to me, a sinner,' I tell you, this man went down to his house justified rather than the other; for everyone who exalteth himself shall be abased and he that humbleth himself shall be exalted." The story would have been familiar to most educated Victorians.

4. *usher:* an unqualified junior schoolteacher, usually very badly paid.

5. *Allecompain Major:* If two or more brothers were pupils in the same school, they would be known by their surnames plus a Latin suffix. The eldest Allecompain would be Allecompain Major, the second Allecompain Minor, and the third (if there was one) Allecompain Minimus.

6. *organ of conscientiousness...phrenology:* Phrenology was the "science" of making deductions about a person's character from the shape of his or her skull. Different parts of the head were thought to correspond to different character traits. Most Victorians believed strongly in this "science," which has now been discredited.

7. *jack-towel:* towel hung on a roller for communal use.

8. *drab:* prostitute.

9. *copper-plate:* a type of elegant handwriting taught in Victorian schools. A typeface based on copper-plate handwriting was often used for business cards.

10. *Virgil:* Publius Vergilius Maro (70–19 B.C.) was a Latin poet, most famous for his epic poem the *Aeneid,* which recounted the adventures of Trojan hero Aeneas, who traveled the world after surviving the fall of Troy. The *Aeneid* was commonly used for teaching Latin in Victorian and early-twentieth-century schools.

11. *construe:* translate from Latin into English.

12. *acid rock:* Victorian term for what is now known simply as rock, or seaside rock. It was traditionally made from sugar, water, and tartaric acid.

CHAPTER II. GOOD FOR NOTHING

1. *East Indies:* India, so called to distinguish it from the Caribbean islands, which were known as the West Indies.

2. *half-caste:* person of mixed race—in this case half-Indian, half-white.

3. *lacs of rupees:* Rupees were the currency of India. Lac, or lakh, is a Hindi word for 100,000.

4. *liver:* In Victorian times, Englishmen who had spent many years in India were usually assumed to have liver problems as a result of drinking alcohol in the heat.

5. *Anglo-Indian:* Nowadays this term is used to denote a person of mixed race (Indian and British), but in Victorian times it meant an English person who had spent most of his or her life in India.

6. *Havannah:* cigar from Havana.

7. *sea-coal:* Today this term is only used to describe coal gathered from beaches, but during the nineteenth century it was often used to describe all coal.

8. *still a little boy in a pinafore and frock:* In the nineteenth century it was the custom for the English upper classes to dress boys and girls in the same way until the age of about seven, when the boy would be given his first pair of trousers.

9. *Lascar:* an East Indian soldier, sailor, or servant.

CHAPTER III. THE USHER WASHES HIS HANDS

1. *smock-frock:* a loose, baggy overshirt (usually white) worn by male farmhands and other countrymen.

2. *gaiters:* a leather or waterproof cloth covering for the lower leg and ankle, worn over shoes.

3. *scratch wig:* a wig covering only part of the head.

4. *"Opium—Poison!":* There was no legal restriction on the sale of opium in the U.K. until 1868, and it was often prescribed by doctors as a painkiller. Opium-taking was not made illegal in the U.K. until the 1920s.

CHAPTER IV. RICHARD MARWOOD LIGHTS HIS PIPE

1. *sovereign:* gold coin, with a value of one pound sterling.

2. *commercial traveller:* traveling salesperson.

3. *cursed Jews:* moneylenders.

4. *writ:* legal document demanding money.

5. *organ of adhesiveness:* See note 6 on p. 429.

6. bijouterie: jewelry or small, delicate trinkets.

7. *Wictoria Theayter:* the Victoria Theatre, in New Cut, in the Waterloo area of London. Showing mainly melodramas, the theater was notori-

ous for its rough, noisy, working-class audiences. In 1861, John Hollingshead wrote, "It is a large, well-built house, and has been celebrated, in its time, for good acting; but it is now one of the 'three-penny theatres,' giving a very coarse kind of drama, suited to its audiences. The fittings are faded, the walls are smeared with greasy dirt, the pit floor is muddy and half covered with orange peel and broken bottles, and the whole place is a little cleaner than the courts and alleys at its back, but nothing more. The audience are worth looking at; and on the night of a popular drama, such as 'Oliver Twist,' or 'Jack Sheppard,' the gallery presents a most extraordinary picture. Half the evil, low-browed, lowering faces in London are wedged in, twelve-hundred deep, perspiring, watchful, silent. Every man is in his yellow shirt sleeves, every woman has her battered bonnet in her lap. The yell when Bill Sykes murders Nancy is like the roar of a thousand wild beasts, and they show their disapprobation of the act, and their approbation of the actor, by cursing him in no measured terms" (Hollingshead, John, *Ragged London*. London: Smith Elder & Co., 1861).

8. *the 'Suspected One,' or 'Gonsalvo the Guiltless':* These are evidently the titles of stage melodramas. There is no record of either title in the British Library Catalogue, so it is likely that either the scripts were never officially published or that Braddon invented the titles.

9. *scrub:* a person who is insignificant or of low social rank.

Chapter V. The Healing Waters

1. *after the manner of the mythic frog that wanted to be an ox:* In *Aesop's Fables,* the fable of the frog and the ox tells how a frog tried to inflate himself to the size of an ox, but burst in the attempt.

2. *gentleman on the pale horse:* from the Bible: "And behold, a pale horse, and he who sat on it, his name was Death" (Rev. 6:8).

3. *Old Tom . . . Mountain Dew:* alcoholic drinks.

Chapter VI. Two Coroner's Inquests

1. *three-halfpence per line . . . penny-a-liners' copy:* Journalists on the cheap papers were paid per line of copy. "Penny-a-liner" was a disparaging term used to describe such writers.

2. *merciful verdict—"Found drowned":* This verdict was often given in cases of suicide by drowning, to save the feelings of the deceased's friends and family and to ensure that the body could be buried in consecrated ground.

CHAPTER VII. THE DUMB DETECTIVE A PHILANTHROPIST

1. *"cakes and ale"*: from Shakespeare: "Dost thou think, because thou art virtuous, there shall be no more cakes and ale?" (*Twelfth Night* II.iii. 106–7, Modern Library ed.)
2. *yclept*: named.
3. *Dutch oven*: either a large cast-iron pot with a tight lid, used for slow cooking, or a metal utensil open on one side and equipped with shelves, which would be placed before an open fire for baking or roasting food.
4. *red herring*: a herring that has been cured and smoked to a dark reddish color. During the nineteenth century this term began to be used to describe a false clue in a criminal investigation. This usage stems from the fact that a red herring drawn across a trail would put a hunting dog off the scent.
5. *fondling*: foundling, i.e., an orphan or illegitimate child.
6. *brought up by hand*: bottle-fed rather than breast-fed. In Dickens's *Great Expectations* (1860–61) there are frequent references to the hero, Pip, having been brought up "by hand" by his foster parents.
7. *high-lows*: ankle-boots that fastened at the front.
8. *pea-jacket*: a coat of coarse woollen material, usually worn by sailors.
9. *long-clothes*: clothes worn by a very young baby, extending below the feet.
10. *He who provides for the young ravens*: a reference to a hymn by William Cowper (1731–1800). Written in 1779, the hymn begins "Sometimes a light surprises / The Christian while he sings." The third verse ends:

> Beneath the spreading heavens
> No creature but is fed
> And he who feeds the ravens
> Will give his children bread.

11. *scragged*: hanged.

CHAPTER VIII. SEVEN LETTERS ON THE DIRTY ALPHABET

1. *contumacious*: obstinate in resisting authority or refusing to obey.
2. *rue*: plant with bitter leaves, traditionally a symbol of repentance.

CHAPTER IX. "MAD, GENTLEMEN OF THE JURY"

1. *brain-fever*: This mysterious, life-threatening ailment is mentioned frequently in Victorian novels. It is usually stress-related and occurs

after a person has suffered a great trauma. Audrey Peterson ("Brain Fever in Nineteenth-Century Literature: Fact and Fiction," *Victorian Studies* XIX, no. 4 [June 1976], pp. 445–64) suggests that it may have been a form of meningitis or encephalitis. An earlier definition can be found in *The Working Man's Model Family Botanic Guide; or Every Man His Own Doctor*, by William Fox, M.D. (Sheffield, 1904), p. 149ff. Fox writes:

> Typhus, Nervous, or Brain Fever.
> Symptoms.—...stupor, this being the characteristic symptom of the disease; and it is also called Putrid Fever. The slow or nervous is distinguished from other kinds of fever by its effects on the nervous system, by a torpid state of the brain, prostration of muscular power, and more or less delirium. It is preceded by a slight indisposition for several days, succeeded by chills, debility, sighing, and oppression in breathing, with nausea, loss of appetite and an uneasy sensation at the pit of the stomach.

2. *unmentionables:* trousers.
3. *under-coat:* jacket.
4. *Blue devils:* depression, despondency.
5. *whitlow:* an inflammation of the fingernail or toenail.
6. *divers:* diverse.
7. *green fat of the turtle:* Turtle fat was used to make turtle soup, which was considered a great delicacy in Victorian times, and was often served as one of the first courses of a banquet.
8. *I have won the battle of Arcola:* The Battle of Arcola took place from November 15 to 17, 1796, in what is now northern Italy. Under Napoleon's leadership, the French army defeated the Austrian forces.
9. *Napoleon the First:* Napoleon Bonaparte.

BOOK THE SECOND.
A CLEARANCE OF ALL SCORES
CHAPTER I. BLIND PETER

1. *chandler:* Nowadays this term denotes a dealer in ships' or boats' supplies and equipment, but in the nineteenth century it was also used in a broader sense as an alternative word for "shop."
2. *going into the* Gazette: being declared bankrupt. There were three official journals that published notices of bankruptcy—the *London Gazette, Edinburgh Gazette,* and *Dublin Gazette.*

3. *Alsatia:* London slum district between Fleet Street and the Thames. It was notorious for its high crime rate, and it was said to be unsafe for anyone to venture there alone.

CHAPTER II. LIKE AND UNLIKE

1. *boned my mug:* stolen my face.
2. *rheumatic fever:* a disease caused by a streptococcal bacterium that destroys blood cells. In its most extreme form it can cause fever, arthritis, and heart failure.

CHAPTER III. A GOLDEN SECRET

1. *born to be drowned:* There is a proverbial English saying that a person is born to be drowned or born to be hanged.

CHAPTER IV. JIM LOOKS OVER THE BRIM OF THE TERRIBLE GULF

1. *the first murderer:* in the Bible, Cain, who murdered his brother Abel (Gen. 4).

CHAPTER V. MIDNIGHT BY THE SLOPPERTON CLOCKS

1. *the nobleman that wrote the letters:* Lord Chesterfield (1694–1773), English statesman whose *Letters to His Son* (1774) was published as a guide to good manners.
2. Rasselas: novel by Samuel Johnson (1709–84), published in 1759.
3. *Mercury:* In Greek mythology, Mercury was the messenger of the gods.
4. *Œdipus:* In Greek mythology, Oedipus won a kingdom by solving a riddle posed by the Sphinx. He later blinded himself in a fit of despair when he realized that his wife, Jocasta, was in fact his mother, from whom he had been separated at birth.

CHAPTER VI. THE QUIET FIGURE ON THE HEATH

1. *matutinal:* during the morning.
2. *short-coated:* a child dressed in short clothes.
3. *the Lady's Mile:* the part of Hyde Park where upper-class women rode their horses. One of Braddon's novels is entitled *The Lady's Mile* (1867).
4. *Parthian:* comment or gesture made on departing. This expression came into common use in the nineteenth century. It refers to the practice of the horsemen of ancient Parthia, who would turn to shoot arrows at enemies as they rode off.

5. *gentlemen who wore white neckcloths:* clergymen.
6. fête champêtre: In France, this term describes village fêtes, but in nineteenth-century England it usually referred to upper-class garden parties where food was provided.
7. *farinaceous:* containing flour or starch.
8. *Barcelona nuts:* hazel nuts.
9. *story of the lion and the mouse:* from *Aesop's Fables.*
10. *vesper:* evening prayer or evening service.
11. *seven sleepers:* According to an early Christian legend, seven Christians of Ephesus were walled up alive in a cave on Mount Anchilos by order of the Emperor Decius (249–251). When the cave was opened, over two hundred years later, they had miraculously survived, having slept for the entire time. Similar legends appear in the Koran and in the writings of Aristotle.

CHAPTER VII. THE USHER RESIGNS HIS SITUATION

1. *pound-cake:* a rich fruit cake, so called because it contained one pound of each of the principal ingredients—flour, butter, sugar, and fruit.
2. *sal-volatile:* a carbonate salt formed by the reaction of ammonia with acid. It was often referred to as "smelling-salts." A bottle of sal-volatile would be held beneath the nose of an unconscious person to revive him or her.
3. *red lavender:* Tincture of red lavender was a medicinal cordial composed of oils of lavender and rosemary, mixed with cinnamon bark, nutmeg, red sandalwood, and wine. It was used as a stimulant and a cure for indigestion.
4. *three volumes a day from the circulating library:* In the 1860s, novels were usually published in three volumes. A circulating library was a library run by private subscription where members paid a membership fee that entitled them to borrow a certain number of books. Two of the most popular circulating libraries of the nineteenth century were Boots and Mudies, which had branches throughout Britain.

BOOK THE THIRD. A HOLY INSTITUTION

CHAPTER I. THE VALUE OF AN OPERA-GLASS

1. *La Vallière:* Louise-Françoise de La Baume le Blanc, Duchess of La Vallière (1644–1710), was a mistress of King Louis XIV of France. She

bore him four children. When Louis abandoned her for another woman, he compensated her by making her a duchess (1667). In 1674, she retired to a nunnery in Paris, where she remained until her death; *Scarron:* Paul Scarron (1610–60), French poet and novelist; *Bossuet:* Jacques-Bénigne Bossuet (1627–1704), French Catholic bishop and tutor to the eldest son of Louis XIV.

2. bon mot: witticism, epigram.

3. *Ninon de Lenclos:* Anne de Lenclos (1620–1705), known as Ninon de Lenclos, was a high-class French courtesan, famed for her many aristocratic lovers. She was popularly reported to be taking lovers even when she was in her seventies and eighties; *Beaumarchais:* Pierre-Augustin Caron de Beaumarchais (1732–99), French playwright and political satirist. His best-known plays are *The Barber of Seville* (1775) and *The Marriage of Figaro* (1784), which inspired operas by Rossini and Mozart; *Marmontel:* Jean-François Marmontel (1723–99), French writer and historian; *Philippe of Orleans:* Duke Philippe of Orleans (1641–1701), son of King Louis XII of France and Anne of Austria; *Voltaire:* Voltaire was the pseudonym of François-Marie Arouet (1694–1778), a leading French writer and atheist whose ideas were highly influential in the years leading to the French Revolution; *Ferney:* Voltaire spent the last twenty years of his life at his château near the town of Voltaire-Ferney. He was visited there by many distinguished literary figures, including James Boswell, Lord Chesterfield, and Edward Gibbon; *Madame du Deffand:* French woman of letters (1697–1780). Her literary salon attracted distinguished figures from all over the world, including Benjamin Franklin, Horace Walpole, and Jean-Jacques Rousseau; *Mademoiselle de l'Espinasse:* Julie-Jeanne-Éléonore de l'Espinasse (1732–76), French woman of letters famous for her literary salon; *Horace Walpole:* Horace (or Horatio) Walpole, Fourth Earl of Orford (1717–97) was an English writer and M.P. His novel *The Castle of Otranto* (1764) set the fashion for Gothic romances. He converted his house at Strawberry Hill, near London, into a small pseudo-Gothic castle.

4. ce cher: dear

5. *Bailly:* Jean-Sylvain Bailly (1736–93) was a French astronomer and politician. He was president of the National Assembly and mayor of Paris during the French Revolution in 1789, and was guillotined after allowing soldiers to fire on anti-Royalist demonstrators; *Madame Roland:* Jeanne-Marie Roland de La Platière (1754–93) was the wife of Jean-Marie Roland de La Platière (1734–93), who became minister of

the interior in the French revolutionary government. The couple fell foul of Robespierre *(see note 7 below)*, and were threatened with execution. Jean escaped from Paris, but Jeanne-Marie was arrested and guillotined, after which Jean committed suicide; *Marie Antoinette:* Louis XVI's queen, guillotined on October 16, 1793; *Princess Elizabeth:* one of the many aristocrats killed in the French Revolution; *son of St. Louis:* King Louis XVI of France (1754–93), who was guillotined on January 21, 1793. The phrase "son of St. Louis" refers to his descent from St. Louis of France, King Louis IX (1214–70).

6. *that terrible machine invented by the charitable doctor:* The guillotine was invented by Joseph Ignace Guillotin (1738–1814), a French doctor and revolutionary. Adopted in France in 1791 and named after him, the guillotine is a decapitating instrument used as a means of execution.

7. *Robespierre:* Maximilien-François-Marie-Isidore de Robespierre (1758–94) was one of the leaders of the French Revolution. In 1793, he instituted a reign of terror, but not long after this he fell from power and was arrested and guillotined on the orders of the Revolutionary Tribunal.

8. *Marengo ... Lodd, Arcola, Austerlitz, Auerstadt, and Jena:* battles fought by Napoleon.

9. *Citizen King:* Louis Philippe I (1773–1850), King of France (1830–48). Eldest son of Louis-Philippe-Joseph de Bourbon-Orléans (Philippe Égalité)*(see note 2, Book the Third, ch. IX [p. 440])*, he became king after Charles X was deposed in a rebellion in the summer of 1830. He styled himself the "Citizen King" and swore to observe the Constitution, but alienated many of his subjects. Faced with growing unrest, in 1848 he abdicated in favor of his nine-year-old grandson, Philippe. He spent the rest of his life in England.

10. *La Sonnambula:* opera by Vincenzo Bellini (1801–35), first performed in 1831. The title means "The Sleepwalker." The heroine, Amina, is accused of infidelity when she sleepwalks into the wrong man's bedroom on the night before her wedding. Her fiancé, Elvino, spurns her until a second sleepwalking episode proves her innocence.

11. *coryphée:* ballet dancer who ranks above the corps de ballet but below the soloists. Coryphées perform small ensemble pieces.

12. *Don Giovanni:* an opera by Wolfgang Amadeus Mozart (1756–91), which concerns the adventures of a philandering nobleman. First performed in 1787; *La ci darem la mano:* "There we'll hold hands," a duet from *Don Giovanni,* sung by Giovanni and Zerlina, the peasant girl he is attempting to seduce.

13. *Phædra:* In Greek mythology, Phaedra was the daughter of Minos and the second wife of Theseus. She fell in love with her step-son Hippolytus. When Hippolytus rejected her, she accused him of trying to rape her. Theseus called on Poseidon to punish Hippolytus with death, after which Phaedra hanged herself. Her story is the subject of a play, *Phèdre,* by French dramatist Jean Racine (1639–99), which was first performed in 1677 and is still performed today.

14. *Messalina:* The notoriously violent and promiscuous Roman empress Valeria Messalina (c. 22–c. 48 A.D.) was the third wife of the emperor Claudius, whom she married at the age of fourteen. She instigated a reign of terror, but was eventually betrayed and put to death.

CHAPTER II. WORKING IN THE DARK

1. *the celebrated aphorism of one of our English neighbours, 'Knowledge is power':* This saying is attributed to English philosopher Francis Bacon (1561–1626). In *De Haeresibus* (1597), he wrote "nam et ipsa scientia potest est," which is usually translated as "for knowledge itself is power." In his *Essays* (1598), he wrote "Knowledge it selfe is a power." The phrase was quoted by Braddon's friend and mentor Sir Edward Bulwer Lytton (1803–73) in *My Novel,* serialized in *Blackwood's Magazine* during 1850–53.

CHAPTER III. THE WRONG FOOTSTEP

1. *"Louis the Well-beloved":* Louis XV of France (1715–74). The term "well-beloved" is also sometimes used to refer to two other French kings, Louis XIII (1610–43) and Charles VI (1380–1422).

2. *Bourbon:* the French Royal family.

3. *Boucher:* François Boucher (1702–70), French painter of pastoral and mythological scenes in a delicate, sentimental style.

4. *Versailles Olympus:* Versailles is the French royal palace. In Greek mythology, Mount Olympus was the home of the gods.

5. *recherché:* rare, exotic, or exquisite.

CHAPTER IV. OCULAR DEMONSTRATION

1. *pot à feu:* probably a misprint for *pot au feu,* beef stew.

2. *quarterings on your shield:* line of descent as indicated in armorial bearings.

CHAPTER V. THE KING OF SPADES

1. *Lucretia Borgia:* Lucretia, or Lucrezia, Borgia (1480–1519) was a famous poisoner who lived in Italy during the Renaissance. She was the illegitimate daughter of Cardinal Rodrigo Borgia (later Pope Alexander VI), and the sister of Cesare Borgia. She married three times to further her family's political ambitions. She is the subject of an opera by Donizetti *(see note 2 in ch. VII below).* Braddon appeared several times in a play based on the life of Lucretia Borgia. (For details, see Carnell, p. 369.)

2. aqua tofana: a poisonous arsenical solution invented by infamous Italian poisoner Teofania (or Toffa) de Adamo, who sold small bottles of it at a high price to her clients. She was executed at Naples in 1709. The poison is odorless, colorless, and tasteless, and only four to six drops are enough to kill. It has been suggested that Mozart was killed by a dose of *aqua tofana.*

CHAPTER VI. A GLASS OF WINE

1. *Baron Munchausen:* a German soldier famous for telling exaggerated, untruthful stories. His exploits were first published in English as *Baron Munchhausen's Narrative of His Marvellous Travels and Campaigns in Russia* (1785), by Rudolf Erich Raspe (1737–94).

2. *Charivari:* a popular Parisian satirical magazine, founded in 1832. The name comes from a traditional ritual that involves blowing horns and banging pots and pans in order to express disapproval of an adulterer. The custom was practiced in much of Europe under different names.

3. *Gennaro in Lucretia Borgia:* In the opera *Lucrezia Borgia,* Gennaro is Lucretia's long-lost illegitimate son. In poisoning a group of her enemies at a banquet, Lucretia accidentally poisons Gennaro as well. She begs him to take an antidote, but he refuses, preferring to die with his friends.

CHAPTER VII. THE LAST ACT OF LUCRETIA BORGIA

1. *Victor Hugo:* French novelist (1802–85), now chiefly remembered for *The Hunchback of Notre-Dame* (1831) and *Les Misérables* (1862).

2. *Donizetti:* Gaetano Donizetti (1797–1848) was an Italian composer of operas. His work included *Anna Bolena* (1830), *Lucrezia Borgia* (1833), and *Lucia di Lammermoor* (1835).

3. *'Pescator ignobile':* literally, "despicable fisherman." An aria from Donizetti's *Lucrezia Borgia.*

4. *Maffeo Orsini:* a young nobleman in Donizetti's *Lucrezia Borgia.* Maffeo encourages guests at a banquet to drink heartily, unaware that Lucretia has poisoned the wine. Although a male part, this character is usually sung by a contralto.

5. *brain-fever:* See Book the First, ch. IX, note 1 (p. 432).

CHAPTER VIII. BAD DREAMS AND A WORSE WAKING

1. *Caen:* a port in Normandy, France.

2. *ormolu and buhl à la Louis Quatorze: ormolu* is a gilded metal alloy of copper, zinc, and tin used in France and England for decorating candelabra, clocks, elaborate furniture, and other luxury objects; *buhl:* wooden furniture inlaid with ornamental patterns in brass or tortoiseshell; *à la Louis Quatorze:* in the style of King Louis XIV.

3. *the ardent hue which prejudice condemns:* red. Victorians disliked red hair, which they regarded as ugly.

CHAPTER IX. A MARRIAGE IN HIGH LIFE

1. *Faubourg St. Germain:* a rich neighborhood of Paris, inhabited mainly by aristocrats.

2. *Philip Egalité:* Louis Philippe Joseph, Duke of Orleans (1747–93). A libertine, he squandered his immense wealth and joined the leaders of the French Revolution. He voted for the execution of Louis XVI, but was himself guillotined in November 1793, during the Reign of Terror. His son became King Louis Philippe.

3. *the Madeleine:* a large, fashionable Parisian church, consecrated in 1842.

4. *Asmodeus:* in Christian mythology, a demon who prevented the consummation of marriages. He appears in the book of Tobias, which is in the Apocrypha (books included in older Bibles between the Old and New Testaments). Asmodeus is sexually obsessed with the Virgin Sara. Sara marries seven times, but each husband is killed on the wedding night before the marriage can be consummated. Sara's eighth husband, Tobias, realizes that this is because of demonic intervention. With the aid of his guardian angel, Raphael, he drives Asmodeus from the bridal chamber by burning a fish's heart and liver there. On returning to his family home, Tobias puts the fish gall on the eyes of his blind father, Tobit, and restores his sight.

CHAPTER X. ANIMAL MAGNETISM

1. *animal magnetism:* This term was usually used to refer to a form of hypnotism developed in the late eighteenth century by Anton Mesmer. However, Braddon seems to be using it here to refer to psychic communication.

BOOK THE FOURTH. NAPOLEON THE GREAT
CHAPTER I. THE BOY FROM SLOPPERTON

1. *congé:* order to depart.
2. *Maria Martin... Red Barn:* one of the most notorious murder cases of the nineteenth century. On May 18, 1827, twenty-six-year-old Maria Marten (or Martin) of Polstead, Suffolk, was murdered by her lover, William Corder, who hid her body in a barn. Corder told her family that she had left for London. They suspected nothing until Maria's mother had a dream in which Maria told her of the murder and the location of the body. Maria's father then searched the Red Barn and found the corpse. Corder was convicted on August 7, 1828, and executed on August 11 in front of a crowd estimated at ten thousand people. The story caught the public imagination. Numerous books, broadsheets, and engravings about the murder were produced almost immediately. A pamphlet describing the trial sold over a million copies. An anonymously written novel called *The Red Barn* (London: Knight and Lacy, 1828) was published in serial form starting soon after the trial and became a bestseller. Melodramas based on the case remained popular for many years. As a child, Braddon was taken to see a melodrama entitled *Maria Marten and the Red Barn* (Carnell, p. 7).

    For details of the case, see Altick, Richard D., *Victorian Studies in Scarlet* (New York: Norton, 1970), and Peter Haining, *Buried Passions—Maria Marten and the Red Barn Murder* (Suffolk: Neville Spearman, 1980).
3. *third daughter of Henry the Eighth's seventh wife:* This is a joke on Braddon's part. Henry VIII had six wives (Catherine of Aragon, Anne Boleyn, Jane Seymour, Anne of Cleves, Catherine Howard, and Catherine Parr) and two daughters (Queen Mary and Queen Elizabeth I).
4. *William the Conqueror:* King William of Normandy (c. 1028–87), who conquered Britain in 1066.

5. *Fair Rosamond:* Rosamond Clifford (c. 1140–75 or '76) was the mistress of King Henry II of England. She died in mysterious circumstances, possibly poisoned by Henry's wife, Queen Eleanor of Aquitane. She is the subject of an 1861 painting by Pre-Raphaelite artist Dante Gabriel Rossetti (1828–82), which can be seen in the National Museum of Wales, Cardiff. Braddon was familiar with the work of the Pre-Raphaelites, and may have had this painting in mind.

6. *Emperor Napoleon the First:* Napoleon Bonaparte.

7. *St. Helena:* the island to which Napoleon was exiled after his abdication in 1815.

8. *Sir Hudson Lowe:* British Lieutenant-General who was governor of St. Helena during Napoleon's exile, 1815–21.

9. *water on the brain:* Now known as hydrocephalus, water on the brain was the accumulation of cerebrospinal fluid in the ventricles, or cavities, of the brain, causing enlargement of the head, convulsions, and mental difficulties.

10. *meerschaum:* a type of pipe. Meerschaum takes its name from the material used for the bowl, a hydrated magnesium silicate mineral, which is similar to white clay and is easily carved.

11. *bluchers:* workmen's boots, a cheaper version of Wellington boots; named after General von Blücher (1742–1819), the Prussian general-in-chief at the Battle of Waterloo.

12. *orders of the Bath and the Garter:* The Order of the Bath is a British Order of Chivalry established by King George I by letters patent under the Great Seal dated May 18, 1725. Its title refers to a medieval ritual of purification. It is usually awarded to high-ranking officers in the armed forces and senior civil servants. The Order of the Garter is the oldest and highest British Order of Chivalry, founded in 1348 by Edward III. The Order of the Garter consists of Her Majesty the Queen, who is Sovereign of the Order, His Royal Highness Prince of Wales, and twenty-four Knights Companions. The symbol of the order is a blue "garter" with the motto *Honi Soit Qui Mal Y Pense.* According to legend, the motto and order originated in the fourteenth century when Joan, Countess of Salisbury, dropped her garter at a ball and King Edward, seeing her embarrassment, picked it up and bound it about his own leg saying in French, "Evil [or shamed] be he that thinks evil of it." Although now highly anachronistic, both orders have survived into the twenty-first century.

13. *Pinnock's Goldsmith:* William Pinnock (1782–1843) was the author of revised versions of Oliver Goldsmith's histories of Greece, Rome, and England. These revised versions were used as textbooks in schools from the 1830s onwards.

14. *the Medes and Persians:* from the Bible: "the law of the Medes and the Persians, which altereth not" (Dan. 6:18).

15. *Lord Castlereagh:* the title given to Robert Stewart, 2nd Marquis of Londonderry and Chief Secretary for Ireland, 1798–1801. He quelled the 1798 rebellion and formed a political union between Britain and Ireland in 1800. Castlereagh became infamous after the 1819 "Peterloo Massacre" in which British soldiers attacked a crowd attending a Radical political meeting at St. Peter's Field in Manchester, killing eleven and injuring another four hundred. The poet Percy Bysshe Shelley (1792–1822) responded to the event by writing "The Mask of Anarchy," which includes the lines:

> I met Murder on the way—
> He had a mask like Castlereagh—
> Very smooth he looked, yet grim;
> Seven blood-hounds followed him;
>
> All were fat; and well they might
> Be in admirable plight,
> For one by one, and two by two,
> He tossed them human hearts to chew
> Which from his wide cloak he drew.

CHAPTER II. MR. AUGUSTUS DARLEY AND MR. JOSEPH PETERS GO OUT FISHING

1. *St. Mark's:* a basilica in St Mark's Square, Venice.

2. *Bridge of Sighs:* covered footbridge over the Rio di Palazzo, in Venice. Designed by Antonio Contino, it was erected in the year 1600 to connect the prison with the inquisitor's rooms in the Doge's Palace. It was given the nickname "Bridge of Sighs" in the nineteenth century, when Lord Byron helped to popularize the belief that the bridge's name was inspired by the sighs of condemned prisoners as they were led through it to the executioner. *Childe Harold's Pilgrimage,* by Lord Byron (1788–1824), begins with the lines: "I stood in Venice, on the Bridge of Sighs; / A palace and a prison on each hand:"

3. *penny numbers:* In this era, novels were often published in weekly installments at a penny per installment.
4. *"Bravo":* a daring villain or reckless desperado.
5. *caravansary:* In Persia, a *caravanserai* was an inn with a central courtyard for receiving caravans crossing the desert. Here, Braddon uses it to mean a public house.
6. *mark with a white stone:* from the Latin *Albo lapillo notare diem*—To mark the day with a white stone. This refers to the ancient Roman custom of marking each happy day by dropping a white stone into an urn, and each bad day by doing the same with a black stone. At the end of the month the urn would be emptied and the stones counted to determine what kind of month it had been. The 1898 edition of *Brewer's Dictionary of Phrase and Fable* cites an additional custom, that of marking good days on a calendar with white chalk and bad days with black charcoal.
7. *ha'porth of Epsom salts:* halfpenny's worth of hydrated magnesium sulphate, sold as a laxative.
8. *three-farthings' worth:* A farthing was a coin worth a quarter of a penny.
9. *rhubarb and magnesia:* a purgative consisting of rhubarb mixed with magnesium carbonate.
10. *the legend of the mistletoe bough:* a folktale concerning a bride who hid in a large trunk as a joke. Unable to get the lid open again, she died, and her body was not found until many years later. A folk song based on the story was popular in the nineteenth century, and goes as follows:

> The mistletoe hung, in the old castle hall,
> The holly branch shone, on the old oak wall,
> And the baron's retainers, were blythe and gay,
> All keeping their Christmas holiday.
> And the baron beheld, with a father's pride,
> His beautiful child, young Lovell's bride,
> While she with her bright eyes, seemed to be,
> The Star of the goodly company.
> Chorus: Oh the mistletoe bough, Oh the mistletoe bough.
>
> "I'm weary of dancing now" she cried,
> "Here tarry a moment, I'll hide, I'll hide,
> And Lovell, be sure thou'rt the first to trace,
> The clue to my secret hiding place."
> Away she ran, and her friends began
> Each tower to search, each nook to scan.

And young Lovell he cried, "Where dos't thou hide.
I'm lonely without thee, my own dear bride."
Chorus: Oh the mistletoe bough, Oh the mistletoe bough.

They sought her that night, they sought her next day,
They sought her in vain, till a week passed away.
In the highest, the lowest, the lonesomest spot,
Young Lovell sought wildly, but found her not.
And years flew by, and their grief at last,
Was told as a sorrowful tale long-past.
And when Lovell appeared, all the children cried
"See the old man weeps, for his fairy bride."
Chorus: Oh the mistletoe bough, Oh the mistletoe bough.

At length an old chest, that had long lain hid,
Was found in the castle, they raised the lid.
A skeleton form lay mouldering there,
In the bridal wreath of a lady so fair,
Oh sad was her fate, in sportive jest,
She hid from her lord, in an old oak chest.
It closed with a spring, and the bridal bloom,
Lay withering there, in a living tomb.
Chorus: Oh the mistletoe bough, Oh the mistletoe bough.

11. *eel-spears:* forked or pronged instruments about six feet long, used to catch eels by transfixing them as they lie in the mud. They look like tridents, hence the joke about Peters looking like Neptune.

CHAPTER III. THE EMPEROR BIDS ADIEU TO ELBA

1. chevaux-de-frise: glass or spikes set into the top of a wall to make it more difficult for anyone to climb over.

2. *darkened glass:* from the Bible, First Epistle of Paul to the Corinthians: "For now we see through a glass, darkly; but then face to face: now I know in part; but then shall I know even as also I am known" (1 Cor. 13:11).

3. *Abd-el-Kader:* Abd-el-Kader (1807–83) was an Algerian nationalist who led the rebellion against the French conquest of Algiers (1832–47).

4. *Terp—what-you-may-call-her, the lady who had so many unmarried sisters:* In Greek mythology, Terpsichore was the Muse associated with dancing and lyric poetry. There were nine Muses, who were conventionally depicted as unmarried young women.

5. *muffins:* In England, a muffin is not the type of sweet cake that is known by that name in America, but is a kind of thick, pancakelike savory bread that is eaten toasted and buttered. It is also known as a crumpet.

6. *Alfred the Great:* According to an English folk tale, King Alfred the Great (c. 849–900) once took refuge in a poor woman's cottage while fleeing from a battle. She asked him to watch her baking for her while she went out, but he was so absorbed in thinking out battle strategy that he forgot to do so and the cakes burnt. This, presumably, is why the madwoman thinks King Alfred invented muffins.

7. *"Do you know the muffin-man?"* ... *"He lives in Drury Lane":* English nursery rhyme:

> Oh do you know the muffin man
> Oh do you know the muffin man
> Oh do you know the muffin man
> who lives in Drury Lane.

The rhyme may have a secondary, obscene meaning—"muff"—this being a slang term for female pubic hair.

8. *Lord Chesterfield never advised his son to do that:* See Book the Second, ch. V, note 1 (p. 434).

CHAPTER IV. JOY AND HAPPINESS FOR EVERYBODY

1. *bitters:* alcoholic liquid made from herbs or roots and used to flavor drinks. First made in Venezuela in 1824, today it is mainly used in cocktails.

2. *turned up:* put up in a bun.

3. *leger-de-main:* sleight-of-hand.

4. *Tripe:* offal, which consists largely of parts of the stomachs of cows and sheep; usually served with onions.

5. *taters:* potatoes.

CHAPTER V. THE CHEROKEES TAKE AN OATH

1. *his dexter fist ... Left-handed Smasher:* "Dexter" is the Latin for "right," so this may be a misprint in the original text. The Latin for "left" is "sinister."

2. *grimalkins:* greymalkins, i.e., cats.

3. *Welsh rarebit:* a type of cheese on toast. Before cooking, the cheese is grated and mixed with mustard, salt, pepper, and either milk or beer.

4. *Lindley Murray:* Quaker grammarian from Pennsylvania (1745–1826); author of *English Grammar* (1795), *An English Spelling Book* (1804), and

other books on grammar and spelling, which remained in print well into the 1840s.

5. *mawley:* fist.

CHAPTER VI. MR. PETERS RELATES HOW HE THOUGHT HE HAD A CLUE, AND HOW HE LOST IT

1. *transpontine:* on the south side of the River Thames, in London.
2. *that circular chapel some time sacred to Rowland Hill:* Surrey Chapel, in Blackfriars Road. Rowland Hill (1744–1833) was a popular Methodist preacher who built the chapel at his own expense. It opened in 1783, could seat up to three thousand people, and had what was probably the first Sunday school in London. Hill's services attracted large congregations, and he preached six or seven times a week until shortly before his death.
3. *Sir Benjamin Brodie:* Benjamin Brodie the elder (1783–1862), surgeon to the Queen.
4. *Herring:* John Frederick Herring (1795–1865), British artist famous for his paintings of animals.
5. *Landseer:* Sir Edwin Landseer (1802–73), British artist known for his paintings of animals. He modeled the four bronze lions that stand at the foot of Nelson's Column in Trafalgar Square (unveiled in 1867). He was knighted in 1850.
6. *jujubes:* a generic term for sweets.
7. *tartaric acid:* acidulant (i.e., something that turns things sour) derived from argol (a sediment found in wine vats).
8. *seidlitz-powders:* laxative made from tartaric acid, potassium tartare, and sodium bicarbonate.
9. *'steriky:* hysterical.
10. *Marengo:* battle at which Napoleon-led French forces defeated the Austrian army. It took place on June 14, 1800, in what is now northern Italy. Approximately 5,800 French and 9,400 Austrians were killed.
11. *sup-boned-aed:* subpoenaed, i.e., summoned to appear in a court of law.

BOOK THE FIFTH. THE DUMB DETECTIVE

CHAPTER I. THE COUNT DE MAROLLES AT HOME

1. *tallow:* animal fat melted down to make candles or soap.
2. *Park Lane:* expensive, upper-class residential street on the edge of Hyde Park in London.

3. *Mangling:* drying and pressing clothes by putting them through a mangle. A mangle was a hand-operated device consisting of two rollers. Wet laundry was fed between the rollers to squeeze most of the water out.
4. *Mayfair:* expensive, upper-class residential area of London.
5. *St. Giles:* a notorious London slum.
6. fêtes champêtres: *See Book the Second, ch. VI, note 6 (p. 435).*
7. thés dansantes: tea dances.
8. *Louis the Sixteenth:* Louis XVI was the king of France at the time of the French Revolution. He was executed in 1793; *Madame Elizabeth:* Louis XVI's sister; *the unfortunate boy prisoner of the Temple:* Louis Charles, the son of Louis XVI and Marie Antoinette. The family were imprisoned in the Temple on August 12, 1792. After Louis XVI's execution on January 21, 1793, Louis Charles was taken away from his mother and his sister, Marie Therese Charlotte. According to popular folklore, he was imprisoned in a cell nearby, where they could hear him crying but could not go to him. Louis Charles died of tuberculosis in prison in 1795.
9. *Canovo:* Antonio Canova (1757–1822), Italian sculptor who carved a huge head of Napoleon that he could not bear to part with. Canova is best remembered for his sculpture of the Three Graces, which was the center of great controversy in 1995 when the U.K. government in 1995 paid £7.6 million to prevent its being sold to a museum in America. It is now displayed in London's Victoria and Albert Museum.
10. *solfeggi:* scales, intervals, and melodic exercises.
11. *Cherubino:* Valerie has evidently named her son after one of the characters in Mozart's opera *The Marriage of Figaro.* Cherubino is a flirtatious young man. The role is usually played as a "travesti" role, i.e., sung by a women dressed as a man.

CHAPTER II. MR. PETERS SEES A GHOST

1. otium cum dignitate: Latin expression meaning "ease with dignity" or "leisure with dignity."
2. do for: do the cooking and housework for.
3. *New Road:* a major road connecting Paddington with Islington. It consisted of what are now Euston Road and Marylebone Road.
4. *Mazeppa:* The eponymous hero of Byron's *Mazeppa* (1819) is sentenced to death by being bound to the back of a wild horse, which is then whipped to a frenzy. The horse gallops itself to death. When it

collapses, Mazeppa, who is himself at the point of death, is rescued.
5. *saveloys:* spicy sausages made from smoked pork or offal.
6. *porter:* a type of weak beer.
7. *Kidderminster carpet:* a two-ply or ingrain reversible carpet, named after the Worcestershire town of Kidderminster, where this type of carpet was originally made.
8. *Old Lady of Threadneedle Street:* the Bank of England.
9. *buried... between four cross roads with a stake druv' through him if he'd poisoned himself fifty years ago:* In England before 1823, the bodies of suicides were usually not buried in consecrated ground. From the sixteenth century to 1823, it was common practice to bury them at a crossroads, often with a stake driven through the heart. An act of 1823 decreed that they could be buried in churchyards, but that the burials had to take place between 9 P.M. and midnight, without any religious service. The law was altered in 1882 to allow burial at any time and with a religious service. Suicide remained a criminal offense in England until 1961.
10. *levanting:* leaving secretly, or fleeing, to avoid paying debts.
11. *downy:* clever, alert. A "downy bit" was nineteenth-century slang for a prostitute.

CHAPTER III. THE CHEROKEES MARK THEIR MAN

1. *fop's alley:* in a theater or opera-house, a passage between the tiers of benches, frequented by fashionable young men.
2. *Pandemonium:* name given by John Milton (1608–74) for the capital of Hell in *Paradise Lost,* from Greek *pan* (all) and *daimon* (demon).
3. *Colchesters:* oysters from Colchester, in Essex.
4. *Lucia:* Donizetti's opera *Lucia di Lammermoor* (1835).
5. *Edgardo:* the hero of *Lucia di Lammermoor,* with whom Lucia is in love.
6. *Porte-St.-Martin:* a theater in Paris.
7. *Hessian boots:* high boots with tassels on the front, as worn by Hessian troops (Hesse was a state in what is now central Germany). They were fashionable in the early nineteenth century.
8. *quadrille:* a popular dance.
9. *knowledge-box:* head.
10. *bunch of fives:* fist.
11. *Newmarket:* racecourse near Cambridge, about sixty-five miles from London.

CHAPTER IV. THE CAPTAIN, THE CHEMIST, AND THE LASCAR

1. *Newton:* Sir Isaac Newton (1642–1727), physicist and mathematician chiefly famous for discovering the law of gravity.

2. *Leplace:* The Marquis de Leplace (1749–1827) was a French mathematician and author of mathematical treatises. He was said to have presented one of his books to Napoleon while on board ship on an expedition to Egypt. When Napoleon complained that there was no mention of God in the book, Leplace replied, "Sire, I have no need of that hypothesis."

3. *Albertus Magnus:* philosopher and churchman famed for his learning (c. 1200–80).

4. *kitmutghar:* an Indian servant whose duties were connected with serving meals and waiting at table.

5. *Punjaub:* The Punjab was a state in northwest India that was annexed by the British after the Sikh Wars (1845–46 and 1848–49).

CHAPTER V. THE NEW MILKMAN IN PARK LANE

1. *tiger:* pageboy.

2. *Calting or the* Anthinium: The Carlton and the Athenaeum were exclusive gentlemen's clubs.

CHAPTER VI. SIGNOR MOSQUETTI RELATES AN ADVENTURE

1. *point-d'Alençon:* a type of needlepoint lace.

2. *Lyons and Spitalfields:* areas of France and London where many silkweavers lived and worked.

3. *buffo duet:* a comic duet, usually sung by two deep male voices.

4. *the Cenerentola: La Cenerentola* is an opera by Rossini (1792–1868), based on the Cinderella story. It was first performed in 1817.

5. *Erard:* Sebastien Erard (1752–1831), maker of high-quality pianos and harpsichords.

6. *Charlemagne:* Charles the Great (742–814), who united and expanded the Frankish Empire.

7. *Louis XV:* King Louis XV of France (1710–74), who ascended to the throne in 1715 while still a child.

8. *lower House:* House of Commons.

CHAPTER VII. THE GOLDEN SECRET IS TOLD, AND THE GOLDEN BOWL IS BROKEN

1. *the golden bowl is broken:* from the Bible: "Or ever the silver cord be loosed or the golden bowl be broken" (Eccles. 12:6).

2. *Lawrence Sterne on a sentimental journey:* Laurence Sterne (1713–68) was the author of several novels, including *A Sentimental Journey through France and Italy* (1768). He is best known for his comic novel *The Life and Opinions of Tristram Shandy* (1761–67).
3. *Seven Dials:* notorious slum area of London, near Covent Garden. It is now a fashionable shopping area.
4. *comes to Lambeth and murders an Archbishop of Canterbury:* The Archbishop of Canterbury is head of the Church of England. His (or her) official residence is Lambeth Palace, in London.
5. *Atkinson's:* This reference has not been satisfactorily identified. It would appear to refer to a beautician or supplier of stage makeup.
6. *Burlington Arcade:* an expensive shopping arcade in central London.
7. *'Marquis of Granby':* a common name for public houses in the U.K.

CHAPTER VIII. ONE STEP FURTHER ON THE RIGHT TRACK

1. *Cavendish: Cavendish* refers to a brand of strong American tobacco sweetened with molasses; *bird's-eye:* cheap, strong tobacco (Braddon, *Lady Audley's Secret,* chapter 4: "Who could have ever expected that a dragoon would drink sixpenny ale, smoke horrid bird's-eye tobacco, and let his wife wear a shabby bonnet?"); *Turkey rhubarb:* a plant of the dock family (*Polygonaceae*), also known as East Indian Rhubarb and Chinese Rhubarb. The root can be used to make a laxative, and is still used today in alternative medicine; *otto of roses:* attar of roses, a fragrant oil or perfume essence obtained from rose petals.
2. *Doctor Dee:* John Dee (1527–1608), English alchemist, geographer, and mathematician who was astrologer to the court of Elizabeth I.
3. *Mokannah:* Mokanna (usually spelled without the *h*) is the eponymous protagonist of "The Veiled Prophet of Khorassan," the first "poetical tale" in Thomas Moore's book-length poem *Lalla Rookh* (1817). According to Moore, Hakim ben Allah, surnamed "the Veiled" (Mokanna), was the founder of an eighth-century Arab sect. He wore a silver veil over his face to hide the fact that he had lost an eye in battle, but he told his followers that he was veiled because his face was too radiant for them to see safely. Moore describes him as:

> … the Prophet-Chief
> The Great Mokanna. O'er his features
> The Veil, the Silver Veil which he had flung
> In mercy there, to hide from mortal sight
> His dazzling brow, till man could bear its light.

Mokanna led a revolt against Islam. When he was defeated he threw a banquet at which he poisoned all his followers, then committed suicide by throwing himself into burning acid.

4. *Pinnock: See Book the Fourth, ch. I, note 13 (p. 443).*

5. Bragelonne: *Le Vicomte de Bragelonne,* French title of the novel *The Man in the Iron Mask* (1846), by Alexandre Dumas (1802–70). The book was not published in English until 1858, which is why Darley has it in the original French. Victorians regarded reading French novels as a sign of dissipation and lack of moral fiber, as they were considered to be highly immoral.

6. *Michel Lévy:* nineteenth-century Parisian publisher whose authors included Dumas and Flaubert.

7. *Tony Johannot:* nineteenth-century French illustrator.

8. *Monsieur d'Artagnan:* hero of Alexandre Dumas's novel *The Three Musketeers* (1844) and its sequels, *Twenty Years After* (1845) and *The Man in the Iron Mask* (1846).

9. olla podrida: (Spanish) assorted mixture, miscellany.

CHAPTER IX. CAPTAIN LANSDOWN OVERHEARS A CONVERSATION WHICH APPEARS TO INTEREST HIM

1. *Wouvermanns:* Philips Wouwerman (c. 1619–68), Peter Wouwerman (1623–82), and Jan Wouwerman (1629–66) were Dutch brothers who painted small landscapes and battle scenes.

2. *a marriage only in name:* i.e., unconsummated.

BOOK THE SIXTH. ON THE TRACK

CHAPTER I. FATHER AND SON

1. *not enough blue in the gloomy sky to make the smallest article of wearing apparel—no, not so much as a pair of wrist-bands for an unhappy seaman:* An English folk saying is that cloudy weather will turn fine "if there is enough blue in the sky to make a pair of sailor's trousers."

2. *Old Parr:* Thomas Parr, a Shropshire agricultural laborer, said to have lived 152 years and 9 months. He died in 1635 and is buried in Westminster Abbey. According to folklore, he married his first wife when he was eighty, and fathered an illegitimate child when he was one hundred. He said that he maintained his good health by abstaining from smoking, and living on a diet of cheese, onions, bread, buttermilk, and mild ale, with the occasional drink of cider. His recipe for a long life

was reputed to be "Keep your head cool by temperance and your feet warm by exercise. Rise early, go soon to bed, and if you want to grow fat [prosperous] keep your eyes open and your mouth shut."

3. *Oliver Goldsmith:* English novelist (1728–74), chiefly famous for *The Vicar of Wakefield* (1766).

CHAPTER II. RAYMOND DE MAROLLES SHOWS HIMSELF BETTER THAN ALL BOW STREET

1. *Mephistopheles... Doctor Faustus:* In *The Tragical History of Dr. Faustus* (c. 1592), by Christopher Marlowe (1564–93), Faustus sells his soul to the devil, Mephistopheles.
2. *Mr. Carlyle:* Thomas Carlyle (1798–1881) was an essayist and historian who held that the past was superior to the present.
3. *Jardin des Plantes:* zoo.
4. *that dreadful Corsican person:* Napoleon.

CHAPTER III. THE LEFT-HANDED SMASHER MAKES HIS MARK

1. *white-cliffed Albion:* England. The white cliffs of Dover were the first part of England seen by passengers traveling on the cross-Channel ships.
2. *the blue-coated British Sbirri of Sir Robert Peel:* the police. Sir Robert Peel (1788–1850) was the founder of the London police force. The police wore blue uniforms and were sometimes derogatively known as "blue-bottles." The Sbirri were a Papal police force domiciled in private houses in the Papal dominions.
3. *votaries of Thespis:* actors and theatergoers. In Greek mythology, Thespis was the muse of acting.
4. *free trade:* an economic doctrine that trade between different countries should not be restricted in any way; there should be no tariffs or other barriers. This doctrine was hotly debated in the early Victorian era, and led to the repeal of the Corn Laws in 1846.
5. *tuft-hunter:* a toady—one who tries to curry favor with the rich and powerful.
6. *Lady of Lyons:* a play by Braddon's friend and mentor Sir Edward Bulwer Lytton (1803–73), first performed in 1838. Braddon was a member of theater companies that performed this play several times during 1850–59. In June 1858, it was performed at the Theatre Royal, Coventry, with Braddon in the role of Widow Melmotte. (For details, see Carnell, pp. 339–40.) Bulwer Lytton's prolific output included numerous

novels, plays, and poems. Nowadays he is chiefly (if unfairly) remembered as the author of what is regarded as the worst opening line in literature, "It was a dark and stormy night and the rain fell in torrents—except at occasional intervals, when it was checked by a violent gust of wind which swept up the streets (for it is in London that our scene lies), rattling along the housetops, and fiercely agitating the scanty flame of the lamps that struggled against the darkness" (*Paul Clifford*, 1830). Bulwer Lytton became a member of Parliament in 1831, and was colonial secretary during 1858–59. He was knighted in 1866.

7. *Bobby:* policeman. Policemen were given the nicknames "bobbies" and "peelers" because the founder of the police force was Sir Robert Peel.

8. *Republic of Plato:* ancient Greek philosopher Plato wrote about the ideal society in his *Republic.*

CHAPTER IV. WHAT THEY FIND IN THE ROOM IN WHICH THE MURDER WAS COMMITTED

1. *Rosicrucian:* a mystical movement founded by Christian Rosenkreutz (1378–1484). Its adherents called themselves Brothers of the Rosy Cross, Rosy-Cross Knights, and Rosy-Cross Philosophers; its adepts were called Illuminati. A version of the society still survives today.

2. *Freemasonry:* a fraternal order officially known as the Free and Accepted Masons, or Ancient Free and Accepted Masons. Only men are accepted into the order, which mainly flourishes in the U.K. and the United States. Members are sworn to secrecy about the Masonic rituals.

3. *Hebe:* in Greek mythology, the goddess of youth and beauty, daughter of Zeus and Hera.

4. *Plancus:* Lucius Munatius Plancus, ancient Roman politician, general and friend of Julius Caesar and the Emperor Augustus. His mausoleum at Monte Orlando overlooks the city of Gaeta on the Mediterranean and is considered to be the best-preserved Roman tomb in Italy.

5. *Beulah Spa:* a spa and pleasure resort in the London suburb of Upper Norwood. Founded in 1831, it covered thirty acres and included a maze, camera obscura, and archery ground. The pump room and other spa buildings were designed by Decimus Burton. It closed in 1855, and most of the buildings were demolished in 1879. The name Beulah originated in the Bible as a name for the land of Israel. In John Bunyan's *Pilgrim's Progress* it is the name of a land of peace next door to heaven.

6. *Mr. Robson at the Olympic:* Actor Frederick Robson (1822–64) appeared at London's Olympic Theatre in plays ranging from melodramas to Shakespeare. Queen Victoria admired him greatly and referred to him as the "Great Robson." For details of his career, see Mollie Sands, *Robson of the Olympic* (London: The Society for Theatre Research, 1979).

7. *mean-spirited Stuart... death of a traitor:* Sir Walter Raleigh was executed for treason in 1618, by command of James I (James Stuart).

8. *scroop:* creak, squeak, or grate.

9. *damask:* type of linen used for tablecloths.

CHAPTER V. MR. PETERS DECIDES ON A STRANGE STEP, AND ARRESTS THE DEAD

1. *unbranded forehead:* According to the Bible, Cain, the first murderer, was marked by God with a brand on his forehead (Gen. 4:15).

2. *I should glory in seeing him hung:* In Victorian Britain, the punishment for murder was death by hanging. Hangings were held in public until 1868. They drew large crowds, who were often badly behaved. After attending a public hanging in 1846, novelist Charles Dickens wrote to the *Daily News:* "I did not see one token in all the immense crowd; at the windows, in the streets, on the house-tops, anywhere; of any one emotion suitable to the occasion. No sorrow, no salutary terror, no abhorrence, no seriousness; nothing but ribaldry, debauchery, levity, drunkenness, and flaunting vice in fifty other shapes. I should have deemed it impossible that I could have ever felt any large assemblage of my fellow-creatures to be so odious" (*Daily News,* February 28, 1846).

3. *third state:* the common people. The Third Estate was the collective title taken by the French revolutionaries.

4. *Oath of the Tenis Court:* oath taken by the leaders of the French Revolution on June 20, 1789. The oath legalized the Revolution and committed its leaders to providing France with a constitution.

5. *Battle of Waterloo:* the 1815 battle at which Napoleon was finally defeated.

6. *Astley's:* a theater in London.

7. *Jenny Lind:* Jenny Lind (1820–87), born in Stockholm, was known as the "Swedish Nightingale." A soprano, she appeared throughout Europe in concerts and operas and became one of the best-known singers of her day. After 1856, she lived in England and became professor of singing at the Royal College of Music (1883–86).

8. Figlia: *La Figlia del Reggimento* (The Daughter of the Regiment), an opera by Donizetti, was first performed in 1840. The heroine, or-

phaned from birth, was brought up by a regiment of soldiers. She falls in love with a man suspected of being a spy for the enemy.

9. *brown stouts:* beer similar to Guinness.

10. *Liza:* The character is referred to by the much more upper-class name of "Sophia Maria" on p. 228. One of these names is presumably a nickname. Alternatively, Braddon, who was writing under pressure, may simply have forgotten the name she had originally given this character. This character also appears under the same two names in the novel's earlier version, *Three Times Dead.*

11. *the* Life: the *Sporting Life,* a newspaper devoted solely to sport.

12. *Rhadamanthine:* severe, inflexible. In Greek mythology Rhadamanthus, son of Zeus and Europa, was one of the judges in the lower world.

13. *"keeping company":* courting.

14. *Mr. Calcraft:* William Calcraft (1800–79) was England's longest serving public executioner, holding the post from 1829 to 1874. He carried out several hundred hangings, including Britain's last public hanging, that of the Fenian bomber Michael Barrett, outside Newgate prison on May 26, 1868.

15. *Vidocque:* Eugène François Vidocq (1775–1857), famous French detective. Formerly a convicted criminal, he joined the French police in 1809 and rose to become head of the detective branch. He published the first volume of his memoirs in 1828, and an English translation was published in the same year. His adventures remained popular with the British public, and a two-act melodrama, *Vidocq! the French Police Spy!,* appeared in 1852. A film, *Vidocq,* based on his adventures, was released in 2000, starring Gerard Depardieu. For further details of Vidocq's career, see Stead, J. P., *Vidocq. A Biography* (New York: Staples Press, 1953), and Gerson, Noel Bertram, *The Vidocq Dossier: The Story of the World's First Detective* (Boston: Houghton Mifflin, 1977).

16. *blushing unseen and wasting his stamina, if not his sweetness, on the desert air:* a parody of well-known lines from "Elegy in a Country Churchyard," by Thomas Gray (1716–71): "Full many a flower is born to blush unseen, / And waste its sweetness on the desert air."

17. *devilled kidneys:* kidneys cooked with a spicy seasoning.

18. rifacimento: renaissance.

19. *afflatus:* divine guidance, inspiration.

20. *Chevalier Bunsen:* Christian Charles Bunsen (1791–1860), Prussian scholar and diplomat, who was ambassador to England and a friend of Florence Nightingale.

21. *three-per-cents:* shares yielding a profit of three percent per annum.
22. *ferrule:* metal ring or cap protecting the tip of an umbrella.
23. *protean:* changing shape frequently. In Greek mythology, Proteus was a sea-god who could change his shape at will.
24. *something like that of Lancaster, and distinguished for its tendency to mount:* In Shakespeare's *King Henry IV Part 2*, Lancaster says that Falstaff's blood is "too heavy to mount" (IV.iii. 52, Modern Library ed.).
25. *animadversions:* criticisms, censure. From the Latin *animadvertere,* to turn the mind to something.
26. *Mr. William Macready:* William Charles Macready (1793–1873) was an English actor-manager who became the manager of several Covent Garden and Drury Lane theaters.
27. sotto voce: quietly, in a whisper; from Italian, meaning "below the voice."

CHAPTER VI. THE END OF THE DARK ROAD

1. *a bob:* a shilling (twelve pence in pre-decimal U.K. coinage, five pence in decimal coinage).
2. *a tanner:* sixpence.
3. *cabbage-net:* a small net in which cabbage leaves are shaken to dry after they have been washed in preparation for eating.
4. *the execution of the Frenchman Joseph Lesurges, for the murder of the Courier of Lyons:* The Courier of Lyons* was a play by French writers Moreau, Siraudin, and Delacour, based on a crime that had taken place in France in 1795. It was first performed in France in 1850 and in England, in 1851, in translation. In the play, a thief called Duboso robs the night-mail from Lyons and murders the courier. He bears such a strong likeness to the innocent Joseph Lesurques that Lesurques is arrested and sentenced to die in his place. One of the witnesses against him is his own father, who cannot tell the two men apart. In the actual case, and in the French version of the play, Lesurques is guillotined, but in the English translation he is saved at the last minute. Braddon appeared in *The Courier of Lyons* at the Theatre Royal, Brighton, in September 1858, taking the role of Janette, who exposes the murderer's true identity. (For details, see Carnell, p. 342.)
5. *Elizabeth Canning:* Elizabeth Canning was an eighteen-year-old London servant who disappeared on January 1, 1753. She reappeared a month later, emaciated, dirty, and in rags, claiming that she had been abducted and forced into prostitution. She identified her abductor as Mary Squires, a seventy-five-year-old gypsy. Squires denied the

charges and produced an alibi, but was found guilty at the Old Bailey Sessions before the Lord Mayor, Sir Crisp Gascoyne. She was executed, and her alleged accomplice, Susannah Wells, was branded and imprisoned. But Gascoyne later obtained a Royal Pardon for Squires and had Canning prosecuted for perjury. Although thirty people gave evidence of her good character, she was found guilty and sentenced to the penal colony in Australia for seven years. The case caused great controversy. According to *The Newgate Calendar,* "No affair that was ever determined in a judicial way did, perhaps, so much excite the curiosity of the public, as that in question. The newspapers and magazines were for a long time filled with little else than accounts of Canning and Squires." (Wilson, George Theodore, *The Newgate Calendar* [1816; reprinted London: Cardinal, 1991], p. 290.)

6. *Stultsian:* clothes made by high-class London tailors Stultz, Binnie & Son of 10 Clifford Street. Stultz clothes were the height of upper-class fashion during the Regency (1811–20), but were less fashionable by the time Braddon was writing.

7. *the unities of time and space:* conventions of drama as set down by ancient Greek philosopher Aristotle (384–322 B.C.) in the *Poetics.* The unity of time is that all the events in a play should occur within a short time frame (i.e., that the plot's time span should be a matter of hours, not years). The unity of place decrees that all action should take place within a single location. The unity of action decrees that all action should directly further the development and resolution of the work's central theme.

8. *Aristotle's ethics:* Aristotle's *Nicomachean Ethics* (c. 350 B.C.).

9. *"Zaire, vous pleurez!":* "Zaire, you cry!" is a line from Voltaire's tragedy *Zaire* (1732).

10. *"Qu'il mourut!":* literally, "that he died!" from the classical tragedy *Horace* (1639), by French playwright Pierre Corneille (1606–84): *"Que vouliez-vous qu'il fît contre trois—Qu'il mourût?"*

11. *blue fire:* a blue light used on stage to produce weird effects. It was often used in sensational melodramas.

12. *Corneille:* Pierre Corneille (1606–84), French playwright, known as the father of French comedy and tragedy.

CHAPTER THE LAST. FAREWELL TO ENGLAND

1. *Jack-in-the-green:* this folk figure dates back to Pagan times. In a fertility ritual, performed on May Day, Jack-in-the-Green, a man dressed

in a frame of greenery, was led in procession around the village. This ritual was revived in Victorian times as part of May Day celebrations.

2. *George Barnwell: The London Merchant, or The History of George Barnwell* is a morality play by George Lillo (1693–1739), first performed in 1731. It tells of a young apprentice's downfall as a result of his love for a beautiful, but wicked, courtesan, who incites him to kill his rich uncle for his money. It is based on a sixteenth-century ballad that begins:

> All youths of fair England
> That dwell both far and near,
> Regard my story that I tell,
> And to my song give ear.
>
> A London lad I was,
> A merchant's prentice bound;
> My name is George Barnwell, that did spend
> My master many pound.
>
> Take heed of harlots then,
> And their enticing trains,
> For by that means I have been brought
> To hang alive in chains.

The ballad goes on to tell how Barnwell carried out the murder:

> Sudden with a wood,
> He struck his uncle down,
> And beat his brains out of his head;
> So sore he crack'd his crown.
>
> The seizing fourscore pound,
> To London straight he hied,
> And unto Sarah Millwood all
> The cruel fact descried.

The ballad ends with Barnwell and Millwood being hanged for murder. Braddon was part of a theater company that performed a play entitled *George Barnwell* at Brighton Theatre Royal in February 1858. The author is not known. (For details, see Carnell, p. 332.)

3. *parliamentary train:* one of the trains that, by Act of Parliament, the railway companies had to provide for the benefit of third-class passengers, who traveled for a reduced fare.

4. *declensions...ablative:* terms used in the teaching of Latin grammar.

5. *dropsical:* suffering from edema, or dropsy, an accumulation of fluid within body tissues or serous cavities that causes excessive swelling.

6. *East India Company:* A shameless exercise in commercial imperialism, the British East India Company was set up by Royal Charter in 1600 to ensure a British trading monopoly in Asia and the Pacific. Despite competition from the French and Dutch, it traded successfully for over two hundred years, providing Britain with a range of goods such as pepper and other spices, silk, cotton, indigo, and sugar. Its monopoly was broken in 1813, and its powers handed over to the British Crown in 1858 following the First Indian War of Independence (the "Indian Mutiny"). It ceased to exist as a legal entity in 1873.

7. *Sikh campaign:* The first Anglo-Sikh War, 1845–46, ended with the Treaty of Lahore, under which the Sikhs ceded large amounts of territory to Britain. When the Sikh Wars broke out again, in 1848–49, the Sikh forces were defeated and Britain took over the Punjab. The Sikhs' child ruler, eleven-year-old Maharajah Duleep Singh, was forced to surrender his kingdom, his sovereignty, and the Koh-I-Noor diamond to the British in return for a pension.

8. soi-disant: self-styled.

9. *Madame du Barry:* Jeanne Bécu, comtesse du Barry (1743–93), mistress of King Louis XV of France. She left the court in 1774, when Louis XV died. In 1793, she was arrested for treason and guillotined during the "Reign of Terror."

10. *Choiseul:* Étienne-François, duc de Choiseul (1719–85), French statesman and diplomat who negotiated the marriage of Austrian noblewoman Marie Antoinette with the future Louis XVI. Madame du Barry's influence led to his exile from court in 1770.

11. *D'Aiguillon:* Emmanuel-Armand de Wignerod du Plessis de Richelieu, Duc d'Aiguillon (1720–82), French statesman heavily involved in court intrigues.

Reading Group Guide

1. How would you characterize the town of Slopperton and the river Sloshy? How do these two elements function as characters in the novel?

2. Along with Wilkie Collins and Mrs. Henry Wood, Mary Elizabeth Braddon is widely credited as a founder of sensation fiction. Drawing on the introduction, the biographical note, and the novel itself, how would you define this genre? What traits does sensation fiction have in common with today's detective novel or mystery?

3. On pages 29–30, when Mr. Peters spells out NOT GUILT, Mr. Jinks dismisses his lowly assistant's assessment of Richard Marwood. Braddon writes, "Mr. Jinks was a distinguished detective, and prided himself highly on his acumen; and was therefore very indignant that his sub and scrub should dare to express an opinion." Over the course of the novel, how does Mr. Peters demonstrate his superior abilities? Why do you think Braddon chose to deny him the power of speech?

4. On page 320, the Marquis de Cevennes tells Jabez, "You are a very clever fellow...but you would never have got Desdemona smothered. Othello would have seen through you—as I did!" How would you compare Jabez North to Shakespeare's Iago?

5. How are women portrayed in *The Trail of the Serpent*? Consider Sloshy's mother, Valerie, Kuppins, Isabel Darley, the old woman of Blind Peter's Alley, Sillikens, and Mrs. Marwood. Which of these characters show strength in adversity? Which of them fall victim to "oppressive social forces" as described by Sarah Waters in her introduction?

6. Describe the unusual team of helpers that Mr. Peters and Daredevil Dick assemble to help them catch the true murderer of Mr. Montague Harding. What function do they serve in the novel?

7. Who should rightfully be blamed for the poisoning of Gaston de Lancy?

8. On page 333, when Jabez North reveals his true relationship to the Marquis de Cevennes, his estranged father replies, "So, you are my son? Upon my word I thought all along you were something of that kind, for you are such a consummate villain." According to Braddon's narrative, what role does heredity play in a person's destiny? Does nurturing affect the outcome of an individual's moral fiber? Consider young Sloshy and his adopted father, Mr. Peters, as well as Jabez and his twin brother, Jim.

ABOUT THE EDITOR

DR. CHRIS WILLIS works at the Centre for Gender Studies at London Metropolitan University. Her co-edited books include *The Fatal Marriage and Other Stories, The New Woman in Fiction and in Fact*, and *Twelve Women Detective Stories*. She lives in London.

A Note on the Type

The principal text of this Modern Library edition
was set in a digitized version of Janson, a typeface that
dates from about 1690 and was cut by Nicholas Kis,
a Hungarian working in Amsterdam. The original matrices have
survived and are held by the Stempel foundry in Germany.
Hermann Zapf redesigned some of the weights and sizes for
Stempel, basing his revisions on the original design.

MODERN LIBRARY IS ONLINE AT
WWW.MODERNLIBRARY.COM

MODERN LIBRARY ONLINE IS YOUR GUIDE
TO CLASSIC LITERATURE ON THE WEB

THE MODERN LIBRARY E-NEWSLETTER

Our free e-mail newsletter is sent to subscribers, and features sample chapters, interviews with and essays by our authors, upcoming books, special promotions, announcements, and news.

To subscribe to the Modern Library e-newsletter, send a blank e-mail to: join-modernlibrary@list.randomhouse.com or visit www.modernlibrary.com

THE MODERN LIBRARY WEBSITE

Check out the Modern Library website at
www.modernlibrary.com for:

- The Modern Library e-newsletter
- A list of our current and upcoming titles and series
- Reading Group Guides and exclusive author spotlights
- Special features with information on the classics and other paperback series
- Excerpts from new releases and other titles
- A list of our e-books and information on where to buy them
- The Modern Library Editorial Board's 100 Best Novels and 100 Best Nonfiction Books of the Twentieth Century written in the English language
- News and announcements

Questions? E-mail us at **modernlibrary@randomhouse.com**
For questions about examination or desk copies, please visit
the Random House Academic Resources site at
www.randomhouse.com/academic